JACQUELINE FARTHING GALVIN

Murder for Afternoon Tea

Episode I – The Last Cup of Tea

First edition

Cover art by Jenn Z. Cordell

This book was professionally typeset on Reedsy.
Find out more at reedsy.com

This series is dedicated to tea rooms and bed and breakfast establishments around the world. Where would we be without the solace of tea?

I

Part One

Chapter 1

What we have here is a failure to communicate.
-Cool Hand Luke, 1967

Tucker Elliott smiled to himself.

"Ah, yes, the dreaded summons to the boss's office."

He knew this portion of the meeting would not be recorded in the minutes. Alene Elliott shut her office door and took her place behind the power desk.

"Alright, Mother, out with it."

"Sit, please."

"Bugger. You haven't had this chair electrified since our last chat, have you?" asked Tucker, patting the cushion.

The cold stare from behind the desk could have frozen the English raindrops before they hit the pane.

"I have a new assignment for you."

"Really?"

"Despite your...indiscretions... you have a most uncanny way of making money. We have a new venture in the States. It has fabulous potential, but the man at the helm has driven it into the ground faster than your Aunt Frederica, who can go through a buffet line."

"Lord, not even I can save that then. Thanks for the chat, Mother. I'm off."

"Freeze, you. And let go of that door handle. You're not leaving just yet."

She held out an accordion file to Tucker, who reluctantly walked back to the desk.

"You can at least tell me what I'm supposed to be resuscitating."

"Footwear."

"Oh, well, that's altogether different. What are they: stiletto heels, sexy boots, what?"

"Flip flops," said Alene, leveling her gaze at Tucker.

"What? You can't mean it. I won't do it."

"Alright, then, I shall tell your father about Las Vegas."

"Oh, that's evil. Good one. Alright, when do I leave and where have you put me? I hope it's a decent hotel."

"I've bought you a nice little house in Palm Beach."

"Is this a business trip or a sentence?"

"I'm not interested in your sarcasm today. God has already canceled my golf match."

"Who goes to Florida in late summer? Besides, I have obligations here."

"Your obligations, such as they are, have been reassigned. Now go, restructure, and make profits. It's what you're hired to do."

"I am still family, yes?"

"For now. Go make me proud. And no headlines."

"You take the fun out of everything," said Tucker, heading down the hall.

"Not everything. I did give you an assistant.

"Now, why would that be considered fun?"

"You'll see," cooed Alene to no one in particular.

* * *

"Damn. Now I have to figure out what she's up to. I guess I'll find out when I get there. How do you stand the heat this time of year?"

Tucker was throwing clothes into a bag, trying to find items to pack for the oppressively hot weather in Florida. Dahlia Porter, his best friend since diapers, was languishing on the other end of the line listening about yet another battle in the war of the Elliott's.

"Wait a minute, when did you say you were coming?" she asked.

"Tomorrow. She doesn't waste time, you know."

"Wonderful! I have a surprise for you."

"Sorry, full up on surprises for the day. You'll have to wait till tomorrow, thanks."

"This'll be brilliant, really. Once you settle in, call me. Your timing is perfect."

"I assure you it isn't."

"You're going to love this. Will you be able to get away for a few days for a visit?"

"Not sure. Haven't even met the assistant and don't have the slightest idea what to do with flip flops."

"Flip flops? The things on your feet?"

"Yes, the things on your feet. Look, I'll call you when I get in. We'll figure it out."

"Alright, love. See you then."

"Dulcy!" screamed Dahlia. "Tucker's coming for our grand opening."

From somewhere in the quaint tea room came a faint acknowledgment.

"Thank God," said Dahlia to herself. "Hopefully, he can help me sort out this awful mess. And an assistant as well. That could be bloody useful. Dulcy! Where are you?"

Dahlia raced up the tea room stairs to the alcove where she remembered last seeing her manager.

"What have you done with yourself?"

"Dahlia! I'm in the kitchen. You know, where we keep that intercom thing for when one of us is upstairs and the other is down?"

"You know how I loathe those things—nothing like a good yell. I'm going out. You take lunch for me, please."

"Where are you going?"

"It's nothing for you to worry about, I hope," she finished under her breath.

"You're not going out to 'tea' again, are you? It's always such a mess when you do."

"No, but that's a lovely idea. Call the Plank House and tell them to have my scotch ready at 4 p.m. sharp. See you later."

Dulcy threw down the dishrag and called for reinforcements.

* * *

Tucker viewed the new surroundings with approval. There was a slight aromatic breeze dancing through the topiary and flowers lining the over-sized double front doors. He squinted toward the water, inhaling the salt air and cutting through the ninety-degree slog of heat. When he turned back, the double doors were wide open, and a faint lilting sound was spilling onto the drive. Tucker marched into the foyer, halting sharply in front of an elderly couple, hands clasped in front, staring with mild curiosity. Just a hint of a smile pierced their stony features.

"Hello. Hmmm, there's a rugby pitch for a living room. Do you come with this museum, then?"

"We are Stanley and Ivey, and we are at your service, " the old man said.

"Which is which, eh?"

Tucker excused himself and meandered out to a private, well-groomed rose garden at the side of the house. He seated himself on a wrought iron bench and drank in the sea breeze while dialing the string of numbers to England.

"Alright, Mother, hilarious," chided Tucker. "You've had your laugh now. Remove the antiques, please."

"The house came furnished. Everything stays."

"I'm talking about the two who greeted me by the football field living room. I'll hire my staff, please, and after reading this file, it looks like I'll need an emergency response team to raise a pulse on this thing you call a 'new venture.'"

"Those two are your house staff. Your assistant will be arriving within the hour. Now see your office and relax. This is supposed to be enjoyable, dear."

"This is punishment, and you know it; those two nannies especially. But not to worry, I have plans for my fun."

8

"Tucker, no media or police. I do not want to add to your... scrapbook."

"Never. Police and media are the last things you have to worry about this time."

Tucker had toured the massive kitchen and dining room, which comfortably sat forty, and each of the nine bedrooms and baths was complete with gold fixtures. The pool wing, with its bedroom, living room, wet bar, and kitchen, was what Tucker chose as his refuge while exiled from the Motherland. The office was tucked in an upstairs corner and had been given a state-of-the-art makeover. Displayed on the back credenza were sets of styled flip-flops. Tucker surveyed the contents and grunted.

"Now I think we know why the flip-flops flunked."

He sat down at the rectangular Lucite desk and wondered where one put things when there were no drawers.

"Hello?" echoed a voice from the hall.

"Enter at your own risk," said Tucker.

The door opened and admitted a tall, young woman who stood expectantly at the entrance. Tucker did his usual split-second assessment. She was about five foot, eleven inches with long, thick auburn hair and green eyes, which shone with a crystalline essence he found slightly disconcerting. She was dressed fashionably but correctly for her build, which was angular if not athletic. Her skin had a porcelain sheen to it, suggesting she rarely saw the sun. She wore limited makeup that was expertly applied, and Tucker concluded that she probably didn't even need that.

He glimpsed at her shoes out of curiosity and was pleased to see a conservative yet sexy pair of high-heeled, quality pumps in the shade matching her business casual shirt dress. She looked suspiciously like a model. Tucker decided immediately that she would not do it.

"So, you are my assistant."

"Yes, and I was instructed to report here to begin work. Reggie Winter," she said, extending her hand.

Tucker met it and was impressed by the firm grip that matched his own.

"So, how did you get here? Because I didn't hire you."

"Well, someone did. Tucker Elliott, President of Elliott Enterprises, Sussex, England," she said, holding out a letter. "Are you him?"

"Am I he," he corrected. "And I was the last time I looked," he said, taking the letter.

He recognized the standard issue his mother used, including the scrawl that was supposed to represent his signature. Tucker laughed and sat back against the flip-flop display, surveying the strong features in front of him.

"Sorry, have a seat. So, what are your qualifications? What makes you the one to be my personal assistant? I can tell you the hours are erratic, the work is nonstop, and you must put up with me. Trust me, I am not always this charming."

He was hoping to dissuade her quickly so he could get in nine holes.

"Because your mother said so," she announced, stifling a giggle. The amusement sparkling in her eyes reminded him of emeralds. "I'm not sure I understand all this, really."

"Well, you haven't met my mother then, have you, love?"

Tucker stood, glared at the shoes behind him, then at the woman seated before him.

"I'm sorry, but I don't believe this is going to work out. You're not right for the job, I'm afraid, but thank you. If you'll excuse me, I have some things to tend to that don't have to do with tartish footwear. Nice to have met you."

He walked around the desk, shook her hand again, and exited the room, leaving her still seated in front of the drawer-less desk. Reggie smiled and rummaged through her purse till she found another smaller, handwritten letter bearing the same West Sussex postal mark as the one she gave Tucker.

Regina, there is one thing; he will tell you that you're not suitable for the job and that it isn't going to work out. Go home, relax, get rest, and go back the next day, ready to work. All will be well. He always takes time to digest things. It's his way. Give your mother my best and good luck. You are the one for the job, trust me. I know you'll whip him into shape.

Cheers

Alene Elliott

Reggie slid the note back into her purse and grinned. This was going to be fun.

* * *

Chapter 2

Dora Charleston: Is he dead?
Sam Diamond: With a thing like that in his back, in the long run, he's better
off.

−Murder by Death, 1976

Tucker woke up feeling sluggish and fuzzy. He padded from his cozy nook, shoved the sliders open and dove naked into the pool. He sank to the bottom, contemplated the number of scotches he consumed the previous evening then rocketed to the surface. He floated to the edge and rested his head on his forearms, letting the blaze of morning rays warm his face. Opening his eyes, he lazily watched the sunlight sparkle off the inter-coastal waters.

"Good morning. I see you're taking advantage of the beautiful day."

"Ah, Miss Winter, is it? You're back. Here to make me reconsider?"

"I thought we got off to a bad start yesterday and I wanted to apologize. Shall we start over?"

"Absolutely. Apology accepted."

Reggie smiled and held out her hand to shake on their new start.

"Thanks," grinned Tucker.

He clasped her hand and sprang from the pool.

"You're naked."

"Thank you for noticing. I'm naked and difficult. So, what would Mrs. Elliott say about that since she seems to be telling us both what to do these days?"

"She'd say 'I told you so.'"

"About being naked or difficult?" he asked dripping on her shoes.

"Can I get you a towel?" she asked, staring into his eyes.

"Yes. We have lots to do today. You'll need luggage and someone to keep your cats."

"I don't have cats."

"See then? We're already ahead of schedule."

"Wait, why do I need luggage? Don't we have files to go through?"

Tucker had made a skirt with his towel and was heading into a gold-fixtured bathroom with Reggie on his heels.

"Unless you're showering with me, I suggest you go pack," he grinned. "Have you seen these fixtures? Do you think they're real gold?"

"What am I packing?"

"Dunno. Bring everything, you know, casual, golf, swim, cocktail. See you in an hour?"

And with that, he slammed the door and began singing loudly and off-key. Reggie smiled and pictured fish belly-up somewhere in the nearby bay waters.

***

Reggie was leaning on the car observing the landscape. There were statues of naked cherubs dotted along the hedges and peeking out from corners of the house.

"At least he must feel at home here," she said, staring at the cherubs.

Stanley had delivered a neatly packed bag to her, retreating into the house with his serene smile spread across his creased features. As she checked her watch for the fourth time, the front door opened and out popped Tucker, casual, smart, and handsome.

"Where did you find those?" he asked, staring at her feet.

"Do you like them? I think they're groovy."

"I'm not sure. I think I liked you better dressed. In work shoes, you know."

Reggie was wearing flip flops decorated with peace signs on the point and rhinestones along the straps. They were hot pink and hurt Tucker's eyes. He was repelled by them and forced to look elsewhere when he noticed that the attractive peasant sundress she was wearing accentuated her more feminine features. Her thick hair hung loosely over her pretty shoulders and when she seated herself on the driver's side, he was given a glimpse of slender thighs and shapely calves. As she settled in, it dawned on him why the footwear glaringly stood out - her narrow but very large feet.

"So, where are we going?"

"Out of town."

"Do we have a direction?"

"Away from the water."

"Alright. Just let me know when to turn."

"Head west, and before you hit the Gulf of Mexico, make a sharp right.

* * *

"Yes, love, it's going brilliantly. Yes, I've met my assistant. She's very keen, notices every detail, a driving personality, good sense of direction, oh, and a nice dresser."

Reggie rolled her eyes but felt a flush spreading to the roots of her hair. He noticed quite a bit for a cavalier individual.

"Yes, Mother," Tucker droned on. "A full day of slogging through files and sales statistics. You know, we'll probably never see the light of day, but we've had our exercise. You know, our naked swim."

"Our naked swim?"

Tucker grinned and winked at her.

"Yes, Mother, I promise we'll take a break and do something fun. Don't work too hard today. Cheers."

"A driving personality?"

"Well, I must say you're doing brilliantly, and you are a nice dresser."

"We might as well go through those files and at least accomplish something."

"No need; I've tossed them in the bin. They were dismal and depressing."

"They were also our map to getting started."

"I take back my compliment on your sense of direction. They pointed us the wrong way. Please don't fuss, new assistant. I went through them, took what I needed, and put the rest in storage."

"Oh, so I got the job?" she said innocently.

* * *

They had driven across the state, rounding the corner outside of Naples and proceeding straight up the west coast. Tucker had filled her in on all the scandals of the previous management and how they had ruined a perfectly good business model by greed and mismanagement. There were no survivors; they would start fresh. They had also taken in a few of the tourist traps and eaten at an historic inn where the food was good but the atmosphere better.

"Everglades City was interesting. What about the massive alligator on the wall? Is that common?"

"In some parts. Do we know where we're going yet?"

"Of course we know where we're going. How else would we have gotten this far?"

"By sheer prayer?"

"Ironic that, seeing as how you seem to have very little faith. Take this exit, please."

Reggie swerved across three lanes just managing to make the ramp before running out of time and space.

"Ah, I see you've driven in London. Try not to kill me on our first day, please. Take a right there, now follow the one-way street till you find a two-way. Let's see... then turn right, go down two houses, turn into the alley and park in front of the B&B," said Tucker.

Reggie found the two-way street and entered to find it completely blocked.

"Hmmm," said Reggie. "Something's going on. We'll have to see if we can get around it. It almost looks as though it's right where we're heading."

"Bollocks. It is where we're heading. Pull over, please."

Scattered directly in front of the Sea Gables Tea Room and Bed and Breakfast was an assembly of emergency vehicles.

"This looks a bit serious. Let's run find Dahlia, shall we?"

He was fighting the fear growing steadily in his heart. He could see the concern in Reggie's eyes and wondered if she had caught sight of the coroner's van parked at the corner.

"Let's try this entrance," he said, turning her away from the back and steering her to the front door.

Before they could even knock, it opened revealing a uniformed officer peering over the shoulder of a woman almost as tall as Reggie but with darker curly hair peeking out from underneath a wide-brimmed hat, bright blue eyes and cheeks that resembled those on the cherubs back in Palm Beach.

"Tucker! Thank God. It's alright, Officer. I'm expecting them."

Tucker ushered Reggie over the threshold into a beautifully preserved foyer of a 1910 Victorian manor. Uniformed and white coated individuals were crawling over the place like ants looking for crumbs.

"Dahlia, what the bloody hell is going on here?" he said, hugging her tightly.

"Well, you know I was telling you I had a surprise for you."

"If this is the surprise you needn't have gone…"

"Well, no, not exactly. Your surprise was much better. Your surprise was a lovely garden party with food and music and lots of cocktails."

"And this?"

"Was in the garden, just without the party. You see, I found…"

"A body?" supplied Tucker

"Exactly. A dead body!"

* * *

Chapter 3

Richard: Oh, will you look at that, girl talk and me without a uterus.
—Caroline in the City, 1995

Tucker entered the tea room to the hum of muted conversation and classical music in the background. He rounded a corner and came upon two stunning women dressed in black and deep in conversation.

"Reggie?"

Reggie and Dahlia wheeled around and stared at Tucker expectantly. Tucker gazed at the two, shook his head and ventured forth with a grin that took up most of his face.

"You caught me off my mark for a moment, ladies. Is it me or does there seem to be two of you?"

Dahlia squeezed Reggie's arm as she reviewed Tucker from head to toe, letting out a long whistle.

"My, aren't you the one. Brilliant aren't we in our dress togs? Was there something in particular you wanted or were you waiting for that compliment?"

Tucker grinned sheepishly joining the two by the fireplace. Funny, he thought, she managed to get the last laugh again.

"Just roaming about looking for the two most lovely women I know. I was hoping for a crash course in invited guests for the evening."

"Ah, just what Reggie and I were discussing. They're friends and investors. I had a crib sheet with some notes on it, but it seems to have gone missing. What I'll do each time one comes our way is give you a brief description and you can go on from there. Will that do?" said Dahlia and moved off toward her office without waiting for Tucker's reply.

Tucker eyed Reggie who managed to smile sweetly, while also reprimanding him. He was amazed at how she carried off the same look his mother had perfected. He wondered if all women had this capability in their genetic mold. He decided it was time to change the subject when Reggie did it for him.

"By the way, Mr. Elliott, how do you like the way everything turned out?"

"Well, Reggie, I think you look smashing, and I just want to say that I think all the gents here will make themselves silly over you."

"How poetic," she said working her way around him, "but I was referring to the tea room and the kitchen mess. Nice of you to notice my evening dress, thank you."

Tucker remained rooted, hands in pockets, silly grin fixed on his face. Reggie smiled and moved into the foyer where she could stifle her laughter away from him. Tucker waited until she had completely disappeared, then backed himself out onto the porch into the evening air. It seemed to have become oppressively hot inside the tea room.

* * *

"Oh, Dahlia! We've just come from the B&B tour. Everything is so beautiful. You've done a marvelous job. I just hope everything's going well, you know…better."

"Oh, Betty, everything is fine, really. It's so nice of you to be concerned but things are going very well, love. You need to try some of the rumaki," Dahlia said, steering her friend toward the food table and away from other guests. "It's fabulous and I know you'll love it. Here's a plate and napkin and you help yourself to all these lovely hors d'oeuvres and we'll talk in a bit."

"Alright, Dahlia, but you know, you don't have to be brave with me. It's Betty you're talking to now and …"

"And who have you been talking to!?" laughed Dahlia as she turned Betty back toward the table and slithered out of her grasp.

She forced a big smile as she floated her way through guests till she reached Reggie and Tucker in the foyer.

"Ah and there she is, woman of the hour, hostess extraordinaire."

"Do shut up Tucker, please."

Dahlia glared into the crowd then said, "Sorry about the shut-up thing, Tucker. It's that Lehern woman. She would have to be the first person I set eyes on. Worst gossip to ever walk in heels. If Bill wasn't such a great supporter, I'd have to lock her in a closet somewhere. Ghastly tongue."

Reggie gave Tucker a nudge in the ribs which erupted as something between a wheeze and a cough. Dahlia took it as agreement and slapped him across the shoulder blades.

"I think I shall mingle before I have no breath left to speak of," sputtered Tucker and sauntered off toward a friendly looking gentleman standing solo at the bar.

"Tell me about the lady gossip and her other half and also who the woman is standing by herself by the fireplace," said Reggie.

"The gossip is Betty Lehern. She's the wife of Bill, that nice looking man standing at the head of the food table tucking into the rumaki and looking like a sheep. He always does that when he doesn't want to speak to the person who's talking at him, which at the moment is Mercedes Castner, Attorney Roderick's wife. She's probably making him miserable by chewing his ear about some misfire of justice with one of her juvenile delinquents again."

"Hello Mercedes, dear," waved Dahlia as Mercedes flashed a brilliant smile in their direction.

"Bill and Roderick are golfing buddies," continued Dahlia, "and I know he just detests hearing her go on like she does. Roderick has to send the little devils up and his wife goes around trying to reform the unrepentant. It's rather like watching a game of dominoes that starts to fall before it's completely set up. Okay, what else did you want to know?"

"Well, I was curious about Betty's husband Bill. If she gossips, what does he do?"

"Bill really is a nice man, rather tolerant with his silly wife. So tolerant that I think he rather ignores her completely. Much easier to just say 'Yes dear' than to get mired in her endless droning. Luckily, I don't think anyone ever takes her seriously. Lucky for me, that is. No one is really sure how he made his money, but he seems to be dripping in it. He's one of those quiet types - sort of like an owl. Only lets out a hoot every now and again and blinks a lot," giggled Dahlia.

"The younger woman standing in front of the fireplace," nodded Reggie, "just being joined by the rather good-looking, darkish man. Now who is she?"

"That would be the sad and forgettable Mrs. Nelson Platt, or Peggy Platt. Peggy, or Pea, as we affectionately call her, when she's not present, that is, is Nelson's third wife and another in a succession of dull females he's swept off their feet. I think he only likes the chase. Then he becomes bored and starts shopping around for a new victim. His forte is painting a romantic picture of himself. He's head of the historical society and fancies himself monumental in the eyes of the community, mostly the female community. I think he's an old relic if not a complete bore," said Dahlia acidly and Reggie wondered if she had been snared by the womanizing net of Nelson Platt at some point.

"We should mingle," cried Dahlia. "Come with me, love, and I'll introduce you to the rest of the clan. Some of them are quite agreeable actually," and she looped Reggie's arm around hers and led her through the crowded room.

As she neared the bar, Reggie managed to catch Tucker's eye hurling him a meaningful glance toward Bill Lehern. Tucker gracefully excused himself from his cocktail companion and managed to land alongside Reggie and Dahlia when there was a great commotion in the outer room at the entrance. Dahlia let out a yelp and swooped towards the foyer and the newest arrival.

Reggie and Tucker leaned around a tall woman in a gaudy hat and suit and peered at a rather queenly figure now the focus of the guests' attention. People parted like the Red Sea and left standing in the middle was a neatly packaged and compact individual. She held her head high with grace and dignity and reviewed the attendees of the party like royalty viewing her subjects. She was commanding if not intimidating and her presence created an awe amongst the crowd that was palpable. Standing in the dim foyer light was the one and only Mavis Hatfield, former owner of the present Sea Gables.

* * *

Chapter 4

Lawson Russell: Drink, Detective?
Clifford Dubose: Nah. Never touch it. Makes me happy.
—A Murder of Crows (V) 1999

Dahlia removed the mass of straw and chiffon from her head and gently laid it on a nearby lampshade in a uniquely decorated office. She stretched out her long legs and propped them on a stool nearby.

"So, fill us in. What's going on here?" asked Tucker, pouring himself a scotch.

"I went out before the lunch crowd to throw a pill in the fountain and found this...man...in my begonias. Horrifying sight. He's smashed the entire new bed, flat."

Reggie stared.

"Alright," said Tucker standing. "Drink this down," he said, handing her a snifter of what appeared to be brandy.

"Shocking," he remarked.

"That's what I thought. They were brand new."

"Not your begonias, you twit, your awful attitude. I take it you didn't know this man."

"No. They don't know who he is. He was just some person lying in my flowers with a great bloody knife in his back. Literally," she said with a high-pitched giggle.

"More brandy I think," said Tucker, topping her off. "Is there someone in charge here, love? Someone official maybe; badge, gun, notepad, pencil?"

"There's an inspector in the kitchen. Sounds like a murder mystery, doesn't it?"

"Look after her, will you Reg, while I run find the law? This is Reggie, my new assistant, courtesy of Alene."

Tucker dropped a kiss on Dahlia's head and plunged out the door leaving Reggie and the frazzled Dahlia staring appraisingly at each other.

"So, you've been friends since diapers?"

"And you've just got hired on, poor thing. Are you sure about this? I think you need this more than I do," she said, holding out the brandy.

"Are you okay? I know this has been an awful shock; would be for anybody. Anything I can do for you, get you?"

Dahlia thought about it and decided now was as good a time as any.

"There's another reason I hoped you would come. I'm having a spot of trouble here in my little Eden."

"I noticed. Do bodies show up frequently, or is this an isolated occurrence?"

"I'll go with isolated, but I'm afraid it may not be random."

"Oh. Go on."

"Well, the real reason for the party is to do a little investigating, maybe flush out someone who's trying to flush me out...of my business as it seems."Reggie remained silent which Dahlia took as her cue to continue.

"I've been having...incidents. The help is starting to gossip and some of the guests have heard bits and pieces, and you can add up the rest. It's an older place with a somewhat colorful past, perfect for an English tea room, I thought. Only now people are beginning to think the place is haunted or odd and they're not sure if it's quaint or just dangerous. And now this. My investors were already becoming concerned. With this they may draw out altogether."

"Tell me more about the incidents, then we'll worry about the investors."

"It's basically the sabotaging of my events like private parties, weddings, you know. Things that make us look incompetent."

"And what else? Because there is more, yes?" said a voice from the doorway.

"Break-ins, vandalism if you like, to the property. Things torn up and broken, and well, gone through. Each incident is a little more serious than the one before. I was a bit afraid of how far they'd go, quite honestly."

"But you haven't spoken to the police?" asked Tucker.

"I spoke with them a while back when the alarm went off one night and we found an upstairs window pried open. Other than that, no."

"Sounds as though someone is looking for something," said Reggie. "Do you have any idea who or what it might be?"

"No," she said hesitantly. "Not that I could name. I was starting to make a plan. I had some information from..."

"Dahlia, do you have a minute to speak to Detective Laird?" Dulcy said backing up against the door to reveal a large man filling the space.

He was a tallish, decent-looking person whose gaze penetrated to the bones. What caught their attention, however, was that he seemed rather warmly dressed for so hot a day. He was wearing a suit, a long-sleeved shirt judging by the cuff links, and a coat hanging off his massive shoulders. It was like a robe hanging off the back of a chair. He seemed fresh and unconcerned given the heat and the circumstances.

"Miss Porter? I just wanted to clarify a few things before leaving."

He stared openly at Tucker and Reggie and waited patiently.

"Oh, sorry. These are my visitors, Inspector, Tucker Elliott and his associate, Regina."

"It's Detective. I just wanted to let you know that we're finished out here. We've identified the man and basically what we believe we have is a guy with a long rap sheet who finally upset the wrong person. Unfortunately, your property was the choice for dumping the body."

Dahlia winced but Detective Laird made no apologies for the details. Tucker observed quietly while Reggie stared at the floor trying to be invisible.

"If I need anything else, I'll be in touch. Nice to meet you."

He was terse, expressionless, and then gone. Dulcy shrugged her shoulders and retreated to the kitchen leaving the three alone. Tucker made himself comfortable with another scotch to take the sudden chill out of the air.

"You really know how to welcome guests, love. What's next, armed robbery?"

"You haven't been funny since nursery school, so quit trying."

"C'mon, I'm a little funny," he said, reaching around and tickling Dahlia's feet.

"Actually, that's a good question. Now what? What can we do to help? Are you still going to have your party?" asked Reggie.

"Of course; it's way too late to cancel. Oh, bugger," she sighed.

"What?" said Tucker and Reggie as one.

"I'm going to need new begonias!"

* * *

Chapter 5

"For fifteen years, everybody told me I was making it up. Everyone said it was just a story. There's no such thing as the Boogeyman. But I was right."
—Boogeyman, 2005

"Are you going to tell me about the agenda, or do I just guess at it?" asked Tucker.

They were relaxing in the luxurious B&B sitting room on a glorious Florida morning. The night before had been fun and festive considering their welcome, but the light of day brought reality and work. Reggie exposed a pair of almond-shaped eyes over her paper and Tucker could see their corners crinkle in a grin.

"Do we have enough time today to poke our noses where they don't belong?" he asked.

"Yes. It should be exciting as well as educational," and with that she raised the paper back up to block Tucker's intense gaze.

He continued to stare at the sheet, willing it down so he could continue his appraisal of her; rather like deciding if you like the artwork you just bought. She could definitely be exasperating, taking pleasure in it even. This frustrated yet attracted him, but even more disturbing was that he was beginning to like it.

"Shall we discuss strategy?" she said, holding out the agenda.

"Thank you so much. Alright, big events look like a cocktail party, a political luncheon, and the grand opening, correct? So, time to poke around and get ourselves into loads of trouble. My kind of vacation."

"I wasn't aware we were on vacation. Just a side note in case you were interested. By the way, any history on this place, you know like when it was built, by whom, any feature articles, that sort of thing? That could be a place to start."

"I don't know but I suggest the library, say fifteen minutes?"

"Will there be any actual work done today?" she asked.

"Oh, no, there wouldn't be today, sorry. Maybe tomorrow."

Tucker waved Reggie out the side door to her room then wandered back and sat heavily on the couch. Even after sifting through the details from Dahlia's evening, Tucker still couldn't make everything add up.

* * *

"What do YOU have?" asked Reggie, shoving aside her papers in favor of what Tucker had. They had been consuming every article and piece of scrap paper since they arrived.

"I'm not sure, but it seems as though there was some trouble at the Sea Gables a while back. Probably nothing to get too excited over. I'll let you know in a minute."

Tucker slid the bulk of the papers aside and concentrated on a more recent work.

"This is an interview with the daughter of the original owner, a Miss Mavis Hatfield, but it's very disjointed. I mean, it barely makes sense. It's almost as if something's missing," he said, handing it to her.

"Let me read while you see what else we have to work with here. What do you think we have to go on?"

"Well, we have deed, architect, a historical preservation declaration... nothing unusual except for something about Miss Hatfield and a man named Perkins. He's the historian listed as a source that helped with research. My guess is we start with him and the daughter," decided Tucker.

Reggie was no longer listening as she scoured the papers before her. She saw what Tucker meant by the incongruity of them. There were obviously pieces missing but she couldn't decide if it was something lost or purposefully removed. Maybe the historian would know.

* * *

"This is a bit of an odd place, eh?" said Tucker.

They were waiting for Forrest Perkins, historian, in his "research room". It was nothing more than a small space at the back of a shabby house in one of the lesser appreciated neighborhoods. A sour-faced woman had led them into the hovel, then abruptly exited leaving them to a seat on the dirty stacks of media scattered throughout. The light was dim, and the air was filled with the mustiness of a lifetime of collecting useless refuse. There was a grotesquely huge cobweb stretching across a locked wooden cabinet and a soot-encrusted fireplace.

"This seems a bit eccentric," mused Reggie. "We did mention to someone where we were going, I hope?"

"You know, if we do too much nosing about, he might just brick us up in his fireplace. We could be unearthed sometime in the next century by some archaeologist looking for clues to twenty-first century society."

Reggie was about to comment on his gruesome imagination when she was interrupted by the entrance of Mr. Perkins, curator of the bizarre gallery on which they were seated.

"So nice to see you, uh, Mr. uh...

"Oh, sorry, Elliott, and this is Regina Winter," said Tucker, extending his hand.

Mr. Perkins ignored Tucker and kissed the back of Reggie's hand instead, fixing his gaze on her in a most unsettling manner.

"You must excuse my somewhat unorthodox library of records," he said, still gazing at her. "I never seem to get around to cataloging them these days. So busy with other tasks. Much more enjoyable to receive visitors between projects, you know."

Tucker pulled Reggie down next to him onto a stack of tattered filing boxes, extricating her hand from the historian's.

"What we mainly came to see you about," began Tucker, "was some information on a historically preserved house which is now the Sea Gables

Tea Room. We were wondering if you could provide us with the more personal details of its history."

"You know, details about the people who lived there; the owners, their children, gossip, scandals, births, deaths," added Reggie.

Perkins cut quite a figure staring straight through Tucker with his black beady eyes, pursed lips and set jaw. Tucker glanced nervously at the fireplace and waited for the old man to speak.

"I'm sure a man of your stature and accomplishments must have a wealth of knowledge no one else would begin to have," said Reggie sweetly. "Your name was at the top of the list for the most important history of this town, and we'd love to hear some of the special stories only you can tell."

The old man's face softened and spread into a mass of layered lines and shadows of age. Reggie had a flashback to Dr. Seuss's Grinch.

"Well, uh, yes, there are a few things about that particular piece of property which bear noting," he said gradually.

He managed to seat himself on one of the rickety filing boxes, laying his palms on his thighs and draping his knotted fingers over his knees.

"Now, let me see. Mr. Hatfield was the owner and manager of the only market in town. He was quite prosperous, you know, and his assets grew quickly with the rest of the town during the boom era. He married a beautiful girl and built her the house on Fourth Avenue. It was a show place although they had a lot of trouble during construction. It took longer to build than they had hoped, but in the end it was worth it. They had large parties, fashionable events, and the house assumed a character all its own. I attended a few of the galas there. They were something to see."

They sat in silence for a moment while the old man relived his memories.

"They had four children, two boys and two girls, and were very happy until the accident. Then everything just sort of stopped," finished Perkins.

"I haven't heard of any accident," said Reggie, wondering if this could be the subject of the missing sections. "I didn't see it in the papers we read. It was serious then?"

"Well, yes, it was fatal. I'm sorry, but I thought you'd have heard that part of the story. It was Mrs. Hatfield, you see. She was coming home from a social with two of the children when a storm blew up. They had a new automobile that she was not especially fond of. The driver couldn't see well and slid in the mud and water, running the car into a tree. The children were thrown clear, but she was caught underneath. She was pulled from the wreck and taken to the house which was just around the corner. She died there holding onto Mr. Hatfield's hand. And from then on everything just sort of stopped," repeated Perkins.

"What happened after that?" prompted Reggie.

"After that, there weren't any more parties. Mr. Hatfield stuck to his store and his house and buried himself in different business projects. He took up painting for a while. The children stayed in the area until their father died years later. The place was turned into a boarding house by the oldest daughter so they could stay where they'd grown up. Times were of course hard for everyone then."

"It sounds to me like the Hatfield's were rather wealthy people. Wasn't there a legacy or a will? Seems like there should have been some money left from a man who started the only market, even in tough times," said Reggie.

"There should have been more than what they found, seeing as how well he did. He was a good businessman and gave away a lot of his money, but it still wouldn't account for all he must have made. Still, the children didn't seem to be left with much all the same," said Perkins.

"You mentioned trouble during the construction of the house. What sort of trouble?" asked Tucker.

Mr. Perkins glanced quickly at Tucker then at the floor. A flicker passed over his face, then he stood up straight, dusted himself off, and stared uneasily at the two.

"The only thing I know is that there seemed to be a lot of arguments about how Hatfield saw the house and how the architect saw it. Hatfield liked space and areas for storage. He wanted safes concealed in the walls, secret panels, and passages, that sort of thing. The architect was against this because it compromised the structural parts of his plans. I guess he didn't want Hatfield telling him how to design his own work. In the end, though, he got his way, and they went on with the building. Wasn't anything in them, by the way," he said.

"In what, please?" asked Reggie.

"In the safes, in the hiding places in the walls. They were all gone through when he died. Nothing in them but a few papers and some of Mrs. Hatfield's jewelry he hadn't had the heart to get rid of. Rather sad, really. I'm sorry I can't tell you more; it was rather a long time ago and I was very young."

He reached for Reggie and again kissed the back of her hand in the same old-fashioned gesture. Tucker extended his hand and this time the old man took it, shaking it with a strong, short shake. He beamed gracefully, nodded, and retreated from the room. They watched him disappear then gathered themselves to leave. Reggie stooped for a moment in Tucker's path and nearly sent him headlong over her.

"What the devil are you doing down there? You nearly sent me into the next day."

"Nothing, sorry. Let's find our way out of here, please. I'm dirty and I'm hungry and we have a party tonight," said Reggie.

They walked along in silence for some time and were within a couple of blocks of the tea room before either of them spoke.

"What bothers me," said Reggie, "is why a supposedly well-respected historian lives in a broken-down ramshackle house with an old crank of a housekeeper in a bad area of town."

"Don't know about that, Reg, but I do know that I'm starving. We need food in order to think. We eat or I go on strike and do no more work."

"You haven't done any work yet," said Reggie, reminding him of their mission.

They rounded the corner and heard raised voices working their way out into the open.

"Well, let's see what they're on about," said Tucker.

He grasped her arm and crossed the street over to what looked to be the tea room cook and Dahlia under full steam of a most intense, ear-splitting disagreement.

* * *

Chapter 6

Violet: Good afternoon, Mr. Bailey.

George Bailey: Hello, Violet. Hey, you look good, that's some dress you got on there.

Violet: This old thing? Why I only wear it when I don't care how I look.

— It's a Wonderful Life, 1946

"May we help Dahl?" offered Tucker as he and Reggie headed straight into the storm.

Dahlia's creative, yet temperamental cook Frieda, turned a rather cold eye on them from under drippings of a few dozen eggs covering her. She passed judgment, then made an untimely and inconvenient decision.

"I quit!" spat Frieda, only cook to the Sea Gables tea room. "You can find someone else to put up with all the monkey business here. I won't have my kitchen interfered with by these pranks. I quit and I quit now!"

And with that she stomped her massive, egg-filled boot on the porch, turned on her heel and was gone. Dahlia, Reggie, and Tucker watched her fade into the distance before anyone could find anything useful to say.

"I'll get you some tea, Dahlia," said Reggie as she disappeared around a gable while Tucker stared after her.

"Alright then, what was that all about? And why was she dripping in premature poultry?"

"Oh, Tucker, it's another of those pranks. This time, they've demolished the kitchen and now I'm short one cook with guests, reservations, and two parties. I may quietly go off and have a breakdown."

"Well, let's survey the ruins," said Tucker. "Then we'll have to figure a way out of this mess in time."

Tucker straightened Dahlia's hat, gave her a pat, and ushered her in the back door where they found Reggie standing amidst a baker's ingredient bomb.

"You look like a human cookie."

Poor Reggie was covered in sugar and flour from head to toe. She had triggered a last booby-trap washing everything in eggs, flour, sugar, and shells. It was a culinary war zone.

"I came to get the tea and ...ugh!"

"I'll get the tea, Reg, you run along and clean up," offered Dahlia.

"Oh, hold the sugar for mine, Dahl. I'll just have Reggie stick her finger in it," grinned Tucker as she plodded through the destruction.

"I hope she goes around the fence. I think the gardener's watering the roses," said Dahlia thoughtfully.

Together they examined the mess and did a preliminary clean up, looking for clues to the culprit.

"Would you care to have your tour of our facilities now, Mr. Elliott?" teased Dahlia.

"This, as you can see, used to be the kitchen. Now it's a pastry coating. As we leave the ruins, you may observe our downstairs loo, where I may lock myself in for the duration."

Dahlia snorted and swung into her office while Tucker followed.

"Dahlia, who all is coming this evening? Maybe you can push it back an hour or so?"

"Actually, I could delay it an hour and have Dulcy call the agency. I'm hoping Frieda calms down and changes her mind. Anyway, we'll manage. We'll just have to be quick about it," bustled Dahlia.

And while she proceeded to make her phone calls, Tucker continued his now self-guided tour of the tea room. On rounding the stairs, he ran into Reggie looking scrubbed and polished and very attractive in a wholesome sort of way.

"Dahlia said I'd find you wandering about on your own. Have you found anything interesting?"

"No, Reg, I've just begun to look round. I think maybe we should concentrate on what's going on this evening. I'm always fascinated as to why people take an interest in a place like this. It's charming, except for the kitchen. Speaking of, Reg, looks like I'll be taking you out for a late snack since there's no cook and no kitchen."

"I am still starved and taking a bath in sugar and flour did little to kill my appetite. We can at least review the guests' names and maybe Dahlia can fill in the details. You don't think she'll need us?"

41

"No, she's doing her best to salvage things and we can help by staying out of her way."

And with that, they slid through the side entrance in search of a quiet corner.

* * *

Reggie and Tucker had settled themselves into a roomy booth in a pleasant garden café around the corner from the tea room. They ordered the day's special and began the dissection of the cocktail party list.

"And I assume that all these same people will be present at the events tomorrow as well?" asked Reggie as she munched on a bread stick.

"Yes, it's all by invitation plus any guests at the inn, local celebrities, family, and our guest of honor, Miss Hatfield, original owner of the place."

Reggie scanned the list then handed it to Tucker who gave it a quick once over.

"Where did you get this list, Tucker?"

"Stole it off Dahl's desk, of course."

"You big thief. Must've forgotten to wash the sugar off your sticky little fingers."

Tucker smiled handsomely at Reggie and continued with his report.

"From the looks of it seems like she was trying not to mix too many personalities."

"I can't say it tells us much, can you?" Reggie asked.

Tucker slid the list off to the side brushing a crumb off the end of the table just as the food was delivered by a large woman with sensible shoes and scary hair hiding who knew what in the midst of it.

"Get y'all anthin' else, honey?" said the vision.

"I rather don't think so, love, thank you though," beamed Tucker, fascinated by the cartoon-like features before him.

"We'll get the rest of the details out of Dahlia before we continue," said Tucker.

"Well, bon appetit," she said and dove into the greasy special with gusto.

Tucker followed suit occupying his mind with lawyers, doctors, and a few stray thoughts of Miss Winter in a fashionable cocktail dress in the dim light of the enchanting Victorian tea room. These he dismissed immediately and wondered what was for dessert.

* * *

They approached the B&B with trepidation, but all seemed calm and tranquil as they made their way through the garden to the kitchen. They opened the door onto a quiet and clean scene showing no traces of the earlier ravages.

"Seems a calm and peaceful place, eh?" observed Tucker as he searched the area for Dahlia. They passed someone in the breezeway heading into the kitchen and a few preliminary staff primping the interior but no presence of the bonneted lady herself. They wandered into her office for one last look.

"She doesn't seem to be here, Tucker. She's probably gone off to get ready for the party like we should do."

Tucker scanned her desk but found only the open address book from the calling frenzy she had begun as they were leaving. As he glanced at the addresses, his eyes fell on a datebook flipped open to today's date and a heavily lined, but unreadable name listed at the 4:30 p.m. slot. He casually gazed at his watch, saw 5:10 and moved back to the front of the desk.

"Well, we should probably be on our way to freshen up a bit."

Tucker pressed the guest list back on the edge of the desk, stuffed his hands in his pockets, and marched out.

* * *

Reggie collapsed on her settee for a minute before dressing. She let her heavy eyes rest and settling her head back on the couch began thinking of the night ahead. As she leaned back in meditation, she had the nagging feeling of having forgotten something. She breathed deeply, opened her eyes, and stared across to the old-fashioned closet. She was zeroing in on what it was. She had the perfect dress to wear for the party and realized it was hanging on the closet door in Palm Beach.

She thought quickly, threw on a robe, and ran to the tea room. Dahlia was close to her size although shorter. She bolted into the kitchen where smells of mushroom, garlic, and onion were prevailing over the sweetness of the late afternoon garden blooms. She found Dahlia arranging a few last-minute flowers in the foyer and noticed just how much like her she looked from behind without her usual hat and flowing summer dress.

"It definitely would work," she thought.

"Dahlia, I'm glad I caught you."

"Why Reggie, what a unique idea for party wear. A dressing gown!"

"I seem to have no cocktail dress and not much time to work with. I noticed you and I might be the same size. Is there something we can do?"

"I have just the thing," smiled Dahlia and immediately started for the door. "You go back to the B&B, and I'll be along with a lovely piece for you."

Reggie watched her disappear through the front then started back to her room. In the kitchen, she saw what could only be the replacement cook searching through cupboards and rummaging about in the freezers. She was glad to see there had been someone available at such short notice. She had finished her bath and was touching up her hair when Dahlia blew in looking glamorous in her slinky black dress with her hair in a flowing cascade. She held out another similar little black dress and measured it against Reggie.

"Thank God for the universal black dress. It's brilliant but a shade short, you know. It should be alright. I'll leave you to it and if you need anything else just call me, love."

Reggie tossed off her robe and climbed into the dress. To her delight it fit like a g love and looked even better for being a shade short. She reviewed the person in the mirror with detachment and wondered if what she saw was what others saw. She ran a quick eye over the shoulder-length wavy hair, the large almost-too-far-apart eyes, the small tippy nose, and the wide mouth set in the long, oval face which sat atop a well-proportioned five-foot nine-inch frame. The only exception was feet that sometimes looked too large for their own good. Overall, she was not displeased with what she saw. She fastened the last hook, smoothed out the front and with a satisfied nod, made her way out into the world.

* * *

Tucker basked in the hot water with his thoughts on the upcoming evening. He wished Dahlia's notes on the guests hadn't been so cryptic. He leaned back and let the heat of the water penetrate his tired and aching muscles. Tucker thought back to when he was eleven years old. He had accompanied his family to one of the special tea events which were highlights of the family business. At this particular gala, there was a beautiful young girl there whom Tucker didn't recognize. He crossed the room, marched directly up to her and to his horror, she lifted her eyes and proceeded to burst into laughter till the tears stained her cheeks. Tucker gazed at her in confusion. As he eyed her more closely, he realized it was Dahlia Porter, his friend since birth, having a laugh at his expense. The tomboy he was used to seeing was so different in her beautiful gown with her hair swept up, he hadn't even recognized her. Tucker wondered after all these years why he had never told her what a profound effect she had on him. Or maybe she already knew. Dahlia was an insightful and perceptive one from the beginning.

He dressed quickly and stood admiring his form in the full-length mirror. Looking back at him was a tallish man, six-foot three inches with dark hair combed straight back on his head. He was muscular though thin, with an angular face and strong jawline. His prominent cheekbones reached almost up to the long, luscious lashes that had always made his sisters jealous. It was a nice frame that held a well-tailored suit with style and was only marred by the presence of two oversized feet. He finished with a nod and a sigh of satisfaction.

"Let her giggle over this," he said and set out to find Miss Winter.

* * *

Chapter 7

Reggie was mesmerized by the elderly woman and found herself staring openly. The searching glance of the old woman found Reggie and held her in a momentary lock. Reggie veered away, turning toward Tucker and the impenetrable gaze moved on. A chill ran through her body, and she felt as though the woman had laid bare her soul. She was shaking the feeling away when she realized that Tucker was speaking to her.

"Reg, that's our target, the Hatfield woman. Reg? Reg, are you alright?"

He peered anxiously into her face for signs or symptoms.

"May I be of assistance?" said a calm and low voice next to Reggie.

"Oh, yes, Dr. Landry. Seems to be a bit peaked," said Tucker.

Reggie, whose color had all but vanished, felt it coming back in surplus and immediately began to sputter like a stopped-up sink.

"I am so sorry, I'm really fine. It was a momentary thing; really, it's nothing. I just became a little warm, that's all. I'll be fine. No need to worry, Dr. ..."

"Landry. George Landry. You're sure you're alright?"

"Oh yes, quite, thank you."

"I was just discussing town history with Mr. Elliott here. Lots of it, you know. You are Miss Winter I presume? Mr. Elliott's right hand man, so to speak?"

"Yes, and we are so pleased to be here. We're so proud of Dahlia and Sea Gables. We were thrilled to be invited. It's been very exciting so far. We've heard so much about Miss Hatfield and her family," said Reggie, happy to relinquish the attention to someone else.

"Oh, yes, isn't she marvelous?" chimed a voice behind Reggie, giving her the sensation of being surrounded.

"Oh, Miss Winter, please meet my wife, Gloria. Gloria, this is Miss Regina Winter, assistant to Mr. Elliott.

Gloria moved in and enveloped Reggie's hand in both of hers.

"How pleased I am to meet you," said Gloria with a pleasant smile. "I hope you're enjoying our little village?"

As she pressed her hands, Reggie was at once aware of a strong warmth and comfort exuded by Gloria. In just one clasp, she felt completely at ease and safe. Reggie thought this to be a rather appealing quality for a doctor's wife and wondered if he found it beneficial to his practice.

"Yes, we are. It's a lovely spot and the house is quite interesting. I'm very anxious to meet Miss Hatfield and to hear all about her childhood here."

"I do see she's working her way over, so you should get your chance very soon," said Gloria.

Reggie turned sharply to see the old woman who had stirred such a strange feeling in her greeting guests, meeting new faces, and masterfully handling the part of charming hostess and ambassador.

"What did I think I would see?" Reggie murmured aloud.

"Now you're holding conversations with yourself. Are you sure you're alright or just telling me so to keep me quiet?" asked Tucker.

"Oh, I'm fine, really," laughed Reggie, suddenly feeling foolish. "Just a little melodramatic is all. I think I'll get a drink. I see Dahlia at the cocktail table. I'll see you later, boss," she said, raising her eyebrows and winking her large almond eye at Tucker before sweeping towards the bar.

Tucker felt a momentary flush from head-to-toe as she moved off. He was surprised and annoyed at this reaction. He decided the best way to reduce its effect would be to ferret out Mr. Roderick Castner, Esq., and see what he might learn from the honorable attorney, and if he was indeed honorable. Reggie maneuvered through the now lively throng managing to settle in next to Dahlia at the bar. When she realized Reggie had joined her, she let out a loud and gleeful exclamation.

"My dear Miss Regina! How wonderful of you to join us. Have you met these lovely creatures? You must!" and she positioned Reggie ahead of her to make introductions.

"First, we have the one and only Letitia Mahoney, my former partner, sad faces everyone, and her current partner, Mr. Dennis Mahoney. This is Mr. and Mrs. Ross Carpenter. Kitty here is with the Historical Society, and over here is my dear friend and neighbor Miss Rebecca Carlisle, owner of the precious shop next door. We lovingly call her Bucky, don't we?"

Bucky was aglow in a large, toothy grin and Reggie again felt a rush of warmth from her new acquaintance. It made her wonder what overtook her so powerfully just a short time ago when Miss Hatfield entered the room. As if on cue, she turned to see the elderly woman with a small group by the fireplace and while she seemed to be listening attentively to the chattering female bent toward her, she was gazing intently in Reggie's direction. Had that gaze prompted her to turn around? Miss Hatfield nodded and squeezed her eyes at Reggie like a cat acknowledging a pat. Reggie smiled back wondering what produced such a strong draw between her and this woman.

The sound of her name close at hand brought her attention back and she leaned over to tune into the conversation she had abandoned.

"Is it exciting to work with such a famous company and such a handsome employer?" Mrs. Mahoney was saying.

Reggie detected a hint of wistfulness in the woman's voice, which was followed by a grousing grunt from her husband who loomed with his drink in the background like a bat. Reggie wondered if he was the reason she was no longer Dahlia's partner.

"Oh, it is quite a rewarding job," Reggie said. "It's business and charity and Sea Gables is especially pleasant as it's in our own backyard, so to speak, since the US offices are just on the other coast."

"I've recently started stocking the tea in my little shop next door and I can hardly keep it on the shelves," Rebecca was saying. "It has been tremendously successful for me. I just wanted to tell you that while I had you here."

Dahlia poked her cherubic face into their midst with one of her huge smiles.

"May I borrow our guest from you? We won't be a second."

Dahlia led Reggie away from the group who resumed chattering amongst themselves, taking little notice of what the two women were doing.

"Is everything alright Dahlia? Nothing wrong I hope?"

"No, thank God. I did just want to check on things and was wondering if you might help."

"Oh, certainly," said Reggie, trying not to sound too relieved. "I'm happy to help. What do you need me to do?"

"I'll check the kitchen and see how things are going in there if you would just pop upstairs and make sure everything is tidy in case some of these people decide they're going to unofficially tour the premises."

"My pleasure. Meet you back here in a few minutes?"

"Oh, no, love. I'll meet you back at the cocktail corner. You've yet to have that drink you came over for. We'll have to take care of that straight away you're back," and she wrinkled her nose at Reggie making off for the kitchen greeting and grinning as she went like a politician on the campaign trail.

Reggie climbed the two short stair sets to the private tea rooms. She wandered into the east room, which was bathed in the streetlamp glow, reminding her of a picture book Victorian setting. She passed through the alcove leading to the children's tea room and then into the sun room bordered by large paned and shuttered windows. All seemed serene and she was almost to the last room when she was halted by a slight sound from behind. She instinctively shot out a hand to the wall panel. Before she could hit the switch, a sweaty hand covered her own and she felt the rapid and hot breath of someone directly behind her shoulder. The hair on her neck rose and her sharp intake of breath winded her with a spasm before any sound could escape her lips.

"Looks like you don't take a hint very well, Dahl dear. You've had more than your share of warnings and I'm losing patience with this. You're running out of luck and the next time even your fancy English friend won't be able to help you. You understand my meaning? Better think real hard about your future... love."

Reggie nodded shakily, and even though frightened, was dying to turn around for a glimpse of the owner of the menacing voice. She stood rooted to her spot until she realized that whoever had been there had noiselessly slipped out and had by now rejoined the others at the party.

She leaned against the wall to regain her composure. She did not want to upset Dahlia with this until she could tell Tucker. She smoothed the front of her dress once again, ran her hands through her hair and with a deep breath, marched off to rejoin the party. When she reached the foyer, she saw Dahlia waving her back over to the bar. Reggie took another deep breath and plunged her way through the crowd. She eyed the rest of the noisy guests for surprise on seeing her descend the stairs instead of Dahlia but could detect nothing out of the ordinary.

"There you are, come right over here, and let's put you right between Kitty and me," she laughed.

Reggie reclaimed her spot next to Dahlia and scanned the room for Tucker. She located him off to her right cornered by the gregarious Mercedes Castner who was no doubt giving Tucker a well-rehearsed lecture on crime and punishment with the fervor of a religious fanatic meeting a new prospect for the flock. He gave her a pleading grin and Reggie waved and smiled in return then casually turned her back to his plight, deciding that it was not the right time to have any kind of chat. The conversation had taken a turn to local events and the current political scene of which Reggie could only listen politely.

"Reggie, would you please hold this drink for me? I do need to run over and check on Mavis. I won't be a minute," and she was off before anyone but Reggie noticed.

She watched her retreating back and considered just how easy it would be to mistake her for Dahlia. She looked down at the full scotch that had been entrusted to her. It looked quite refreshing especially after her ordeal upstairs. She never had gotten a cocktail as promised so she'd replace Dahlia's when she returned.

Reggie sipped the strong liquid and listened to the buzz of conversation. She kept one ear tuned to the historical topics of her group and one ear to the snippets from passing guests. It was a beehive of activity with people refreshing their drinks and passing by on their way to the powder room or the porch. She swirled the amber liquid in the tumbler and surveyed the room for Tucker and the Castner woman. Tucker had managed to escape but only to be captured by the sour-faced Dennis Mahoney.

Reggie was speculating about their discussion when Dulcy appeared from behind Tucker, waving and making her way toward her. Reggie was glad to see Dulcy. She felt grateful to her for the loyalty and devotion she poured into Sea Gables. Dahlia was lucky to have such a capable manager. As she watched her thread through the room she wondered where she had been all evening. This was the first time she had seen her.

"Well, Reggie. How are we doing? Are you enjoying the festivities?"

"I really am," said Reggie, meaning it, "but I wondered where you were. I haven't seen you all evening. Where have you been hiding?"

"Well, I've been doing a little kitchen duty. Just keeping an eye on the agency woman. She was the only one they had to spare so I suppose we're lucky to get anybody at the last minute. Dahlia has more help coming in for tomorrow, but someone must have an idea of what's going on. I don't want to try to break someone else in right before guests start arriving."

"Well, I think everything has turned out beautifully," said Reggie and shifted her weight more comfortably against the bar flipping a platter of peanuts, sending them flying every which way.

"Oh, how stupid of me. I am so sorry!"

Several guests paused briefly to appraise the situation then went back to their conversations.

"Oh, don't worry Reggie. We'll push them aside for now. It's okay."

"Maybe I should have something else to eat. I guess Dahlia's drink was a little stronger than I thought."

"I'll go with you," said Dulcy. "Have you gotten a chance to meet Miss Hatfield yet? You'll have a wonderful time chatting with her. She's a walking history reference. She tells stories in a way that makes you feel like you were actually there."

They wound their way to the food table and Dulcy deposited Reggie in front of the plates before picking through the desserts and coffees. Reggie gazed at the loaded platters, yawning as she stared over the mushrooms. She had the queer sensation of floating and when she raised her eyes to speak felt as though she lifted the weight of the world. She squinted to get a better view of Dulcy and teetered a bit as she leaned closer to her.

"Reggie? You look strange to me. Stay here and don't move. I'm going to get Tucker."

Reggie watched her go wanting to speak but feeling too lazy to do so. She looked down over the wavering mushrooms as if expecting them to speak for her. She shifted her eyes in slow motion to the half-filled drink glass she had set down. There was something about that glass she was trying to remember. She stared at the empty plate in her hand then back to the drink glass. She felt an odd rising and falling sensation though she was sure she hadn't moved. She struggled to find Tucker in the crowd but couldn't concentrate on what she was seeing.

"Just for a minute," she said aloud, and the plate fell crashing to the floor with her right behind it.

She could hear the clamor of feet and hollow voices ringing in her ears. She knew she had to get up, to stand up and shout something at someone, but couldn't pinpoint what. She pried her eyes open to see Tucker leaning over her, his handsome features close to hers fading in and out.

"My glass...I want...my glass...I..."

"Lie still, Reg. I've got you," she heard him saying.

She tried to raise her head, to make him understand that she needed the glass. She turned her head toward the table and felt heavy sleep pressing her down. She rolled her eyes upward and saw the last thing she would see for a while – the quiet and concerned expression of Miss Mavis Hatfield.

* * *

Chapter 8

The Book: [T]his is the time for maintaining a cool head, and following the one simple rule: put the blame on somebody else.
– How to Succeed in Business Without Really Trying, 1967

Tucker backed away from the ministrations of the doctor and his assistants. He eyed the crowd closing in on Reggie trying to glean any meaning from their faces other than genuine concern and curiosity. He glanced at the bartender who manned his post with only a modicum of concern. This was obviously something he witnessed regularly. A young girl gets into the swing of things, drinks too much, and takes a nap on the floor. Only this girl was Reggie and Tucker didn't believe she was in the habit of overindulging.

He examined the area by the food table where she had been. He hovered over the mushrooms in much the same way as Reggie. They looked like mushrooms to him. His eyes roved over the table until they rested on a half-empty highball glass. A scene flashed through his mind of Reggie lying on the floor pleading for something, possibly a glass. He nonchalantly glanced at the drama before him and shot his hand out for the tumbler. He sat his own in its place and returned to view the proceedings. Reggie was conscious but not lucid and Dahlia had arrived and taken charge with Landry.

"Move her to my office, George. It's alright everyone; just a touch of faint. Everything will be fine. Please go on, we'll be right back."

Reggie was gently lifted from the floor and carried into the privacy of Dahlia's office. She was situated comfortably on the Victorian chaise and was now sporting a cold compress covering her beaded forehead. Tucker straggled in after the others after having given the once over of the party attendees.

It was an interesting scene he encountered in the makeshift sick room. Dr. Landry was busy with the examination of his patient; the timing of the pulse, the blood pressure, temperature, state of the pupils, and reflex reactions, all with which he seemed acutely dissatisfied. Dahlia was pacing in front of the chaise in an agitated state which Tucker could see was annoying Dr. Landry. Gloria Landry was compassionately holding one of Reggie's hands and watching the movements of her husband with intent but accustomed interest.

The presence which arrested Tucker's attention was the quiet figure seated by herself in the corner also intently watching the proceedings. Miss Mavis Hatfield had followed the others in and inconspicuously seated herself away from the action. Tucker could not decide if this was to be out of the way or to detract attention from her presence. As though reading his mind, she slowly turned her pale countenance from Reggie to Tucker and held him in her gaze before returning to Reggie. Tucker was unable to interpret the expressionless stare but decided he would question Miss Hatfield away from the others. Tucker returned his attention in time to see the good doctor giving Reggie an injection. She slowly began to focus, trying to see where she was and why.

"Ouch!" she cried.

"Now don't you go moving about like that, young lady," said Dr. Landry.

"You may have quite a headache for a while. You just lay here and rest now."

Dr. Landry rose from the chaise beckoning Tucker into the hall with a meaningful stare. Tucker checked the room again before following Landry. Dahlia and Gloria were tending to Reggie, oblivious to them, but Mavis Hatfield's eyes followed them through the door into the hallway before Landry pulled the door shut. He stood there, silent, hands in pockets staring hard at the floor. He warily turned his eyes to Tucker and stared again at the floor before trying to speak.

"Has Miss Winter had any recent surgery or been in any accidents of late?"

"Not that I know of, but I don't know her well. Look here, what are you on about?"

Dr. Landry stared fixedly at Tucker as if deciding whether he was worthy of his confidences.

"It's just that she doesn't strike me as a drug user."

Whatever Tucker was expecting, this was not it.

"Dr. Landry, you can't expect me to believe that Reggie's condition is due to drug abuse?"

"This is a drug overdose, Mr. Elliott, whether you find it believable or not. The injection I gave her was to counteract the effects of what appears to be a heavy dosage. Knowing what I do of you through Dahlia, I find this a difficult explanation to swallow. That leaves an accidental overdose which is worrisome but possible, or the thought that someone slipped her something. I must come up with an explanation for my records as to why she would have a prescription narcotic in her possession. It is illegal to have drugs without a prescription, you understand."

"Did you find any on her?" demanded Tucker, "Because I find it hard to believe that she uses drugs of any kind. We'll have to stick to one of the other explanations and I suggest we start with you telling me about some of the people in the other room. What's going on with this inn? Who's trying to discredit Dahlia and what is it that someone is so interested in finding here that they're tearing apart the house to get at it?"

Whatever shock value Tucker had hoped to have on Dr. Landry was only slightly gratified.

"I don't know what you're talking about, Elliott. Whatever you seem to think is 'going on' here is obviously the result of Dahlia's rather overactive imagination. She does tend toward the dramatic on occasion. I have heard of 'incidents' but I had put them down to being part of the renovations of an older and compromised structure. You're an intelligent man; surely you don't believe that bricks just fly out of their moorings for no reason? And I hardly think that any of the people here are involved in anything so sophomoric as practical joking."

Tucker held the medical man in his steady gaze trying not to reveal his surprise. He was not aware that Dahlia had confided details of the incidents to anyone but himself.

"I'll just keep note of the specifics until Miss Winter is well enough to straighten them out. I'm sure she can give us her list of medications, if any."

"Alright, Landry. Let me know what I can help you with, eh?"

"Of course, Elliott. I'll just be getting back to our patient if you don't mind."

"Oh, yes of course, by all means. Please continue. I'll stop on later if I may?"

With a curt nod, Dr. Landry strode back into the sick room to tend to his newly acquired patient. Tucker glanced up to catch sight of Reggie before Landry sealed off his territory. He felt the hair on the back of his neck rise. Landry's expression belied a momentary lapse of bedside manner. What was it he saw there? And why did it bother him so? Tucker stared at the closed door reconstructing the doctor's expression. How did he know about the bricks in the fireplace? Didn't Dahlia say she had told no one about that?

He absently shifted Reggie's drink glass in his hands and was reminded of another tricky little problem. He stared down into the diluted liquid, then raised it for a closer inspection. He was beginning to wish he'd studied harder in chemistry class when the door to the sickroom flew open and out shot Dahlia.

"Tucker! That man has turned me out of my own office. Says I'm disturbing his patient and would I please take my colorful self elsewhere. At least you're here on the spot and with a spot of just what I need," she said, shooting her hand out to seize the glass from his hand.

"Don't touch that glass!"

Tucker managed to whisk the tumbler out of Dahlia's reach and back into his protection in one swift movement.

"Well. Chivalry is bloody well dead, I can see."

Tucker motioned her to be quiet and guided her into the recess by the kitchen.

"You can't have this glass, you can't have what's in it," Tucker hissed. "Do you know a reliable chemist by any chance?"

"Whatever are you babbling about!? I simply do not..."

"Stop for one second and let me finish."

She stared back at him defiantly then slowly grew quiet.

"What's happened, Tucker? What is it this time? Just tell me straight out."

Tucker peeked into the kitchen and saw only a short, stocky woman arranging food on a platter and eyeing them occasionally as she reached for garnishes.

"You've got to listen to me, Dahlia," he said as he pushed the glass up in front of their faces. "This was the one Reggie had. When she collapsed, she was frantically going on about a glass. When I examined your buffet, this is what I found where she was standing before she fell. There must be something in this drink. Reggie's drink. And we have to find out who put something in it. Because I know you don't accept the good doctor's drug abuse theory any more than I do."

Dahlia's eyes widened and stared blankly at the half-empty tumbler. The light from the kitchen bent around the corner just far enough to illuminate the pale glass as she turned it in her hands. When she looked back to Tucker, it had diminished into a very cold and sober stare.

"Not Reggie's drink," she sighed and blinked. "Mine. I gave it to her to hold for me while I rounded up Mavis. She must have drunk my drink and whatever was in it was not meant for her, it was meant for me."

CHAPTER 8

* * *

Chapter 9

"That was close, God."
— Scary Movie, 2000

Mavis Hatfield had been quietly observing the drama unfolding before her. It seemed surrealistic, as something shrouded in a twilight mist. This episode had piqued her curiosity. She had to know more about Miss Regina Winter. Despite how discreet Dr. Landry had tried to be, she had heard the murmurings to his wife suspecting Reggie of abusing drugs. Mavis did not believe this conclusion and envisioned this young woman enlisting any means available to find the cause of her collapse.

Mavis's curiosity had drawn her to the sickroom. She was convinced that there was an additional explanation for the presence of Mr. Elliott and his capable associate. What was it Dahlia had said that stuck in the back of her mind like an irritation? There was something about Tucker Elliott; something suggestive in his mannerisms that kept tugging at her subconscious. The ever-growing curiosity was overwhelming. She felt compelled to find out more about both these people. She would formally meet this young woman in more agreeable circumstances. Right now, it was her duty to return to the party and mingle among the guests who had shown loyalty to Dahlia and patronage to herself.

"Miss Hatfield? Miss Hatfield, are you alright, dear?"

Mavis looked up to find Gloria Landry bent over her with respectful concern.

"Is there anything I can get you? I know this is upsetting but she'll be fine, you know. She just needs a little rest now and with what George gave her she should sleep for some time."

"Oh, no, no. I was just getting ready to return to the party. She seems to be doing much better. Do you need any help getting her to her room?"

"No, Miss Hatfield, we'll let her rest here for the time being. We'll only disturb her when it's absolutely necessary."

"I'm sorry I didn't have the chance to be introduced to her but I'm sure I can see her tomorrow perhaps?" asked Miss Hatfield.

"Oh, yes, she'll be good as new by then and I know she'd love to meet you, too. Are you sure I can't get you anything?"

"No, thank you, Gloria. I'll be on my way. Thank you for letting me sit in."

"Oh, no trouble at all, Miss Hatfield," she said as she ushered her through the door and into the corridor before returning to help her husband tidy the room.

Reggie's even breathing came quietly from the chaise and Gloria was satisfied she was fast asleep.

"Odd, isn't it George," she remarked as she returned the chairs to their respective locations. "A nice young girl like that experimenting with drugs. She seems to have an exciting, glamorous job with a handsome and famously wealthy eligible bachelor, you'd think..."

Gloria prattled on while George sat on the end of the chaise with his arms folded holding his head in his thumb and forefinger watching her. He glanced again at Reggie, satisfying himself that she was resting comfortably. He turned his attentions back to his wife. This was a delicate situation and although everyone saw, it should all be shrugged off as over excitement or exhaustion. He couldn't afford to have drugs enter into it. He would talk to Gloria.

"Alright, Gloria, let's get back to the others if they're still there. And Gloria, let's not talk about the girl with anyone, shall we?" he said as he took her arm and steered her to the door. "You know we have to keep the sacred trust now, don't we?" he said smiling.

"Oh, of course, George. You know I wouldn't break a confidence where a patient is concerned. I am the doctor's wife you know," she said brightly.

But the good doctor could tell there had been a momentary flash of disappointment before Gloria remembered the reality of her situation and quickly dismissed a juicy topic for the daily coffee klatch.

"There's my girl," smiled Dr. Landry as he held the door for Gloria.

He threw a quick glance back at the chaise, then proceeded to follow his lovely wife into the hall.

"That," he thought, "was a close one," and he clapped his hand over the switch and pulled the door closed.

* * *

Chapter 10

HAL9000: Will I dream?

Dr. Chandra: Of course you will dream, all intelligent creatures dream.

– '2010', 1984

Reggie woke and found herself walking through the most amazing home she had ever seen. She was wandering through it passing huge tables with layers of food, ice sculptures, and champagne fountains. She heard muffled voices and laughter and the faint clinking of glasses somewhere. She tiptoed through the foyer, moving cautiously along the corridor as if the slightest noise might scare the laughter away. The hallway became a huge ballroom where there were hundreds of people talking and laughing, but the silence was deafening. No one noticed her until she passed her mother who cried out, " Where on earth have you been? We've all been waiting for you. It's time to make your speech."

She had to climb a narrow staircase to get to a podium. She clung to the sides as she flattened herself to safely crawl up them. When she reached the top, she could only make out silhouettes. A brilliant spotlight was blinding her to the features of the waiting audience. She tried to speak but couldn't understand her own language. The guests were now wearing masks, faces up, taunting, and teasing her. She tried to speak but was drowned out by their laughter. She covered her ears and closed her eyes to block them out.

Reggie sprung up and gazed wildly around in the dark. She was not in the ballroom, yet this place was just as foreign. She did know that she was finally awake. The minute she sat up an intense pounding wracked her head. Her hand weightlessly reached up to stop it. She imagined her head to be a large, unwieldy object and was genuinely surprised to find it quite small instead.

She groaned as she focused on her surroundings. It was dark except for a shaft of light from under the door. She could barely make out the fixtures when her eyes rested on a slouching figure seated directly beside her. Reggie leaned closer and recognized it as a sleeping Tucker Elliott dressed in disheveled evening clothes and making a sound close to that of steam escaping a tea kettle at the beginning of a rolling boil. Reggie was confused about this when memory began creeping back, first slowly, then in a flood. She stifled another groan remembering the night's events as they began to take shape. She was mortified at the thought of having passed out in front of Dahlia's guests.

She relaxed her body limb by limb as if the slightest noise would wake him. She rubbed her temples and tried to recall the events but to no avail. She took several deep breaths and began to feel the cobwebs loosen. She opened her eyes and let them rest on Tucker. He was leaning at an awkward angle with his head lolling to the right, arms crossed around his chest, and long legs crossed over each other. It looked a most uncomfortable position, but he was sleeping a deep, undisturbed sleep.

She studied him closely; at the usually carefully groomed hair that now lay loosely across his forehead, the long, soft lashes that rested languidly on his cheeks, and the shine of a scar on his forehead. She smiled thinking about a tired but worried Tucker Elliott sitting up all night with her.

Reggie reddened at the thought of it possibly being him who carried her to this room. How impressive she was fainting in front of her new boss! She was thankful for the darkness in case he woke. She was thankful to the light now and could see they were in Dahlia's office. She noiselessly slid off the chaise and found her shoes. With a last look, she tiptoed through the door and out into the hall.

She wandered toward the kitchen bathed in security lighting. All was quiet and clean, not a spec to suggest that there had been anyone there let alone a well-attended cocktail party. She slipped through the swinging door into the tea room and relaxed. All was well here too, as she stood in the middle of another clean and tidy room.

She was overcome by a tidal wave of exhaustion and wanted nothing more than to be in her own bed. She was rubbing her head to rid the lingering ache when she spotted something small and shiny in the glow of the streetlamp. She begged herself to run to the B&B, but her mind said otherwise, and she found herself in front of the fireplace.

She closed her hand around a small object and carried it to the window for a closer look. Reggie thought this was not a momentous discovery but just a small piece of metal, twisted and torn on one edge. She was about to toss it aside but thought better of it. Maybe she should find out what it belonged to. She gripped it tightly and scuttled down the path to the B&B and bed.

* * *

Tucker woke to the sound of clinking dishes and the smell of fruity, sweet muffins. He had spent a fitful night and was now feeling kinked, crooked, and cranky. He had also been having a dream that tested his better humor. This dream irked him as it was not only recurring, but it involved a woman whose face he could never bring into focus. She was always the center

69

of a brilliant light where everyone else was fuzzy. The light smeared her features and kept her face unrecognizable. Just as he would try to touch her, he would be back in his office reaching for a file folder.

This was typical of how the dream progressed only this time there was something new. As he reached for the file, he came back instead with a glass. It was an ordinary highball glass with no distinction other than being wrongly placed in his files. But this time, he found himself back at the ball. He scanned the crowd searching for the girl and noticed them all looking at something on the ground.

He followed the circle of gazes to the girl lying on the floor. A moment of panic consumed him, and he knelt beside her to wake her and bring her back to safety. When he lifted the soft shoulders, it was Reggie's face, clear and distinct in the paling light. People were backing away now and he shook her and called her name. The noise of clinking glasses and chattering receded with the crowd.

Tucker realized he had been slowly waking and his remembrances were overtaking his dreams, pushing him to reality at the start of a new day at the Sea Gables Tea Room. His first thought was for Reggie. He unfolded his cramped limbs and leaned into the chaise. It was empty. It was also cold and carried a slight trace of Reggie's perfume leaving Tucker to believe she had been gone for some time.

He stood, stretched, and brushed himself down before leaving. He felt rather exposed knowing that she had woken, watched him as he slept, and tiptoed out before disturbing him. He sighed, glanced around, and made for the door. He opened it wide and was face to face with Dahlia in all her morning glory.

"Well, good morning, you. And how did you sleep all crumpled up in my lovely wing back? And how is our patient feeling today?"

She peeked around the door and gazed fixedly at the vacated chaise.

"Well, what have you done with her? I should think it would be simple to keep an eye on a rather tall, attractive girl. Did I mention unconscious?"

"She must have slipped out a little bit ago. Awfully embarrassing, you know, knotted up in a frilly chair looking like I'm spying on her," said Tucker.

"Well, come on. Have some breakfast and then we'll look in on her. It's early yet but we've got a big day, and a lot of questions to be answered. I've been at it since daybreak with Dulcy getting this place ready for a reception. Maybe I should hire police protection."

"One of the first things we need to do is run that glass round to your chemist friend," said Tucker. "I want to know as soon as possible what was in that tumbler."

Dahlia set a laden tray in front of him and poked at the steaming muffins.

"Well, let's dig in, then we'll get cracking!"

* * *

Reggie rolled over on her side and punched her pillow. Everything about this bed felt hard and uneven, like she was lying on a pile of rocks. She gingerly opened her eyes and again felt disoriented. She focused on one piece of furniture at a time until the glaze left her eyes and she remembered where she was and why.

She thought about getting up then decided it might be better to lie still for a while. It would be good to marshal her thoughts. There were a few things she had not told Tucker, and after last night, he would not be pleased that she had kept them from him. She still had the square of newspaper she had picked up from historian Jenkins' floor. She would have to bring it to Tucker's attention now.

She felt foolish thinking back on how she had scooped him on a clue and how she was going to triumphantly supply the answer to the puzzle with her stolen treasure. She had no idea things would become so complicated. She had no idea they would become dangerous. As if the stolen article wasn't enough, she didn't think she had told him about the stranger in the upstairs hallway. And now another unexplained detail was the sharp metal object found by the fireplace. The metal object occupied the ashtray on her nightstand and her head hurt trying to decipher what this piece might mean.

She thought back to the dimly lit room, turning it over in her hands. How long ago that seemed. How far away the shadows of night and the closeness of darkness were. She leaned on one elbow and noticed how brilliantly the sun shone through the sheers. It must be a beautiful day as well as warm. She would have to think about getting up and joining the rest of the world.

She would recall this quiet time later envying how calm and tranquil it had been. The disastrous events that were to cloud their lives indeed were nowhere on the horizon.

* * *

There was a sharp wrap on Reggie's door. She pulled the covers to her nose and prayed as the visitor entered.

"Good morning, love!" trilled Dahlia as she marched in with a beautiful wicker tray of fresh baked goodies.

"How are you feeling this morning? You gave us a nasty turn last night dropping all over the floor like that."

She set the tray down in front of Reggie with a wink.

"Yes, I know. I gave myself a scare as well," she said as she glanced around Dahlia at the doorway.

She felt herself redden and noted a flicker of amusement on Dahlia's face before she perched on the edge of Reggie's bed.

"I um...noticed that...uh..."

"Mr. Elliott," pronounced Dahlia regally, "is performing his morning ablutions following his rather undignified repose of the previous evening."

Reggie burst out laughing and the embarrassing overtones of Tucker's nightlong vigil dissipated.

"I woke up at some point in the night and had no idea where I was and then, there he was sitting next to me fast asleep. Did you know he snores, Dahlia?"

Dahlia roared with laughter and nearly toppled off the bed. This was better than any tonic she might have taken.

"I dare say he'd be properly pink if he found that out," giggled Dahlia. "It wouldn't do for his image, you know."

They chuckled over the visual of Tucker and his snoring till the laughter subsided and they faced each other in silence.

"Dahlia, what did happen last night? I mean, how did I come to wake up in your office with Tucker sitting watch? I don't remember much after my run-in upstairs and coming down to find you. I remember you went away for a while; that's when Dulcy came in. I think we were having our drink together."

Dahlia stared at Reggie. Normally her first question would be to know what she meant by "run-in" but decided to let it go. What was she talking about? She snapped back into conversation as though a spell had been broken.

"I think what you need to do is eat up all these goodies and then rest a while longer. Things are well in hand for this evening, and I think Dr. Landry would prefer you relaxed for the time being."

"Oh, no!" protested Reggie. "There's a million things to do; lunch with the city, your grand opening and reception. I will not sit by like an invalid and let the world proceed without me!"

Dahlia was not up to matching the high spirits of Regina Winter this morning and she decided to consult Tucker before questioning Reggie further.

"Tell you what. I'll go find Tucker and we'll speak to Dr. Landry and see if he won't grant you an early release. You seem to be better. Eat up and I'll be back in a bit."

She smiled at Reggie and let herself out. She headed straight for Tucker's room and knocked as lightly as possible as if Reggie might hear her. A freshly scrubbed Tucker finally popped the door open with one of his most handsome smiles.

"Dahlia, love! I feel like shit. Come in, darling. How's our patient doing? Progressing nicely, I hope."

"Yes, she's doing quite well, although she has questions and seems not to remember much. I just couldn't continue without knocking you up first. I think we need to talk. I didn't let on, but she mentioned something about a run-in while on her go-round upstairs. I think she thought she had told me about it. I said we'd call Dr. Landry to see if he would parole her today. Maybe it would be better than being stuck in her room."

"Yes, well, there's a few things needing cleared up, eh?"

Dahlia could only nod.

* * *

Chapter 11

Marion Cobretti: You wanna talk, we'll talk. I'm a sucker for good conversation.
— Cobra, 1986

The three of them gathered around an old oak table at the far side of the porch.

"So, what does all this mean?" Reggie asked.

She had gotten a reprieve from Dr. Landry provided that if she felt ill, she would banish herself to her room.

"I don't know yet," ventured Tucker.

Dahlia sat consumed by her thoughts running her finger along the edge of the table.

"I'm trying to understand all this," said Reggie. "I came downstairs and met up with you, Dahlia. Then you went off to tend to Miss Hatfield. I was holding your drink and decided to drink it. I spilled a tray of peanuts, went to the buffet with Dulcy, tried to take some food but only managed to fall to the floor instead. I'm beginning to vaguely remember this now. And what you're saying is that there was something in that drink meant for you and I drank it," she said waving her hand at Dahlia.

"Exactly. We just haven't found out what or who could have been responsible. I thought I kept track of everyone quite well. Someone managed to pull this off right under our noses," said Tucker.

Reggie thought about her incident up in the tea room but wasn't sure what to say. She decided it would be better to talk to Tucker first. She looked up to find them both watching her. She assumed it was out of concern for her condition and she smiled wanly as if to punctuate her weakened state.

"Well, what's next then?" she asked.

"Dulcy is handling last minute details for me so I can do my social duties this afternoon and then we'll be receiving guests in the garden starting at 4 p.m. This is an important event," said Dahlia, "and everything must go perfectly. We're booked solid and everyone is turning out from the local set. I've received almost no regrets."

Tucker wondered callously if this had to do with friendship or morbid curiosity from the nosy townspeople.

"What's the schedule today?" asked Reggie.

"We'll be starting the garden reception around four. Tea and food will be served just off the porch, the bar will be set up at the northeast corner of the garden, and the girls will be conducting tea room and B&B tours continuously. Dulcy will be manning the information booth, and the agency woman will be tending the kitchen."

"And what do you want us to do?" asked Tucker.

"Just be your charming selves. You know, Tucker, your usual dog and pony show and then you're free to um...work the room with Reggie?"

Tucker knew this meant that they were to investigate the guests. He had already decided his line of attack. He nodded and wondered if Dahlia had anything else to mention, such as with whom her 10:30 appointment was today. She apparently had no intention of mentioning it and it made Tucker uncomfortable thinking she was keeping something from him.

He shifted his thoughts to Reggie and her secrets and wondered when and if she would confide in him. His talk with Dahlia made him wonder what possible "episode" occurred while he had been chatting at the bar below. He had faith that she would eventually tell him.

He was stirred from his thoughts by a bellow from inside and looked up to see Dahlia legging it through the front door.

"Oh, Tucker, we'll meet in the foyer to go to the lunch. If you need me, I'll be popping in and out. Don't let me miss anything, now!"

Tucker and Reggie sat in awkward silence till he could bear it no longer.

"Are you sure you're up to it, Reg? I mean, you look well enough, but be honest."

"Oh, I'm fine really," Reggie said blushing. "Just a slight ping in the upper temple but nothing that some good detective work won't cure."

Tucker said nothing and steadied his gaze on her. She shifted in her seat feeling the cushion-less wrought iron furniture making quite an impression on her. Tucker, continuing to stare in an unnerving manner, let her know it was time to own up to her actions.

"Uh... Tucker, I haven't kept you up on everything."

Tucker continued his challenging gaze, though softening it a bit.

"There are several things I need to catch you up on, to be exact," she said.

"Oh, several things," thought Tucker.

It was his turn now to shift in his chair, and he too felt the impression Reggie had.

"Okay, let's chat. Maybe we should walk. I feel as though we shouldn't speak so close to the tea room," Reggie said.

She looked at the structure as if it was staring back at her. Tucker ushered Reggie gentlemanly before him from the porch. Reggie headed for the sidewalk as Tucker casually massaged his backside and followed her down the steps. He met her at the corner, hands in pockets, face turned to the bright sun and vivid blue summer sky.

"Alright, Miss Winter, let's have it."

"I'd like to first say that I didn't mean to not tell you these things, it's just that that's how it came about, you know."

"Go on, please."

She passed over the newspaper article saving it for last and started with the upstairs encounter.

"Last night, when I went to run rounds upstairs for Dahlia, I was met by someone."

Tucker slowed his gait and looked in her eyes.

"I went up the stairs and started room by room, as anyone would do," began Reggie, "and as I was on my tour, I thought I heard a noise, but before I could turn on the lights..."

"Reggie, you were walking about in the dark? Why ever would you?"

"It was really quite beautiful. The light shining in through the windows... It didn't seem right to turn them on. Besides, Dahlia didn't want anyone wandering around up there and turning on a light seemed like an invitation."

Tucker levied a stern look at her.

"And as it happens, turning on the light would have let someone know who I was in which case..."

"Yes?"

"They wouldn't have come up from behind and threatened me."

"Because they thought you were Dahlia."

Clarity was dawning now.

"Ah, now it all makes sense," he said as he cut off Reggie's path stopping before her.

"And what exactly did this person say to you, Reg?"

"Well, it ended with 'and next time even my fancy English friend won't be able to help me'."

"Of course it only stands to reason Miss Dahlia is leaving out a few details of her own, I'm afraid. It's obviously a scare mission to get her out of here. There's something either worth money or someone's reputation. What else?"

"Nothing, really. He left and I stood there afraid to breathe till I was sure he'd gone."

"It was a man, then?"

Reggie wasn't quite sure; she had just assumed it was a man.

"I don't know whether it was a man or a woman, really. They were whispering, so I suppose it could have been either."

"Well, that's clear as mud. Are you sure there wasn't anything else helpful?"

Reggie shut her eyes to picture the scene, but her mind was still foggy from the drugs, and she was no longer certain if what she pictured was true or part of the haze.

"I'm sorry. I can't seem to get it to focus," she said feeling frustrated.

"Never mind, love," said Tucker gently. "It'll pop back in your head when you least expect it."

He led her through the B&B to the salon and guided her to the sofa.

"Alright, we'll just move on. What else did you have to tell me?"

Reggie weighed the two, then decided.

"Well, it was something rather odd. Something I found," she announced.

* * *

Mavis Hatfield leaned in closer to the mirror to check her carefully sculpted hair. She could not help thinking that life was cruel at times, yet kind. It tended to rob you of your youth in a long drawn-out fashion, while dimming your eyesight so that you couldn't really see it. That had a certain symmetry to it, and she grinned at the thought. She tucked up a stray hair and craned back her neck to survey the results.

She thought about the young girl from the night before. She would call the tea room to ask after her. She needed to check on Mazie's reservation and hoped Dahlia would have remembered to put her sister on the first floor. Mazie didn't get around as well as she did and climbing stairs was not an option.

It had been a long time since Mazie had visited home and Mavis had finally convinced her it was time. It had been best for all concerned when she left for the north, but Mavis knew that one day she would return. Mazie had been pleased and proud, fluttering with excitement when she learned of all the attention the family and their childhood home were receiving.

"Of course I'll come," she had responded.

How could she resist with the interest in their home and history and Mavis knew she would not refuse Dahlia's personal invitation. Mavis drifted back to happier times when the house was in its heyday. She chose only to dwell on the fond memories rather than the unpleasantness which eventually enveloped the family. The accident seemed to trigger a chain of misfortunes which would devastate and decay the family past repair.

She had been the anchor for them in their times of need, sacrificing most of her life for their welfare. That part of her past couldn't be helped but there was a part that could. It was the reason she felt so drawn to Regina Winter. Reggie reminded her of herself, and she knew she had made the right choice with her and Tucker. She hoped she was a fighter. Mavis counted on these qualities to help her finally uncover the truth behind her family's past.

* * *

"Yes, Mavis dear. We're all finished. Mazie will have the suite on the bottom but away from the noise and we've planned some wonderful goodies for her. Dulcy will be keeping an extra eye on her to make sure she doesn't want for anything, and Linda, our assistant, will be on site for anything else."

Dahlia was trying not to be short with Mavis but was pressed for time as the elderly lady prattled on.

"Yes, Mavis. I'll be there shortly. I was trying to catch up with Tucker and Reggie, but it looks like I'll have to meet them at the luncheon. They had an important errand to run and must have gotten caught up."

Dulcy poked her head out of the kitchen and Dahlia eagerly waved her to the foyer.

"Yes, Mavis, Miss Reggie is feeling much better. A good night's rest has done wonders. Thank you so much. Bye bye now."

"Oh, bollocks! Now I really am late. Dulcy, would you be a love and call the mayor and let him know I'll meet him at the luncheon rather than his office? I have one more stop to make."

Before Dulcy could utter a sound, Dahlia was out the door, crossing the street, hat teetering and dress flapping in the summer breeze.

"That's odd," thought Dulcy. "Where could she be going at the last minute? And now I have to tell the mayor she's standing him up. What's with everyone today?"

* * *

Mavis gave a once over to her tidy sitting room. Satisfied that it was presentable, she went out the front door and down the brick path. She pondered the fact that Tucker and Reggie were "errand running" and wondered what it was about. She had to know what happened at that party. It would be significant to both her and Reggie. As she walked, she began to formulate a plan and was thinking quite highly of it when she spied Forrest Perkins strolling in her direction. She stopped and leveled a gaze on the little man that would have frozen an iceberg. He slowed and came to a halt, leaning casually on a mailbox. He watched Mavis turn on her heel and march down the sidewalk, head high, walking straight as an arrow without so much as a glance back.

* * *

Chapter 12

"Realizing the importance of the case, my men are rounding up twice the usual number of suspects."
– Casablanca, 1942

"Oh blast! Look at the time. We'll have to continue this on the way if we want to get to the chemist before lunch. C'mon, Reg."

"Tucker, wait!"

"Oh, Reg, I'm sorry. I'm not even thinking. Are you alright?"

"I'm fine," she said, brushing him aside as she went for the stairs.

"I just need my bag before we go. I'll meet you on the porch."

Reggie ran upstairs, grabbed her purse and was halfway out the door when the glint of shiny steel pierced her vision. She stared at the jagged metal remnant and grabbed it up.

"I'll not have this wandering off from me, will I?"

Tucker was holding the scrap in the palm of his hand examining it as a jeweler would examine a questionable gem.

"Hmmm. I must say it's awfully difficult to place. Mind if I keep it, for now anyway?"

"I would prefer it, to tell the truth. I'm beginning to feel a little paranoid."

Tucker slid the scrap in his pocket and grinned at Reggie.

"Not to worry, love. Safe as houses with me."

They followed Dahlia's cryptic directions and entered the chemist's shop excited but nervous.

"Thank you for your time, Finch. We appreciate such a quick turnaround."

"My pleasure, Mr. Elliott. But you know I will have to document this as a matter of policy, especially if there was a medical emergency involved."

"I understand, but could you please give us just a day or two? I can put you in touch with the attending physician. He can supply any missing details," said Tucker, sliding a folded banknote into the man's palm.

"I'm not sure we should trouble Dahlia with this lab report just now," said Tucker as they rushed to the banquet hall.

"I agree," said Reggie. "After all the festivities are over tonight, we'll get with her and show her the results. You know it'll need looking into."

"I've a good mind to call the police this minute, but I know how she would react. And I still feel it's just another amateur attempt at scare tactics."

They had reached the steps of the landmark. Tucker was holding the door for Reggie when he saw a billowing hat in the next block gesturing animatedly to a small, dark man in the doorway of a local antique shop.

Tucker wondered what part in all this he could possibly have.

"Coming Mr. Elliott?"

"Yes, straight away," said Tucker, casting one last glance down the street.

For a moment, he considered waiting to confront her, then thought better of it.

"Drinking in the breeze?" asked Reggie.

"No, Reg, just catching some of the local sights."

* * *

It was a spacious room with the unmistakable design of a gentleman's club. Gliding through the crowd were smartly dressed young men and women with silver trays bearing champagne cocktails and pre-luncheon nibbles. Tucker and Reggie were heading towards the bar when they were hailed from behind.

"Mr. Elliott and Miss Winter! How are you, dear? I've been worried about you. I must say you look marvelous. Not feeling any ill effects, I hope?"

"Other than a slight ping now and then, you wouldn't even know I'd gone faint. Thank you, Mrs. Castner."

"Oh, I'm so glad to hear it. And it's Mercedes. We were all so worried about you. Look after yourselves now."

Reggie thought it sounded like a warning. She was beginning to wonder what Alene Elliott had gotten her into and if they were ever going to do what she was hired for. She followed Mercedes' catlike gaze till she was staring at Tucker, who was not staring at them, but straight at the door.

"Oh, Dahlia's here. I must speak to her. Excuse me, will you please?" and she wriggled off in hot pursuit.

"What's she up to?" queried Reggie.

"Which one?" was Tucker's reply.

The room was at capacity, and the servers were working overtime. Tucker and Reggie found their seats at a table near the front where their names were neatly stenciled on placards in front of the plates. They circled the table reading off their seatmates. Dahlia would not be sitting with them as she was at the head table with the mayor as part of a group of local men and women who had contributed to the restoration and preservation of historical landmarks. They sipped their drinks and reviewed the crowd.

"Did you notice that Mavis Hatfield is at our table?"

"Yes, I wondered if Dahlia had something to do with that," said Tucker. "I remember some of these people from last night. We really must mingle, Reg. Maybe you'll recognize the voice of your stalker."

"All we have to do is get him to talk in a low and menacing tone and we've got him," she teased.

They wound their way through the sea of faces, recognizing some, thinking they knew others until they rubbed shoulders with one they definitely knew.

"Regina! I trust you've recovered sufficiently? I hope you're not overexerting yourself."

"No, thank you Dr. Landry. I'm quite well. All the effects seem to have disappeared with a good night's rest."

Mrs. Landry had joined her husband and was peering anxiously into Reggie's face. Reggie felt Gloria's eyes bore through her as though she was evaluating her for an experiment.

"We're so glad you're feeling better," she said, stretching both her hands to clasp Reggie's.

Reggie felt none of the warmth from the night before and wanted nothing more than to escape from both the Landry's.

"Landry, something I must talk to you about later. I have some information I'd like you to look at if you would. Technical piece of rubbish, you know. Wonder if you could decipher it for me," interrupted Tucker.

"Oh, uh, surely. Glad to help if I can, Elliott. I wonder if you would excuse us. Our table mates have arrived," he said as he guided Mrs. Landry to the newcomers hovering at the bar.

"How strange that all was!" said Reggie. "I must truly be becoming paranoid."

"No, Regina. There's something different about those two today. Not to worry, we'll run it down, whatever it is."

They were watching their retreat when Tucker spotted Nelson Platt coming their way.

"Hello there! I think you'll find our program quite interesting today. It's a tribute to the historical good works going on here such as Bill's pet project."

They turned to acknowledge Lehern but caught only the tails of his coat disappearing into the bar crowd on the other side of the room.

"Oh, well, he's quite modest about his contributions to the various organizations. Rather shy about talking about them."

"What exactly does he contribute to, Nelson?" asked Tucker.

"Quite a variety of things. Let's see; our historical preservation projects, housing projects, outreach programs, hospital functions, those types of things."

"I'm afraid we didn't catch his line of work before, is he a local business owner?" this time from Reggie.

"Why yes, he does a bit of everything, you know, some real estate development, special projects, he owns a dealership, and an interest in local sports."

"I wonder if you could tell me..."

"Oh, Miss Hatfield! How nice to see you again," said a swooping Nelson.

The little old woman had weaved her way through the crowd to meet them head on.

"My dear Miss Reggie. How are you feeling today?" she asked as she brushed through the foursome and wedged herself between Reggie and Tucker. "I wasn't sure you'd be here after your ordeal last night. Looks as though you're doing fine. I'm sorry we didn't get a chance to formally meet last night."

"It was a bit out of the ordinary. I don't normally faint in the middle of a party."

"Good afternoon, Nelson. Such a nice turnout for you. I hope we can chat later. I do so wish to spend a few moments with Miss Reggie while I have the chance."

"Of course, Miss Hatfield. Tucker, Reggie. Thank you for coming. We'll see you this evening," and with that Nelson Platt graciously took Miss Hatfield's dismissal and continued greeting his guests.

Miss Hatfield watched the retreating Nelson Platt as though waiting for safe distance between them. She turned back to Reggie beaming at her.

"Now, let me look at you. You do look well. I'm so glad. The whole experience gave me quite a turn."

"And I as well," said Reggie.

"I must say, Miss Hatfield, you did show a great deal of concern and Reggie and I wanted to share our thanks for your assistance," said Tucker.

"Oh, my pleasure, dear. I wanted to keep an eye on things for my piece of mind."

"Really, Miss Hatfield? How curious. Honestly, I wanted to talk to you about some of the events last night. There are things that I'm curious about."

Reggie felt like an outsider watching the exchange between the two. Once again, the queer overwhelming sensation stole over her as it had last night.

She drew closer to the pair feeling awkwardly out of the conversation.

"Please do go on, Mr. Elliott. I am most anxious to hear what you have to say."

Tucker glanced at the crowd, but they were oblivious to their conversation. They appeared to be moving in another sphere, in another time.

"Miss Hatfield, I don't want to alarm you, but I think you must know that Reggie didn't just have a fainting spell or a spot too much of the good scotch. We have every reason to believe that she may have been deliberately poisoned by an attendee of Dahlia's reception."

Reggie and Tucker watched and waited for Miss Hatfield's reaction. She gazed intently into their faces and slowly began to nod her head.

"That's what I wanted to speak to you about as well, yes."

"Yes?" echoed the pair.

"Of course she was deliberately poisoned. I don't think that she may have been, I know that she was!"

* * *

"It was most kind of you to see me back so I could check on Mazie. She should be here any time," mused Miss Hatfield.

Tucker waited for Linda to leave by the garden before tipping the door shut with his toe.

"Miss Hatfield, you must tell everything you know. You would be helping us, and Dahlia, a great deal if you have any information about what's happening around here," said Tucker.

They were seated comfortably in the B&B salon where they could talk without prying eyes or ears.

"Well, Mr. Elliott, what I know comes from in here," Mavis said as she pressed her chest. "I can't tell you cold facts, but I have lived here all my life and I do see quite a bit more than most give me credit for."

"What I will tell you is this: I have always suspected that there was something more to this house than what was confined to the public records. It seems to me that lately someone else has been having those same thoughts. I was hoping that you might be able to help me in some way."

Tucker and Reggie quickly exchanged glances and came to rest on the penetrating eye of Miss Hatfield.

"Oh, it's not just the things happening to Sea Gables or to Dahlia. I have had the opportunity, or rather have created the opportunities to assist Dahlia in some of the planning and execution of this opening, hoping that I may be able to discover some secret I may have missed over the years. I have provided her with the background concerning the history of this house and its grounds."

"Oh, then you must have been working with Mr. Perkins," said Reggie.

Miss Hatfield froze, and Reggie instantly regretted her comment. For whatever reason, the mention of Forrest Perkins turned Mavis into stone. She raised her chin and narrowed her eyes at Reggie.

"I do not associate with Mr. Perkins. Mr. Perkins is a charlatan and a fraud.

I would not use him as a resource in your research."

Reggie now understood the import of the article she had swiped from the historian's floor. She still did not know the reason for his professional exile but made it a point to find out.

"Miss Hatfield, we have visited with Mr. Perkins, and he seemed to be not only..."

"What Mr. Elliott means, Miss Hatfield, is that although there are many sources for information on the area, we did learn something from him which maybe you can elaborate on. It seemed a rather important piece of information at the time," finished Reggie.

"I can try," said Miss Hatfield.

Tucker watched Reggie. He had no idea what was going on but felt it was in his best interests to keep quiet for now.

"There was an accident involving your mother?" said Reggie delicately. "Were you with her?"

They watched Miss Hatfield closely, afraid to move or breathe for fear of scaring her off.

"Yes, I was there," she answered flatly. "I was so little, and Mazie was even smaller. We had gone to a social event with her. We were there with Mother's friends. We should have waited till the storm passed before we went home. Mother died that night, you know. And father was never the same."

Reggie waited respectfully while the old woman dealt with her childhood demons.

"Miss Hatfield, you were the daughter who ran the boarding house, correct?"

"Yes. Those were hard years, but we managed to keep the house and the family together," she said proudly.

"During that time, did you ever find anything hidden away in any of the secret passages or cubby holes your father had built?"

"No, dear, I did not. I looked whenever I had the chance, but if there were any hiding places, I never found them."

"So, you don't think there are any others then?" asked Tucker.

"Oh, no, I believe there must be. Everything points to it. I have to admit it must be beyond me. I never was able to find anything even though I really looked."

Miss Hatfield smiled and sat back and once again looked to be reliving old memories.

"Mr. Elliott?"

"Yes, Linda, what is it?"

"Miss Porter thought you might like to know that Mazie Cavanaugh has just arrived. She said she'd be looking for Miss Hatfield and checking into the B&B."

"Thank you, Linda," said Mavis as she rose.

"We'll finish our chat some other time, shall we? Would you like to meet my sister?" she said with an impish grin.

* * *

Chapter 13

The garden had been transformed by an efficient team into a fairy tale dreamscape. There were beautiful bouquets, lace-draped tables, and soft music all with a backdrop of a sky of blending blues, wispy clouds, and the late afternoon sun. Leafy trees were billowing in the late afternoon breeze, framing the picture-perfect setting. As they surveyed the preparations, they ran into Dahlia ordering a gangly, freckle-faced boy about with a great shock of lilies in a monstrous vase. She waved the youth on and came to meet them.

"Hello, hello, are you all ready for the celebration? Mavis, Mazie should be coming out any minute, love. She looks marvelous. It's wonderful to see her here."

"I think I'll just go up and get her. I'll be right back," said Miss Hatfield.

She weaved her way through the ivied path and disappeared into the tea room.

"Well, you're showing quite good form, Dahl," said Tucker. "I thought you might be nervous."

"I should be, but things are going well so I really have no need. I did have a spot of trouble in the kitchen with that agency woman but if that's the worst thing that happens today, I will consider myself blessed."

Just then, a mirror image of Mavis Hatfield started down the porch steps on Mavis's arm while a tall and courtly gentleman followed. All three were amazed at how alike the sisters were even in old age. Mavis beamed and held Mazie out to them as though touching her would bring them divine grace.

"Miss Reggie, Tucker, I would like you to meet my sister, Mrs. Mazie Cavanaugh. Mazie, Mr. Tucker Elliott, and Miss Regina Winter."

Mazie greeted them graciously then parted the way revealing the stately gentleman who had silently followed.

"And this is my husband, Cord Cavanaugh."

"How d'you do, Miss Winter, Mr. Elliott. Very pleased to make your acquaintance."

Tucker noted the slow southern drawl and wondered exactly from where he hailed.

"We're happy to meet you also, Mr. Cavanaugh. We're pleased you could be part of our celebration."

"We don't travel much these days, but this is special. Wouldn't have missed it."

"You must be tired after your trip. Let's get you to your rooms to freshen up before the party," said Dahlia.

Dahlia led them towards the B&B with Cord trailing the women, hands clasped behind his back, nodding congenially as they proceeded through the terrace to the inn.

"So, what do you suppose is wrong with her, other than old age I mean?" asked Reggie.

"Anybody's guess, Reg. Quite a difference from her sister. Could be a way of garnering all the attention."

"How very cynical of you, Mr. Elliott. Although she has managed to do just that," said Reggie.

"Hmmm, I wonder," said Tucker.

"Seems we have quite a bit to find out about those two."

"Mind you there's a good story there, but right now I really would like a minute before everything starts, wouldn't you?"

"Meet you in the sitting room for a spot before it gets going, Miss Winter? I just need to run up to the room for a minute."

"It's a date, boss," said Reggie jauntily.

Tucker blushed and turned so Reggie didn't notice. He waved her in front of him to the B&B.

* * *

Reggie was first to the sitting room and hoped she didn't appear too anxious. She was surprised she was alone and decided any other guests must be out in the courtyard. She situated herself comfortably amongst the lush cushions and waited for him. As she was readjusting herself for the fifth time, a handsome Tucker breezed into the room and faltered as he caught sight of her.

"Well, you've turned out stunningly. You'll make every flower in the garden wilt in jealousy."

"Oh, go on," she said as she waved him away and batted her eyelashes. "No, I mean it. Go on. You don't think you're done with just that, do you?"

Tucker laughed and took a seat next to her. Out in the garden, there were beautifully coiffed, appareled, and hatted guests milling about enjoying the late afternoon sun, the expensive aperitifs, and the soothing sounds of the stringed quartet. Wine and tea were flowing freely as were the tongues of the guests. Reggie and Tucker exited into the blinding sunlight and burrowed into the bar area to observe.

"See Dahlia yet, Reggie? I would think she would be snuggling up to some of the more demanding souls of the city at this point, eh?"

Reggie was methodically examining the perimeter to catch all the attendees. It felt like the first act of a play to her. This thought amused her, and she smiled as she worked her way past the trees, the concrete benches, the gazebo, the buffet, and back to the bar and Tucker Elliott. She had caught Dulcy's eye for a moment among the chatting guests and gave her an encouraging smile. Dulcy beamed back then was enveloped into the group of women showering her with hugs.

"I haven't. She must be inside seeing to last-minute details. Look, over there. The Cavanaugh's and Mavis. He certainly is a dapper old gent, isn't he?"

Tucker was gazing sharply at Cord Cavanaugh who was stationed outside the sisters and looking much like one of the old oaks surrounding the grounds; solid, a bit bored, and wavering in the breeze. The women were tittering happily with each other and receiving guests like queens at a coronation.

"May I offer you something to nibble on?" asked Tucker.

"I believe I'll watch you eat first," she said, passing a hand over her fluttering stomach. "I don't much care to be the fainting guest again."

"Come on, then. I'm sure if we mix, we'll pop into her sooner or later."

Following the brick path, they spotted familiar faces from the cocktail party and then the mayoral lunch. Reggie spied Betty Lehern and deftly steered Tucker toward the less treacherous Bucky Carlisle chatting with Gloria Landry. Bucky saw them and lit up with her toothy grin. Gloria rolled gracefully around to face them.

"Good afternoon, ladies," smiled Tucker. "You're looking brilliant this afternoon. And how is everyone?"

"Oh, we're fine," beamed Bucky. "Watching all the activity. We were just discussing Mavis and her sister, weren't we Gloria?"

Bucky giggled and Gloria smiled politely feigning interest though it was clear to Reggie that her attentions were engaged elsewhere. She strained her eyes to follow Gloria's. She was just about to give up when she spied Dr. Landry and Attorney Castner, heads bent and eyes in their highball glasses, Landry's lips joined to Castner's ear. Reggie floated toward Gloria who was trying to engage Tucker in conversation regarding the philanthropic duties of a small-town doctor's wife.

Since no one was paying her much attention, she inched her way toward the bar and the two men whose conversation had captured her interest. She was almost within earshot when she felt a tap on her shoulder. She turned to see Pea Platt smiling at her from under a large, broad-brimmed hat of indeterminate color. Reggie wondered if this was Peggy's way of hiding out in a crowd.

"This is quite exciting, isn't it?" she gasped.

Reggie could see she had already become friends with the bartender.

"Where's Nelson, Peggy?" Reggie asked then instantly regretted sounding like a scolding babysitter.

Peggy shyly grinned and let out a mischievous giggle.

"I'm not supposed to say," she let slip then placed her hand over her mouth.

"But since it's you...It's to be a big surprise for Dahlia for the party. I'm not really sure what it is but I was sworn to secrecy and if he knew I'd said anything, he'd be awfully upset..." she said trailing off miserably before brightening again.

Reggie was smiling knowingly even though confused when she spotted Dahlia rummaging around on the porch resplendent in another chiffon dress with billowing wide-brimmed hat. She appeared to be desperately looking for something. Reggie watched her poking through the small tables while graciously smiling and greeting guests and friends. The preoccupied expression surfaced again, and Reggie decided it was time to help. Peggy would hardly notice her leaving since she had caught sight of Nelson glad-handing his way through the men and kissing his way through the women.

"Excuse me, Peggy. Duty calls!" and Reggie was off before Pea could lower her glass.

She fell in step with Tucker just as she was about to reach the porch stairs.

"Saw her about the same time you did. Looks a bit off kilter to me. Let's see if we can help."

"My thoughts exactly."

* * *

Chapter 14

Norman Kane: Interesting group of people.
Frank Dooley: Yeah, to Freud, maybe.
– Armed and Dangerous, 1986

Tucker and Reggie watched Dahlia's skirts disappear through the kitchen door followed by a series of screeches and screams.

"Things are running smoothly, I see," mused Tucker as they reached the open doorway.

In the middle of the kitchen was a reeling Dahlia surveying the remains of what looked like canapes spread eagle on the floor. A stocky-looking matron in full kitchen garb was plastered against the refrigerator door balancing a now empty tray with one hand.

"Where did they find you, you twit!"

"May we help?" ventured Tucker.

Dahlia jerked her head toward the retreating figure while kicking a couple of canapes toward the trash.

"I don't know where they get these people at this agency. This woman is as incompetent as they come. I'll have to get this mess cleaned up before anyone sees it. You just know the Health Inspector is probably hiding in the rose bushes waiting to pounce."

"I think maybe we have a rather rampant case of nerves, my dear. Let's let Dulcy deal with the agency ass and we'll just go have a nice little chat out in the lounge, shall we? Reggie, go gather up Dulcy and see if she can't manage things in here for a bit."

Tucker led Dahlia into the foyer and planted her on the hall seat as constant commotion continued behind them.

"Come on, love. Pull yourself together. Shall I get you a spot of something? Could be just the thing."

"I'll get something in a minute. You're right. It's just a pinch of nerves. I'll be better once things get moving. Remind me not to use that agency again for kitchen or any other kind of help ever. Silly old cow doesn't even know one end of a cooker from the other. I've a mind to chuck her out if I didn't actually need another warm body."

"Well, buck up. Dulcy will shape her up long enough to make it through the day and then you'll never have to see her again."

Dahlia grinned up gratefully at Tucker.

"You are surely right about that," she announced.

* * *

Reggie found Dulcy smoothing out creases in the tablecloths. The starched white tables gleaming in the sunlight gave a formal air to the garden festivities. Guests were hovering in the rustling breezes of the courtyard while mixing with nature and their fellow man. She hated prying Dulcy away from the mundane to take on the insane, but time was wasting.

"Dulcy. The tables are gorgeous. Really lovely. You're doing a wonderful job."

"Oh, dear, what's the matter now? Not that I mind the compliments, but..."

"Alright, you're on to me. I hate to take you away from here, but Dahlia needs help in the kitchen. The agency woman..."

Dulcy raised her hand to halt her.

"Say no more. See you later, Reg," and with that Dulcy was enveloped in the crowd like an apparition in the fog.

Reggie let out a breath and surveyed the scenery. It was a great turnout, the presentation was breathtaking, and the guests seemed to be enjoying themselves. But something about the picture was amiss. She was gripped in a sense of foreboding and unreality that she would always remember. Viewing the party goers, she couldn't see anything or anyone untoward, but the backdrop of dread would not be shaken.

A server appeared with a tray full of brimming champagne glasses. Reggie absently took one, thanked the man, and meandered into the crowd. She spied Mavis and her family holding court by the rose garden. Reggie smiled at Bucky and Gloria who appeared to be swapping gossip with Betty Lehern. Gloria was no longer monitoring her husband who had left Roderick Castner in the capable hands of Nelson Platt. Peggy was making garrulous conversation with the bartender who kept an eye out for whomever it was that could send him packing for fraternizing with the guests.

Bill Lehern joined Nelson and Roderick in order to keep a safe distance from his gossiping wife, Betty. Castner was clipping the end of a cigar the size of a gift wrap tube. Reggie was glad she was on the other side of the garden and could smell the scent cast off from the roses rather than the pungent odor of Attorney Castner's favorite pastime.

She searched the crowd unsure of what she was looking for. The feeling had not subsided when she saw it was time to find Tucker to prepare for the upcoming ceremony. She would talk to him about this later.

As Reggie elbowed her way through a group on the stairs, she ran into Tucker.

"Hullo! lovely job with Dulcy. She's in the kitchen with the woman now taking charge like a general. Shouldn't wonder if one day she ends up masterminding this whole operation. Just the thing for Dahlia. Always good to have an efficient right-hand man, or woman as it were."

Tucker eyed Reggie closely and realized she was not listening.

"Have I said something to offend? You're looking at me as if I've just made off with the family silver."

Reggie's narrowed gaze on Tucker quickly softened.

"Sorry. I was having a thought, and not a very good one at that. I think we need to look up our notes and start getting ready. I don't want to be the one who throws off the schedule."

"Right. You will fill me in later on your black thoughts when we have a spare moment, I assume? Otherwise, I agree; let's move on. As far as Dahlia is concerned, I left her heading upstairs to freshen up. Let's just gather the troops and give this little oasis a send up it will never forget.

* * *

Mavis sneaked a glance at Cord Cavanaugh catching his eye then quickly looking away, embarrassed for having been caught. She felt as though her murderous feelings toward him were apparent to the entire courtyard. Her guilt commanded her to steal a glance at Mazie, always cheerful and vulnerable in the way that some invalids can be, yet fully in control when it came to commanding attention. Mavis sighed and noticed that Cord was also checking up on Mazie. Mavis straightened her back and put the image of days long gone out of her mind. She often marveled at Mazie's expansiveness in forgiving Cord his betrayal to her family.

Mazie had worshiped Cord since the day they met and even his lies and deceit weren't enough to taint her devotion to him. Mavis knew her true feelings were jealousy of the fairy tale life she had been robbed of that caused her to be so unforgiving toward them both. She sighed and wondered resignedly when the dedication was to begin and asked the woman next to her if she had the time.

"I'm not quite sure, Ma'am, but I can find out if you'd like."

"Thank you so much."

She was sure she should be getting ready to say her few words but did not want to be a bother. Dahlia always had things well in hand on these occasions. She spotted Reggie and Tucker moving to the back of the dais and decided to join them.

She excused herself, feeling eyes on her back as she disappeared in the throng of party goers. She would not look back to catch his gaze. She reached Reggie and Tucker deep in consultation over some small note cards.

" lovely turnout, don't you think?" she asked as she caught their attention.

"Oh, wonderful," said Reggie. "I'm thrilled it's come together so nicely. Dahlia is very pleased," she added, eyeing Tucker as he smiled gently at Mavis.

"Where's our hostess?" she asked. "I really haven't seen her at all. Would you like me to check on her?"

"Oh, no, no, no," blurted Reggie and Tucker together with a sharp look at each other.

"Dulcy will be bringing her out shortly," added Reggie. "Just putting a last pat of lipstick on I should think."

"Perhaps we should make sure you're comfortable up here, Miss Hatfield," offered Tucker. "Make sure the microphone is the right height, step is close enough, all that sort of thing."

As Tucker assisted Mavis to the podium, Reggie watched Dulcy move rapidly and purposefully through the crowd toward them. She felt a rush of adrenaline that peaked and ebbed leaving her dizzy. Dulcy flashed a forced smile and asked Reggie if she could see her for a moment behind the food table. Reggie casually moved off behind the display. At least it was a barrier between the two of them and the guests, and Tucker and Mavis, for that matter.

"Did Dahlia come this way?" Dulcy asked abruptly.

Reggie was surprised but checked herself before answering.

"I thought she was up in the tea room with you. Please don't tell me we've lost her," smiled Reggie, eyeing the crowd.

"No, no, maybe just misplaced a bit. But I know she was upstairs. She called down through the laundry chute looking for clean towels, which I swear I took up there, and then I looked upstairs, in her office, and couldn't find her anywhere. Did she say anything to you about running out?"

"Not a word, and I would have seen her. I locked the front door to keep strays from wandering in alone up there."

Reggie decided not to mention what Tucker had witnessed which was Dahlia quietly sneaking out of the tea room. She leaned up to see what Tucker and Mavis were doing. They were consumed with the notes and the podium. Reggie decided not to alarm Mavis or crash Tucker's party, at least until she had good reason.

"Dulcy. You stay here, keep an eye on Tucker and Mavis and if they ask you anything, just say I had to go in and help Dahlia with a last minute something or other."

"Alright, if you think…"

Dulcy stopped short and Reggie pressed closer to hear her over the laughter at the food table. She did not at first follow her gaze but soon fell in with Dulcy's line of sight. As a large-hatted woman shifted to one side, she spied a billowing dress in graceful progress from the B&B back door, leisurely making her way to them. Dahlia was wending her way through the crowd like a beauty pageant contestant.

"But I know she was in there," said Dulcy pointing to the tea room. "I heard her in the powder room. I heard her slamming cupboards, moving things on the shelves, and talking to herself."

"Well, she'll be here in a second," sighed Reggie.

Dahlia floated closer each second, barking polite instructions and greet- ings to those in her path. When she reached Reggie and Dulcy, she glistened with excitement, nearly bowling them over as she slid behind the table.

"I've got a secret!" she sang and then bounced up to the dais, winking at Dulcy and Reggie and wearing a smile the Cheshire cat would have envied.

* * *

Chapter 15

Reggie and Dulcy stared at Dahlia, then each other. They watched as she whispered in Tucker's ear and then winked. She looked down at them and arched her perfectly shaped eyebrows.

"So, what do you suppose is going on?" whispered Reggie.

"I have no idea, but we need to find out. I think she may have finally found something," said Dulcy.

As they mounted the dais toward Dahlia, Tucker blocked their way. Reggie didn't want to be rude, but she was set on finding out Dahlia's secret.

"Tucker, we must talk to Dahlia. It's very important. We think she may have just found something. She practically..."

"Right ladies, I know, I know," said Tucker quickly. "Nothing to be alarmed about and there's plenty of time after the presentation to chat."

"But we…"

"We're running late, and you know the natives are getting restless. Dahlia took her time getting over here and now we're off schedule. The press is here, and they won't wait…"

"That's what I mean. Dahlia knows something and we need to find out what it is. Damn the media vultures. Let them wait."

For her efforts, Reggie received a quiet and disconcerting beam straight from Tucker's narrowed black eyes. She felt very much the employer and employee at the moment and knew she had overstepped her bounds. She knew she must back down and let the proceedings begin, curiosity satisfied or not.

"Sorry," she pronounced. "I'm just worried about this and if she knows…if she's found… we'll just speak with her later."

Tucker gave her a curt nod and moved off toward the reporters now milling about like tigers around their prey. The two women moved aside and watched as he masterfully briefed the crew jockeying for position. Reggie shot a quick glance at Dahlia and Mavis who were in deep conversation. She suddenly felt rather stupid.

"I'm going to try to make amends, Dulcy."

Dulcy had been trying to appear invisible but now came to life to assist Reggie. She had felt an intruder in their confrontation and did not know whether to move off or stay still. She was glad she had decided to stay for Reggie's sake even though it had been most uncomfortable.

"He probably thought I was just being nosy," Reggie groaned. "I feel such an ass. I'm going to see if I can get Dahlia anything before she goes on," she muttered.

Reggie sidled up to the dais before Dulcy could reply, leaving her relieved to not have to find the appropriate thing to say. She decided to check the food tables instead. Meanwhile Reggie had climbed halfway up the dais to get to Dahlia and Mavis, balancing herself by the podium.

"Dahlia, can I get you anything before you go on? A nice 'cup of tea'? Miss Hatfield?" she asked.

"Oh, no thank you, dear," said Mavis. "It's very thoughtful of you but I'm much too nervous to think about anything but my speech. I hope it will express our gratitude."

"It'll be fine, love," said Dahlia as she gave Mavis a quick hug around the shoulders.

"I'm fine, Reggie," she said as she waved a glass in Reggie's direction. "I grabbed my 'cup of tea' on my way by the bar, so I'm good for now."

Reggie had the split-second opening she was looking for. Should she ask Dahlia about her secret now? In that same split second, she saw Tucker's face with the warning stare and decided against it wishing to preserve her dignity, her job, and her relations with Alene Elliott. Reggie glanced at the contents of the highball glass and noticed the ice was melting.

"Can I get you some fresh ice? Yours is melting away."

"Oh, no, this is how I like it. I don't usually drink it till it's melted just right," she said laughing and tapping the microphone.

Reggie looked over and saw that Dahlia was taking her cue from Tucker who was now at the far end of the garden. She took the cue as well and moved off the dais to her place behind the food table.

"I'll just be a good girl and wait," she decided. "There'll be plenty of time later for all this."

And with that, she leaned against the fence and relaxed for the last time that week.

* * *

Tucker made his way back to the podium to introduce Dahlia. He could hear the insistent tapping at the microphone as he weaved through the crowd. As he approached the dais, he caught Reggie's wary eyes and gave her a thumb's up. Maybe he had been too hard on her. Reggie broke into a pleased grin and relaxed from head to toe. Dahlia was chatting nervously with Mavis, awaiting Tucker's arrival.

"Ready love?" Tucker whispered as he passed her.

"As ever. Shall we?" she replied toasting Tucker with her "tea" as he slid by her.

Mavis smiled and moved further aside. Tucker gave her a gentle pat on the arm as he stepped to the microphone.

"Good afternoon and thank you for coming to the grand opening of the Sea Gables Tea Room and Bed and Breakfast!"

Applause filled the garden and ladies could be seen removing their g loves and clapping loudly.

"I also wish to thank the honorable Mayor Callahan for his support, our investors, supporters, and all the ladies and gentlemen of the press for being in attendance today. This afternoon, we witness the fulfillment of one woman's dream, a lifetime in the making. I also would like to take a moment to thank a very special and honored guest today, Miss Mavis Hatfield!"

Applause broke out again and Mavis stepped forward with a queenly bow and nod of her head.

"Miss Hatfield was gracious enough to agree to come today to enlighten and entertain us with stories of this magnificent house. Without further adieu, I'd like to introduce you to that remarkable woman whom I feel has added so much to my life – and so much to the community with her preservation of this historical landmark. Miss Dahlia Porter!"

Applause and cheers rang over the garden as Tucker regally ushered Dahlia to the microphone. He gave her a large hug and kiss as she stepped up, eyes welling with tears.

"Hang on to this, please love," Dahlia murmured as she passed the highball glass to Tucker.

Tucker grabbed the tatty cocktail napkin and peered down into the half-empty glass, smiling over their long-standing "tea" joke. Dahlia had taken her place and was waving to the crowd as she adjusted the microphone.

"Thank you. Thank you so much," she said as she viewed the crowd. "I'm just so...uh...excited you could all be here...uh...to ...see...my big day!" she finished breathlessly. "It's quite something...for me."

Tucker looked up sharply. He had never seen her so nervous. He shot a look at Reggie who was staring quizzically at Dahlia. He turned back toward her as she abruptly and loudly continued.

"It really has been...a...uh...lifetime...um in the...um...making," she stammered as she reached up to rub her temples. "You'll have to excuse me. I...I...It...must be...all the ...excitement."

Tucker watched closely as Dahlia swayed, then caught herself with the podium, knees buckling in turn then straightening with her erratic attempts at steadying herself. Tucker shoved the highball glass into Mavis's hands and caught the fear in her eyes before rushing the podium. In two steps he was catching Dahlia as she crumpled. He gently lowered her onto the platform.

"Dahlia! Dahlia, can you hear me? Reggie!" yelled Tucker, but Reggie was already at his side gazing wildly down at her.

"911! 911!"

Reggie turned to find Dulcy, but Dulcy was already in sight, phone in hand, screaming frantically into it.

"Hold onto her, Reg," he commanded as he scanned the crowd for Dr. Landry.

Landry was already pushing his way through the mass that had rushed the stage and was demanding the area be cleared. He jumped onto the platform and bent over Dahlia, hands working quickly in search of clues to the collapse.

"Clear the area," he barked.

Tucker moved Reggie and Mavis to the dais' end and rejoined Landry as he started the rhythmic movements of resuscitation. Tucker watched horrified as the doctor repeated the movements and checked her pulse. Tucker grabbed her arm as if to fill her with his energy then realized it was as much to steady himself as it was to will her conscious.

"Dammit, come on," Landry growled as sirens blared through the distance.

It was like a slap across the face to the shocked crowd.

"There's no pulse, I'm losing her! Dammit where is that ambulance?" moaned Landry, his voice as rhythmic as the movements he did to revive her.

He continued feverishly, checking pulse, heartbeat, and pupils, grunting, and cursing as the motionless body failed to respond with each frenetic attempt. He lifted a lid and peered into her eyes. Tucker choked as he glimpsed the fixed and dilated pupils. He stole a miserable glance back at Reggie who was backed up against the fence, holding Dahlia's wide-brimmed hat against her chest. Tears were streaming over her cheeks.

"Landry!" he gasped.

Landry ignored Tucker as he checked for the pulse and was about to begin the rhythmic shoving again when the ambulance crew with stretcher banged onto the dais and took over.

"What's the situation, Landry?" asked an EMT.

Landry stared in disbelief at Dahlia and then at the EMT.

"My God, I think she's dead!"

* * *

Tucker grabbed both of Landry's arms and swung him around as the EMTs pushed past to Dahlia.

"You'll have to clear the area, sir," said the EMT who had spoken to Landry.

Tucker watched helplessly as the technicians quickly snapped the legs down on the stretcher and were gone before he had a chance to even touch her hand.

"Where are they taking her? We've got to follow."

Dr. Landry was staring at Tucker with a glazed cast to his eyes.

"Don't you understand, boy, she's gone. I couldn't do anything for her."

"And I refuse to accept that, doctor. No offense, but what you could do versus a medical team does not stand out as a final declaration for me, I'm afraid."

"Yes, of course. They'll be taking her to Northside General. It's not far from here. Let's go."

Tucker turned for Reggie, but she was already gone. Mavis was hovering at the back of the dais, a small, feminine handkerchief stretched between her fingers. She gazed sorrowfully at Tucker and moved to take his hand.

"I'm so sorry, Mr. Elliott. I'm so very sorry."

"It's not over yet as far as I'm concerned. I need your help, Miss Hatfield. Please let the guests know that the event will have to be rescheduled.

They're welcome to stay; I know Dahlia would hate for all this to go to waste. She'll be screaming mad when she comes round," Tucker said, forcing a grin.

Mavis nodded at him, returning a weak smile.

"This is a speech I would never have dreamed I'd be giving," she said quietly as she tucked her handkerchief up her sleeve and took a deep breath.

"I'll be in touch as soon as I know anything," said Tucker as he grabbed Dr. Landry to go.

Mavis watched them hurry away then calmly took her place at the podium. Tucker and Landry shoved their way through the crowd now demanding to know what had happened.

Tucker ignored them as they ran for the street, reaching it in time to see a yellow streak with deafening sirens swerving wildly around the corner. Standing alone gazing after it was Reggie, still holding the large hat and twisting it repeatedly by the brim. She wheeled around when she heard them running toward her.

"They wouldn't let me in. They wouldn't let me be with her," she said angrily. "They wouldn't even let me in the ambulance. Why wouldn't they let me in the ambulance? She needed someone with her!" cried Reggie.

Tucker and Landry looked at each other and when Tucker stayed silent, Landry stepped up to take her hand.

"I'm sorry, Regina," he said softly, "but it just doesn't look good for her. I couldn't even raise a pulse. They need room to work, to maybe do the job I couldn't."

Tears were spilling down her cheeks as she watched a squirrel in the distance gnaw a nut, expertly extracting the meat from the shell cracks. The sound of Mavis's commanding, steady voice could be heard over the startlingly loud birds, a car, and a neighborhood kickball game. Reggie listened to the quiet tones of Mavis's voice clash with the children's laughter and wished she was playing kickball with these carefree children. She knew she must pull herself together, if only for Tucker's sake. She felt horrid for this man she hardly knew, standing bewildered in the street.

She looked at Dr. Landry and then at Tucker. She also was aware of Dulcy standing quietly on the porch unwilling to intrude but displaying a palpable sense of urgency. In the distance, sirens were again evident, growing stronger, racing to only one likely stop.

"I'll hold the fort," promised Dulcy.

"Let's get on, then," announced Tucker and he took Reggie by the arm towards Landry's car.

Reggie glanced over her shoulder at Dulcy who was holding onto the railing watching them go. Dulcy gave her best attempt at an encouraging smile, waved once and was gone. Reggie watched her leave, envious of her ignorance and angry at the knowledge she had. For one thing she knew in her heart, life would never be the same, just in how many ways she could never have guessed.

* * *

Chapter 16

"Hal 9000: Look Dave, I can see you're really upset about this. I honestly think you ought to sit down calmly, take a stress pill, and think things over."
- 2001: A Space Odyssey, 1968

Dulcy took the shortcut through the kitchen. She found it rather irritating to walk into an empty room with no food prep and no staff. Where was that woman anyway? She leaned over the sink craning her neck for a better view of the garden. Mavis was finishing at the microphone and a slow hum was beginning to issue from the guests.

Dulcy wondered what they would all do. Would they leave? Would they stay? Maybe eat, drink? Or just ghoulishly gossip and wait for news. She was surveying the proceedings with a strange detachment which surprised and disturbed her. She should be feeling something more. There should be something other than just curiosity about the crowd, shouldn't there?

She watched the guests milling about trying to think what it reminded her of. Something base like cows in a pasture or birds on a seashore. She was contemplating this and did not hear the clattering of feet on the porch. Footfalls sounded outside the kitchen and turning she found her path blocked by a familiar, rather tallish, decent-looking man whose impenetrable gaze again bore down to her bones. Her first thought was of having to deal with him without Dahlia. Her second thought was just exactly how long had he been outside?

"Hello, Miss...uh..."

"Dandeneau. I'm sorry, your name again?"

"Detective Laird. I'd like you to answer a few questions, bring me up to speed if you would."

"I really should be checking on the guests in Dahlia's...until...in case, they're leaving. Someone at least should see them out."

"Uh...I'm thinking that won't be an issue Miss...uh...Dandeneau. No one is permitted to leave the premises until we've had a chance to speak to them and get their names and addresses."

"Well, you certainly are making quite a fuss," Dulcy said, in an annoyed voice. "I'm not even sure why you're here. If you'll excuse me, I really feel I need to make sure my guests are seen to. We can't just let them tromp around out there like cattle stuffed in a pen."

Detective Laird had a mental image of cows swatting flies and sniffing each other's back sides.

"I'm afraid we can't let them do much of anything except be interviewed. Nothing can be touched, cleaned, or consumed for now. My men are out there informing the guests of the situation. As long as everyone is calm and cooperative, it shouldn't be long."

Dulcy glanced over her shoulder out the window to see several uniformed officers herding the guests into groups. Her stomach lurched and she shivered involuntarily with a pang of raw awareness. She had no news of Dahlia's condition and now the police were taking over the garden.

Detective Laird was commenting on the number of guests, who they were, and how they knew Dahlia.

"We're not sure what we have here yet, Miss Dandeneau, whether it's an accident or perhaps foul play. We will need everyone's name including all kitchen, cleaning, and bar staff, and of course anyone who may have slipped out before we came. Do you have a formal guest list? That would be a great help in sorting some of the people out quickly."

Dulcy had not heard much of what he had said after "accident or foul play" and now slid her gaze over his face in a slow searching way.

"What are you talking about, 'accident or foul play'? They took her to Northside General. No one has said whether she's…"

Dulcy's voice was raising an octave with each word. Detective Laird was silently staring at her waiting.

"Dispatch spoke with you on the phone, Miss Dandeneau. Twice, the first call for the ambulance and the second call for the police for a death. Or am I missing something?"

Dulcy's voice stuck in her throat. She couldn't seem to breathe, much less speak. And when she did, it sounded far away and not like her own.

"But…I didn't … I only called once. When she was falling at the podium. I called for an ambulance. She was having some sort of seizure. Anxiety or nerves or heat or something. No one said anything about a death."

"Well, looks like we may have a place to start. Why would anyone call back to report a death if there wasn't one, accident or not? We need to find out who made that second call and where they are now. Meanwhile, I'm proceeding here with caution, just to be sure. We can't lose evidence because of ignorance."

His pronouncement seemed quite final to Dulcy, and she now didn't know what was happening or what to believe.

"Do you have a guest list?"

"Yes, it's in Dahlia's office."

"What about a list of staff and servers? Same place?"

"No, no, I have that in my pocket."

"I would assume they are all still here?"

"Yes, I can see most of them except for a couple of servers and the kitchen woman. She wasn't here when I came in from outside. She may have gone out to the garden to listen to Mavis. I'm sure everyone wanted to hear her."

"If you would be so kind as to find her, please, and gather her with the other staff. Now, is there anyone that you know of who left?"

Dulcy hated to tell him about Tucker, Reggie, and Dr. Landry but knew he would find out anyway. If she didn't tell him, he would think she had lied to him.

"Well, of course Mr. Elliott, Miss Winter, and Dr. Landry took off after the ambulance to follow it to the hospital."

"Dr. Landry. Okay. The other two, Elliott and Winter? And they aren't family members, correct?"

"No, they...well he, Tucker...and Dahlia are very old friends. Grew up together. Reggie Winter is his assistant."

"We'll see to them later. Anyone else you know who may have left?"

"No, I haven't really looked."

"Okay. I'm sorry, Miss Dandeneau. I know this is hard, but we'll get this over quickly, I promise."

"Okay, boss."

Laird nosed around the podium and the back of the dais before proceeding to the next food table and the bar. The wait staff had been grouped awaiting Dulcy's return and the assistance of the next available officer to begin their interrogation.

The bar area was semi-enclosed so that one or two people could be behind it, but guests would be blocked from any contact with the staff or contents. Laird had seen bar setups where drunk guests took it upon themselves to help the bartenders if they could get access. This was professionally laid out to discourage any misbehavior.

A couple of the servers were bent together whispering behind cupped hands and eyeing Laird as he meandered through the mix. He casually observed the area wondering if Dulcy had gotten everyone or if this was it.

Dulcy entered the B&B and went straight for the kitchenette thinking maybe the woman had gone here in search of something. The area was empty except for a few glasses, a couple of serving trays, and two empty ice trays. She went to touch the glasses, then deciding better of it, proceeded to the sitting room. The area was perfectly arranged and unruffled. She mounted the stairs to the guest rooms noting a patch of wallpaper that had come loose.

With each room she passed, she felt an increasing sense of pointlessness knowing there was nothing to be found. She decided to go back to the tea room. Maybe on her way there she would see the woman corralled with the other staff.

She weaved her way through the neatly arranged groups and peeked over at Detective Laird before climbing the stairs. She knew he could see her though he was not being obvious. She surmised that probably not much got by him. She felt the list in her pocket and checked to see if there was a number if she needed to call the agency. She found it on the bottom with an after-hours service number as well. She had an uneasy feeling about this woman, figuring she would need to make the call after all.

She wandered back through the kitchen hoping that just maybe... But it stood empty and expectant as if confused by the interruption. She veered left into Dahlia's office and dropped the paper on the desk as something shiny and metal caught her eye. She halted in mid-sit wondering if she had really seen something or if the light was playing on the nick-knacks.

She moved a couple of pieces of paper aside and the shiny object came into full view. It was one of the prettiest keys she had ever seen. It was bronze with carefully shaped ornate rings on the handle and carved niches like flowers on the shaft. The actual key itself looked hand-formed and had one bent and jarred prong. She had never seen it before and wondered if it was Dahlia's or something she might have been given for safekeeping.

She eased herself back into the chair pulling the phone to her while grabbing the paper. She read down the list of names and landed on Nora Ramirez, kitchen assignment, and began to dial the after-hours number while fingering the intricate ironwork on the key.

She left a message and pushed the phone aside. She rolled the key in her palm leaning back in Dahlia's favorite old chair to wait for a callback. She noticed the worn spots on the arms where Dahlia always patted it while making a point. The castors were rickety and squeaky and had worn grooves in the bare floor where Dahlia had refused to place a mat.

Dulcy was thinking back to the other day when Dahlia had hitched up the chair and rolled over her own foot, when the violent trilling of the telephone nearly catapulted her out of it. She stared at the phone, let it ring once more, then finally answered.

* * *

Dulcy was sitting and staring, staring, and thinking, and trying not to panic. A voice from the kitchen jolted her back to reality and she absently dropped the key in her pocket. Detective Laird met her in the doorway and was giving the kitchen a cursory examination, looking expectant but not fulfilled. He motioned her outside toward the waiting staffers.

Dulcy floated out the porch door and slowly made her way over to them. Detective Laird finished copying the last address of a neat, primly-smiled server and Dulcy waited silently for him to finish.

"I'm through here if you have anything you need to talk to them about," said Laird.

Dulcy took a deep breath and quietly dismissed the group apologizing for the uncommon events which led to their early dismissal. The servers gave hurried thanks and quietly turned to go, eyes lingering on her before merging into the rest of the groups.

"Now if you'll just give me the name and address of your missing server, we'll tidy her up and head on to other things," said Detective Laird, eyes on his notepad and pencil poised.

Dulcy did not answer him, and he finally peered up senses alert.

"Um," Dulcy began.

She was actually wringing her hands, which Detective Laird had never seen before except in movies.

"I called the agency," she said as if reciting. "And they told me they had sent three servers and two bartenders but no kitchen help. The person we engaged called the agency earlier and told them we'd canceled her booking for today. They said they called here and confirmed that with us. I never took that call. Our kitchen woman wasn't from the agency. I don't know where she came from."

* * *

Chapter 17

Topper Harley: You've got to be joking.
Ramada Thompson: Look, if I were joking, I would've said 'what do you do
with an elephant with three balls? You walk him and pitch to the rhino.'"
- Hot Shots, 1991

Dr. Landry sped down the street in pursuit of the fading sirens. Reggie sat stiffly in the back wishing she could see Tucker, braced and tense riding shotgun. She had read nothing in his face and decided to concentrate on what she could remember that might help. Images flashed through her mind like poorly edited reel-to-reel film. She was angry with herself for being so self-involved with her spat with him.

What was Dahlia doing before she stood up to speak? She was talking to Tucker, no, she was talking to Mavis. She looked up to see the street blur by and the hospital loom up in a surrealistic landscape. She swayed off balance as Dr. Landry swerved into the drive and screeched to a stop in front of the ER. The ambulance was still, no personnel, no Dahlia. Just a few people milling about outside the automatic doors looking expectant.

"Let's go," snapped Tucker.

Landry was already out of the car as Reggie extricated herself from the back seat in time to see Tucker cover the entrance to the ER in two strides.

Landry wordlessly hustled Reggie before him and the two caught Tucker at admitting where a sallow-skinned woman in scrubs was peering over the rims of her large spectacles at the three of them.

"Woman. Just brought in. Very critical. Came from the Sea Gables Tea Room, name of Dahlia Porter," spat Tucker.

"Just a minute, please."

Landry shoved through Reggie and Tucker announcing himself to the spectacles. He conjured a badge from inside his jacket and made his way around the desk and towards the back.

"Wait here," he said.

The Spectacles reviewed a clipboard and lifted a phone handset, punching at the keys with her pencil.

"Have a seat please. Someone will be right with you."

"But we've..."

"Have a seat, please. I have no information for you. You'll have to wait," she admonished.

Dr. Landry was gone, and Reggie knew they could only do as they were told until he came back. Tucker took Reggie by the hand and led her to a row of chairs against the windows where they could be somewhat distanced from the melee of Saturday catastrophes. He placed her in a chair and started to pace.

"Tucker, do you think she's alright?"

"Dunno. I usually trust my feelings when it comes to this sort of thing, Reg, but this time, I don't have a clue. It's not a bad feeling but it's not a good one either."

"It's not a typical situation, Tucker. I was trying to think of what was happening those last minutes before she fell. Something struck me but I've lost it now. It was something she said. Something I should remember. Something that's very important."

"Well, keep working on it, Reg. I was going over the conversation with Dahlia and Mavis and I didn't notice anything other than how excited Dahlia was. She was toasting the opening, us, and herself. She was absolutely reveling in the moment. Sort of like the cat who's caught the canary."

Reggie suddenly jerked her head up to meet Tucker's eyes.

"Wait a minute. Say that again. The cat that's caught the canary?"

"Ye...es."

"I know what it is," she announced. "There is a canary," said Reggie, "and she had just found it!"

* * *

Dr. Landry sped down the terrazzo floor and grabbed an intern as he came around the corner.

"I'm looking for an emergency case. Just brought in. Woman in her early thirties, possible poisoning. Which room, son?"

"Oh, yeah, Dr. Landry. I saw that one come in. Over in ER 12. They were working her pretty good. Hope it turns out okay," he yelled at Landry's back retreating through double doors.

He ran down the corridor and slipped through the ER 12 opening. Several heads snapped around meeting his gaze with the hostility reserved for interruptions, which eased only slightly when they recognized their colleague. Dr. Landry stared openly before he was able to grasp the situation. Comprehension spread slowly like a cold mist. There was a big piece missing in this puzzle and Dahlia knew what that was. He could only watch in confusion.

"What canary?" asked Tucker. "What are you talking about, Reg?"

"When we were having our, uh.. little spat," she said reservedly, "Dahlia had breezed by Dulcy and me on her way to the podium. I wanted to get up there and talk to her but I didn't want to make you angry, so I stayed put."

"Alright, Reg. Where does the canary fly in, please?"

"As she went by, she was teasing us. She said she'd got a secret. Sort of in that sing-song voice you did when you were a kid, you know? 'I've got a secret, I've got a secret.'"

Tucker eyed Reggie as though he was thinking about admitting her to a different wing of the hospital.

"She sang at you then, on the way to the stage?"

"She had found something, Tucker. Probably something important. Maybe she knew who had been causing all the trouble."

"And she didn't tell either of you anything? Not even a hint?"

"No. Oh, God, what if she never can tell us?"

She gazed imploringly at him as he stared without seeing her. Reggie followed his gaze to see Dr. Landry coming toward them. They could read nothing from the medical man coming to deliver the news to the waiting family.

"What is it, Landry?"

Landry struck the pose of the messenger, hands clasped in front, then fanned out in a helpless gesture of resignation.

"I'm sorry, Tucker. She didn't make it. They pronounced her at 4:43. Cardiac arrest. All attempts to help just didn't work. She was already gone. I can't believe it myself. She's gone."

* * *

Chapter 18

Detective Laird sprang into small quick movements. Dulcy didn't even hear him as he beckoned to several people then began dispensing instructions like an orchestra conductor. One by one his staff acknowledged and darted off in different directions, fading into the crowd to their missions.

"Are you alright? You're looking a little off. Come in here with me and tell me about this phone conversation."

He led her through the crowd, stopping to tell his sergeant he could begin dismissing the guests at his discretion. Dulcy cast her eyes over the crowd urgently seeking out the elusive woman. It made her head hurt and she allowed Laird to lead her to Dahlia's office. Laird gently placed her on the same chaise Reggie had occupied so recently. She sat down slowly, thinking how long ago that seemed. She could hardly believe it had been just hours and so much had happened since.

Detective Laird was poking around the desk with his pencil, lifting papers and folders then letting them fall lightly back into place. Something about the slight movement of a paper falling made Dulcy remember what was hiding in her pocket and she felt a guilty flush cover her face. She peeked at Laird to see if he noticed but he appeared to be engrossed in Dahlia's datebook and its various entries.

He had found a few interesting notations in her calendar but nothing quite as interesting as the look he had just witnessed from the chaise. Obviously, something had struck Dulcy as she watched him. He hoped she would volunteer it rather than him having to work it out of her.

Dulcy hunched her shoulders forward, sliding her hands in her pockets as if a sudden chill had overtaken her. She felt the smooth part of the key on her palm and the prongs dig into her fingers. She leaned forward and rested her eyes on Laird with a slight smile. He hadn't noticed anything after all. She would just wait for him to open the conversation, which wasn't long. He slid his pencil back into his pocket and smiled at her. It was a nice smile, she thought and one she was sure worked quite well at disarming his victims.

"Now why don't you tell me what happened with your phone call. It would now appear that we have a missing person. We won't discuss just yet what that means if Ms. Porter does not return," he said, leveling a strong, steady gaze at her.

"Well, I uh...called. And they told me who they had sent out and I accounted for them and then I asked about the awful kitchen woman, and they told me that they didn't have anyone by that name working for them and that the person they had hired for today had called in to let them know she would be available for other jobs because we had called her and canceled."

"You mentioned that they said they had confirmed with you. It was a call you obviously didn't take. Do you have any idea who might have?"

"I never took a call from them but then I wouldn't have expected one either since I didn't know there was a change. We don't normally call one of their workers directly. We almost always go through them with any questions or changes, but the name on the confirmation sheet was mine."

"I'm sorry, but how does that work?" said Laird sharply.

"Well, when they call to confirm anything, they're required to take down the name of the person who takes the call to go into the records in case there's any...sort of...problem...or..."

"And the name on the confirmation sheet was yours."

It was a statement rather than a question and Dulcy knew what he was getting at.

"Yes, it was mine. Whoever answered the phone said they were me and confirmed the cancellation."

"Who would have taken that call besides yourself, Miss Dandeneau?"

"Well, it would have only been me or Dahlia."

"Does that sound like something Miss Porter would have done, or would have done without telling you?"

"You mean answer the phone and give the agency my name? No. No, she wouldn't have done that, and if she had taken a call confirming the cancellation, believe me, I would have been the first to hear about it no matter what."

Detective Laird continued to level his gaze at her for a long and uncomfortable pause before either spoke.

"Well then, I have a guess as to who took that call, don't I?" he replied dismissively.

* * *

Mavis sat down on the seat the sergeant gave her and waited for Laird to come back. She watched with great anxiety as he led Dulcy quickly through the crowd into the tea room. She wondered what development had taken place or if it had even been news of Dahlia. She was greatly worried, and no one seemed to have any information.

As she watched the crowd slowly disperse, she wondered where her sister and Cord had gone and whether she should leave her spot to find them. As she peered over heads of guests, she caught a glimpse of Cord standing off to the side on the B&B stairs. Mazie was not with him, and Mavis figured he had settled her into her rooms for a rest following such an upsetting experience.

Not feeling as though she could leave her station, she stood and waved her handkerchief in his direction, hoping he might see her and follow her lead. The white cotton fluttering in the breeze caught Cord's attention and he removed his hands from his pockets and headed in her direction.

Mavis felt a twinge of gratification then put her mind back on finding out about Mazie. Cord drew up alongside her and crouched in an uncomfortable squat close enough to hear but not be overheard.

"And how is Mazie? I assume you've taken her to her rooms to settle down. How awful for her to see all that."

Cord remained wordless next to Mavis gazing out over the garden, the

138

walk, and the lovely tree-lined fence and marveled at how something so serene could have been disrupted by something so vivid and abrupt.

"Cord, I know this must be strange for you after all these years, but we're here and it looks like we will remain so for some time until they find out what happened today. Tell me, how has your life been all these years?"

"You never did waste words or time did you, Mavis? I suppose that's one of the things that drew me to you... and away from you in the end. We've been happy, Mazie and me. I manage the doting devoted husband role quite well and if it were suddenly gone, I probably wouldn't know what to do after all these years of servitude."

Mavis eyed him with a cool glare trying to decide if he was being sincere or just confessing for effect.

"Oh, are we telling the truth these days or are we still manipulating others?"

Cord met her eyes and felt a pang of regret for the walls they had built around themselves but could only feel responsible for placing the first brick there to start with. He could never repair the past damages. Mavis watched the hurt spread over Cord's face and felt surprisingly sorry for her callous remark. She had expected to gain satisfaction from it rather than regret and guilt.

"I can't pretend to know what your life is like now, Cord. I only know that you made your choice and we've all lived with it whether happily or not. It doesn't seem to matter now. I'm also not going to pretend that what happened didn't hurt. But it all just seems so pointless now. I can't even think why I've wasted so much time on it."

The gratitude in Cord's eyes was overwhelming and all Mavis could do was smile shyly. As they watched the scene around them, a chamber maid came charging toward the dais aiming straight for Cord. The alarm in her eyes was palpable and he straightened in anticipation, waiting for the expected announcement of yet another spell or calamity with Mazie. She was waving and motioning him to come.

"You stay here, Mavis. It's probably another one of her spells."

He started towards the maid and by the time they met were turning and covering the garden space in huge strides before breaking into a run into the back entrance. Mavis watched their backs disappear through the banging screen door and felt a cold shiver run down her spine even as the late day warmth enveloped her. What could it be this time?

* * *

"Miss Hatfield! Pardon me, Miss Hatfield!"

Detective Laird was making his way through the crowd toward Mavis surveying as he went, greeting personnel and answering questions from subordinates. He reached the dais without much difficulty, but before he could pose his first question, the back door of the inn sprang open, and Cord bolted through it heading straight for them.

Detective Laird watched expectantly as Cord covered the distance in a run that belied his age. Looking at Mavis he saw only a concerned and surprised expression. Cord reached them in record time, shockingly pale and obviously distraught.

"You must come. It's Mazie. She's not breathing. I've called 911 and have the maid waiting with her. I would have gotten Landry, but he went after the ambulance. She looks so frail this time. I'm just afraid..."

"Patrick!" yelled Laird. "I need you over here now!"

"Let's go. Miss Hatfield, I want you to stay with Patrick until we call for you."

"Oh, no, young man. That's my sister and I'm going with you!"

At that moment, a crisp young man in uniform came bounding up the platform. Taking a visual cue from Laird, he gently took Mavis by the elbow and turned her toward the stairs.

"I'm sorry, Miss Hatfield, but I must ask that you stay with Patrick until we can sort this out. If she's ill, too many people will hamper our attempts to help her."

Mavis shot a pleading look at Cord and was wrenching her elbow from Patrick when Cord held up his hand and stopped her cold.

"Mavis, I'll come get you when she's come out of it. Believe me, this is best right now."

The urgency Mavis felt subsided as she read the resolve in Cord's eyes. She would not get anywhere with these three and to try would be futile.

Detective Laird stepped through the suite door with Cord closely on his heels. What he saw there saddened and reminded him of the many unintended victims of incidents he had witnessed over the years. Poor Mazie, tired and overcome by the events of the day, had retired to nap in her suite. Only now it would seem that the nap was never-ending, and she had passed on to a gentler world where hopefully peace was finally found.

Mazie did indeed look peaceful, stretched out attractively on her duvet, but still and quiet as obviously death was beginning its metamorphosis. The maid Cord had left Mazie with had finally let go of her hand, crossed herself again, and rose to her feet. She said something in Spanish that Laird did not catch and faded into the background as the two men moved further into the room.

"I'm sorry, Mr. Cavanaugh, but this does not look good. There was a heart condition if I'm not mistaken?"

"Yes, among other things," Cord stated. "I would never have thought her heart would go first but who am I to know," he murmured.

Laird glanced at the woman standing respectfully in the background. She would need to be questioned.

"Are you alright, Ma'am?"

"English no good. Only little. Sorry," she said and moved further away to make room in the cramped and uncomfortable space.

"We'll have to get someone to interview her," he told Cord. "We need to know if there were any last words."

"I understand," replied Cord.

Laird thought he looked ten years older in the last five minutes and once again thought about how many more victims there always were in these instances. Several people had gathered outside the suite door. Laird spotted a female officer in the distance keeping an eye on the proceedings alert for any call to duty.

"Officer Runey," he said as he beckoned her towards them.

She pushed through the gathering crowd and stood awaiting instructions.

"Please take this woman over to the tea room, find Officer Vasquez and send him to me. I'll get back to you shortly."

"Yes, sir," she stated and headed for the woman in the corner staring sadly at the still figure.

Laird took Cord by the arm maneuvering him forward to move the onlookers further from the scene.

"Danny! Do me a favor and get these people out of here," he said to a young man pushing through onlookers towards him.

"Call forensics and Chris and don't let anyone near her until we've had a good look. I need you with me for the time being," he said to Cord. "I realize this is a very difficult time but there are a few questions I need to ask and it's best to do it now."

Sensing confusion, Laird mollified Cord with the official speech.

"Mr. Cavanaugh, I wouldn't be doing my job if I didn't lock it down and investigate. I don't believe there's anything unusual, but we just have to go by the book. I'm sure you understand."

Cord nodded wordlessly and let himself be steered through to the front where they side-stepped the remaining curious guests and stepped out onto the porch. There was a slight breeze brushing across the hanging flower baskets. Something was bothering Laird about the death scene, but he couldn't put his finger on it. He didn't believe there was "nothing unusual", but whatever it was eluded him for now.

As he grasped for thought, for the third time that day, sirens could be heard in the distance increasing in volume as they neared a very busy and disjointed crime scene.

* * *

Chapter 19

"Sometimes I don't know where the bullshit ends and the truth begins."
–All That Jazz, 1979

Reggie and Tucker stepped into the blast of tropical air from the polar confines of the ER, Dr. Landry close on their heels. Landry had taken care of Dahlia's paperwork and conferred with the police sergeant who had followed them. Tucker and Reggie had stood by shell-shocked and wounded. A fun diversion had turned costly, deadly, and had forever changed their lives. Tucker squinted toward the sky and rubbed his lower back. It ached from sitting in the rock-hard seats of the hospital. He sighed and turned to Reggie, wordlessly took her arm, and slowly began to cross the street. Reggie let herself be guided off the curb only to be shoved back harshly by Tucker out of the way of a fast-moving car. Dr. Landry stepped back quickly to avoid being stepped on and the three watched the vehicle fade down the street before continuing to the parking lot.

"Sorry, Reggie. We don't need an accident to go with the day. It's already just been murder."

Dr. Landry looked up sharply at this, eyed Tucker for a minute and continued to follow the two. Reggie felt tears stinging again, blinked them back and heaved a long, tear-rattled sigh. Tucker searched the parking lot before spying the car. As they approached it, he grabbed a piece of paper from underneath the wiper and threw it aside before opening the door for Reggie.

"What is this fascination you Americans have with clipping things under the windscreen wipers?" he asked.

Landry bent to pick up the paper Tucker had so carelessly tossed aside and scanned it quickly before placing it in his pocket. He had no intention of showing this to Tucker who was occupied with settling Reggie and himself into the back seat. Landry sat with his hands on the wheel before turning to face the two.

"I just want to let you know they did everything they could for her. We won't know exact details till after the postmortem but they're going to initially go with cardiac arrest. I promise you we'll know everything when this is over. I know you don't believe this to be the real cause, but it's all we've got for now."

"You're right. I don't believe the cause, but I do have a good idea what the reason is. And I will find out who and what is behind it before I leave here," stated Tucker as he tossed the keys to Landry who clumsily caught them.

Reggie narrowly eyed Dr. Landry from the back seat. She was physically tired and emotionally spent but she did want to see the look on his face. Did she see a flicker of some kind? She glanced at Tucker who was twisted in his seat eyeing Landry challengingly.

"You have every right to feel as you do with all the things that have gone on here since you arrived. I promise you that I will do everything in my power to help you."

Tucker nodded at him and glanced meaningfully at Reggie before straightening out and leaning back. His thoughts turned to the piece of paper he had thrown to the ground, only to see Landry silently slip it into his pocket. What was on that missive that was important enough for him to keep? Tucker knew it wasn't an ad. He wondered who it was meant for.

"Let's get out of here," he sighed.

* * *

Mavis was sitting in the tea room foyer when she heard the sirens scream around the bend and pull up outside the B&B. She cast a frightened look at Patrick who was already on the radio to Laird for instructions. After a brief conversation, he stood with an official air and smiled curtly.

"I have been asked to escort you to the B&B, Ma'am. If you would please come with me."

Mavis already knew the reason and silently let the young man assist her from the tea room to the garden. She could see Detective Laird and Cord standing on the porch and the foreboding that had been seeping into her consciousness filled her entire tiny frame. Cord and Laird turned quickly when they saw her. Cord's eyes locked with hers and she could read the events as if she had seen them herself.

"Please, may I see her?" she said quietly.

"Patrick, please take Miss Hatfield in but make sure nothing is disturbed. Have you seen Vasquez anywhere? I need that woman interviewed now."

"No sir. I haven't seen him."

"Doesn't matter. I sent someone to find him for me."

Mavis moved to the door when Cord joined her.

"Would you like me to accompany you, Mavis?"

"No, Cord. This is something I need to do myself. I'll see you out here in a few minutes."

She reached out and patted his arm and managed a small smile as she went through the door Patrick was holding for her. Detective Laird was feeling the effects of a long day and more work to come as he watched the neatly uniformed men step efficiently to the back and pull the gurney from a heap into a transport.

He stepped back to let them pass as he rubbed the back of his aching and stressed neck. He squinted at the sun then flinched as it seared his eyes. Cord wandered over to him, having watched Mavis tread silently through the door.

"So, what now?" he asked.

"For now, we wait."

* * *

Dr. Landry pulled up to the curb between the two buildings. The three of them sat silently watching the gurney rolling up the brick path. Landry jammed the car into park and stared straight ahead.

"I can't believe it," said Tucker flatly.

Reggie leaned up and peered over the seat to get a better view. She felt her heart sink and her stomach lurch as she watched Laird talking to a very solemn-looking Cord Cavanaugh.

"Let's go," said Dr. Landry.

As they approached the two, Detective Laird snapped to attention. His sergeant had already radioed the outcome from the hospital. They stood facing each other, each waiting for the other.

"I'm sorry," said Laird. "I want you to know that I really am very sorry."

Reggie was moved by the genuine sympathy and felt a wave of gratitude toward him for being so human in the face of what must be an everyday occurrence.

"What's going on here, Laird?" asked Dr. Landry.

"Unfortunately, I must tell you that you all must remain close at hand till we can question everyone about their actions today. In the midst of everything, Mrs. Cavanaugh has passed away. The maid went into the room and was unable to get a response and when we arrived it appeared to be too late. The EMTs had been called but now we're waiting on the coroner so she can be released."

At this statement, Cord flinched, and Laird remained motionless for a second before continuing.

"I'll need to take statements from all of you. At the moment, I have a few things to wrap up here and then I'd like to get this underway. I'll arrange transportation for anyone that needs it. I realize this is a tough time and I promise we'll make this as quick as possible," he stated leaving them rooted in shock.

He motioned to an officer standing nearby and with a few discreet words, once again starting the frenetic motion of activity that had defined his presence all day.

"Landry, a word please. Excuse me folks, just remain here for a moment if you would."

Cord, Reggie, and Tucker watched him lead Landry aside, conversing in low tones and shaking heads as they moved to a more private spot.

"What happened here, Cord?" asked Reggie, no longer able to contain herself.

"I don't know," replied Cord. "I was having a chat with Mavis when the maid came running. Mazie was just there on the bed. She looked so beautiful, so peaceful," he said, his eyes welling with tears for the first time.

He stopped to take a deep breath.

"I guess her heart stopped," he said and then shook his head sharply as if to make it go away.

"I just wouldn't have thought it would be her heart in the end with all the other conditions she had. Doesn't matter now though, does it?"

She reached out and grabbed his hand hoping to raise a shield of human warmth. She felt a shiver pass through her and hoped he had not noticed. Tucker's fractured thoughts were interrupted by the banging of the screen door, and they all turned to see Mavis standing alone on the porch. Cord stepped up and gently guided her down the walkway. He brought her to meet them and as they stood in a bubble of grief, Laird rejoined them, Landry at his side.

"We'll need to take everyone's statements now, Miss Hatfield. You'll be excused to go home after that but I'm afraid not before."

"It's quite alright Detective. I require no special treatment. I'm anxious to be away from all this evil. I'll manage just fine."

Reggie thought it a strange thing to say but made no comment. She noticed that Mavis did not look as grieved as she would have expected, in fact almost smug. She was contemplating this when Mavis asked the question Reggie had been dreading.

"Please tell me what has happened to Dahlia," she demanded.

Laird and Landry eyed each other briefly before the detective took his cue and relayed the news to Mavis. She maintained her calm and respectful demeanor, far from the melodrama that Reggie knew to be many people's reaction to such events. It seemed a bit cold to her, but Miss Hatfield was of the old school. Even though she didn't know Mavis well, Reggie felt a miscue somewhere. There was something quite odd about her reaction to the day's events. Something quite odd indeed, and she aimed to find out what.

* * *

Chapter 20

Harry: I don't think I've ever had this effect on a woman before.
Erica Barry: What effect do you think you're having on me?
Harry: I don't quite recognize it. That's how I know I never had it before.
−Something's Gotta Give, 2003

The day dawned with a brilliant blue sky, warm early on with expected showers later, typical of the daily pattern for the time of year. The lovely garden party atmosphere had been replaced by the hubbub of the forensics units in their cordoned off areas performing their tests, continuing to photograph, and scraping for the tiniest pieces of evidence. Statements had all been taken and the exhausted and mournful group had finally been allowed to escape late in the evening.

But now, as darkness mellowed to light, those staring at the unending patterns on the ceiling were free to rise and determine how to begin their day. Tucker and Reggie were two of these people, dressed and ready for whatever would happen next. As Reggie slipped out the back of the inn, she saw Tucker striding towards the kitchen door, and skipped to a short run to catch him.

"Tucker! Wait!"

Tucker squinted in the sunlight and veered to double back to her.

"Let's go into town and have a good breakfast, Reg," he said quietly as he slid his hand under her elbow and guided her away from the tea room.

They were some ways away before Tucker relaxed and slowed his pace. Reggie was thankful for this as she was struggling to keep up with this long-legged man. Neither had said a word since leaving Sea Gables and Tucker gave her one of his warm and captivating smiles. She felt as if someone had knocked her in the knees when he did this, a reaction she found irritating.

"So, how are you feeling today, Reg? Better after a little rest?"

"Very little, I may say. I tossed and turned all night. I just couldn't get the image of Dahlia out of my head. And poor Mazie. And Mavis, which is something I need to talk to you about as well, but I feel like everyone can hear even out here in the middle of the street. I think I must be getting paranoid."

"Well, Reg, that doesn't mean they're not out to get you, as they say."

"I get your meaning. Did you sleep any?"

"Not much. I made the call to Dahlia's parents last night. We've begun arrangements for her to go home. We'll have a nice memorial service here but she's going to be shipped back to go in the family plot. She had a good will by the way that her parents had a copy of. Up to date and such. Didn't realize she was so organized, but she was a good businesswoman."

"How did they take it; I mean it must have been an awful shock."

"Of course it was but you know us Brits. Stiff upper lip and all. Anxious to find out the answers to everything as we all are."

"Speaking of which, there are a few answers I'd like myself."

"Okay, that makes two of us. There are some things I don't understand. Maybe you can help me with them, but honestly, I really needed to get out of there."

"Well, I understand one thing and that's that I'm absolutely starving. I never ate anything yesterday during all the fuss. I think I could actually eat a horse."

"I don't know if they serve horse, but I heard of a great little café we can visit that should do the trick," he said.

He guided her around the corner and stopped in front of a small store-front with ice cream tables outside and a breakfast menu chalked on a blackboard.

"How does this look, Reg?" asked Tucker.

"It's good with me as long as they have food. Doesn't matter what kind."

Tucker reached for the door and held it for her as she read the chalk menu. He glanced around the tree-lined street into the green complete with gazebo and bandstand. As he took in the view, he caught sight of a familiar figure crossing the street and disappearing into a travel agency. Curiosity piqued, he ushered Reggie into the café, followed her to a table and asked her to order him a coffee, black.

"Where are you going? We just got here."

"I'll be right back, Reg. There's something I have to look into."

Tucker rushed to the travel agency to catch up to his quarry. He peered through the window to double check what he saw, opened the door, and headed straight for a corner desk. As he approached it, the customer turned, face flushing with surprise and guilt.

"Going somewhere?" smiled Tucker.

"Elliott! What a surprise. You're certainly out and about early. Thought you might be taking it a bit easy today. How are you doing?"

"Oh, I'm bearing up. You're out and about early as well. Planning a vacation?"

"Oh. No, just a medical convention coming up. Continuing education courses and all. You know, we medical men must keep our hours up or they sideline us."

Tucker smiled and gazed even harder at Dr. Landry. He dug his hands in his pockets deeper and widened his grin as he watched sweat break out over the vast expanse of Landry's forehead.

"How are things going at the inn? Have you seen the detective this morning?" he asked as he took out his handkerchief and patted his face.

"No, Landry, not yet. I'm sure I will at some point. There are some things to discuss about Dahlia after having spoken to her parents last night. Arrangements and all that you know."

Tucker watched quizzically as Landry was squirming where he sat. He was starting to enjoy this scenario when the efficient woman behind the desk decided it was time to intrude.

"I'm sorry to interrupt Dr. Landry, but do you wish to book these flights today or should we wait?"

"Oh, uh...I'll be right with you, Marie," he said as he turned to dismiss Tucker.

Tucker leaned over Landry and stuck out his hand to the impatient travel agent.

"Hello, Tucker Elliott, how are you? I'm just here for a visit but I love the quaint town and may be staying on a bit. Looking for a possible permanent residence, you know."

He could see Landry out of the corner of his eye and noticed with pleasure that he was again mopping his brow.

"My friend Dr. Landry here will be introducing me to some fine estate agents, I'm sure, so I may be doing a bit of back-and-forth business you know. Could be helpful to have a good travel agent on hand."

"It's nice to meet you, Mr. Elliott, "she said, focusing all her attention on her new prospect. "Do you travel widely, or would this just be a regular routing?"

"Actually, a little bit of both. My main offices are in West Sussex, England so there would be a lot of that leg plus the additional business travel to wherever the call comes, you know," he said with a casual hand flick.

"Isn't that a coincidence?" she fluttered. "That's what I'm looking up for Dr. Landry as we speak. You didn't say you were doing business together, you old silly," she said, slapping his hand.

Dr. Landry cast a cold glance at Maria before turning to meet Tucker's stare.

"This is not the time to discuss this, Elliott. We'll talk soon, alright? You know, you really don't know what's going on here. And don't even try to figure it out. It's none of your business."

"Like it wasn't Dahlia's?"

"I have nothing more to say to you," and he rose and stalked from the premises.

"Bye Dr. Landry! We'll finish this later. Have a good...day."

She drew her eyebrows together in a confused knit, then turned her attention back to Tucker.

"I'm sorry, we were talking?"

"Oh yes, love. You were just about to help me with some detailed travel arrangements for Dr. Landry and myself," he said with his most charming smile.

"Uh-huh," she breathed.

* * *

"So, what was so urgent that you streaked off down the street without a word? I've been sitting here for the last half hour wondering if I'd been abandoned. What have you been up to? I'm really jazzed up now, I've had two cups of coffee and yours is cold."

"I'm sorry, Reg, but I've been having the most fascinating experience. It appears Landry and I are now in business together."

"Not to be disrespectful to my employer, but you're not even working the business we were sent here for so what the hell are you talking about, please?"

"Landry is up to something and I'm going to find out what it is. He certainly didn't want me meddling in his business over there. That much was clear."

"Meddling in what business where? Tucker, would you please explain what you seem to be so involved with that I'm clueless about, even though it's only been …twenty minutes," she said, and she smacked her watch to check it. "I have a couple cups of coffee and I'm hopelessly out of date now."

"I've just been having a most interesting conversation with our friend Landry over at the local travel establishment. Seems the good doctor was making a reservation to jolly old England, as he so desperately tried to avoid me finding out."

"Why would he be going to England?" asked Reggie.

"Well, I had an enlightening conversation with a cooperative young woman named Marie who has apparently made these arrangements for Landry before. It seems he has interests in, of all places, Sussex."

Tucker waited for the reaction and was not disappointed.

"But that's your area. What would he possibly be doing there? That's too coincidental, Tucker. Sorry, I just don't believe it."

"I do," said Tucker flatly. "Reggie, it may be time to let you in on a few things I've been discovering about my friend Dahlia."

* * *

Mavis awoke with a lead-like sense of gloom and loss, but also with a sense of purpose. She had a mission to complete, and nothing would stop her. It was all too surreal to think that Mazie was gone now, too. Cord was in shock, as to be expected, but wasn't there something else? Maybe a sense of relief? A relief from years of servitude and cowering. She had to be honest, she and Mazie hadn't really been close in many years, but she had been the only family Mavis had left. She felt an increasing sense of guilt that she wasn't more distraught.

She struggled to wrestle her weary, aging body out of her comfortable bed and trudged towards the bathroom. As she passed the mirror, she caught sight of herself. She was always surprised to see the face that stared back looking so old when she felt so young. She was also alarmed at the naughty smile that lit her features. As she crossed the old, creaking floorboards, Mavis halted as if at a stop sign. Floorboards. She must tend to that. That piece of paper needed to be moved from under there and soon. It was not an impending issue at the moment.

What was though, was Mazie, Cord, and God help her, Dahlia. She needed to dress, breakfast and now that she was wide awake, answer the telephone she had been ignoring all morning as it started to ring again. Mavis about-faced and headed toward the nightstand.

"Hello?" she answered tentatively.

It was a short conversation. One she would remember for some time.

"I cannot talk to you at this moment. Have you no respect? Do not contact me again until I decide I wish to speak to you," she said haughtily.

She hung up with decision, smiled ever so slightly, and continued to her original destination.

* * *

Dulcy was going through the motions of her usual morning tea room routine. She was alone there with no one to tell her what to do now. Dahlia would never again flounce down the stairs, hat askew, running scattered between schedules and duties. She had so many things to ask her. She wondered what would become of them all. Would Sea Gables even survive?

Dulcy sat down in the foyer and stared at the ceiling. It was 9:30 a.m. and she already needed a break. She remembered the key in her pocket. She felt down in the apron folds and pulled out the ancient piece. She turned it over, wondering where it could possibly fit. She slid languidly down in her seat, relaxed and closed her eyes. What was it about this house that was significant? What had she missed, probably even while staring straight at it? She opened her eyes and let them rove around the room, starting at the far corner and heading clockwise. She noted a few small things she never paid attention to such as a stand with a "for sale" sign on it, teacups in need of dusting, and some unsold tea cozies.

She noticed nothing else out of the ordinary. She felt disgusted with herself for not being more observant. She closed her eyes again letting the inn float through her mind when a slight cough caused her to snap them open. Standing before her with hands folded in front like a choir boy was none other than Detective John Laird.

"I hope I'm not disturbing you, Miss Dandeneau. Anything I can help with?"

"No, nothing," said Dulcy guiltily. "I was just...um... thinking about things."

"I understand," he said quietly. "Anything come to mind? Maybe something that had escaped you yesterday?"

His eyes were piercing making one feel exposed. They rested on the balled-up hand in her apron pocket. There was obviously something tucked away in there. He would get her to give it to him whatever it was. She released the key and stood abruptly.

"What can I do for you, Detective?"

"I need just a minute of your time, if you don't mind."

The compassionate man had disappeared, and the police detective had returned in full force, and they were at opposite ends of the spectrum. Both knew an opportunity had passed and wasn't to be regained. They stood staring at each other before Dulcy gave in.

"Would you like a cup of tea or coffee maybe? I can have one of the girls get it for you," she said.

The college help had turned out in force with ghoulish curiosity about their now former employer.

"I would like that, Miss Dandeneau. We can sit down and have a little chat. I'd like you to spare me the time if you would."

Dulcy knew this was not charming southern manners. The hard look that accompanied the request spoke volumes of what was to come and what was expected. Three tittering girls stopped cold when Dulcy and Laird entered the kitchen. They finished their assigned tasks and hurriedly excused themselves, whispering and casting curious glances over their shoulders as they exited.

"It's comforting to know that some things never change," remarked Dulcy as she turned on the kettle and pulled two decorative cups from their island hooks.

She busied herself with the various tea canisters hoping to buy time before Laird started his interrogation.

"Miss Dandeneau, we've questioned the staffing service and they can't explain the chain of events which led to there being an impostor here yesterday. Have you remembered anything since our talk? Nothing is too small to overlook, or to be important."

Dulcy stared defiantly at him as he held his cold, gray eyes on her until she sighed and turned back to the kettle.

"There's nothing I can remember large or small," she said decidedly and sloshed the giant tea ball into the teapot's boiling water.

"I'll be outside with the forensics team, checking on what they've discovered. They're very good at finding key evidence in a hurry."

Detective Laird heard a loud crash from the kitchen as he rounded the porch door to the garden.

* * *

Tucker received a fresh cup of coffee and ordered a large breakfast platter. Reggie, who had been ravenous, was now not terribly hungry. She attributed it to the three cups of coffee she had consumed. They handed the menus back to the server and sat silent until she could stand it no longer.

"So, what have you been finding out about Dahlia?"

"Well, Reg, it seems our Dahlia has made a couple of trips home recently," replied Tucker.

"So? Why would that surprise you and what does that have to do with Landry?"

"Well, she's visited her Mum and Dad and done some traveling around Sussex. My new friend Marie has been telling me all sorts of information I'm supposing Landry would rather I not know."

"But why would she tell you anything about her clients? Isn't there some sort of agent/client privilege she's violating?" she said with a raised brow.

"I think you're thinking of attorney/client privilege or doctor/patient privilege, Reg, and she didn't as much tell me as I got her to confirm a few well-placed shots in the dark."

Reggie began to picture a scene where Tucker was all but seducing this young woman to divulge private details of her clients. She was appalled, and to her surprise, a bit jealous at the thought of him cozying up to the unsuspecting travel agent.

"Okay, so what earth-shattering facts did you learn?"

"For starters, it appears there may be some major support coming from someone other than me and the original investors as I am seemingly the last to know."

Reggie watched Tucker as he continued to thoughtfully sip his coffee and waited for the punch line.

"And?" she asked impatiently.

"Well, not so much 'and' as 'why', I think," he said as he stared at the paneling by Reggie.

Confused, Reggie hitched her chair and clasped her hands together staring at Tucker.

"I don't understand. What do you mean support? She has investors other than you; we all know that."

Tucker narrowed his eyes and opened his mouth to speak when the breakfast dishes plopped down in front of them with the ceremony of laundry down a shoot. Tucker backed away from the table and narrowly missed the sloshing sausage gravy now resting where his hand had been.

"Thank you so much," he said, smiling at the server.

She smirked and moved off haltingly, unsure as to whether she had been appreciated or not.

"You were about to say?" she said, staring at the pile in front of her.

"Well, why would Landry make her travel arrangements for her? What's in it for him? I would have thought she would have mentioned it to me if they were business partners of some sort. He just seems to be too tied up in all this to be just the local doctor. He's in this up to his stethoscope and we need to find out what's going on. He was very unprofessional on that podium yesterday. You don't see medical men showing raw nerves like he did. He was in shock, which is fine for onlookers, but he was the attending physician."

Reggie turned her mind back to the blurry scene trying to piece together the events on the dais. She ran them in her mind but couldn't conjure anything meaningful.

"So, you think he's the root of what, some big intricate plot to defraud Dahlia or steal something?"

"Yes, Reg, that's exactly what I think. So, now all we need to do is prove it. All we need, is a plan."

"A plan. Okay, Mr. Elliott, so what sort of plan did you have in mind?"

Tucker was staring at a spot behind Reggie's head and a slow, sly grin was spreading over his handsome features as he returned his eyes to hers.

"A simple, yet slightly evil plan would be my guess. Whaddya reckon?"

* * *

Chapter 21

Dulcy stood in the kitchen watching Laird weave through the specialists in the garden. Her interesting secret was becoming a burden. She pulled the key out again and examined it closely. There was a tiny spot of paint on one prong. She scratched her fingernail along the surface and the spot came off under her nail. She rolled it between her fingers. It was old and rubbery and did not match any paint in the redecorated inn.

Something told her to squirrel this piece away, so she found a baggie and slid it back into her pocket. She absently watched the events in the garden while deciding to ask Tucker and Reggie for advice. She didn't quite know why she was hiding this from Laird. Her eyes rested on the clock above the door until the time sank in and she realized that lunch began in ninety minutes. She whistled for the girls to begin prep for the incoming crowd. In her mind, she rehearsed what she would say to Tucker and Reggie and imagined their reaction. She also imagined the reprimand she might be entitled to for withholding information.

She blanched at the thought but busied herself with the day's salads to occupy her mind. As she was mixing the vinaigrette, Tucker and Reggie appeared in the doorway. She threw her spoon in the dressing, peered out the window for Laird and motioned them into the hallway. The two glanced at each other but followed Dulcy, her eyes darting over her shoulder toward the garden. She beckoned them into Dahlia's office and shut the door. They surveyed the office then looked at Dulcy wondering what revelation was next.

"To what do we owe the secretive pleasure?" asked Tucker.

"There's something I have to tell you," shot Dulcy.

"Well, there seems to be a lot of that going around," said Tucker.

Reggie shrugged her shoulders attractively and blinked at Dulcy and Tucker waiting for the bomb to drop.

"Well... it's something I probably should have shared with Detective Laird, but I just can't seem to get myself to hand it over. Every time I think about it, something stops me, and I shove it back in my pocket and think about it some more and..."

"Out with it, Dulcy," commanded Tucker.

She sighed and drew her hand from her pocket holding the battered key in the crumpled baggie. Tucker and Reggie leaned in peering questioningly at the object. Tucker lifted the key from the bag and turned it over from every angle. Shivering at the sight of it, Reggie felt a chill plunge down her spine. She drew back from the key and looked from Dulcy to Tucker.

"What is it, Reg? Do you recognize this?"

"No. No, I don't but... I can't explain it. It's just an eerie feeling. Like it's a major piece of the puzzle. Like it's the key to the whole thing."

"You have such a way with words, Reg. So, what you're saying is that you think this is the 'key' to the mystery, eh?"

Reggie gnawed on her lower lip and nodded. All her instincts were on fire. There were so many weird pieces scattered out there. She felt like she needed to clear her head and think. If she could just manage the parts, she felt she could come up with the whole.

"I think we've come to the part where we sit down and assess the information we have. I think we need to set a trap. To capture the killer. And then everyone lives happily ever after," she finished.

"Everyone except Dahlia," sighed Tucker.

***

Dulcy headed back to the kitchen to continue with lunch. Tucker and Reggie retreated to the B&B. They sat on the fluffy couches in privacy and laid the pieces on the table in front of them.

"Wait a minute," said Reggie.

"What's the matter?" asked Tucker sharply.

"Have you seen Cord Cavanaugh today? I know we've been busy, and I haven't even given him a thought till now, but I just feel like this isn't something I want him or anyone else walking in on."

Tucker reached over, scooped the key and the baggie off the table, and slid them into his pocket.

"Right, well I guess we can't be sure about anyone at this point. Better to keep it quiet till we have some ideas."

Reggie nodded and propped her head in her hands. She stared into space then eased back into the voluminous cushions.

"I think we can map it out now," he said.

Tucker took out a small black book and handed it to Reggie who began to jot notes, hunt and peck fashion. She studied her handiwork then passed it to Tucker.

Pranks at inn and tea room
   Newspaper clipping – Perkins' house
   Mystery voice in upstairs of tea room
   Mickey in drink meant for Dahlia
   Metal fragment
   Dahlia's death
   Mazie's death
   Landry – travel agency – money?
   Key and paint chip!

Tucker perused the list, reading and rereading it. Reggie began to feel uncomfortable and was about to speak when he cleared his throat and peered over the top of the book.

"Why do I feel like there's a brick about to drop?" asked Reggie.

"Ha. Funny. Brick. Like the one that fell out of the fireplace Dahlia told us about. Well, love, there are a couple of things that aren't on the list. And...uh...they would be things that I haven't made mention of just yet."

Reggie glared at him and sat silently, arms folded across her chest.

"Let me make a couple of additions here."

She watched as he ran the pen across the paper, stared it down, then handed it to her. She eyed him severely, taking the pad and studying it before letting it fall in her lap. Tucker smiled and stretched back against the settee.

"These are rather large additions," she said accusingly.

"Now, Reg, it's not like they were things that I could get my arms around till maybe now. I couldn't be dead sure of how they fit so why add more fuel to the fire when it seems to be big enough already."

Reggie looked down at the list and read:
   Appointment at 2:30
   Meeting with man in front of shop before luncheon
   Dahlia's secret

* * *

Cord Cavanaugh was sitting in the Washburn-Harrelson funeral home eyeing the surrealistic events with curiosity. Mavis was talking with brother Washburn while brother Harrelson nodded appropriately beside him. The sympathetic tones of Vivaldi were wafting through the background while the W-H staff of motherly attendants were busy with preparations for the day's ceremonies.

Delivery men bustled by under the weight of extravagant flower arrangements while bleary-eyed and shell-shocked customers wandered miserably through the rabbit warren to the sales rooms. Cord had waited for this day to come. Callously, he had hoped he would still be young enough to enjoy the life he would have left. Still, it would be an adjustment after years of playing nursemaid.

He turned his thoughts again to the surroundings of the opulent, old-fashioned funeral home, another in the long line of rescues by the Historical Society. He marveled at the money it must have taken to restore such a large and intricate structure. As he watched Mavis, he noticed something else as well. There were people watching them and whispering; talking about them as they conducted their business. They were the day's top story, and he hadn't considered that until now.

He shifted uncomfortably in the high-backed chair and eyed a young couple outside a parlor standing in what looked to be a receiving line. They averted their eyes at his stare and read the program a smartly dressed child presented to them. He needed to get Mavis alone and have an enlightening discussion.

He looked up to find her shaking hands with Washburn and Harrelson and being presented a business card. It had seemed a brief meeting and Cord was confused as to how arrangements could have been made so quickly. Mavis headed towards him reading the card. She stood before him, a peculiar expression on her face.

"That was quick. You couldn't have possibly finished," he said.

He was aware of a change in the atmosphere; the funeral home had grown chilly indeed.

"This card belongs to Detective Laird. We've been asked to call at his office to discuss Mazie's autopsy."

Cord stared at Mavis, unable to comprehend this turn of events.

"I don't understand. Why are they doing an autopsy? Is there some question about her death?"

"Apparently, it's standard procedure in a case like this. There will be no funeral for the time being, but I have decided that she will be buried here with father and mother. I'm sure you have no problem with that, Cord," she said warningly.

"No, no problem," he said, rising without looking at her and ushering her towards the polished double doors.

"I wish to go straight to the police station and get this over with," she said.

Cord nodded and followed Mavis as she turned left out of the home and marched towards the station.

* * *

Detective Laird was in and available to see them. He was actually awaiting their arrival, knowing that the news from the funeral parlor would send them immediately his way. He was anxious to see them. He still had a nagging feeling about the scene from the night before. He had been sorting through his paperwork and finishing up a phone call when they arrived. A smart, efficient-looking female officer led the pair into his office and showed them to seats directly in front of his massive desk. The chairs looked comfortable but low, a worthy tool in the detective's bag of psychological tools.

"I understand you are now doing an autopsy, Detective," began Mavis.

"Yes, Miss Hatfield. It is standard procedure in death cases," he said as he shuffled papers and stacked them in a tray. "I also would like you to know that I feel this death is not what it appears to be, and I am bound by my position to find out why that is," he said, easing back in his leather chair.

He folded his hands in his lap and waited patiently. Mavis and Cord sat stonily watching him. Neither broke the silence until Mavis cleared her throat and sighed.

"Just what do you think happened, Detective Laird?"

Laird leaned up and gazed at Mavis through clasped hands.

"You know Miss Hatfield when you have a terrible nagging feeling about something? Like when you just feel like something's missing or something's wrong with a picture? That's how I felt."

"Felt, Detective? Do you not feel that way now or am I misunderstanding your meaning?"

"I just had a phone call, Miss Hatfield, actually two. The Hispanic woman on the scene we wanted interviewed yesterday."

"The maid who came to get me," added Cord.

"That's the one. Officer Vasquez was sent for to question her before she was dismissed. Somehow, she managed to slip out of the B&B and is now gone. We have no record of her amongst the staff lists and Miss Dandeneau does not recognize her description. So, I now have two missing or nonexistent workers; one chambermaid and one kitchen woman."

"Do you think she has something to do with this?" said Mavis horrified. "But why?"

"Well, that's what I aim to find out. And I'll have lots of time to do that now, after my second phone call," glared Laird.

"And why is that, Detective?" asked Mavis hesitantly.

173

"Because I've just been removed from the Dahlia Porter case," stated Laird peevishly.

* * *

Tucker and Reggie stared silently at each other from their respective couches. It was something of a standoff with Reggie feeling wronged and out of sorts and Tucker grinning amongst the cushions as if settling in for a good movie.

"You seem to think this is funny," accused Reggie.

"Oh, on the contrary. I find nothing funny about this at all. What I do find is that we, as you say, may now have the 'key' to this mess. And I'm glad you recognize that. It makes what we're about to do so much easier."

Reggie stared down Tucker and shifted in her seat. Suddenly, the fluffy couch didn't seem quite so fluffy.

"What kind of trouble are you about to get us into, Mr. Elliott?"

"If we place our shots right, it won't be us in trouble."

"Famous last words, Mr. Elliott, famous last words.

* * *

Mavis and Cord sat stunned staring at Detective Laird. As annoyed as he was with his superiors for interfering with his work, he at least gained a modicum of satisfaction from their reaction. What was it he saw in their eyes? Was it curiosity, bewilderment, fear? He still had to deal with Mazie Cavanaugh's death and that kept him in the thick of things as far as he was concerned.

Besides, while he thought about it, it also gave him the opportunity to spend a little more time with Miss Dandeneau. She was hiding something, but maybe there was also something else. He thought he might like to get to know Miss Dulcy a little better. She intrigued him and he planned to make what was under that luxurious mane of curly hair part of his investigation.

No matter what, his part in this was far from over and the outcome was likely to be interesting indeed. It was clear that his guests were through with this discussion. They had been stunned into silence and Laird knew from experience that no more was to be gained from continuing the interview.

"Well, be that as it may, I hope I find it unnecessary to caution you against taking any trips outside the area," warned Laird.

"No, no Detective, I have no trips planned," said Mavis.

Laird moved his gaze off Mavis to Cord who remained blank and unread-able.

"Of course," he stated.

Laird noticed his charming southern drawl had lost a little polish.

"I have no plans of returning home any time soon," he said as he stuck out his hand to meet Laird's.

Laird was amused by the fact that if a stone could talk, this is what it would look like.

"I'll be in touch," he said as the couple exited the room with one quick glance back.

* * *

Chapter 22

Dr. Raymond Stantz: I think we better split up.
Dr. Egon Spengler: Good idea.
Dr. Peter Venkman: Yeah, we can do more damage that way.
-Ghostbusters, 1984

Cord and Mavis marched down the sidewalk without a word. As they rounded the corner to Mavis' street, Cord steered her across the road. Mavis stepped off the curb, jaw set and mind to match. When they reached her front door, Cord took the key, inserted it in the lock, and held the door for her while she stepped through. She tossed her purse on the table and headed for the kitchen.

"I could use a little something, Cord, and you?"

"That would be lovely, Mavis, thank you. Bourbon, neat, if you don't mind."

Cord could hear the muffled clinking of glasses and ice from the kitchen as he surveyed the old-fashioned living room. Mavis quickly reemerged, handed Cord his cocktail, and seated herself primly on the edge of a stark, hard-backed chair. This suited her as well, as she was not planning a comfortable conversation.

"Well, that was quite an interview."

"Yes, it was, Mavis. And somehow, you didn't seem too shocked at what he had to say."

"We would both be fools to pretend we didn't expect some investigation. It was an unexpected and tragic event. Wasn't it Cord?"

"Now, Mavis, you sound as though you're accusing me."

"I've never trusted you in all the time I've known you, so why would I start now?"

"Now, Mavis, honey..."

"Oh, stop patronizing me, Cord. I'm not a silly schoolgirl anymore."

"No, no, you're not, are you, Mavis? So maybe it's time we have a little comin' to Jesus meeting."

"That suits me just fine, Mr. Cavanaugh. I'll go first if you don't mind."

Cord nodded to Mavis, crossed his legs, and sat back on the couch, a mocking grin spread across his distinguished features.

"You think I don't know what you're up to? Well, I do. And I want you to know right now that you will not cut me out."

Cord gazed at Mavis, a mocking grin frozen in place as he processed her words. Mavis set her glass aside, stood, and crossed the room to a small box resting on the mantelpiece. She pulled a necklace from under the prim blouse and worked the key into the small hole. She withdrew a shriveled, yellow piece of paper and returned to sit across from Cord.

"Now, what's all this about, Mavis?" he said as he tried to maintain his cavalier posture.

"You forget I still have the letter. You forget I know what you did to Mazie and to me all those years ago, not to mention Forrest Perkins. You've made ruining lives your casual hobby, but you won't have the last say on this, dear, mark my words. I know what you've been up to, and I know you're on to where the money is and if you don't give me what's rightfully mine, I will make sure you rot for everything you've ever done," she finished, flushing, and settling back in her chair.

"Why, Mavis. I think you overestimate me. Whatever it is you think I know, I am positive you are laboring under a grave misapprehension."

"And I am not. We're about to be true partners at last, Cord. Isn't that what you've always wanted? Don't you remember how I was the one you really wanted? But you had to settle for Mazie after the truth came out, didn't you? Wel,l now, you'll finally have your wish. But it will be my way this time, Cord, my way."

Cord returned her cold, malicious stare and leaned forward.

"What is it you really want, Mavis? Revenge, lost time rewarded back, things you can't have? What makes you think I know anything?"

"Because I know where you were the night of the cocktail party. The night before you were supposed to have arrived with Mazie. I saw you. You were there. You didn't see me, but I saw you. And your confidante – you think he's loyal to you? Well, you couldn't be more wrong."

Cord considered her for a moment then gave a slow, resigned smile.

"Well Mavis, looks like we are, as you say, partners. Now just what do you think it is we should do?"

"I think you need to be on the next plane to London and get that paper before someone gets wise and beats you to it. Without that, there's no proof."

"But Mavis, dear," Cord said with a leer, "I'm not allowed out of the city, much less the country. How do you suppose I can leave?"

"You're a slippery, ingratiating manipulator; you'll figure a way. Now tell me just how much you're involved in all this, Cord. And you can drop the doting widower pretense. I need to know everything if we're going to get our money out of that tea room. Now start talking."

* * *

The woman in seat 9A was settling in for the long flight. She was feeling surprisingly relaxed despite the turmoil of recent days. It would be nice to get away. She gently toed her bag further under the chair in front of her, dug her seat belt parts out of the sides of her cushions and stretched her feet in front of her.

She was comfortably dressed in jeans, a loose sweater, tennis shoes and a low fitting ball cap. She reached up to remove her sunglasses then decided against it after glancing into the setting sun beating through the plastic window. She picked up the in-flight magazine and propped it up in her lap while she listened to the passengers being greeted by the corps of attendants manning the doors. She could hear the lilt of their polished accents directing traffic behind her, pointing out forward or rear cabins.

"Good evening, sir, and where do we have you sitting today?"

The same lilting accent answered her back and made the woman in 9A peek over her shoulder, curious as to the particulars of the owner of such cultured speech. The man was older, handsome, and had the cosmopolitan air of a seasoned traveler, and she desperately hoped he would be turning the opposite direction, away from her seat section.

She let out her breath as the passenger veered off and away. She remained alert, thumbing absently through the magazine, her mind on the man in the other cabin. She would try not to worry about it now but think about some of the fun things she'd be doing once in the UK.

She adjusted the blinders over her eyes, inserted the ear plugs and turned her face to the window. She would not be concerned with small details. With a slight thump against the window, she fell into much needed sleep as the plane climbed higher into the late evening sky.

* * *

The woman was jarred awake by the skidding of the wheels on pavement and brakes jamming her forward in her seat. She removed the blinders and earplugs and blinked. Her neck was stiff from where her pillow had collapsed underneath her dead weight. She stretched, reached for her bag, and slid the window shade up to its limit.

"Welcome to Gatwick Airport, ladies and gentlemen," droned the attendant while others prepared the passengers for deplaning.

Her mind wandered back to the man in the rear. She would be first off and able to backtrack around to where she could follow him. Once out of the jet way, she sidestepped into the ladies room, tidied her makeup, shoved her hair into her cap, and reemerged into the throng just as the man appeared at the jet-way door.

He took no notice of anyone but made his way straight to the concourse toward customs and baggage. He mechanically breezed through the passport booth, and without a backward glance, swung his carry on over his shoulder and strode out into the London morning haze. Clearing customs quickly herself, the woman jogged out the doors and scanned the sidewalk, catching sight of him disappearing into a taxi, which quickly pulled out and was lost in traffic.

The woman retreated into baggage claim, retrieved her lone bag, and headed back to the taxi stands. Wherever the man was headed, he had lost no time in clearing the airport like a pro. The lack of luggage left her puzzled and she concluded that he either kept a home here or hated checking bags.

"Alright there, Miss? Need a taxi?"

"Oh, no thank you. I'm heading for the train," and she smiled and pulled her bag toward the station.

Gazing up at the boards, she found the next available time for Hayward's Heath and made her way towards the track. She hadn't long to wait as it was pulling in and chugging to a stop as she stepped onto the platform. With a surveying glance, she pulled up her bag, stowed it at the front, and chose a seat in the back. She took out paper and pen and jotted down a few cryptic notes. The pen swayed as the train fell underway and she looked up to see the station signs begin to move down the line.

It wasn't a long ride, and she soon became lost in her thoughts. As the metropolis turned to small villages, the outer city boundaries of Gatwick became rolling green hills and the open pastureland of one long moving picture. In no time at all, the conductor was booming out "Hayward's

Heath, Hayward's Heath. Coming into Hayward's Heath."

As she stepped off the train, the woman sited a man by the post office getting into an old, but functional mini. She crossed the street, catching the man before he could drive away.

"Excuse me, is your car for hire?" she said warmly.

"Why yes, Miss. Would you be wanting a lift, now?"

"That would be lovely, thanks ever so much."

The rickety mini chugged down the street and off into the lush landscape.

"Will you be staying with us long, Miss?"

"No, just for a bit."

"Well, have a lovely visit all the same, Miss."

The mini strained up the drive and the man tooted the horn and gave the woman a wide grin.

"Thank you again."

The old man waved and drove off leaving the woman standing alone staring up at a huge house. She made her way up the walk looking out over the downs and the gardens until she arrived at the front door. She smiled nervously and rang the ancient bell. She waited, rang it again, and stepped back as the door swung open to reveal a tall, stately gentleman wearing an apron over a shirt and tie and removing polishing mitts.

"Oh, Jennings! It's so good to see you. It's so nice to be home."

"Miss Dahlia. There you are. We've been waiting for you.

* * *

II

Part Two

Chapter 23

Elaine Dickinson: You got a telegram from headquarters today.
Ted Striker: Headquarters – what is it?
Elaine Dickinson: Well, it's a big building where generals meet, but that's not important right now.
-Airplane, 1980

Dahlia hitched up her bag and crossed into the foyer. Jennings rushed to take it from her while she fondly glanced around the familiar entranceway.

"It's funny how you know some things will always be there for you," she said, drinking in the smell of aged wood, antique carpets, and a mixture of polishes.

He watched her gaze at an old portrait of the Porter family, waited deferentially, then escorted her to the next room.

"Your mother and father have been waiting anxiously for you, Miss Dahlia. They're in the conservatory. Breakfast will be served momentarily. Is there anything I can get for you, Miss?"

"I would love a good cup of tea, Jennings. Not to be confused with the other tea," she added, laughing.

"Oh, no, Miss. Not to worry."

Dahlia watched Jennings retreat, then entered the plant-filled room. Amidst the vast amount of greenery sat an older couple at a small mosaic-topped table, spectacles perched atop their noses and sunlight streaming over their newspapers and coffee cups.

"Hello, Mum, Dad. I made it," she said, exhaling.

"Oh, Dahlia!"

Her mother jumped up and enveloped her in a tight hug while her father waited his turn.

"Hello, Popkin," he laughed. "How was the trip?"

"Alright, Dad. A bit tiring, but pleasant."

She decided not to worry them with the irritating presence of the man on the plane and pulled up a seat next to her mother.

"So, darling. How are things going?" she asked.

"Well, Mum, so far, it's gone beautifully. I hate doing this to Tucker, but the less who knows, the better. I adore Reggie, but the two of them with this information are just too many. I only brought George Landry in on it because he tripped over it. The police have been wonderful, though. How was the call from Tucker?"

"Oh, Gawd. I do feel just awful. He's in utter misery, darling. I hope all this is worth it. I can't bear to see him like this. And it's been horrible lying to the Elliott's this way. Poor Alene is beside herself. It took an immense amount of persuasion by your father to keep her from running for the

188

airport when he called."

"It was a bit tricky, but they saw reason in the end," he said. "I may have missed my calling, you know. I could have done wonderful work on the stage."

"Well, Dad, we could get an act together. You've never seen a more convincing death scene. And in front of loads of people as well. Landry almost had to be put in hospital himself when he walked into that emergency room, I can tell you," she finished, looking pleased with herself.

"If it hadn't been that they've been trying to pin this other case down for so long, they might never have agreed to work with me. I have some very good friends in the right places. Some of the benefits of living in a small town," she added.

The door opened, and Jennings entered with a beautiful cart filled with all kinds of goodies. The smells of bacon, cinnamon, coffee, and syrup made Dahlia realize just how hungry she was. She found it hard to remember the last time she had eaten anything substantial. She gazed longingly at the plates of food being deposited in front of her.

"Well, dear, tuck in and then get some rest. You'll have plenty of time to hunt through things once you've had some sleep."

"Oh, actually Mum, I was thinking I would get a breath of fresh air. Sitting on a plane and all. You know how positively claustrophobic I get when I'm confined like that."

"Well, alright, darling. Just try and get some rest. It's not that urgent that you run right off now, is it?"

"Oh, no. Not to worry. Just feeling a little restive, that's all. Just going to take a spin through the garden," Dahlia replied, feeling as guilty as a child trying to hide candy before dinner.

"Jennings will fix you a nice snack later when you feel more like eating again. You look awfully thin, dear."

"Thanks, Mum. I'll run up to bed shortly. See you later, Dad."

Dahlia was out the door before her father could even acknowledge her.

"Yes, well. So, when do you suppose she'll tell us what she's really up to?" said Mr. Porter.

"No bloody idea," mused Mrs. Porter over her paper. "Trust, my dear, trust."

* * *

"Oh, honestly, did you think I knew about this? Why didn't you know about it? You were there, too. I thought you had one of your labradors keeping tabs on everyone. Now I'm on another continent, and so is he, and no one seems to be able to tell me why. You missed this, didn't you?"

Dahlia Porter was wending her way through the late summer gardens of her childhood home. Having always been a peaceful place, it was now quite disturbing to her to be ripping through the hedges trying to get out of earshot of the household staff and her parents.

"Well, I don't know that right now, do I?" she spat after a long pause of listening to the other end. "He went into London and probably checked into a cheap hotel. All I know is that I need to get to Bournemouth before he does. If he's here for what I think he is, I need to beat him to it. He doesn't know I'm here, so I'm sure I can get in and out and gone before we have to deal with him."

"If only I could have checked out that room more before I ran out of time," she thought dejectedly.

For some reason, she found herself keeping this tidbit from the police commissioner. She'd have to rely on Tucker and Reggie.

She poked her head over a hydrangea bush and peered through the window. She could see Jennings polishing some sort of artifact. She only hoped he was really concentrating on that and not keeping an eye out for her. She didn't think for a minute; she had fooled her indulgent parents as she whisked out the door, cell phone in hand.

"And Laird is off the case? Do you think that will stop him? Alright. Just keep me informed," she said as she lowered off her tiptoes from the window.

She stuffed the phone back in her pocket and quickly strode to the front of the house. She veered to the potting shed where she kept her ugly little bicycle with the bell and the basket. She looked back at the house, grabbed the bike, and wheeled it, wobbling back down the drive.

She drove back the same route as the old man's mini skidding in front of the local postal shop. She heaved her bike onto the rack and glanced at the sign in the window. They were having a sale on late summer merchandise. She looked up the street and then pushed the door open, bell jingling as she entered.

She viewed the greeting cards, box selections, and wind chimes as she approached the desk of the solitary attendant. The pimply youngster was leaning against the shelving, reading the latest gossip rag. Dahlia cleared her throat politely and waited for her to take notice. She was relieved that it was no one she knew and smiled warmly as the young woman came to greet her.

"Sorry, Miss. Can I help?"

"Yes, love," chirped Dahlia. "I need to send a telegram, of all things!"

* * *

Cord Cavanaugh settled himself into the seedy little room and pulled out the yellowed letter his mother had shown him so many years ago. How many was it now? He read over the details and let his eyes rest on the name. Clinton Miller Peters. That name had almost ceased to exist for him. He had lived so many years as Cord Cavanaugh that the name Clinton Peters held little significance for him now.

He glanced at the rest of the paper and folded it in two. Forrest Perkins had been a thorn in his side before. He just hoped he wasn't going to be one again. He had needled him every chance he had for as long as he could remember: the notes, the letters, the insinuations over the years.

He began having murderous thoughts toward him. After all, what was one more if it came down to it? But the more he thought about it, the more he knew he needed to keep his head and do what he came to do.

Once his job was finished, he would deal with Mavis. She was becoming tiresome now. He had once harbored strong feelings for her. Only now, he didn't feel much at all except the squeeze of the iron fist from an iron maiden who was greedier than he. He noted the time. He was in a hurry, on a deadline. But he was there finally, and he was the only one who knew it. He relaxed and congratulated himself on his brilliance. As he sat reflecting on the intricacies of his plans, his eyes wavered, then flickered, then finally closed, and he slept a most fitful and tortuous sleep.

* * *

Dahlia smiled and thanked the young woman behind the counter. She glanced once more at the sale merchandise and banged the shop door shut, bell tinkling.

She surveyed the street, deciding which direction to turn. What she really needed to do was go straight to Bournemouth rather than wait. Knowing that Cord was in England after the same thing, she needed to get a jump. He thought she was dead. There were some advantages to that. She had time on her side since he didn't know she was there. She began to feel her confidence seep away, and she turned north to the train station. With each step, she felt her anxiety deepen. It was mid-morning, and the small early rush had gone, leaving the depot quiet and lonely with only a trickle of traffic heading to spots of no consequence.

"One ticket to Bournemouth, please," she said breathlessly.

"Next train 11 a.m., Miss," said the clerk.

"That's lovely, thanks," said Dahlia, peeking at her watch.

She thanked the clerk and headed toward the platform. She looked up one end and down the other, noted no one of significance, and boarded the train to whatever she would find on the other end.

* * *

Tucker and Reggie were in the B&B sitting room pouring over details and deciding on a game plan. Reggie still felt miffed that Tucker had held things back, but what could she say when she had done the same?

"So, where do we look first?" ventured Reggie.

Tucker sighed and passed his hands over weary eyes.

"Let's think about this. There's a cupboard or something hidden here. That in itself is astounding because how does that happen? How do we find something that no one else has been able to?"

"Let's look at it all again," said Reggie. "Maybe we can get some help from that."

Tucker picked up the list and reread it.

"You know all these things go together," he said.

"Well, let's take the bigger things first," said Reggie. "Let's pick those apart, then see how the smaller things fit in."

"Right. Dahlia's and Mazie's death, then what next?"

"I know what's next," said Reggie. "And I've looked at it till I'm purple. It's like one of those Dali paintings. You look at it one way, and then all of a sudden, you see a whole other picture where you were just looking.

It's really quite amazing once you figure out how to view them," she said, amused.

But Tucker wasn't listening. He was still, staring straight ahead with an alarming quality.

"Tucker, what is it?"

"Paintings! There were paintings here. What did Hatfield's will say about the paintings?"

"The paintings on the walls here?"

"Yes. There used to be a lot of paintings here that were done by Mr. Hatfield. Didn't Mazie say that was how Daddy would unwind at night? He would paint pictures for Mrs. Hatfield."

"Yes, but what do you think those paintings have to do with this?"

"I don't know, but they're worth looking at. Everyone thinks there's something here that's worth money. But what if what was worth money is now someplace else?"

"Didn't she say those pictures were donated?"

"I'm not sure, but I know who would. How about our good friend Nelson Platt?"

"What do you think, Tucker, that those paint-by-numbers are worth real money?"

"I don't know, Miss Winter, but I think we need to pay a visit and find out."

* * *

Tucker and Reggie were marveling at the wonders of the Nelson Platt Historical Society's 1880s foyer when Nelson himself rounded the corner. He rushed to greet them and deliver his well-known welcome speech heard by all who ventured into the preserved landmark.

"I was wondering when you might get a chance to come see us. It's something I knew you would want to do since Dahlia was such a large part of what we do here. She was a great supporter and gave us a lot of volunteer hours, which we greatly appreciated."

"Actually, Nelson, that's one of the reasons we came. We were curious as to what kind of help Dahlia gave you. We're trying to put together everything she was doing before her, well, anything that can help us figure out what might have happened."

"Exactly," said Reggie. "Every little bit 'paints a picture' if you follow me."

Tucker grinned at the reference and watched Nelson to see if anything registered. If they were waiting for a monumental moment, they were disappointed as he did nothing more than smile politely and nod.

"Would you like to take a tour, or would you like to start with questions? I'd be happy to take you through it personally. You know, everyone's version is a little different depending on their association with the story or storyteller, as it were. For example, every Wednesday, Forrest Perkins comes in and does a brown bag lunch program on various aspects of life in the early days here."

"Hmmm," ventured Tucker, "I think we'd like to just take a quick look around and come to you with our questions afterward. We hate to take up your time. I know how busy you must be."

"Not to worry. Rather a slow day today. I do have a call to make, so if you'd like to just start over there, I'll catch up to you and see what you think."

He handed them a four-sided brochure and steered them to the first room, which held collectibles ranging from dolls to musical instruments to farm implements. Reggie scanned the brochure and finally pointed to a section of artwork donated over the years.

"Look, Tucker, there's an art gallery on the second floor. That's where we need to be."

"Right. Which way?"

They passed an elevator, obviously installed for handicap use, and rounded the bead-boarded back hall to a large banistered staircase. The steps creaked as they climbed and after consulting the brochure, they turned right to a ballroom with high ceilings, paintings, sculptures, and ironwork.

"My, lots of local artistry here, isn't there? Let's see what we've got," smiled Reggie.

They rounded the sculptures of Maryann Denton, the ironwork of Thomas J. Potter, and various works on canvas from a number of individuals, none of whom they recognized.

"I would have sworn we were on the right track. I thought all we'd have to do was pop up here and be standing right in front of them," sighed Reggie.

Tucker scoured the rest of the room, searching the pieces, hoping to stumble on something from the Hatfield home.

"Nothing. I guess we're on the wrong track after all," she said.

As they stared at the brochure, Nelson Platt walked by but backed up and smiled when he saw them.

"There you are. Quite a collection, isn't it?" he said proudly.

"Yes, it's brilliant. This must have taken quite some time to put together," praised Tucker. "We did quite think, though, that we would see some things from the Hatfield estate here. I may have been mistaken, but I thought there were some paintings he had done that might have eventually come to you."

"Oh, yes!" said Nelson. "But those wouldn't be in this room. They'd be in the Hatfield-Brown room. He was an important factor in the development of this town. There's a room devoted entirely to the family and the history of the contributions they made. Come this way, and I'll take you to it."

Nelson about faced and headed toward a smaller staircase leading to another level. Tucker and Reggie followed in silence as they mounted the rickety stairs to a loft and a smaller room filled with memorabilia spanning any number of years.

Nelson ushered them in and grinned like a Cheshire cat as they stared openly at the expanse of trinkets covering the walls, tables, and floor.

"I'll be downstairs if you have any questions," he added. "I have a meeting with Attorney Castner that I'm preparing for."

And with that, he was gone, leaving them in awe of the mountain of collectibles. As they wound their way through the tables, chairs, pottery, and music boxes, they stopped in front of a tidy display of watercolors and pencil drawings bearing the name John Alexander Hatfield.

"Here we are, after all, Reg. Now, if only we knew what we were looking for."

* * *

Detective Laird had watched as Tucker and Reggie entered the Historical Society. His inscrutable face gave no indication of his thoughts as he continued on his way. He tromped over acorns scattered along the sidewalk, enjoying the crunch under his shoes until he found himself staring at the B&B and the adjacent tea room.

He pushed open the garden gate, deciding on the element of surprise. What he hoped to accomplish, he wasn't sure. He noted a few cars on the side street and glanced at his watch, calculating the timing of the thinning lunch crowd.

He entered the kitchen and experienced déjà vu as the giggling college girls scattered like disturbed ducks on a pond. He smiled and waited, but not for long, as Dulcy bounded in the door, then stopped short. She casually leaned on the counter, glancing longingly at the carving knife by her hand. He laughed and threw his arms wide.

"I'm harmless," he said. "I've been stripped."

Reddening, he added, "Of my duties. At least where this case is concerned."

"So, I hear," she relaxed and smiled. "I was surprised to hear that. Why?"

"Usually, in this instance, it's because someone up top has decided to put his own man on it. I've been given other tasks. Of course, I'm still on the

Mazie Cavanaugh case, but that seems a bit more straightforward than Miss Porter's."

"Oh, so you have more questions about the Hatfield's?"

'Well, I do have a theory which I wanted to run by you. It's not entirely to do with the Hatfield's. That is if you have the time."

"Actually, I am trying to finish up lunch and then we have to set for high tea, but maybe another time?"

"I was thinking more along the lines of dinner," grinned Detective Laird.

Dulcy stood frozen in shock before regaining speech.

"I, well, I... I don't know... I'm not sure if..."

"As I said, it's not entirely to do with the Hatfield case."

Dulcy's face cleared, and she slowly shook her head knowingly.

"You've been called off, but you're not going quietly, are you now?"

Detective Laird once again became inscrutable and eyed Dulcy.

"Shall we say 7:30?"

Dulcy shook her head once more, trying to suppress the surprising quiver of excitement in the pit of her stomach. Detective Laird smiled pleasantly and let himself out the way he came in.

* * *

Laird was in his office following up on another dead-end tip by the time Tucker and Reggie were leaving the Historical Society. They had studied the artwork for what seemed like hours, trying to find some common thread. Having only come up with sore feet, Reggie bargained with Tucker to come back on Wednesday for Forrest Perkins' brown bag lunch program.

They walked the short distance to the tea room, trying to decide what to do for lunch when they caught sight of Dulcy waving from the front porch. They glanced at each other and marched toward the beveled glass door, which, only a short time ago, held Dahlia's cherub face like an old-fashioned picture frame. Dulcy disappeared through the doorway, and Tucker and Reggie followed her to Dahlia's office.

"Well, love, what's up?" started Tucker.

"Oh, now I'm embarrassed," she giggled. "It's just that I was so surprised by this that I had to tell someone, but now I'm not sure..."

Dulcy was again beating around the bush, and Tucker was losing patience. Her face took on an attractive glow as she blurted out her news.

"I'm having dinner with Detective Laird this evening!"

Tucker and Reggie stared openly.

"You know, Detective Laird," said Dulcy with exasperation.

"Well, that is exciting. How did that come about?" asked Reggie.

"Yes, how did that come about?" asked Tucker.

Reggie sat opposite Dulcy, squeezing her eyes at Tucker until he sat down next to her. She issued him a stern glare to keep quiet.

"He came in today. I wasn't expecting him, and he mentioned something about having been removed from Dahlia's case, which we had all heard, and that he had a theory he wanted to talk to me about."

"What kind of theory?" asked Tucker.

"He wouldn't say. I figured at this point he was butting his nose back into Dahlia's case without permission, but I couldn't get another thing out of him."

"Are you going to go?" asked Tucker.

"Are you excited?" blurted Reggie at the same time.

They shot each other disgusted looks and waited for her reply.

"Yes, I'm going to go," she said to Reggie. "I think he's sort of handsome. In that rugged kind of way," she added.

"I don't see what he's up to if he's supposed to be off the case," remarked Tucker, folding his arms.

Reggie shoved Tucker in the chest until he fell sideways on the chaise in a heap.

"So, what are you going to wear?" she grinned, clapping her hands together.

"Oh, I hadn't thought about that. You know he didn't say where we're going, so now I don't know what to wear," she said dismally.

"Well, I'll help you," said Reggie kindly.

Dulcy gave Reggie a big grin and took her cue to leave.

"Dulcy, a word, please, before you go?" asked Tucker.

Dulcy headed back into Dahlia's office, re-closed the door, and waited.

"We've just been to the Historical Society. It's a brilliant collection they've put together, but we were mostly interested in some pictures donated from here. Do you know anything about them?" he asked.

"I do know there were some things donated, but I don't know if it was Dahlia or the previous owners."

"We were just curious. We thought they might tell us something. Like maybe what that key fits."

"Oh, my goodness," squeaked Dulcy. "I forgot all about it till now. Something came for you while you were gone."

She pulled out a folded yellow paper and handed it to Tucker.

"I didn't open it, but it's a telegram of all things," exclaimed Dulcy.

* * *

Chapter 24

I like your plan, except it sucks.
-The Avengers, 2015

It was while Reggie was lounging in a glorious bubble bath and Tucker was leaning against the wall of a steaming shower that Dulcy decided to use the upstairs bathroom to tidy up and change rather than make the trek across town before her dinner with Laird. She was fishing a towel out of the linen closet when its removal revealed a gap between the shelf and the wall. She put her finger into the hole and wriggled further. This area must have been missed in the recent renovation. From the niche came a large, rubbery chip of aged paint. As she examined it, there was a click and a snap, and the side wall gave way to a hole the size of a small storage door.

She waved her hand in the gap, feeling only stale air. She leaned further into the space to more stuffy air. She inched further into the gap, excited yet fearful. Crouching in total darkness, she lost her nerve and doubled back to the opening, where the fresh fragrant air of her recent bath beckoned her to safety. She climbed out of the hole and wrapped the towel around her more tightly. Should she fetch a flashlight now or leave it for later? She was torn. As much as she wanted to find out what was lurking down this discovery, she was too scared to go it alone.

She grabbed her watch from the tub and made up her mind. She tucked the towel tighter and ran downstairs to the kitchen for a light. As she rummaged through the supply closet, a step on the stairs made her freeze. She backed out of the cupboard and turned to meet Detective Laird's surprised gaze as she set the flashlight down on the counter.

"I seem to be overdressed and possibly a bit early?" he said as he checked his watch. "Is dinner at the local nudist colony?" he asked hopefully.

"No, no, just thinking about setting the traps. You never want to get caught with rats, now do you?" she said as she slipped past him and ran up the stairs.

* * *

Reggie and Tucker noticed the lights on their way out.

"I thought she'd be gone by now," said Reggie. "Maybe we'd better check on things before we leave."

They entered to find Laird examining the supply closet.

"Oh, sorry," said Tucker. "Thought maybe Dulcy had forgotten to turn out the lights. Looking for clues, Inspector?"

"Uh, no. I was just... that is, I was...nothing," said Laird as he rubbed the back of his neck roughly.

"Sorry, I just had to get my purse, my keys, my makeup, my hair, and my clothes," said Dulcy as she rushed into the kitchen.

All three turned as she reddened and looked at Laird. Tucker coughed and grinned. Reggie moved for the door, but Tucker stuck out his hand to Laird, blocking him from further movement.

"Well, now, we're all out to do the same thing, you know. Have a mind to join forces this evening?" he said with a wry smile.

Laird glared at Tucker, hands shoved in his pockets.

"Depends," he stated. "What's the catch of the day?"

* * *

The train puffed and wheezed until it reached an even speed to where Dahlia could settle in and close her eyes. It seemed like an eternity since she had really slept. The rhythm of the rails rocked her, and she barely heard the conductor's echo when he called for the Bournemouth stop. She shook off the sleep and grabbed her bag. This was a quick business trip, not like the holiday revelers off to enjoy the pier and beach even in the less-than-hospitable conditions. She headed toward the pretty town square with its hanging baskets and clean streets. She consulted her map and headed to the town hall. The hall of records was on the second floor, and she was confident that what she wanted could be gotten easily and cleanly. It would only be a problem for the next person who came along.

She was directed to the records section and approached the administrator, mindset and story straight.

"Well, dear, we certainly have those records. Will you be needing any copies? Because that will be an extra fee and that's seen to on another floor."

"Thank you so much. I will need copies. If you could just help me find the original, I'd be very appreciative," she said as she smiled and held out a five-pound note.

"Oh, love. Copies don't cost that much," she laughed gaily.

* * *

Dahlia paged through the records, sighting not one but two names. The man at the antique shop had given her some very interesting information. There had been claims by Cavanaugh that he had a right to the Hatfield fortune. There had also been claims of a forged birth certificate, infidelities, and other ugly rumors. But old man Hatfield was not to be deceived. The threats were finally too great, and Cavanaugh, and Hatfield's daughter Mazie, were gone. They had not been back since, even when John Alexander Hatfield died. Only the real certificate from the place of birth could help determine what the story would be in the end.

"Find everything you need, Miss?"

"Yes, thank you," said Dahlia, glancing into her purse.

"That'll be two pounds for the copy, dear."

"Oh, I didn't need a copy after all. Thank you, though," she said as she shoved the record to the bottom of her purse.

Dahlia smiled and walked quickly out into the mid-day mist. She entered the pub down the street from Farthing's Bed and Breakfast and sat down heavily in a corner booth. The historic pub was full with the lunch crowd.

"Something for you, Miss?"

Dahlia ordered a Shandy and sat back in the old wooden seat, closing her eyes. Her mind felt crowded, and she rubbed her temple,s trying to relax.

"Oh, Gawd," she sighed as she finished her Shandy in one gulp.

As she signaled the server, she glimpsed a familiar figure crossing the high street to the hall of records.

"Time to be off," she said, paying her tab and running for the depot.

If she hurried, she could make the next train back before he even got to the right floor. She rounded the corner and saw the train pulling into the station.

"And the race is on!" she said.

* * *

Once again, she was speeding through the countryside. She had gotten there by a plane, a train, and a car, all rushing her to places she didn't want to be. But she had no choice. Others would have just given in to make it all go away, but she had never been much of a quitter. She found this tendency tedious, tiring, and usually expensive.

She woke to the jarring train pulling into the station. She had slept most of the way home. She glanced around the compartment at the faceless, preoccupied occupants and thought how easy it was to be invisible if you really wanted to.

"Mind the gap, Miss," a porter said behind her as she hurried to retrieve her bicycle.

She turned up the long drive and ran straight into Jennings, pulling bags from a car in the drive.

"Good morning, Miss. Bit of a quick trip, I see. Pleasant, I hope?"

"Oh, yes, Jennings, thanks for asking. Is someone here?"

"Yes, Miss. These would be the Elliott's bags."

"What!? What are they doing here? I thought no one was to know where I was?"

"Well, Miss, they are not aware that you have sought the anonymity of your childhood home. They are here, however, for the upcoming weekend at the lodge with your parents."

"Oh, Gawd. I would have thought they'd cancel that with me hanging about the place."

"Apparently, Miss, your parents tried, but the Elliotts felt it their duty to be present in their hour of need after the tragic loss of their beloved daughter," he said with a penetrating stare.

"Oh, really Jennings. How melodramatic. No way to get them to clear out, I suppose?"

"No, Miss. They are quite set on lending comfort and aid in this desperate hour."

Dahlia hopped off the bike, slapped Jennings on the arm, then turned back to the street. She threw on her hat and lowered her head as she veered away from the house. She peered over her shoulder to make sure she was not being watched. As she turned onto the lane, Mrs. Alene Farthing Elliott stepped out the front door and headed for the car. She stopped and stared at the bicyclist in the lane.

"Oh my, Jennings. It's awful when you lose someone. You think you see them at every turn. I can even see her in that street person on the bicycle. Such a shame."

"Yes, Ma'am," said Jennings. "'Tis at that."

* * *

Dahlia's muscles had turned to lead; she was breathing like an asthmatic and was as dry as the Sahara in summer. She had pedaled so far so fast she hadn't looked back to see what might be happening. She finally pulled off the road a mile away, drew a normal breath, and calmed down.

She scanned the road behind her and saw nothing terrifying, nothing to give her away to the people who would know her for sure. She needed to think, but not here. She walked the bike, then pulled herself astride once more heading to the village. She would find a quiet place with a call box and contact her mother and father. Her cell phone was not an option.

She kept her head down as she rode into town, pulling up in front of the local hotel. The George and Dragon offered nice loos, a restaurant, and staff that wasn't overly interested in your business, considering it was a small town. She parked the bike where Jennings could easily retrieve it. She flew through the lobby to a phone bank around the corner from registration. She had her hand on the receiver when the mention of a name made her stop and eavesdrop on the front desk conversation.

"No, no. I said, Porter. Lives out towards the country."

The desk manager gazed confusedly at the man. Wasn't this, after all, the country? Dahlia drew her cap further over her face and edged around the stalls for a better view. It could only be the man from the train. She was unpleasantly surprised to see none other than Dr. George Landry, her contact and finger on the pulse of the events unfolding at home. Why was he here? There could only be a problem that threatened their plan or exposed her existence.

The only question was how to gather him up without fanfare and keep him from heading to the house. He would trip over the Elliotts before they could get safely off for their lodge weekend, ruining everything. Dahlia lowered her cap again, drew her jacket around her, and marched to the front desk.

* * *

Chapter 25

Carlton Ashby: I don't know how I let you perverts talk me into this.
-Hardbodies, 1984

Tucker, Reggie, Detective Laird, and Dulcy ended up at a pretty little café on the main drag. The others were talking to the maître de as Reggie scanned the quaint storefront. She realized that the windows with the decorative shutters weren't really windows. They were wide open, and if she wanted, she could reach out and touch the young couple dining before her.

She was wondering what would happen if it rained when she saw the others follow the haughty little man. Tucker stood at her side, beckoning her in front of him. It was a romantic venue, and Reggie wondered who had picked it, Laird or Tucker. They were seated in a quiet corner booth, away from the street noise, the lovers, and the kitchen. They ordered drinks, peering distractedly at the listed fare. As they perused the menu, Laird lost no time in diving right into conversation.

"So, what do we all feel like?"

"How about calamari to start, with a side of truth?" said Tucker.

Laird stared, chuckling, then gave in.

"Alright, Elliott, what do you want to know?"

"What's the bottom line here? What are we doing?"

Reggie and Dulcy were staring in silence, as anxious as Tucker was to know what was happening.

"I don't mean to be rude, but we all know we're not here for dinner."

"I beg your pardon," said Dulcy. "I'm starving at the moment."

"And I happen to be quite intrigued with the hungry person across from me if you want to know the truth. As for Sea Gables, it depends on what you think you're going to learn in the end as to where you begin, I suppose," finished Laird.

"I'm only looking for anything that will clear this matter up. And so are you. The fact that you have been officially taken off the case means nothing to me. What's on your mind, Inspector, because you don't strike me as the type just to clear out no matter what the upper powers say."

Laird stared at the hot, inviting bread for what seemed like an eternity, then resigned himself to the fact that he would have to give in.

"Alright. I'll discuss this with you, not because I think you should be involved, but because you are involved. I tried to leave you out of this, but it didn't work. I'll admit that some of your information might be helpful."

"Information such as finding strange keys and, uh, hidden doors?" said Dulcy quietly.

"You want to run that by me again?" asked Laird.

Tucker was glaring at her like she had given away the hiding place to the loot of the Great Train Robbery. Reggie was afraid to move, her eyes darting between the three.

"I'm going to tell him," said Dulcy. "I'm going to tell him everything and quit dancing around. Dahlia is dead, and we're squaring off like one of us did it. I think it's time we teamed up and figured this out."

Tucker shifted slightly in his seat but did not get the chance to give his opinion.

"I think she's right," Reggie blurted out.

Tucker and Laird stared silently, waiting.

"We're wasting time while whoever did this is biding their time waiting to start again with their threats and pranks. That's right. When you all leave, I'm still here. And they've got rid of Dahlia, so what's to stop them from coming after me if I'm in the way next time they go looking for, well, whatever it is they're looking for? I'm a sitting duck," Dulcy said.

"You don't think I haven't thought of that?" said Laird. "People like this don't stop until they've gotten what they want, and I don't believe that's happened yet."

"No, you're right," said Tucker. "So first, what happened with that kitchen woman from the staffing agency? I don't know if she's even involved. It could have just been a coincidence."

"No," interjected Laird. "I don't think it's a coincidence. I can't say she was the one who put the stuff in the glass, but she was there for a reason, hired by somebody. What I really want to hear are the details only you three know. Let's start there."

Dulcy shot Reggie a sharp glance as she took the old-fashioned key from her purse. She laid it on the table between her plate and Laird's. He gingerly examined it before returning it to the table.

"And?"

"I found this the day it happened."

"Well, that is a start. Is that what you've had in your pocket for the last week?"

Dulcy blushed, trying to hide behind her wine glass, but shook her head yes.

"I knew there was something I didn't have my hands on. Where did you find it, and was it before or after Dahlia collapsed?"

"Since you knew there was something, I found it right about the time you came in."

"How's that for timing? Didn't think to tell me about it? So, what do you two know about this?" he said, turning to Tucker and Reggie.

"It came up shortly after Dahlia's death," said Tucker, "and now that I think about it, I may know more about it than I thought."

"What do you mean?" asked Laird.

"She said something to me at the opening. I thought it was a joke at first."

Slowly, Tucker turned toward Reggie and dropped his head.

"You were trying to tell me, and I ignored you. I was trying to keep things moving, but she said something, and so did you, about knowing something, right?"

"Oh, Gosh," said Reggie. "She did. She never got the chance to tell us. I thought she told you about it. You acted like she had said something but that it would have to wait till after the speeches."

"No, sorry, love. She never told me anything. We went over the speech, and then she went to the podium."

"Whatever she was so excited about got her killed," said Dulcy.

"What was she doing right before she got up there? We need to track her movements," said Laird.

"I don't know, but now I guess it was something deadly important. I have a bad feeling about all this," said Tucker.

"Yeah, me too," said Laird.

Dulcy was staring into space. She looked as though she was watching a movie vignette.

"Oh. Oh! I think maybe...Oh! I think I've got it. I think I know! I know what she didn't get to tell us. I can't believe I didn't see it before. Actually, this is where I tell you what I found before we came to dinner."

And in a rush of words, Dulcy detailed finding the hidden entrance in the upstairs linen closet only an hour or so before.

"So, you couldn't find her in the tea room to send her to the podium and went out to ask Reggie where she was when she popped out of the B&B. Meaning that the opening you found is the entrance to something which takes you from the tea room to the B&B without being seen," said Tucker. "So, it's some sort of tunnel. Can't imagine there's a whole lot of room under there."

"That has to be what she knew," said Reggie. "I know it's what she had just found. And the key fits something somewhere down there. This has to be what they're looking for. Someone else knows this exists and has been trying to find the entrance," she finished excitedly.

Tucker pulled a handkerchief out of his pocket. In the middle lay the torn metal fragment Reggie had found the night of the cocktail party.

"I bet that belongs to the opening in the bathroom," said Reggie. "I also bet it only clicked and opened because someone before you, probably Dahlia, had finally found it but broke the latch. You must have hit it just right somehow."

"The paint chip," said Dulcy. "The big rubbery paint chip I pulled out of there must have been jamming the door and when I pulled on it, the spring activated."

Laird had been quiet during these revelations, pondering the new facts.

"What else have you got?" he asked. "I mea,n what other evidential fragments do you have lying around that might complete the picture?"

"That's just it," said Tucker. "We think the pictures could be a part of this as well. We went to the Historical Museum looking for the original paintings of John Alexander Hatfield. We finally found them but then had no idea what they were supposed to tell us. I think maybe someone else is also looking for those paintings. I just don't know if they know why either."

"So, a person or persons is poking around the inn hunting for something of value, and they haven't found it yet. They tried intimidation tactics to get you ou,t and when those didn't work, they killed in order to cut to the chase. They may not make any new attempts right now with our men still investigating, but you're all in danger as long as you stay there. You'll be safer if you leave and let us find what they're looking for before they do."

"I appreciate your concern, Laird, but if we leave your lot to take over, we may never know who's behind it or how and why they killed Dahlia. We have to be a part of this. You're off the case, or had you forgotten? You can give them this information, but they'll sit on it, and we won't know any more than we do now," said Tucker.

"That's right," said Reggie. "No one from your department has questioned us about Dahlia since you left. No one has asked to see us or have access to the tea room. I think they're sweeping it under the rug for some reason, and for all we know, there's someone making decisions who doesn't want the truth found out."

"You mean someone from the commissioner's staff?" said Laird incredulously.

"I think we need to set a trap," said Reggie.

Reggie earned a smirk from Laird for her contribution.

"This is not the movies, Reggie. You don't mess about setting traps to catch the bad guy. But you may be right about the department. I don't see any effort there, either. It does look like they're burying it for some reason."

"Then what do you suggest?" asked Tucker.

"I think we would all agree that we need to find out what's beyond the entrance, and the sooner, the better. Depending on what we find there, we may have all the answers we need. Is there anything we haven't discussed?"

Reggie leaned down and rummaged in her purse, laying the tattered newspaper clipping in front of Laird.

Winner of Sizemore Award Discredited; Alleged Plagiarism Negates University Post

This year's winner of the prestigious Sizemore Award for Historical Excellence has been discredited amongst allegations of plagiarism. Newly appointed Dean Forrest Perkins III has resigned his post at Winston University based on evidence presented to the President detailing passages from his award-winning dissertation as having been copied verbatim from a piece written in the early...

"Uh-huh. And how do you believe this fits in?" asked Laird.

"We're not sure," ventured Reggie," but it's something to look into. It may not mean anything, but we should check it out to confirm or deny his involvement."

"Right," said Laird. "This is a nice tangle. My guess is it goes pretty deep. And there's always the corpse in the garden the day you got here. Probably nothing in that, but... and like you, I'm still bothered by the kitchen woman and not only her but the maid as well. I'm still working on the Cavanaugh death, so there's no question of my being on the premises. That will help. But we're still trying to locate the maid for questioning. The only thing is, I really don't think we're going to find her. You know she is long gone, folks."

"Laird, what if the maid and the kitchen woman are the same?" asked Tucker.

"Well, I think that's just it. They are one and the same. That's why we never found the agency woman. She was there all the time, hiding out in the B&B and the crowd masquerading as the maid."

Dulcy felt a wave of nausea pass through her stomach.

"Dahlia always handled them, and they change out so often. It could be anybody, but I wouldn't know. I feel so stupid."

"No worries," said Tucker. "We may be on to something here."

"Yes," smiled Laird. "Very good," he said, smiling at Dulcy.

"So, what do we do now?" asked Reggie.

"Right now?" said Laird. "We order dinner."

* * *

"What are you doing here?" hissed Dahlia as she sneaked up to Landry at the desk. He found a medium-sized, dark-haired woman in his way as he turned to face the person accosting him.

"Please excuse me," he said to the desk clerk, guiding Dahlia to the fireplace where they could talk in confidence.

"I needed to see you and discuss all of this in person. Didn't you get what you came for?"

"I did, yes. Why didn't you let me know you were coming?"

"I wasn't going to hear you tell me not to, and I couldn't wait any longer. Elliott saw me in the travel agency. I feel like a sitting duck."

"YOU feel like a sitting duck? I'm supposed to be dead. Can't be more 'sitting' than that. And so he saw you in the travel agency. Big deal."

"You're not the one who faked a death certificate with a practice already in trouble."

"I told you for your help with this, the police are going to work with you. Next time, do what you're supposed to, and you won't have to worry about your license."

"It's not the police I need to worry about. It's the medical association."

"And anybody who decides to press charges, seeing as how you weren't cer-tified in Florida when you were writing prescriptions and recommending therapies," she added.

Landry blanched, waving an impatient hand over his head.

"Can we go to the manor and get this over with? You have what you need, so let's go back to the house and discuss it there," he finished, turning her towards the door.

Dahlia stayed still, staring down Landry until he turned and stopped.

"What? What's the matter? What's going on?"

"Look, you, I'm not here having lunch on my holiday. I am here because, at this very moment, back at the house, the Elliotts are having tea with my parents before leaving to go to the lodge for the weekend. Seeing as how I'm dead, it would be poor form to have me walk into the conservatory with the tea cart. 'Cheers, Alene, cheers, Roger. Have a biscuit with your tea or maybe some nice smelling salts'?"

"Oh. Didn't see that coming."

"No, neither did I. I was phoning Jennings to pack my things and bring them to me when I heard you at the front desk. When I got home from my rail trip, he was unloading baggage as I rode up. I made it out of the drive, but only just. I hope nobody saw me. I never looked back."

"I feel like a fugitive," said Landry.

"You? Oh, really, do grow up," said Dahlia. "I'm going back to the phones to try Jennings again and see what we can do about this. Be a good boy, sit, and try not to make notice of yourself. I'll be right back."

Dahlia went back to the phone bank while Landry sat in a large leather chair by the fireplace, trying to be invisible. It was only five minutes before she was back, but to Landry, it felt like an hour. Dahlia plopped down opposite hi,m taking a deep breath and then exhaling.

"Much better," she said.

Landry looked like a rumpled cat in the rain.

"You do look awful, love. Try not to worry. It'll all be over soon."

"That's what I'm afraid of."

* * *

"Well, at least I do have good news," said Dahlia, getting comfy. "Instead of leaving tomorrow morning as planned, my terribly cooperative parents have persuaded the Elliotts to head straight to the lodge tonight. Why waste part of Saturday driving when they can push off this evening and wake up in their comfy eiderdowns tomorrow? Luckily, they're feeling a bit antsy. It seems poor Alene wandered out to the car and caught sight of a street person pedaling by who reminded her of me. She decided that the sooner she quit the Porter household, the better. Thank God for that."

"So, she did see you."

"Yes. It appears I left out just in time. Anyway, Jennings says the coast will be clear in an hour, and we'll be able to stay till they decide to come back, whenever that may be."

"Well, I don't know about you, but I sure could use a drink."

"You know you're right. It is teatime, isn't it?"

* * *

Pulling up to the door, they could see the pointed, birdlike features of Jennings peering through the front window. They eased Landry's rented mini into the garage and locked it up. Jennings was swinging the door wide by the time they got to the stoop.

"Hello Miss, hello Sir. They've only just gone. They were running a bit tardy with the food and the wine choices. But I am now at your service."

"Thank you, Jennings. This is Dr. George Landry. He will be our guest this evening. When do you expect the happy lodgers to head back home?"

"They are expected to stay into next week. I shouldn't anticipate their return till at least Thursday."

"Lovely then. We have some business to attend to, Jennings. Would you please bring dinner into the conservatory?"

With a nod, he disappeared into the vast house while Dahlia and Landry headed in the opposite direction. Swallowed comfortably amidst the foliage, George Landry was finally able to relax. He felt the tension drain from his body as he leaned back in his chair. He inspected the room with its massive plants and tall windows and felt the welcome sensation of the communion of nature with soul.

"So, shall we catch up?" asked Dahlia.

"Well, you first. What have you found out?"

"I now have the original birth record for our friend Cord Cavanaugh, or should I say Clinton Miller Peters? I must say you were spot on with that, but why is this so important? I guess it's a piece of evidence, but I'm even more lost. It's all about as clear as the bog out back. What was this supposed to tell us? Because quite honestly, George, this has been a bit fractious running about the countryside with only a slight idea as to why."

"Sorry to have been so tight-lipped, but I just couldn't chance someone overhearing us. I don't know much more, but I'm sure there's some missing documentation. What I saw looks too disjointed to be the real paperwork."

"That would actually fit, George. When Tucker and Reggie went to the hall of records to go through the paperwork on the house, there were all sorts of inconsistencies. Someone had removed pages, making it incomprehensible. As I well know, it's very easy to do. We have to get those two into that room I found before my 'untimely demise.' I left the key where I'm sure Dulcy has already tripped over it. Once they get into that room, there must be something that will explain all this. What other reason would you have for a place like that unless you had things to hide?"

"A place for hiding yourself as well, I suppose," said Landry. "Lots of people like to disappear to get away from things."

"I'm sure you're right, but it must be more than that. Whatever is there is what they've been searching the house for. There's something terribly valuable down there. I was so amazed to have found the entrance, and of all places, right under my nose in the bathroom. I didn't see a thing on my way to the B&B, but that doesn't mean anything. So, what confirmed that we were on the right track?"

"Well, I had stopped by the inn to check on 'Cord,' and I overheard a very private phone conversation."

"Ooo, so what exactly was said? I'm dying to know."

"That's a good one. They thought you did know, so you did die."

"Or so he thought," chuckled Dahlia. "Gives a whole new meaning to 'what's your poison,' eh? So, if he's the one who thinks he's killed me, then he's the one in back of all of this. If we could only prove that he put the poison in the glass at the cocktail party."

"I knew there was something about him, and the more I thought about it, the odder it seemed. I think he's led a double life and who knows for how long or how many are in on it. But don't think he's all on his own because I would bet against it."

"Oh, I wouldn't bet on anything at the moment. So, what was it he said, and to whom was he speaking?"

"I still don't know who he was talking to. It was the sort of thing where you happen upon a conversation accidentally and are embarrassed at being there. But you don't leave quickly enough, so you hear things. I thought it was the wrong suite. I actually checked the room number. I wasn't there to eavesdrop; I figured he'd be alone, maybe resting. I could tell fast enough that he was on the telephone. What stumped me was his accent. It wasn't the slow southern drawl he's been using. It was plain at points but had English overtones to it."

"What did he say, George?"

"Well, it was something like 'I'm not going over this again. I told you before it doesn't make any difference at this point. What's one more if it comes to that? You didn't seem to have any problem with it then, what's changed your mind now?'"

"Well, that doesn't sound particularly evil. When was this you went round?"

"After you had gone, Mazie had died, he'd been working on the funeral arrangements, and Tucker and Reggie had started plans for your memorial."

"Oh, how sweet. I hope it's going to be a nice service. Maybe it has something to do with the funeral arrangements."

"Dahlia, that's when I knew you were right. You thought he had something to do with trying to kill you. Now I know he had something to do with it."

"That conversation is hardly enough to prove that he tried to kill me," she said with a smile, "because we both know he didn't. What else has happened to send you scurrying over her, hair on fire?"

"It's what I found out just before I came over here. I met with Police Commissioner Hammond. Because of our agreement and the fact that I signed the death certificate, he has shared some very confidential evidence and information."

"What else could he have found? I thought we went over everything that day in hospital."

"I'm not talking about you. I'm talking about Mazie Cavanaugh. I'm talking about the autopsy report and the fact that she did not die a natural death. She was ill and had had a shock, but she did not go gently into that good night. She was helped out of this world, and the only person who could have done it was Cord Cavanaugh. There were only two people who had been in the room with her: Cord and the maid who found her," he finished with satisfaction. Dahlia was speechless.

"I would never have figured she was murdered. She was so sick anyway."

"Yes, but they found oleander in her system. They would have done an autopsy anyway, but now they had to double-check for anything unusual. Their conclusion is still that she died of heart failure, but heart failure brought on by oleander toxicity. It may have been in some tea or honey, making it a double dose of poison. She never knew what hit her."

"So, who gave her tea?"

"Who knows? There was nothing in the room, so either he took it, or the maid did something with it for him for all we know."

"Oh, I don't believe that. Sara would never do anything of the kind."

"It wasn't Sara. This was a Hispanic woman who barely spoke English. When they went to interview her, she had disappeared completely."

"I don't have anyone of that description working for me."

"That's something that's being looked into as we speak. The police feel it could be a major link in the whole case. They never found the kitchen woman, and they never found the chambermaid."

"That horrible kitchen woman?! I knew there was something wrong with her. She didn't know a utensil from a toothbrush. So, you don't think he was talking about funeral arrangements but 'funeral arrangements', as in I'll make sure you actually have one. So," she said, concentrating, "he really does think he's killed me. We can work with this. And he's killed Mazie, his own wife. Anyway, I have sent Mr. Elliott a lovely little missive, which I hope will send them off to find the room before we get back."

"What did you do, Dahlia? Don't risk this whole setup by exposing yourself."

"I beg your pardon. I would never expose myself. I just sent Tucker a little telegram with a couple of hints. He's a bright bulb. He'll figure it out."

"You could have just let me handle it."

"Really, George. You're already well in more than was ever intended. From the minute I decided to do this, there was to be no one else involved. Who knew you would burst into the ER like an outlaw and see the whole thing? I don't want you in any deeper."

"Fine. What do we do now?"

"Well, tell me about my memorial service. Sounds lovely. Will there be loads of flowers and harps and crying children?" she said whimsically.

"I have not heard any of the details, but I'm sure we'll read about them in the papers."

"Really, George. I think not," smiled Dahlia.

"Oh, I really don't care for the look in your eye."

"I think it's time to go shopping, darling."

"For what?" he snapped.

"Why for black, of course. I just can't attend my own memorial service in these old rags, now, can I?"

* * *

Chapter 26

*Dr. Raymond Stantz: You think there's a connection between this Vigo
character and the slime?*
Dr. Egon Spengler: Is the atomic weight of cobalt 58.9?
–Ghostbusters II, 1989

Tucker and Reggie were enjoying the moonlight while Dulcy and Laird
had gone for a nightcap at the new club by the marina. Tucker was as far
away from Reggie as the boats moored in the breeze.

"So, what a dinner, eh?" said Reggie.

"Sorry, what?" said Tucker.

"I didn't think you were with me. I mean, you're with me. You just weren't
with me."

"Have a bit on my mind after that meal. There are still a few things I just
am not satisfied with."

"Like what?"

"It's not that I don't want to tell you. It's just that I don't feel like I can
make any sense of it just yet."

"Well, I have a question."

"Ask away."

"Why aren't we heading down to that hidey hole right now? I can't believe you're not so curious that we're running through the streets making a beeline for that linen closet."

"I applaud your enthusiasm, Reg. And I know there is something amazing at the end of that opening."

"But you're not going down that hidey hole at night, in the dark, for anyone, are you?"

"It's not that, love, but whatever is there will wait. There's nothing in the dark that's not there in the light, eh?"

"Don't believe everything you hear. And have you told the rats, bats, and spiders your philosophy? But really, if it's my sensibilities you're concerned with, not to worry. I am willing to head on in bats, rats, spiders, and all. Well, maybe not spiders, ugh."

"I'm not quite sure, Reg, is all I can say," he muttered as they headed for the B&B.

The lights were out, but for one, on the front porch. It bore a fantastic resemblance to a spook house at Halloween.

"Ah – daunting, eh? What say we stop off for a topper in the salon and then decide?"

Reggie nodded, and they headed for the light at the front. The back was hooded in darkness, and neither of us wanted to go that way. They were engrossed in conversation when they surprised a sergeant posted at the front door.

"Sorry, but I can't allow you to enter."

"I thought your lot was through here. What's happened?" asked Tucker warily.

The sergeant's phone rang, and he excused himself while still barring the entrance.

"Right. Right. Yes, sir. Good. Thank you. You would be Miss Winter and Mr. Elliott?"

"Yes, what is it?"

"Detective Laird has given you permission to enter the premises."

"Well, that's a relief," said Tucker. "I thought we were being evicted."

"Well, sir, actually, you are," said the sergeant.

"Sorry?"

"My apologies, sir, but this is a crime scene, and we have no choice but to relocate you and Miss Winter. Detective Laird has requested that you meet him at the Beach Drive Plaza in the center of town, where he will explain everything to you. You have two rooms booked."

"A crime scene?"

"Yes, sir. Detective Laird asked that you meet him at the Beach Drive Plaza."

Tucker nodded as he guided Reggie through the yellow tape.

"Not a problem, Sergeant, cheers."

The two peeled off in opposite directions upstairs to pack their things and head to the new hotel. Tucker stared around the room. He had an idea forming in his brain. He pulled the telegram from the nightstand and reread it. What was he meant to see? He spread the sheet on the bed, staring intently. Whatever it was he was not going to see it now.

He packed his things taking one last look, then pulled to door to. The sergeant's directions were accurate, and they were standing in front of the Beach Drive Plaza within five minutes. It was a charming boutique hotel, and Tucker and Reggie sighted Dulcy and Laird on the patio.

"Feel like a nightcap, Elliott?"

"I do now."

The server bustled away while the four sat and stared at each other.

"So, we have another crime scene. You can't mean..."

"The report I was waiting for came in while we were at dinner. I asked forensics to be a little extra diligent in checking out Mrs. Cavanaugh, and they found something. I had this feeling I couldn't shake while I was standing on the porch of the inn. There was a siren in the distance, and it made me think of something far off, but I couldn't get it to surface."

"Is this heading somewhere, Laird?"

"On the surface, Mazie's death was straightforward, a bit too straightfor-ward. I asked for an autopsy, which I can tell you was a surprise to the old woman and to Cavanaugh, but it paid off. An examination produced high levels of oleander in her system, which led them to the conclusion of murder. Now we start the process of who had access, a reason, and an opportunity."

"Oh, but that could be anybody. The place was full of people. Wouldn't you start with the most likely persons, which was the maid, or whoever she was, and Mr. Cavanaugh?" said Reggie.

"Yes, and we did. We now have our theory on the maid. And I have sent my men to round up Cord Cavanaugh, grieving widower. And, of course, he is nowhere to be found."

"Maybe he's just taken a long walk. Gone off to be by himself," said Reggie, knowing it wasn't true.

"I really do not think that's the case. I sent a man to Mavis Hatfield's to question her. She said she had talked with him earlier in the day, but she hadn't actually seen him since they went to the funeral home. That's when they were made aware of the autopsy proceedings and were told not to take any sudden excursions. I now have men circulating his picture at the airports and the cab companies. If he turns up, that's fine, but I don't think it's going to work out that way."

"Where do you think he's gone? Maybe he had some business to take care of," said Dulcy.

"Whatever it is or wherever he's gone, we'll find him," said Laird.

"You'll keep us informed, I'm sure. Speaking of business, I have a few things I have to take care of in the morning, so I think I may push off to bed," said Tucker.

Reggie eyed him with curiosity. She hadn't heard of any issues that would require his immediate attention. If so, Alene would have informed her.

"Really, Tucker? What's going on? I haven't been called about anything," said Reggie.

"There's a plant outside of Manchester that's having some labor issues. I may have to intervene," Tucker lied. "Nothing to worry about. I can take care of it easily enough."

"And as far as our flip-flops are concerned?"

Tucker thought of a smart alliteration that fit with the "f" in flip flops but thought better of it.

"I've spoken with Alene on that, and we're reprieved for the time being. What I would like you to do is to continue working with Dulcy and the others on Dahlia's service."

"I did get contacted on that," said Reggie. "I also wanted to go to the Brown Bag Lunch at the History Museum. You know, the one that Forrest Perkins does? Remember we were going to see what that was about?"

"Oh, right, yeah. Really should check into that. When is the next one?"

"Tomorrow."

"We'll see how things go. I have a couple of errands to run as well, so if I can't make it, Dulcy, can you escape the lunch crowd to escort Reggie?"

"Well, I suppose I can. I'll just have to get one of the older girls to take charge for a bit."

"What errands?" blurted Reggie.

"I just have a couple of things I need to review before I handle Manchester. But that does leave one other rather big topic."

"The hidey hole!" said Dulcy and Reggie together.

"Yes, the hidey hole. Laird, we have to get down there and check it out."

"Technically, I shouldn't let you near that, but since I have no ability to request men, my best response is to go with you and see what you find."

"Right. I think we just need to move ahead, and the sooner, the better," said Tucker as he stretched his long legs and rose.

Reggie and the others rose as well, each saying goodnight and heading to their appointed accommodations. Tucker accompanied Reggie to pick up their keys, and they were then pointed to the elevators. Tucker said goodnight as Reggie sighted her room, then turned to find his own. As he read the room numbers, he felt a hand on his arm and turned to find Reggie wide-eyed and whispering frantically at his side.

"There's been someone in my room," she said quietly.

"What do..."

"Ssshh!" she hissed.

"Easy, Reggie. You think they're still there?"

"There's a light on, and the door's cracked. It's a bit strange, don't you think?"

"Reg, I think you're just letting all this get to you. It's probably just the turn-down service. I'll go in with you if you like. C'mon, let's go."

"No, no, you're right. I'm being silly," said Reggie, feeling stupid. "I've let all this make me jumpy. I'm sorry, I'll just go in. I really am tired. Let's get together for breakfast and figure out our day. Thanks for dinner. It was...interesting."

"Alright. You sure you don't want me to walk through the room with you?"

"Nope, just being silly. Go on and get some sleep. Big doings tomorrow," she said, yawning.

"Goodnight, Reggie."

"Goodnight, Tucker."

Tucker watched as she entered the room, quickly glancing back and smiling briefly as she pushed the door shut. He wandered through the corridor and found his room at the corner of the hallway. The secluded spot satisfied him, as he was not only tired but wanted to go over the telegram again in peace.

He inserted the key and pushed the door open. He thought how nice it was to have a real key rather than a bendy piece of plastic that never seemed to work no matter which way you slid it in the slot. He also wondered how many cards he must have lodged in his luggage when he heard a horrendous scream coming from the opposite hallway.

He bolted the length of the corridor to the scream's source. It led him straight to Reggie's room as heads popped out from every entrance. He pounded on the door, yelling to be let in.

"Oh God, let her be alright," he muttered.

"Get the manager," he ordered to a woman staring at him. "Now!" he yelled as the next room's occupant scurried off in frightened silence.

"Regina! Open the door!"

The door finally opened, and he pushed past a white and shaking Reggie.

"What is it? What's happened?"

She could only point to the bathroom, where a low light shone under the door. Tucker gripped her by both arms and sat her on the bed. He pushed the door open, scanning the small space. His gaze rested on the sensible shoes of a chambermaid poking out from under the shower curtain, eerily still and lifeless.

***

"Let's go over it again, Reggie. I know it's repetitive, but we need to make sure we don't miss anything," said Laird.
Reggie once again reviewed the details of what she and Tucker had done after leaving him and Dulcy on the patio.

"Well, there goes our answers from the chambermaid," said Laird, glaring at Tucker.

"It's too bad you didn't get to ask her anything before she..." trailed Tucker.

"That's by design. Whoever did this knew we were almost to her, so she had to go. At least, it confirms we were on the right track."

"I must say, the bodies are starting to pile up here," he mused.

"That is morbid and grotesque," said Reggie, and with that, she began to cry.

"Sorry, Reggie. That was bang out of order."

Tucker and Laird exchanged glances. Then Laird barked to a female officer who led Reggie down to the sitting area.

"This is getting a bit deep," said Tucker.

"Yep, this is one twisted cluster. You know there are no coincidences."

"Yeah, but if I can prove these things connect, they'll have to listen."

Tucker was thinking the opposite as he watched the squad work around him. Laird answered a question from one of his men, then sat and watched Tucker, waiting for the eventual response he knew would come.

"Might I have a word?" asked Tucker.

Laird rose, beckoned one of his men, and followed Tucker into the hallway.

"If you don't mind, let's wander down to my room. Less noisy and rather private, luckily."

Once seated, Tucker and Laird compared notes. After half an hour of theories interwoven with facts, the two men decided their courses of action. Each had their assignments, including guiding Reggie and Dulcy through theirs. The only thing Tucker forgot to mention was the cryptic telegram still folded in his breast pocket.

***

The morning dawned sunny but muggy, and Tucker decided to forego the pretty patio breakfast for the cooler, more comfortable main dining room. Reggie entered smiling and calm but not well rested despite spending the night in a double suite. Dulcy slept shotgun in the other room, steadfastly refusing to leave her after this newest assault.

Tucker rose as they wove their way toward him. He could see through the bright grin to the deep circles and glassy eyes of the restless, interrupted sleeper. She probably had no more than an hour or two of actual rest.

His heart went out to her as she neared the table. He instinctively enveloped her in a warm embrace. Embarrassed, they let go, and Tucker pulled out her chair.

"Well, good morning to you too, Mr. Elliott," said Reggie. "And how did you sleep with all the activity rolling along down the hall?"

Laird's men were combing Reggie's room with special attention to the bathroom. Tucker was seated with his arm around Reggie, who was calmer but still shaking. Laird and Dulcy had barely gotten to the tea room before his phone was pinging, the message labeled 911. The posted sergeant sprinted toward them, directing them back to the Plaza.

"I slept like a baby," said Tucker, "for at least two hours before I couldn't stare at the millions of tiny dots in the ceiling any longer and decided to get up to check on the investigation in your previous room."

"Did you find out anything?" she said eagerly.

"No, they had posted a man at the door, and even though we're acquainted, I was not allowed to enter the crime scene. They really are adding up," he said, instantly regretting it as it was a remark such as this that caused her earlier distress.

"Well, what is our schedule for today since there's so much to do?"

Reggie ordered breakfast while listening to the day's agenda and was quick to note that almost nowhere in the itinerary were she and Tucker together for any length of time.

"I notice you're rather absent in all this. What are you up to?" she said, munching a muffin.

"As I mentioned, I do have some Manchester business to take care of and other errands that need to be dealt with, not the least important being that telegram."

Reggie raised her eyebrows and waited for more information, then resigned herself to having to pry it out of him.

"Have a theory on this, Mr. Elliott, or is that classified?"

"When I couldn't sleep last night, I dug it out and reread it. You know there's something in it, and I rearranged things here and there. I think maybe I've landed on a basic idea. Let me sketch it up for you."

He reread the markings he'd made and turned the paper to her. As she studied it, Tucker could see the comprehension dawn. She laid the telegram back on the table, staring at him.

Important medical news stop Key to death stop Find storage place stop Room to file it away stop See you again on the other side stop Important key find room stop See you on the other side stop

"Who did this, Tucker?"

"One of my errands is to find out where this came from. That could answer everything. Or make it more complicated; I don't know which."

"We know we have to find that room before anything else. Shall we start after breakfast?"

"After breakfast, love, I'm going to run along to see Landry. I have a couple of questions. I want you to get with Dulcy and Laird and head for that room. He'll be waiting for you. Then I want you to go to the Brown Bag and check out Forrest Perkins."

"What do expect to learn from Landry?"

"Maybe where this telegram came from, maybe nothing. By the way, I don't quite feel ready to share this with Laird yet."

"So, we're not going to totally work together then, are we?"

"It's not that I don't want to. It's just that I need to sift through this more before wasting his time."

"You don't want him pulling this from you and taking you out of the picture."

"You know that if he gets his hands on this, he'll use it to try to make them let him back on the case, and I just don't think that's going to happen. They'll add it to the rest of what they haven't investigated, and then we're lost."

"So, when do you want to meet up?"

"I'll be in touch. Now, eat your breakfast. I have a feeling you're going to need it."

***

Tucker gave Reggie a few last instructions, then headed in the opposite direction, checking the address on the hotel notepaper. He climbed old brick steps, pushed open double doors, and stopped at the building directory. He scanned the listings and found the clinical offices of George Landry, MD, on the fourth floor.

He peeled off to the stairs, rhythmically logging the landings until he reached number four. Heavy oak doors marked the entrance to the plush offices of the good doctor. A prim middle-aged woman sat behind sliding glass panels, checking files against insurance forms. She barely raised her eyes to note his intrusion. He couldn't help noticing the waiting room being a bit sparse as he stood expectantly awaiting acknowledgment. Finally, the woman lowered her pen and slid open the panel.

"May I help you?" she said stone-faced.

"Yes, I am here to see Dr. Landry."

"Dr. Landry is not in this week. Would you care to make an appointment for next week?"

"Sorry, just a bit surprised since we had a set appointment for this morning. I would have thought he'd let me know if he was going to be out of the office," he said, acting injured.

"Well, it was a matter that came up suddenly, so Dr. Landry had to cancel some appointments. I'm sorry if he missed yours," she said, checking the book. "Your name, sir?"

"Oh, I don't think you'll find me there," he said. "It was more of a business appointment, you see. I can get with him when he comes in. I hope everything's alright. I would hate to think he's ill in any way."

"Oh, no, he's fine. He just had a quick business trip to make. Everyone's fine," she said, softening.

"Oh, lovely. Don't like to hear of anyone being ill. Thank you for your help. I'll just be running along now."

"Oh, sir. Can I tell him who called?"

"Oh, uh, Pickering. William Pickering. Thanks," he said, hurrying out and grimacing at the fake name.

He stood on the brick walkway, marshaling his thoughts. They were jumbling rather than clearing.

"Quick business trip."

If that was the case, he would see Maria and hope to get lucky. There's a possibility he would have made his arrangements, but a better possibility that he wouldn't. If he got lucky, he could find Landry without losing too much time. Maria was in her element when Tucker entered but rang off her call and walked around the desk to greet him.

"Hello, Mr. Elliott. It's nice to see you again. How are you?"

"Very well, thanks, you?" he said, turning on the English charm.

"Oh, very well," she gushed. "And what brings you to me... uh, to us... today, business or pleasure?"

"An oversight on my part, sorry to say. I should have come in with George so we could have booked at the same time, and then I would have gotten to see you sooner," he said, leaning in closer, hands on the desk, magnetic smile in place.

"Not to worry. I can take care of you now," she oozed. "Are you meeting him there or somewhere else?"

"Bulls-eye," thought Tucker, then quickly bought time with more flattery.

"You do a brilliant job with these things. Please just take the itinerary and place me where I ought to be by tomorrow."

"That should be easy since he's only in one place so far. Right back home for you, I see. Let's find you a nice wide-open flight. First class, I assume?"

"Of course. Wouldn't want to take a jaunt like this in Economy, now, would we?"

"We?" she smiled coquettishly.

Tucker just smiled and gazed intently into her eyes.

"Now you're just being a bad girl," he said. "I like that in a woman."

"Oh, Mr. Elliott. Will that be on Visa or MasterCard?" she said, blushing.

Tucker rounded the desk and leaned closely over Maria's shoulder to read the screen. An evening flight to Heathrow with a train trip to West Sussex. How very interesting. At least he would finally find out about the business dealings of the good doctor. It must have been something he and Dahlia were doing together. One of the unanswered secrets he uncovered before she was gone. He pushed the unsettling thought out and reached for his wallet.

"Do you take American Express, love?"

***

As he walked back to the tea room, his mind reached back to happier thoughts of him and Dahlia playing as kids, helping each other through the awkward dating phases, and trading business stories. His heart ached, and he was only beginning to realize how much he would miss her.

He hadn't really had time to comprehend what her loss would mean to him. There was a surreal aspect that left him with a dawning disbelief that he was finding troublesome to shake. It was as unfamiliar as it was uncomfortable.

Allowing himself these hollow feelings in the midst of the present mess irritated him, and he took a deep breath to clear his mind. Thoughts of his new assistant soon soothed his unsettled being. He found these musings becoming more frequent, and he commanded himself to regain his purpose.

Shortly before he reached the tea room, he swerved toward the residential area and Mavis Hatfield's home. He hoped she could shed some light on the increasingly mysterious events.

Mavis was closing her door as he approached. She was dressed her best as the women of her generation tended to do, even when just going to the local grocer's. She was surprised to see him but not unsettled, and he was more curious than ever to question her.

"Good morning, Miss Hatfield. Hope I'm not buttin' in, but I really hoped to have a word. I see you're on your way out. Do you mind if I walk with you a ways?"

"Of course not, Mr. Elliott, please do," and she offered her hand for him to guide her down the steps.

They crossed the walkway in silence, and it wasn't until they reached the sidewalk that Mavis finally spoke. Tucker had the feeling she was plotting a strategy.

"Well, Mr. Elliott. I have been watching the news this morning and see that we have yet another tragedy on our hands. What is all this coming to?"

"Not to avoid the question, Miss Hatfield, but you've had the opportunity to see these events unfold, and I'd be very much interested in your opinion."

"Well, it's a very sad business. And I keep coming back to the same thing each time, Mr. Elliott. Greed, pure and simple greed. It's a dangerous and evil trait."

"Oh, please continue. I couldn't agree with you more."

"We both know there's something in that house, and someone will find it. I just hope it doesn't cost any more lives. I'm so very sorry about Dahlia."

Tucker had to admit, she was a master. They were both employing their best moves. This was just another chess match, and if he were to outmaneuver her, he would have to be on his best game.

"As well as can be expected, thanks for asking. It's been difficult dealing with her parents, not to mention mine. We grew up together, you know. She was my best friend. Handling her return and not being there has been tough, but I'll be heading home soon. She's in skillful hands," he said with a slight catch in his voice.

Mavis gave him the proper amount of respect for his anguish before making the next strike.

"I have a very high regard for you, Mr. Elliott. I do hope you'll be able to find out who did this. I also hope you'll find out what really happened to Mazie. I should hate to see her death go unpunished."

Tucker gazed at the passing clouds, processing Mavis' statement. That information was not yet released. Was she guessing, or was she just naturally suspicious?

"I know you think I must be just a silly old woman, but I know that something had to have happened to Mazie. She was ill, but not so ill as that. They say the stress of the events caused her heart to give out. Mazie didn't know what stress was. She was well taken care of, and to be brutally honest, those events didn't mean enough to her pampered existence to cause any real harm," she said, gazing defiantly at Tucker.

There was an edge to her voice that Tucker found difficult to interpret; the coldness of the exchange fascinated yet repelled him.

"Have they told you the results of the autopsy?"

"No. I'm not aware if they're available. Are they Mr. Elliott?"

"I don't believe I can answer that, Miss Hatfield," said Tucker evasively. "But I'm sure they'll be contacting you and Mr. Cavanaugh as soon as they're ready. By the way, where is Mr. Cavanaugh? He seems to have gone missing. Any ideas?"

"They asked me the same questions last night, and as I told them, I saw him last when we went to the funeral home to make arrangements. He did not confide in me regarding his plans after that."

"He was told to keep handy, you know. This looks bad for him. If you do hear from him, you might want to explain the position he's put himself in. Right now, he's not being viewed in the best light."

Tucker stared sternly into Mavis' eyes, but she did not waver.

"I'll keep that in mind, Mr. Elliott."

"Is there somewhere I can walk you?"

"Why, yes. I was on my way to the Brown Bag Lunch Program at the museum. Care to join me?"

"I would love to, Miss Hatfield," smiled Tucker. "Lead on."

***

CloseManuscript

Planning
Create boards
Switch themeTrash

Jacquie Galvin

Manuscript

Add

Front matter
  edit
  Copyright

Dedication

Epigraph

Table of Contents

Foreword

Preface

Acknowledgments

Body
   edit
   Prologue

Introduction

1
   Chapter 1

2
   Chapter 2

3
   Chapter 3

4
   Chapter 4

5

Chapter 5

6

Chapter 6

7

Chapter 7

8

Chapter 8

9

Chapter 9

10

Chapter 10

11

Chapter 11

12

Chapter 12

13

Chapter 13

14

Chapter 14

15

Chapter 15

16

Murder for Afternoon Tea
  4

Dr. Raymond Stantz: You think there's a connection between this Vigo
character and the slime?
Dr. Egon Spengler: Is the atomic weight of cobalt 58.9?
–Ghostbusters II, 1989

Tucker and Reggie were enjoying the moonlight while Dulcy and Laird had gone for a nightcap at the new club by the marina. Tucker was as far away from Reggie as the boats moored in the breeze.

"So, what a dinner, eh?" said Reggie.

"Sorry, what?" said Tucker.

"I didn't think you were with me. I mean, you're with me. You just weren't with me."

"Have a bit on my mind after that meal. There are still a few things I just am not satisfied with."

"Like what?"

"It's not that I don't want to tell you. It's just that I don't feel like I can make any sense of it just yet."

"Well, I have a question."

"Ask away."

"Why aren't we heading down to that hidey hole right now? I can't believe you're not so curious that we're running through the streets making a beeline for that linen closet."

"I applaud your enthusiasm, Reg. And I know there is something amazing at the end of that opening."

"But you're not going down that hidey hole at night, in the dark, for anyone, are you?"

"It's not that, love, but whatever is there will wait. There's nothing in the dark that's not there in the light, eh?"

"Don't believe everything you hear. And have you told the rats, bats, and spiders your philosophy? But really, if it's my sensibilities you're concerned with, not to worry. I am willing to head on in bats, rats, spiders, and all. Well, maybe not spiders, ugh."

"I'm not quite sure, Reg, is all I can say," he muttered as they headed for the B&B.

The lights were out, but for one, on the front porch. It bore a fantastic resemblance to a spook house at Halloween.

"Ah – daunting, eh? What say we stop off for a topper in the salon and then decide?"

Reggie nodded, and they headed for the light at the front. The back was hooded in darkness, and neither of us wanted to go that way. They were engrossed in conversation when they surprised a sergeant posted at the front door.

"Sorry, but I can't allow you to enter."

"I thought your lot was through here. What's happened?" asked Tucker warily.

The sergeant's phone rang, and he excused himself while still barring the entrance.

"Right. Right. Yes, sir. Good. Thank you. You would be Miss Winter and Mr. Elliott?"

"Yes, what is it?"

"Detective Laird has given you permission to enter the premises."

"Well, that's a relief," said Tucker. "I thought we were being evicted."

"Well, sir, actually, you are," said the sergeant.

"Sorry?"

"My apologies, sir, but this is a crime scene, and we have no choice but to relocate you and Miss Winter. Detective Laird has requested that you meet him at the Beach Drive Plaza in the center of town, where he will explain everything to you. You have two rooms booked."

"A crime scene?"

"Yes, sir. Detective Laird asked that you meet him at the Beach Drive Plaza."

Tucker nodded as he guided Reggie through the yellow tape.

"Not a problem, Sergeant, cheers."

The two peeled off in opposite directions upstairs to pack their things and head to the new hotel. Tucker stared around the room. He had an idea forming in his brain. He pulled the telegram from the nightstand and reread it. What was he meant to see? He spread the sheet on the bed, staring intently. Whatever it was he was not going to see it now.

He packed his things taking one last look, then pulled to door to. The sergeant's directions were accurate, and they were standing in front of the Beach Drive Plaza within five minutes. It was a charming boutique hotel, and Tucker and Reggie sighted Dulcy and Laird on the patio.

"Feel like a nightcap, Elliott?"

"I do now."

The server bustled away while the four sat and stared at each other.

"So, we have another crime scene. You can't mean..."

"The report I was waiting for came in while we were at dinner. I asked forensics to be a little extra diligent in checking out Mrs. Cavanaugh, and they found something. I had this feeling I couldn't shake while I was standing on the porch of the inn. There was a siren in the distance, and it made me think of something far off, but I couldn't get it to surface."

"Is this heading somewhere, Laird?"

"On the surface, Mazie's death was straightforward, a bit too straightfor-ward. I asked for an autopsy, which I can tell you was a surprise to the old woman and to Cavanaugh, but it paid off. An examination produced high levels of oleander in her system, which led them to the conclusion of murder. Now we start the process of who had access, a reason, and an opportunity."

"Oh, but that could be anybody. The place was full of people. Wouldn't you start with the most likely persons, which was the maid, or whoever she was, and Mr. Cavanaugh?" said Reggie.

"Yes, and we did. We now have our theory on the maid. And I have sent my men to round up Cord Cavanaugh, grieving widower. And, of course, he is nowhere to be found."

"Maybe he's just taken a long walk. Gone off to be by himself," said Reggie, knowing it wasn't true.

"I really do not think that's the case. I sent a man to Mavis Hatfield's to question her. She said she had talked with him earlier in the day, but she hadn't actually seen him since they went to the funeral home. That's when they were made aware of the autopsy proceedings and were told not to take any sudden excursions. I now have men circulating his picture at the airports and the cab companies. If he turns up, that's fine, but I don't think it's going to work out that way."

"Where do you think he's gone? Maybe he had some business to take care of," said Dulcy.

"Whatever it is or wherever he's gone, we'll find him," said Laird.

"You'll keep us informed, I'm sure. Speaking of business, I have a few things I have to take care of in the morning, so I think I may push off to bed," said Tucker.

Reggie eyed him with curiosity. She hadn't heard of any issues that would require his immediate attention. If so, Alene would have informed her.

"Really, Tucker? What's going on? I haven't been called about anything," said Reggie.

"There's a plant outside of Manchester that's having some labor issues. I may have to intervene," Tucker lied. "Nothing to worry about. I can take care of it easily enough."

"And as far as our flip-flops are concerned?"

Tucker thought of a smart alliteration that fit with the "f" in flip flops but thought better of it.

"I've spoken with Alene on that, and we're reprieved for the time being. What I would like you to do is to continue working with Dulcy and the others on Dahlia's service."

"I did get contacted on that," said Reggie. "I also wanted to go to the Brown Bag Lunch at the History Museum. You know, the one that Forrest Perkins does? Remember we were going to see what that was about?"

"Oh, right, yeah. Really should check into that. When is the next one?"

"Tomorrow."

"We'll see how things go. I have a couple of errands to run as well, so if I can't make it, Dulcy, can you escape the lunch crowd to escort Reggie?"

"Well, I suppose I can. I'll just have to get one of the older girls to take charge for a bit."

"What errands?" blurted Reggie.

"I just have a couple of things I need to review before I handle Manchester. But that does leave one other rather big topic."

"The hidey hole!" said Dulcy and Reggie together.

"Yes, the hidey hole. Laird, we have to get down there and check it out."

"Technically, I shouldn't let you near that, but since I have no ability to request men, my best response is to go with you and see what you find."

"Right. I think we just need to move ahead, and the sooner, the better," said Tucker as he stretched his long legs and rose.

Reggie and the others rose as well, each saying goodnight and heading to their appointed accommodations. Tucker accompanied Reggie to pick up their keys, and they were then pointed to the elevators. Tucker said goodnight as Reggie sighted her room, then turned to find his own. As he read the room numbers, he felt a hand on his arm and turned to find Reggie wide-eyed and whispering frantically at his side.

"There's been someone in my room," she said quietly.

"What do..."

"Ssshh!" she hissed.

"Easy, Reggie. You think they're still there?"

"There's a light on, and the door's cracked. It's a bit strange, don't you think?"

"Reg, I think you're just letting all this get to you. It's probably just the turn-down service. I'll go in with you if you like. C'mon, let's go."

"No, no, you're right. I'm being silly," said Reggie, feeling stupid. "I've let all this make me jumpy. I'm sorry, I'll just go in. I really am tired. Let's get together for breakfast and figure out our day. Thanks for dinner. It was...interesting."

"Alright. You sure you don't want me to walk through the room with you?"

"Nope, just being silly. Go on and get some sleep. Big doings tomorrow," she said, yawning.

"Goodnight, Reggie."

"Goodnight, Tucker."

Tucker watched as she entered the room, quickly glancing back and smiling briefly as she pushed the door shut. He wandered through the corridor and found his room at the corner of the hallway. The secluded spot satisfied him, as he was not only tired but wanted to go over the telegram again in peace.

He inserted the key and pushed the door open. He thought how nice it was to have a real key rather than a bendy piece of plastic that never seemed to work no matter which way you slid it in the slot. He also wondered how many cards he must have lodged in his luggage when he heard a horrendous scream coming from the opposite hallway.

He bolted the length of the corridor to the scream's source. It led him straight to Reggie's room as heads popped out from every entrance. He pounded on the door, yelling to be let in.

"Oh God, let her be alright," he muttered.

"Get the manager," he ordered to a woman staring at him. "Now!" he yelled as the next room's occupant scurried off in frightened silence.

"Regina! Open the door!"

The door finally opened, and he pushed past a white and shaking Reggie.

"What is it? What's happened?"

She could only point to the bathroom, where a low light shone under the door. Tucker gripped her by both arms and sat her on the bed. He pushed the door open, scanning the small space. His gaze rested on the sensible shoes of a chambermaid poking out from under the shower curtain, eerily still and lifeless.

***

"Let's go over it again, Reggie. I know it's repetitive, but we need to make sure we don't miss anything," said Laird.
Reggie once again reviewed the details of what she and Tucker had done after leaving him and Dulcy on the patio.

"Well, there goes our answers from the chambermaid," said Laird, glaring at Tucker.

"It's too bad you didn't get to ask her anything before she..." trailed Tucker.

"That's by design. Whoever did this knew we were almost to her, so she had to go. At least, it confirms we were on the right track."

"I must say, the bodies are starting to pile up here," he mused.

"That is morbid and grotesque," said Reggie, and with that, she began to cry.

"Sorry, Reggie. That was bang out of order."

Tucker and Laird exchanged glances. Then Laird barked to a female officer who led Reggie down to the sitting area.

"This is getting a bit deep," said Tucker.

"Yep, this is one twisted cluster. You know there are no coincidences."

"Yeah, but if I can prove these things connect, they'll have to listen."

Tucker was thinking the opposite as he watched the squad work around him. Laird answered a question from one of his men, then sat and watched Tucker, waiting for the eventual response he knew would come.

"Might I have a word?" asked Tucker.

Laird rose, beckoned one of his men, and followed Tucker into the hallway.

"If you don't mind, let's wander down to my room. Less noisy and rather private, luckily."

Once seated, Tucker and Laird compared notes. After half an hour of theories interwoven with facts, the two men decided their courses of action. Each had their assignments, including guiding Reggie and Dulcy through theirs. The only thing Tucker forgot to mention was the cryptic telegram still folded in his breast pocket.

***

The morning dawned sunny but muggy, and Tucker decided to forego the pretty patio breakfast for the cooler, more comfortable main dining room. Reggie entered smiling and calm but not well rested despite spending the night in a double suite. Dulcy slept shotgun in the other room, steadfastly refusing to leave her after this newest assault.

Tucker rose as they wove their way toward him. He could see through the bright grin to the deep circles and glassy eyes of the restless, interrupted sleeper. She probably had no more than an hour or two of actual rest.

His heart went out to her as she neared the table. He instinctively enveloped her in a warm embrace. Embarrassed, they let go, and Tucker pulled out her chair.

"Well, good morning to you too, Mr. Elliott," said Reggie. "And how did you sleep with all the activity rolling along down the hall?"

Laird's men were combing Reggie's room with special attention to the bathroom. Tucker was seated with his arm around Reggie, who was calmer but still shaking. Laird and Dulcy had barely gotten to the tea room before his phone was pinging, the message labeled 911. The posted sergeant sprinted toward them, directing them back to the Plaza.

"I slept like a baby," said Tucker, "for at least two hours before I couldn't stare at the millions of tiny dots in the ceiling any longer and decided to get up to check on the investigation in your previous room."

"Did you find out anything?" she said eagerly.

"No, they had posted a man at the door, and even though we're acquainted, I was not allowed to enter the crime scene. They really are adding up," he said, instantly regretting it as it was a remark such as this that caused her earlier distress.

"Well, what is our schedule for today since there's so much to do?"

Reggie ordered breakfast while listening to the day's agenda and was quick to note that almost nowhere in the itinerary were she and Tucker together for any length of time.

"I notice you're rather absent in all this. What are you up to?" she said, munching a muffin.

"As I mentioned, I do have some Manchester business to take care of and other errands that need to be dealt with, not the least important being that telegram."

Reggie raised her eyebrows and waited for more information, then resigned herself to having to pry it out of him.

"Have a theory on this, Mr. Elliott, or is that classified?"

"When I couldn't sleep last night, I dug it out and reread it. You know there's something in it, and I rearranged things here and there. I think maybe I've landed on a basic idea. Let me sketch it up for you."

He reread the markings he'd made and turned the paper to her. As she studied it, Tucker could see the comprehension dawn. She laid the telegram back on the table, staring at him.

Important medical news stop Key to death stop Find storage place stop Room to file it away stop See you again on the other side stop Important key find room stop See you on the other side stop

"Who did this, Tucker?"

"One of my errands is to find out where this came from. That could answer everything. Or make it more complicated; I don't know which."

"We know we have to find that room before anything else. Shall we start after breakfast?"

"After breakfast, love, I'm going to run along to see Landry. I have a couple of questions. I want you to get with Dulcy and Laird and head for that room. He'll be waiting for you. Then I want you to go to the Brown Bag and check out Forrest Perkins."

"What do expect to learn from Landry?"

"Maybe where this telegram came from, maybe nothing. By the way, I don't quite feel ready to share this with Laird yet."

"So, we're not going to totally work together then, are we?"

"It's not that I don't want to. It's just that I need to sift through this more before wasting his time."

"You don't want him pulling this from you and taking you out of the picture."

"You know that if he gets his hands on this, he'll use it to try to make them let him back on the case, and I just don't think that's going to happen. They'll add it to the rest of what they haven't investigated, and then we're lost."

"So, when do you want to meet up?"

"I'll be in touch. Now, eat your breakfast. I have a feeling you're going to need it."

***

Tucker gave Reggie a few last instructions, then headed in the opposite direction, checking the address on the hotel notepaper. He climbed old brick steps, pushed open double doors, and stopped at the building directory. He scanned the listings and found the clinical offices of George Landry, MD, on the fourth floor.

He peeled off to the stairs, rhythmically logging the landings until he reached number four. Heavy oak doors marked the entrance to the plush offices of the good doctor. A prim middle-aged woman sat behind sliding glass panels, checking files against insurance forms. She barely raised her eyes to note his intrusion. He couldn't help noticing the waiting room being a bit sparse as he stood expectantly awaiting acknowledgment. Finally, the woman lowered her pen and slid open the panel.

"May I help you?" she said stone-faced.

"Yes, I am here to see Dr. Landry."

"Dr. Landry is not in this week. Would you care to make an appointment for next week?"

"Sorry, just a bit surprised since we had a set appointment for this morning. I would have thought he'd let me know if he was going to be out of the office," he said, acting injured.

"Well, it was a matter that came up suddenly, so Dr. Landry had to cancel some appointments. I'm sorry if he missed yours," she said, checking the book. "Your name, sir?"

"Oh, I don't think you'll find me there," he said. "It was more of a business appointment, you see. I can get with him when he comes in. I hope everything's alright. I would hate to think he's ill in any way."

"Oh, no, he's fine. He just had a quick business trip to make. Everyone's fine," she said, softening.

"Oh, lovely. Don't like to hear of anyone being ill. Thank you for your help. I'll just be running along now."

"Oh, sir. Can I tell him who called?"

"Oh, uh, Pickering. William Pickering. Thanks," he said, hurrying out and grimacing at the fake name.

He stood on the brick walkway, marshaling his thoughts. They were jumbling rather than clearing.

"Quick business trip."

If that was the case, he would see Maria and hope to get lucky. There's a possibility he would have made his arrangements, but a better possibility that he wouldn't. If he got lucky, he could find Landry without losing too much time. Maria was in her element when Tucker entered but rang off her call and walked around the desk to greet him.

"Hello, Mr. Elliott. It's nice to see you again. How are you?"

"Very well, thanks, you?" he said, turning on the English charm.

"Oh, very well," she gushed. "And what brings you to me... uh, to us... today, business or pleasure?"

"An oversight on my part, sorry to say. I should have come in with George so we could have booked at the same time, and then I would have gotten to see you sooner," he said, leaning in closer, hands on the desk, magnetic smile in place.

"Not to worry. I can take care of you now," she oozed. "Are you meeting him there or somewhere else?"

"Bulls-eye," thought Tucker, then quickly bought time with more flattery.

"You do a brilliant job with these things. Please just take the itinerary and place me where I ought to be by tomorrow."

"That should be easy since he's only in one place so far. Right back home for you, I see. Let's find you a nice wide-open flight. First class, I assume?"

"Of course. Wouldn't want to take a jaunt like this in Economy, now, would we?"

"We?" she smiled coquettishly.

Tucker just smiled and gazed intently into her eyes.

"Now you're just being a bad girl," he said. "I like that in a woman."

"Oh, Mr. Elliott. Will that be on Visa or MasterCard?" she said, blushing.

Tucker rounded the desk and leaned closely over Maria's shoulder to read the screen. An evening flight to Heathrow with a train trip to West Sussex. How very interesting. At least he would finally find out about the business dealings of the good doctor. It must have been something he and Dahlia were doing together. One of the unanswered secrets he uncovered before she was gone. He pushed the unsettling thought out and reached for his wallet.

"Do you take American Express, love?"

***

As he walked back to the tea room, his mind reached back to happier thoughts of him and Dahlia playing as kids, helping each other through the awkward dating phases, and trading business stories. His heart ached, and he was only beginning to realize how much he would miss her.

He hadn't really had time to comprehend what her loss would mean to him. There was a surreal aspect that left him with a dawning disbelief that he was finding troublesome to shake. It was as unfamiliar as it was uncomfortable.

Allowing himself these hollow feelings in the midst of the present mess irritated him, and he took a deep breath to clear his mind. Thoughts of his new assistant soon soothed his unsettled being. He found these musings becoming more frequent, and he commanded himself to regain his purpose.

Shortly before he reached the tea room, he swerved toward the residential area and Mavis Hatfield's home. He hoped she could shed some light on the increasingly mysterious events.

Mavis was closing her door as he approached. She was dressed her best as the women of her generation tended to do, even when just going to the local grocer's. She was surprised to see him but not unsettled, and he was more curious than ever to question her.

"Good morning, Miss Hatfield. Hope I'm not buttin' in, but I really hoped to have a word. I see you're on your way out. Do you mind if I walk with you a ways?"

"Of course not, Mr. Elliott, please do," and she offered her hand for him to guide her down the steps.

They crossed the walkway in silence, and it wasn't until they reached the sidewalk that Mavis finally spoke. Tucker had the feeling she was plotting a strategy.

"Well, Mr. Elliott. I have been watching the news this morning and see that we have yet another tragedy on our hands. What is all this coming to?"

"Not to avoid the question, Miss Hatfield, but you've had the opportunity to see these events unfold, and I'd be very much interested in your opinion."

"Well, it's a very sad business. And I keep coming back to the same thing each time, Mr. Elliott. Greed, pure and simple greed. It's a dangerous and evil trait."

"Oh, please continue. I couldn't agree with you more."

"We both know there's something in that house, and someone will find it. I just hope it doesn't cost any more lives. I'm so very sorry about Dahlia."

Tucker had to admit, she was a master. They were both employing their best moves. This was just another chess match, and if he were to outmaneuver her, he would have to be on his best game.

"As well as can be expected, thanks for asking. It's been difficult dealing with her parents, not to mention mine. We grew up together, you know. She was my best friend. Handling her return and not being there has been tough, but I'll be heading home soon. She's in skillful hands," he said with a slight catch in his voice.

Mavis gave him the proper amount of respect for his anguish before making the next strike.

"I have a very high regard for you, Mr. Elliott. I do hope you'll be able to find out who did this. I also hope you'll find out what really happened to Mazie. I should hate to see her death go unpunished."

Tucker gazed at the passing clouds, processing Mavis' statement. That information was not yet released. Was she guessing, or was she just naturally suspicious?

"I know you think I must be just a silly old woman, but I know that something had to have happened to Mazie. She was ill, but not so ill as that. They say the stress of the events caused her heart to give out. Mazie didn't know what stress was. She was well taken care of, and to be brutally honest, those events didn't mean enough to her pampered existence to cause any real harm," she said, gazing defiantly at Tucker.

There was an edge to her voice that Tucker found difficult to interpret; the coldness of the exchange fascinated yet repelled him.

"Have they told you the results of the autopsy?"

"No. I'm not aware if they're available. Are they Mr. Elliott?"

"I don't believe I can answer that, Miss Hatfield," said Tucker evasively. "But I'm sure they'll be contacting you and Mr. Cavanaugh as soon as they're ready. By the way, where is Mr. Cavanaugh? He seems to have gone missing. Any ideas?"

"They asked me the same questions last night, and as I told them, I saw him last when we went to the funeral home to make arrangements. He did not confide in me regarding his plans after that."

"He was told to keep handy, you know. This looks bad for him. If you do hear from him, you might want to explain the position he's put himself in. Right now, he's not being viewed in the best light."

Tucker stared sternly into Mavis' eyes, but she did not waver.

"I'll keep that in mind, Mr. Elliott."

"Is there somewhere I can walk you?"

"Why, yes. I was on my way to the Brown Bag Lunch Program at the museum. Care to join me?"

"I would love to, Miss Hatfield," smiled Tucker. "Lead on."

***

Chapter 27

Rosemary Pilkington: Lunch.
J. Pierpont Finch: Huh?
Rosemary Pilkington: I said, "Lunch."
J. Pierpont Finch: What about "lunch"?
Rosemary Pilkington: I'd love to!
−How to Succeed in Business Without Really Trying, 1967

As Tucker was strolling toward Landry's office, Dulcy met Laird and went on to the tea room. The commercial kitchen had taken on an air of homey familiarity for him. The atmosphere was expectant, as if the kitchen itself was waiting for events to continue.

He glanced at the supply closet and grinned. Dulcy set her things in what was now her office and scouted about the tea room. She was finishing her rounds when Reggie popped into the kitchen, anxious for action and gleaming with excitement.

"Are we ready?"

Laird fished the key out and placed it on the island. Dulcy was gathering flashlights, water, bug spray, rubber gloves, and paper towels.

"Are we going fishing or camping?" asked Laird, amused.

Reggie snickered, and Dulcy gave Laird a sarcastic grimace.

"Who knows what we're going to find down there? I just like to be prepared."

"We need to get going if we're going to do this and still make the Brown Bag," said Reggie.

"If worse comes to worse," said Laird, "we'll have to leave the Brown Bag for another day. This is more immediate in my book."

"I'm afraid he's right, Reg. I still have lunch prep, and we have no idea how long this is going to take. I just want to wait a minute till Lisa comes in so I can get her started on things."

"Why not just leave her a note? I would actually like to get down there without anyone else here," said Laird.

"Alright. Hand me a sheet from that pad there."

On their way to the linen closet, the bang of the back door stopped all three dead.

"Go on ahead, " said Dulcy. "It should be Lisa, but I just want to make sure."

Reggie and Laird quietly disappeared into the bathroom, shutting and locking the door behind them. Dulcy rounded the corner to find a young man standing in the back doorway, taking in the kitchen contents in a mildly curious fashion.

"May I help you?" asked Dulcy politely through her annoyance.

"Yes, ma'am. I am here to see Miss Dulcy Dandeneau. Would you be her?"

With growing irritation and a strong desire to correct the young man's grammar, Dulcy smiled through gritted teeth and admitted to being Miss Dandeneau.

"I'm just here to ask you a few questions regarding the sale of this property since the death of Miss Porter."

Dulcy was instantly on guard. As far as she knew, everything was being held up pending the investigation of Dahlia's death. And no one ever said anything about selling.

"I'm sorry, but I'm afraid I can't help you. If you'll leave me your card, I'll have our attorneys get in touch with your company, which is...?"

The young man frowned and backed up a few inches.

"I can pass your attorney's name on to my people," he said flatly.

Dulcy smirked and said, "Laird, Elliott, and Winter. They're in the book," she said, wishing she had a camera.

He thanked her curtly and quickly exited while Dulcy fished out her phone. She ran to the window, sighting the man just before he turned out of sight. She was replacing the note to Lisa when the girl herself rushed in, apologized for her lateness, and set to work. Dulcy gave her a few instructions, then took the stairs two at a time and landed in the bathroom. She tried the door and found it locked. She inserted her key in the lock. The door creaked open, and a rush of stale air greeted her. There was a space cleared in the linen closet, and she could hear faint murmurings from the distance from the opening. She grabbed a flashlight and, with an involuntary shiver, inched her body through the opening and down the narrow path.

***

The opening widened as she found a short flight of stairs. She flashed the light on her surroundings, marveling at how something like this could have remained hidden for so long. She could still hear the voices in the distance but could also hear something closer.

She headed toward the sound, sweeping the torch back and forth like a lighthouse beam. She halted every few feet to listen and mark her progress. She shone the light into the low ceiling and squinted at the pattern before her. She ran her hand over the rough surface and realized she was at the fireplace in the foyer. It was craggy and dust-laden, and she guided herself around it with one hand while holding the torch in the other. She peered up at the structure, noting a tiny glint of light coming through.

As she moved for a closer look, she tripped over something solid and caught herself before pitching over it. The torchlight illuminated yet another short flight of stairs jutting out from the back of the brick face.

She could hear muffled conversation above and was mildly satisfied that at least lunch was going on as planned while she was poking around in the bowels of the building. She tentatively tapped the bottom step, testing it for her weight. She climbed to the next step, then up two more where she could examine the bricks more closely.

She poked, prodded, and pounded but came up with nothing. She pulled out her phone and dropped a step to take a picture of the surface. The light from the flash temporarily blinded her, and she nearly toppled off the steps in confusion.

"That wasn't very smart."

She waited for her eyes to adjust and picked her way back down the stairs. She caught her breath and then proceeded to where she had heard Reggie and Laird. The eerie silence made her uncomfortable. The voices seemed to have stopped. She inched her way down the narrow corridor until she came to a small wooden door with an oversized metal doorknob plate sporting an old-fashioned, looped keyhole.

With a surge of excitement, she turned the knob, and the door gave way under her grasp. It released with a pop and swung open with a whine. Dulcy was standing in a small, round, and sparsely furnished room with no sign of Reggie or Laird.

***

Dulcy was fascinated by the space in front of her.

"This could do with a good cleaning," she thought as she sniffed the mustiness.

Judging from the size and shape, she figured she must be under the garden gazebo. She pointed the flashlight up at the ceiling, letting her eyes adjust. There was a small desk and chair and various other indiscernible remnants. To the right of the desk was an archaic-looking easel.

Although the paint smell had long gone, there were dried paint tubes and rotting brushes lying beside the easel with an air of expectancy as if the artist had only stepped away for a moment. She stepped closer to the perimeter to examine a series of hangings in a patchwork design over a large portion of the walls. As she was leaning in for a closer view, a latch popped opposite from where she entered, and Reggie and Laird stepped in.

"Hey! Where've you been? You'll never believe what I found," said Dulcy.

"You'll never believe what we found," said Reggie.

"This goes all the way through. You go out this door, and the path takes you up underneath the B&B and ends up at the back. The entrance is in the storage closet in the mini kitchen. That's how you saw Dahlia in the tea room, then poof – out she comes from the B&B. Nice to know you're not crazy, eh?"

"Yeah, actually, it is. Well, Detective? What do you make of all this?"

"I haven't formed any opinions yet, but I think this confirms what she found that day but never got to tell anyone. Now all we need to do is figure out what we're looking for and why."

"Well, like I mentioned," Reggie said, looking at Laird, "these walls are covered with the same type of paintings that are in the museum exhibit. Hey, the museum. What time is it?" asked Reggie.

"It's about 12:30. We can still make part of it; let's go, and I'll tell you about the other entrance."

"There's another entrance?" said Reggie in awe.

"You two go ahead," said Laird. "I'm going to pull some of these down. Tell Elliott to get here as soon as he can."

"I don't have the slightest idea where he is," said Reggie as she ran back up the tunnel with Dulcy.

They popped the latch, tidied the disarray in the linen closet, and then checked to see if they were alone. When the coast was clear, both women headed downstairs.

"Where did you go?" asked Lisa. "I've been looking for you everywhere. Lunch is in full swing."

"I have to go out," said Dulcy. "Miss Reggie and I will be back later this afternoon. I know you can handle this. You'll do a great job. But, if you need me, I'll be at the museum at the Brown Bag Lunch Program."

"That's kind of funny. You're leaving lunch to go to lunch," said Lisa.

Reggie and Dulcy were hurrying down the street to the museum. On the way, Dulcy described the fireplace with the attached staircase and her quick examination. She was surprised it had gone unnoticed by the other two. By the time they arrived, they decided they would prioritize finding the latch to the fireplace entrance.

"I'm beginning to feel like the white rabbit jumping down all these holes," said Reggie. "Hope we don't have to shrink ourselves to get through an opening somewhere."

They entered the Brown Bag area to see Forrest Perkins at the podium and the program underway. It was a standing room only and was very warm. There was a small marquee featuring the title "Artistic Periods and Their Impact on History", Forrest Perkins, lecturer.

Mr. Perkins was animatedly pointing to various framed works, each one a representation of a particular period, each one the epitome of achievement for that time. Reggie was taking in the room, absorbing the gist of his message, when she saw a section devoted exclusively to local art through the ages. It would only seem fitting to see a representation of Hatfield's works here, considering his contribution to the community.

As she digested his information, her eyes landed on a familiar elegant figure, legs crossed and politely conversing with the elderly guest next to him. She elbowed Dulcy and pointed at Tucker and Mavis. Dulcy nodded and followed as they slipped through the crowd to stand directly behind their seats. Reggie leaned down and whispered a quick message, then stood and waited. Tucker excused himself and beckoned Reggie to the hallway, leaving Dulcy to take his seat next to Mavis.

"I didn't expect to see you here. I thought you had 'errands'."

"I am on them, Reggie, make no mistake. And nice to see you but I need to be getting back to them. How did it go down below?"

"Amazing. There are all sorts of nooks and crannies in there. I see a few Hatfield's displayed for our lecture today. Wait till you see what Detective Laird has for you."

"What did you find?" he asked, craning around to check on Dulcy and Mavis.

"In the room, which we did find, there are all sorts of these same pictures hanging on the walls. Laird is removing them to sort through. He said when we saw you, he told you to get back there to take a look."

Tucker swore and grabbed Reggie by the shoulders. Something had just clicked.

"We can't let him take those off the walls. The pattern may be important. It was something Forrest Perkins said in his lecture. There may be a message in the way they were hung. Reg, stay here with Dulcy and Mavis. I have to keep him from moving at least some of those pictures."

"Tucker!"

"I'll talk to you later, Reg. I need to get there now!"

Reggie rolled her eyes and weaved through the crowd, only to find two empty chairs. She was sure the two women had been right here. She gazed around in confusion, double checking her location by an especially gripping Dadaism portrait. It seemed to be grinning back at her. Where would they have gone and why?

***

Tucker ran the distance to the tea room and vaulted through the front door. He needed to find Laird. He glanced around at the foyer and the tea room staff while making a sharp right at the stairs. He halted at the bathroom, noting the out-of-order sign on the door.

"Crude but effective," he thought.

He knocked slightly, half expecting Laird to answer. When nothing happened, he retreated and found a pretty, freckled girl rolling a dessert trolley into the dining room.

"Excuse me, Miss, but have you seen an official-looking gentleman moving things around a bit?"

"Oh, you mean Detective Laird," she said.

News of the detective had hit the wait staff and Tucker was glad for once that workplace gossip was alive and well.

"Yes, exactly. Have you seen him?"

"He was just upstairs. I'm sure he's still there because I never saw him come down, and I would have been stationed in this section."

"Thank you so much. What's the special today?" he asked, realizing his hunger.

"Ooh, it's Shepherd's Pie," she said, beaming. "It was Miss Porter's mother's recipe. It's delicious," she said slowly, realization dawning. "I'm sorry, Mr. Elliott."

"No need. I've had the pleasure of it on many occasions," he said. "It honestly is wonderful," and he winked and disappeared up the staircase.

"He must have been down below," he thought as he tested the door again. As he was jiggling the handle, it popped open, and Laird's head poked around the corner.

"About time; get in here," he said.

"Please tell me you haven't taken them all down. It's important."

"No, I only said that to get them to go to the museum. I didn't want anything touched."

Tucker raised his eyebrows, and Laird stared stone-faced.

"Why don't you want them off the walls?"

"I'll get to that in a minute. I have to go to London tonight. I went to see Landry. He was not in his office. His travel agent had booked him into London yesterday, destination West Sussex. I have to find out what he does there. I thought it was something maybe he and Dahlia were doing together, but I need more information. I think he's involved in this somehow, and whatever he's going on is being worked on from there. And no one has seen Cord Cavanaugh. My guess is we'll find them there together."

"Let's not jump to conclusions. Where are Dulcy and Reggie?"

"I left them to finish the lunch program and corner Forrest Perkins for a few questions. That should give us some time to sort through these pictures."

"Well, come on then. Let's get started."

Tucker was impressed with the small space as well as the pathway leading to it. He gazed at the pictures closest to the door, working his way clockwise. His cursory view did no more to give him a direction than Forrest Perkins' insights.

"So, what exactly did he say?" asked Laird. "What are we supposed to be seeing?"

"According to Perkins, back then, when someone wanted to hide something, they used a code or a type of cryptography. The only thing we know is that they may hold information as to where to find something else. Something of value."

While Tucker began his route again, Laird poked around the desk with his pencil. It was an old-fashioned mahogany piece with lots of drawers and compartments. It reminded him of something from an old library or post office.

He fished around the open holes, finding only dust. He tried the front drawer, but it was locked along with the rest of the compartments. He tried the key in the main lock, but nothing happened, and he slid it back into his pocket with a sigh.

"You really didn't think it would work, did you?" asked Tucker.

"No, but you know I had to try. There's got to be another key. Let me do my fingerprint thing, and then we'll see if there's anything attached to these pictures."

While Laird searched for prints, Tucker poked around the desk and checked the chair for anything unusual. It was a basic straight-backed piece with no elaborate scrolling or carvings, and he abandoned it as a lousy job and focused his attention on the desk.

He took out a handkerchief and pushed the desk out to get a view of the back. He thought he could feel a weight difference between the two sides and beckoned Laird to take a look. He wavered back and forth but could find no visual cues.

"Move it all the way out," he ordered.

They pushed the desk into the center of the room, walking around it and knocking on strategic sections.

"There's something on this side of it," said Tucker, pointing to the right row of drawers.

"From the sound, I would agree," said Laird. "I don't want to force it in case we damage any evidence or it's booby-trapped. We have to find the right key. Where would you put it if you were a secretive old man hiding his valuables?"

"To start with, since I've gone to all the trouble of building such a place, I'm banking on no one discovering it, or whatever was here would have been lifted long ago."

"The first key was in a place where someone finally found it, probably while looking for something else. I would put it somewhere personal to me, somewhere I know it would stay hidden."

"I agree. Let's look at the pictures. Maybe there's something there."

The two men started at opposite ends of the room and worked toward each other. They methodically felt around the frame of each print, then carefully lifted them off the wall, checking for breaches in the backing. When they met in the middle, neither had discovered anything more than a fraction of talent for a variety of subjects done in oils, watercolors, charcoal, and pencil. Tucker glanced at his watch and realized he was running out of time.

"Well, let's see the other entrance. Reggie said it was in the B&B."

"Oh, right. It's just out this way. I should be getting back to the office anyway. Should be some information on the maid by now."

"It was wonderful. There is so much history here. I feel like only the surface has been scratched. You have such an amazing personal perspective on all this. I would love to be able to ask you a few more questions."

"Well, I'm free for lunch," he said.

"I have a wonderful idea," she said. "May I treat you to the tea room? They have a delicious menu today."

His face clouded, and she thought she was going to lose him when he smiled kindly and offered her his arm. Exiting the lecture room, Reggie scanned the halls and entrance, hoping to get a glimpse of Dulcy and Mavis. There were only a few student groups and the lecture participants streaming out of the program. She engaged Mr. Perkins in small talk as they strolled to the tea room. Mavis and Dulcy would turn up; she just hoped Dulcy would learn something of value from Mavis to salvage their trip. Only time would tell how valuable it is.

***

Chapter 28

Andy Kaufman: You don't know the real me.
Lynne Margulies: There isn't a "real" you.
Andy Kaufman: Oh, yeah. Forgot.
-Man on the Moon, 1999

Dulcy and Mavis went to the Beach Drive Plaza at Mavis' insistence, claiming their clam chowder to be the best in the city. Dulcy was fretting over leaving the tea room for so long. She put it out of her mind, concentrating instead on having an enlightening conversation with Mavis.

Dulcy asked Mavis a few questions regarding her father's artwork, but found her distracted. She responded politely with short, pat answers revealing nothing more than what they already knew. There was no indication that she was aware of any hidden rooms or entrances, and Dulcy would never compromise their find without more information.

The Beach Drive Plaza was a hopping place with patrons inside and out, eating or waiting at the bar or watching the string of police units performing their investigative tasks in the restricted area. Then it finally dawned on Dulcy why Mavis wanted to come here; a lot was going on, and for a little old, retired lady, it was better than television.

"Would you like to eat inside or out, Miss Hatfield?"

"Oh, I think we can go inside today. It looks crowded out here and seems a bit warm."

Dulcy smiled, signaling to the hostess for two for inside. Mavis observed the festivities with a ghoulish relish, and Dulcy felt the same pang of attraction, yet revulsion Tucker had experienced earlier.

"Well, Miss Hatfield, what do you make of all this?"

Mavis was not to be taken in by Dulcy's small talk.

"You mean the death of the chambermaid, dear."

"So, you've heard about that, I see."

"It is, at best, still a tiny town."

Dulcy was unsure where to take the conversation. She was uncomfortable discussing the dead woman when they weren't yet sure of the connection, if any.

"I'm sorry about your sister. She was your only sister?"

"Yes, that's correct. I still have Cord, though. We haven't been close over the years, but now that everyone is gone, I guess we should put the past behind us and stay strong for the family's sake."

Dulcy thought this a strange remark, seeing as how she just pointed out that there wasn't any family left to be strong for.

"I'm sure you've put together a beautiful ceremony. Will Mazie be staying here or going back north?"

"Oh, she'll, of course, be staying here where she was born. She'll be given the proper burial in the family cemetery once they release her."

"I guess an autopsy is standard practice with something like this."

"Something like what?" asked Mavis sharply.

"There was so much going on that day with Dahlia and the police. I'm sure all the excitement was enough for even the heartiest of people. I know she was trying to rest. It must have just been too much."

"I hardly think my sister was so upset by the events that it caused her to have a fatal attack," said Mavis derisively.

Dulcy was appalled but said nothing, waiting for Mavis to continue her train of thought.

"I know there is more to her death than a mere episode brought on by nerves or shock. If anything, she would have been excited and energized by it, thriving on the gruesomeness. Of course, it also meant that the attention was not on her, which she would have most definitely found annoying. If you hadn't noticed, Mazie was a master at being the center of attention."

Dulcy was again taken aback by the callousness of Mavis but fascinated by this strain of honesty. It was also apparent that she had not yet been contacted with the autopsy results. She wondered what Laird was waiting for.

"I'm sure Mr. Cavanaugh is very distressed by all this. How is he doing?"
"I haven't the slightest idea," replied Mavis. "They're looking for him, you know, and I haven't seen him since the funeral parlor. I don't know if he's in town or gone back home," she said, peering at the menu before

slamming it shut and smiling sweetly.

"I think I'll stick with the clam chowder after all."

* * *

Reggie and Forrest Perkins walked to the tea room, enjoying the warm sea breezes and the beautiful day. Reggie was wrestling with bringing up the clipping but decided to hold off. She needed to take it slowly; she knew he would tell her almost anything if she handled him correctly.

Tucker and Laird were leaving to go back to the Beach Drive Plaza as Reggie and Forrest Perkins were walking to the tea room. Tucker had to pack, make a few phone calls, and leave a note for Reggie. This last task would be difficult as he felt guilty for deserting her. He knew if he told her about Landry, she would want to come along. And he needed her to continue what they had started here. Besides, she was a big girl and more capable than he even knew, he was sure.

Reggie opened the door as Perkins helped her across the threshold. Lisa had been watching them from the hostess stand and had menus and a table ready. Once they sat, Reggie excused herself to find her accomplice.

"Hello. How's it going? Has Dulcy come back yet?"

"No, Miss Reggie, I thought she'd come back with you. But don't worry; we're doing fine. There are no surprises, and there is nothing too difficult for the girls to handle."

"Good, I'm glad," said Reggie, misgivings beginning to return.

She had hoped Dulcy might bring Mavis here for lunch where they could join forces in their questioning. She hurried back to the table where Perkins was enjoying the attentions of the young servers bringing muffins and pouring the day's tea special.

"Ah, Miss Winter. You must try these muffins. They are delicious! We were discussing how beautiful the tea room is looking these days. It's been such a long time since I've seen it."

"This is more like it," thought Reggie. "Now, maybe we'll get somewhere."

"Mr. Perkins, when was the last time you saw this house?"

"Oh, let's see. It was before Miss Dahlia. It may have been before the previous owners to her, I believe. They had called me to ask about some of the pieces they were giving to the museum. You know, the ones you saw today."

"So, it wasn't Dahlia who gave the pictures to the museum?"

"She gave a few to the museum, but the others were given up way before she came."

"Who were the previous owners? I know nothing about the people before her."

"It was a group of investors who had purchased it from a family who had lived here right after the Hatfield family. It had been a boarding house, you know. Mavis did the best she could under the circumstances. It was difficult at that time for a young, single woman to do what she did. She worked so hard to keep that family together. In the end, it must have seemed like a waste of time and energy."

"Do you think she feels that way, Mr. Perkins?"

"I don't have the slightest idea. We no longer have that level of relationship where she would tell me how she felt about anything, either then or now."

Reggie waited for him to continue, but it seemed that he was finished.

"Why didn't she take the pictures with her if they belonged to her father?"

"Oh, it was much too generous an offer to turn down. She had to sell the whole thing off. Furniture, pictures, everything went with the house. I know it was tough on her. She is quite a prideful person, our Mavis."

"What did she do after she sold?"

"She found herself a little place and did some work for the museum and a few other small writing projects, but that was about it. At the time, she had married Mazie off, and the two boys were on their own. She kept mostly to herself."

"And she never married?" asked Reggie.

Forrest Perkins stopped smiling. He slid his chair back, placed his napkin on the table, and stood politely in front of Reggie.

"If you'll excuse me, I'll be right back."

Reggie had hit a nerve, and she only hoped she hadn't gone too far. She would know if he didn't come back. But a few minutes later, Mr. Perkins returned, smiled, and placed his napkin back in his lap.

"Sorry, my dear. Now, we were talking about the pictures from the museum?"

Reggie smiled, turned the slip of newsprint toward him, and crossed her fingers behind her back. He froze in his seat, color draining from his face, eyes fixed on the table.

"So, that's what you picked up that day. It's not true, you know. I can't explain; all I can tell you is that it is not true. What they accused me of, I never did. I lost my post at the hands of Cord Cavanaugh that I will tell you."

"Cord Cavanaugh? I'm afraid I'm very confused."

"And you will have to stay that way, my dear. I said I would never speak of this again," he said, pointing at the cutting. "I was engaged to marry Mavis, was a respected scholar, and held an enviable post at the university. His lies and deceit caused me to lose everything: Mavis, my reputation, and my position. I have never forgiven him for what he did, and she has never forgiven me either."

"I'm sorry," whispered Reggie. "I had no idea. We can talk about something else. Tell me how you became involved with the Brown Bag Lunch at the museum. It's a wonderful program, and you're a very engaging speaker."

"It's not much to talk about, and if you'll excuse me, it's been a lovely lunch, and you are a beautiful companion, but I really must be going. I'm working on a project for someone anxious about the results. Thank you for such a delicious meal, and please give my regards to Mr. Elliott."

Reggie stood and gave her hand to him. He kissed it lightly, displaying the crinkly, wrinkled smile she had previously found so alarming. She found that it made her sad and promised she would get to the bottom of it. Cord Cavanaugh, for such a stately southern gentleman, was turning out to be a rather nasty bit of goods, as Tucker would say.

* * *

Tucker shook hands with Laird and turned to go. Looking back, he witnessed him sign something before marching off. He mounted the stairs to his room, threw a few things in a carry-on, and gave the room a once-over. He learned that what Laird had signed was his room charge. He smiled to himself, making a mental note to ring him with his thanks. He found Laird still on the sidewalk, speaking with a short, rather bookish man. Rather than interrupt, he turned up the street but was halted by a quick, efficient whistle behind him.

"Come on, I'll give you a lift."

"I'm off to the airport. It's not exactly close, you know."

"It's fine. We can talk on the way. That man back there is the medical examiner. She was murdered, of course. Apparently, someone decided to supplement her cleaning supplies. What she had in the bottle wasn't tub cleaner but acetone. Judging from the state of the room, she was fairly disoriented till she fell unconscious. Once she was out, our murderer just had to roll her into the tub, finish the job, and close the shower curtain."

"Horrible! I don't suppose we can identify this person who seems to be so handy with chemicals?"

"No. Can't even tell if it's a man or a woman. No prints, of course."

"Of course."

"I had the sergeant from the B&B identify her as the maid who was with Mazie. That only leaves showing Dulcy a picture to see if she can identify her as the kitchen help, which we're pretty sure she'll be able to do."

"Well, at least that's sorted out. Too bad the rest of it couldn't be so easy. Look, could you do me a favor? Give this note to Reggie. I meant to leave it at the desk. Thanks for the ride. I would have been late if you hadn't driven me. And thanks for paying my bill. I do know about that, and I appreciate it."

"Oh, stop. I'm getting all giddy. It's my tab, you know. You are part of my official investigation whether you wanted to be or not."

"I thought as much. I'll be in touch. Stay out of the closets, eh?"

"No problem. You stay in touch and let me know what you find when you get there. Hopefully, you can help cut this whole investigation short and keep me out of trouble."

"And catch a murderer or two, I hope."

* * *

Chapter 29

Margo Channing: Fasten your seat belts. It's going to be a bumpy night.
-All About Eve, 1950

Jennings was truly enjoying himself. He waited deferentially, expecting action in five, four, three, two...

Six bodies flew past him in a vain attempt to view an automobile that was long gone. As the last in line, Tucker let the rest go while he clicked the door shut and turned to Jennings. Both grinned slyly and relaxed.

"So, how did you do it, Jennings?"

"If you will pardon the liberty, sir, I sneaked the keys from the hook and threw them to Miss Dahlia as she was picking her way through the aspidistras. While we were in the conservatory, she was retracing her route back under the windows and out to the east entrance, where the car had been left for me to put in the garage. In their haste to surprise you, they left their personal gear there to collect later. That's unfortunate, but I'm afraid casualties were inevitable, sir."

"Not a bit of it, Jennings, well done. I'm sure she is at the station and moving along as planned."

A cloud passed over Jennings' face, then cleared as he figured out yet another solution to a posing problem.

"I understand that Miss Dahlia asked that I put her things together and forward them to the station. I hesitate to burden you, Mr. Elliott, but I may require assistance with this request. It will be necessary for me to telephone the constable in about two minutes once the shock of the empty car park has settled."

"No burden at all. Just assure them that you have things well in hand but that I must see to it that there is a time-sensitive issue with one of the memorial committee members during American business hours. I'll nip up to her room, toss her things together, and meet her at the station. Before you phone the constable, please let her know that I'll be along shortly and not to wander off. Tell Mrs. Elliott I will join them later for cocktails."

"Yes, sir. Pleasure, sir."

"Thanks Jennings. You're an ace, mate. Oh, by the way. Brilliant performance for the family. Rave reviews, really. I think you outdid yourself."

"Thank you, sir. My pleasure."

Before exiting, Tucker turned back, picked up the papers and plans, including Dahlia's scrawled notes, and stuffed them in his pockets.

"That would be a bugger to explain," he said, heaving a sigh of relief.

* * *

It had been years since Tucker had been in the inner sanctum of Miss Dahlia Porter's boudoir. It was a trip down memory lane through their childhood. Mrs. Porter had left the room covered in the bluebell wallpaper with matching curtains, chairs, and bed linens. It took him back to their teen years when he was one of the few male guests even to see it. He reminisced about the house parties that bored them up the stairs to her private retreat. As usual, her things were scattered haphazardly, and he had to comb the room to gather them. He came upon a year-old invitation to one of the Farthing Tea Balls and read the yellowed stationery line by line.

He was immersed in his memories when a soft click from behind jerked him back to the present.

"So, where is she, Tucker? Has she gone?"

"You gave me quite a start, Delia. And yes, she's gone. I'm sorry. You know how she is: headstrong and willful and usually unstoppable."

"And thank God she is, or we really would be going to a funeral," she said, gazing at the tatty invitation.

She smiled at Tucker and gave him a tight hug.

"Take her things to her, Tucker," she said with a sigh. "Oh, and bring the car back, for God's sake. The Elliott's will have Scotland Yard down here before you can spit."

Tucker scanned the hallway. No one was in sight. He jogged down the back stairs and exited the mudroom. He did not expect to meet anyone as he made his way to the garages. The household was calming down after a most traumatic evening. He pictured the Porters and Elliott's well cared for in the capable hands of Jennings, who had poured the brandy and nestled them in comfy chairs. He went in through the side door and chose his favorite: a spunky little blue Ducati, which would blend into the crowd of scooters and bikes puttering the West Sussex byways. He then quickly changed to a dark Mercedes sedan, a bland and quiet getaway car.

His heart skipped a beat as he steered It to the roadway, then realized it probably had more to do with the impending call to Reggie than being caught by the family. The ringing seemed incessant, but finally, the cheerful voice of the Beach Drive Plaza staff broke his trance. His disappointment turned to delight when the message to ring her at the tea room was delivered with a smile and maybe a smattering of giddiness.

Dialing the tea room gave him a minute to think about his game plan, and he ended the call and flipped the phone on the passenger seat. It just sounded rehearsed and phony to him. He also wasn't sure what might pop out of his mouth once he heard her voice. He was confused to find out that he missed her presence, which made him feel foreign and out of sync. He hoped she would be the usual commanding Regina and save him from making his typical ass of himself. He plucked the phone from the seat and punched the resend.

"Sea Gables tea room and Bed and Breakfast, Lisa speaking. May I help you?"

"Hello Lisa, Tucker Elliott here. I was hoping you had Miss Winter on the premises. I must speak with her."

"Yeess... She's here somewhere. Dulcy! Do you know where Miss Reggie went? It's Mr. Elliott, and he says it's important."

"Tucker!" yelled Dulcy, grabbing the phone. "How are you? What's going on over there? Reggie's dying to talk to you. Did you hear about Mavis?"

Tucker was holding the phone at arm's length as the volume escalated. He lowered it, but with the amount of information he had to share, he was hesitant to begin.

"Dulcy! I'm heading to the airport. I need to talk to Reggie, but if you can't find her, have her phone me back. As soon as you can, yes?"

"Okay, Tucker. She's uh... down below," she whispered. "She's on to something, too. We're not sure what, but I can't go into it here. I'm going down to check on her, so I'll have her call you back."

"Brilliant, Dulce. I'll be waiting for her call. Cheers, love."

Dulcy slowly lowered the phone, smiled at the arriving dinner guests, and sprinted up the stairs.

* * *

Tucker parked the Mercedes and ran the length of the station to ticketing. He scoured the platforms for Dahlia and even did a once-through of the ladies' loo. All he found was a young, punkish-looking girl who only scowled at his retreating figure. He sighted Dahlia at the other end of the station and ran for her, never taking his eyes off her light tan jumper. He grasped her shoulders and swung her to him, coming face to face with a set of bright blue eyes belonging to an attractive girl whom he had never seen before. He abruptly apologized and searched again, trying not to panic. As he peered in the windows, the train jerked and wheezed with its imminent departure. His quickening pace matched the quickening pace of the train and his heart. His ears were ringing above the station clutter until he realized it was not his ears but his pinging phone.

"Tucker! Turn to your left and start running!"

Tucker jogged blindly into the mass until he saw her just ahead. She was watching the train. He had to get to her before it gained speed, leaving her behind. She caught his eye and, in an amazingly athletic move, bore down on him, stripping him of his bag and shoving the car keys into his hand. With a slight wave, she jumped the train just as it accelerated past the point of access.

Driving back to the Porter's in one of the now two missing cars, Tucker was suffering from a melancholy sense of relief. He was glad she had made the train, but he was worried about her safety and what she would do when she landed. Once again, the ringing started, and he punched the button with trepidation.

"Tucker! I don't think I can wait for you. Send Landry on and get back when you can."

"I don't feel right about you roaming the continents alive and alone. You're supposed to be dead."

"You sound like you're sorry they missed."

"No, no, just worried about what you're going to do when you get back."

"Like you said, it's time to bring in Laird. I'll call back and let you know when I land. What better nanny than a copper, eh?"

"Alright, I'll call him when I get home."

"Did you call Reggie?"

"I tried. We didn't connect. I'll try again, but I've already left a message

305

for her to phone me back."

"You best talk to her soon, or she'll have your guts for garters, love."

"Yes, I know, and when... wait, that's her. Bye, Dahl."

"Ciao."

"Tucker Elliot."

"Well, hello, boss. Remember me? Employee, female type, tallish side, dark hair, a partner in crime? Babysitter," she added for spite.

"I'm sorry, Reggie, it's been outrageous here. This has been the most outlandish afternoon; you can't know."

"That's surprising. I would have expected a slightly more subdued atmosphere in the circumstances."

Tucker caught himself, remembering she knew nothing about the unbelievable events occurring even as they spoke.

"First off, I want to apologize for the nasty way in which I fled off. I know I've landed you in no end of a mess to get on with on your own..."

"No, we're doing quite well without our lord and master, I'll have you know. But seriously, Tucker, I really think we're close. I've been down in the room making notes on the pictures. There's a connection here somewhere. I know if I keep at it, I'll find the key. I have so much to tell you. I don't know where to begin. It's a bit frustrating."

"Let me help you out. How are Dahlia's service arrangements coming along? To me, that's most important now. I was just informed this evening that the Porters and the Elliott's will be in attendance."

"You're kidding," blurted Reggie, regretting it as it came out. "I mean, I'm surprised. I thought they were going to wait for her to... to come home."

"They were, then they decided it was important for them to be a part of her American family and are booking flights as we speak."

"It's Saturday at 2 p.m., and people are coming out of the woodwork to speak about her. We were going to have Mavis talk, but that's questionable now."

Tucker said nothing about his feelings on Mavis lauding someone she may have tried to help "kill." He skipped that point.

"Then, after the tributes, there's a memorial plaque that the historical society will mount by the front door. Nelson Platt will cover that, and then that's about it. There'll be food and drink, courtesy of Farthing's Fine Teas Corporation, and, of course, the usual guest book signing. Oh, I almost forgot, there will be music from a nice chamber group."

"Sounds brilliant. Listen, Reg, I'm almost to the Porter house. I'm going to need to ring off, but I promise I'll call later."

"How are they doing?"

"As well as can be expected. You know, bearing up with the usual English front, but stone devastated as you would expect. Sort of not real, I reckon," said Tucker, getting into the part.

"Anyway, we'll talk more about that when I see you."

"Okay. Do me a favor and give them my best."

"Of course, Reggie. I'll see you soon. I'm getting ready to come home tomorrow or the day after," he said, wondering how he was to extricate himself from the parents so soon after arriving.

"Tucker—what about Landry? You never told me anything about Landry."

"Oh, uh, I'll call you back with that later. I really have to run. Jennings is holding the door for me," he lied.

"I'll talk to you later, then. It was nice hearing from you."

"You also, Reg."

He hit the end key, feeling even lonelier than when he called. While trudging to the door, he noticed a plain black sedan by the garage and figured Jennings had found the constable. If he knew the Porters, they were plying him with food and drink and holding him captive until Tucker got home with the vehicle. All he had to do was explain how he found it so quickly. He was devising a believable story when he heard voices coming from the study. He gathered his thoughts and poked his head in the door.

"Hullo all!"

His parents, looking weary and sad, merely glanced his way while the Porters, Jennings, and the constable nearly jumped out of their skins.

"No one guilty here," he thought.

"How are you, Constable Downs? Nice to see you again. Come to call for the missing car, eh?"

"Well, sir, yes and no."

Tucker went to alert status. He caught a glimpse of Jennings pretending to be invisible in the corner, sporting a tense, strangulated look.

"Sorry?"

"You see, Tucker, Jennings called Constable Downs to report the car. The constable was taking a call from Mrs. Benson, the neighbor down the road?"

"Yes, go on," said Tucker.

He felt as if he was about to be hit with some bad news. Something told him this was far worse than the car and that he wasn't going to like it one bit.

"She had a most incredible story," went on Mrs. Porter, staring wildly at Tucker. "It seems as she was heading into town, she was following our car. Of course, it was a bit dark, so she wasn't completely sure, but then she saw the driving license and knew it was one of us. She thought it was me since she could see it was a female driver."

"Jennings," interrupted Tucker, "would you please fetch me a scotch from the pantry?"

"There's scotch right here, son. Won't that do?" said the senior Elliott.

"No. I have a particular taste for the eighteen-year-old Macallan. That's Glenmorangie - fine scotch, but not what I have a taste for at the moment. I really would appreciate it, Jennings. Thank you."

Jennings weaved through the crowd, looking like a puppet whose legs weren't being worked correctly. He stumped past Tucker, giving him a desperate, pleading look as he exited.

"Hang on a sec," said Tucker, following Jennings out.

"Make that neat, would you, mate?" he shouted as he pressed the keys into his hand and grabbed his sleeve.

"Get it out of here," he said under his breath.

"Yes, that's right. Thanks so much, Jennings."

"Sorry, where were we?"

The six faces were gazing back at him aghast. How could he leave the room at a time like this?

"So, Mrs. Benson followed the car into town, thinking she was going to the store, but the car turned off at the rail station. She figured she'd just ring her later and turned into Waterson's. She looked over to see if she could see Delia, but when the driver got out, she said it wasn't Delia at all but Dahlia! Of all things! Tucker, what do you have to say about that?" cried his mother.

* * *

Chapter 30

The Tracker: Anyone ever tell you too much persistence can make you kind of stupid?
-What Dreams May Come, 1998

Reggie paid her bill and strolled into the foyer. She decided to head upstairs to wait for Dulcy. The bathroom was occupied, so she toured the dining area, noting the romantic tables, the soft colors, and the antique knickknacks and pictures. She greeted a few lingering lunch guests and then headed back to the hallway. As she passed the last table, a tilted picture caught her eye, and she reached up to straighten it. The picture righted with a click, and a thin, crinkled paper floated to the floor. Reggie glanced around, then lifted a corner of the photograph to peer under it. She saw nothing more and let the picture fall back against the wall with a clang. She picked up the paper, straining her eyes to read the worn lettering.

As she wiped at the faded ink, Dulcy's head appeared on the staircase. She carefully folded the fragile paper, slid it into her pocket, and pulled Dulcy into the bathroom.

"I found something. It fell out of a picture in the dining area."

"What? Let's see."

"Not here. Let's grab the lights and head back down below. We can look at it there, and you can show me what you found at the fireplace."

The two women squeezed into the tunnel and made their way to the basement fireplace. Reggie carefully extracted the paper and shined the light on it. It was not in English, and she gave up and handed it to Dulcy, who scanned it with the same quizzical look.

"I haven't the slightest idea what this is. Let's put it in the room where we know it'll be safe, and we can ask John about it later."

"Ooh, it's John now, is it?" purred Reggie.

Dulcy reddened and stood gazing at the back of the fireplace rather than at Reggie.

"Are you going to help me or be snippy?"

"It's more fun to be snippy, but for now, I'll help you. What are we looking for?"

Dulcy was feeling the brick-like reading Braille, looking for an opening to the stair set.

"Something that gives, like a latch or a button, but I just can't seem to find anything. You see anything?"

"Nothing, so far."

She shone her light into cracks, crevices, and crannies but still only saw old, dusty bricks caked with aged mortar and sand. The two finally met at one end and decided to quit. They moved on to the painting room, where they might find something of value.

"We have a hidden room full of original artwork, an old foreign piece of paper, and keys, and we can't make heads or tails of any of it," said Reggie.

"It's very frustrating. And I didn't get a thing out of Mavis Hatfield. That old puss is a piece of work if you ask me."

"Oh! I forgot. I had lunch with Forrest Perkins. That was interesting, let me tell you. Did you know that he and Mavis were engaged once?"

"No! How did you get that out of him? I got nothing out of her other than how good the clam chowder is at the Beach Drive Plaza."

Reggie filled Dulcy in on her lunch as they opened the rusty old door. The pictures still hung full of secrets and history, mocking them from their respective spaces. In the low light, they looked entirely different as their shapes seemed to shift on the wall.

"They have something to do with all this, you just know. Perkins said Dahlia didn't give the collection to the museum. He said she only gave them a few pieces and that the family that owned the place before her gave them the bulk of it."

"Well, if they have the bulk of the collection, then what are these?" asked Dulcy.

"More of the same, just ones that no one knew about."

"I don't know. There's something very familiar about some of these."

Dulcy marched around the room, Reggie in her wake. They walked one after the other, peering up into the still frames.

"This one," pronounced Dulcy.

"What about it?"

"This looks like the same picture Mavis showed me as we were on our way out. She said it was one of her father's favorites. It's the same piece but somehow different."

"Are you sure?"

"There's only one way to find out. We need to go back to the museum and see that picture."

"Fine with me. This is creepy, even in daylight."

They shone the lights across the pictures, each one flowing easily into the next. Dulcy shrugged her shoulders, sliding past Reggie and out of the room. She reluctantly edged out the door, glancing back at the effect of the walls, the pictures, and the lights. There was something there, but she couldn't put her finger on it. As she bounced off the tunnel walls, she had a slow burgeoning thought. She quickened her pace to catch up with Dulcy. She was thinking back to an earlier conversation with Tucker. She suddenly had the urge to read up on Salvador Dali.

* * *

Dulcy and Reggie again excused themselves from the tea room and headed back to the museum. Reggie was beginning to feel like a ping-pong ball bouncing back and forth between the same paddles. Reggie pulled out the worn letter she had forgotten to leave in the room.

"What do you think this is supposed to be?" asked Reggie.

"I don't even know what language it is. We'll give it to John, and he can probably figure it out."

Reggie said nothing feeling guilty that she didn't want to give the letter over to Laird. She couldn't explain it, but she had misgivings. Dulcy pulled her to a halt and stared silently.

"You don't want to give it to him! Why? What's going on?"

"I didn't say that. I just have this awful feeling that if we give it to him, we'll never see it again, and you know it's something important. Sorry, maybe I'm being silly. If he can't decipher it, he'll give it to someone who can, and that'll be it. We'll never find out what happened to Dahlia, and I don't think I could stand that," she finished.

Dulcy led Reggie to the steps of a house and sat her down.

"I know this has been hard on you. But you have to have faith in John. He wouldn't do anything to hinder this. I truly believe he wants to get to the bottom of it as much as we do. It's not a matter of police protocol anymore; it's a matter of pride and what's right, and he's going to do what's right, I know."

"Well, that was a nice speech. Okay, if you feel that strongly, then we'll give it to him, and I'll be fine. Come on," she said, standing, "let's go to the museum. I really want to take another look at those pictures."

* * *

Laird sat in his office reading over the report on the maid: acetone and iodine. You could get acetone anywhere, but iodine enough to kill was a bigger question. He sat back in his chair, clasping his hands behind his head. He closed his eyes and pictured the scene in the bathroom. Was there anything he missed?

Momentarily, the scene shifted and morphed into the pretty face of Dulcy Dandeneau. He let himself linger on that for a minute, then again scanned the initial report. There was nothing in it out of the ordinary except that a maid was murdered in a hotel where she took a job under an assumed name. Why was she even still in town? Why didn't she leave the minute she left Mazie Cavanaugh's still - warm body? Was there another assignment in the offing, or maybe she hadn't gotten her money yet?

No large sums were found among her things so that it could be either. These musings got him nowhere, so he threw the report in his inbox and grabbed his jacket. It was time for a walk. He stomped over to his assistant's desk on the way out.

"I'll be over with Dr. Walker if you need me."

"She said to tell you she's not finished with the autopsy yet, sir."

"That's why I'll be at Dr. Walker's."

* * *

"So, what have you found, Chris?"

"Nothing out of the ordinary. She was doing her job, was probably overtaken by the fumes, and got dizzy and lost consciousness. There's a bruise on her occipital area, so I'm guessing she fell when she passed out, hitting her head. It wasn't what killed her, though. She had some

316

bleeding, but from what I'm seeing, she died of acute iodine poisoning. See this tiny bruise on her neck and the pinpoint? That's the injection site. But no needle, syringe, nothing, and that's what you need to find, and I bet you never will. Whoever did this would have taken that piece of evidence far away. I'm figuring when I take a look at her lungs, they'll be burned from the acetone."

"Okay, well, we don't have a whole lot to go on at this point. No needle, no real exotic murder method, and circumstances in which either a man or a woman could have done it. The only thing I'm convinced of is that these three murders are connected. Couldn't you give me any details on the Dahlia Porter autopsy?"

"Who?"

"Dahlia Porter. The owner of the tea room died on Sunday. The body had to come through here. You must have done the work on her."

Chris eyed him curiously. She grabbed a clipboard and ran down the worksheets. She shuffled back and forth through the papers and then tucked the board under her arm.

"I don't have anyone by that name in the work orders, John. Now, if you'll excuse me, I need to get back to it."

John Laird stared at the retreating figure of Chris Walker, scanned the room, then let himself out the way he came in.

"Maybe it's time to call the commissioner," he thought.

* * *

Dulcy and Reggie were standing in front of the Hatfield pictures, wishing they could talk. The pieces were still in the lecture hall, where they would remain until the following week's Brown Bag event. Nelson Platt provided them with a catalog, making it easy to check them off at the museum and back at the tea room. They roamed from easel to hanging and back again, noting which pictures were duplicates of the ones in the hidden room. By the time they finished, their feet were sore, and they were hungry again.

"I am ready for something good to eat, a drink, and some quiet time with this listing down in that room," said Reggie.

"I can join you after I check on the girls. They've never seen so little of me. What must they be thinking?"

"Probably that you're giving them the space to show you what they can do when you need their help. People like to feel needed."

"I hope so. I know Dahlia always urged them to step up and take responsibility. I think they're doing it for her, you know."

"I think they're doing it for you," smiled Reggie.

"Well, maybe. I like to think..."

Dulcy slowed her pace, staring at something in the distance. Reggie followed her line of sight to see Detective John Laird crossing the street in an apparent hurry to his office. He was on his phone, oblivious to anyone or anything around him.

"Huh. Wonder what's up?"

Reggie grabbed Dulcy's arm and led her across the street to the tea room.

"It doesn't matter. I'm sure he'll tell us later. I've changed my mind. Let's go straight down to the room. It's getting late, and I don't really feel much like being down there in the dark."

"It's always dark down there, Reg. It's underground."

"I know, but I mean at night. It's just a feeling I have. Do you realize I haven't heard a word out of Tucker Elliott all day?"

"Yeah, a little weird, huh?"

"Okay, let me call the Beach Drive Plaza and see if I can track him down. I'll meet you in the upstairs bathroom," she said, heading for the office.

Dulcy wandered into the dining area, observing the proceedings. Reggie punched the hotel number. She prodded a few things on the desk and peered at the pictures on the wall. She was making a mental note to give them a thorough going over when a voice at the other end jolted her back to reality.

"Good evening. Thank you for calling Beach Drive Plaza. This is Traci. How may I help you?"

"Tucker Elliott's room, please."

"I'm sorry, Miss, but Mr. Elliott has checked out. Is there something else I can help you with?"

"No," she said distantly. "Did he leave any messages for a Miss Winter?"

"No, Miss. I'm afraid not, sorry."

"Thank you."

Reggie replaced the phone and stood alone, feeling strange.

"Where could he have gone?"

* * *

"Yes, I understand. No, sir. I just thought a little more information from you on the Porter case would help with the other two. I've got the men going over everything again. I just came from Chris Walker's office, and it's pretty straightforward. No, you'll have it as soon as I get it. Yes, sir. I'm heading back to the tea room now. I'll keep my eye on them, not to worry. They can't get into much trouble with me right there. I'll let you know if anything turns up. They're progressing along just as we want them to. They're getting a lot of work done for us. Yes, sir. Thank you, sir."

Laird ended his call and stomped into his office.

* * *

Dulcy ran into Reggie, leaving Dahlia's office.

"Whoa, look at you. You look like you've seen a ghost."

"Maybe I have," stated Reggie, recovering enough to feel anger surfacing.

"What?"

"I just got off the phone with the hotel. Tucker Elliott checked out earlier with no forwarding address. I'm beginning to get a little irritated," she said as she pushed past Dulcy and headed for the stairs.

Dulcy rolled her eyes and skipped to keep up as Reggie freight-trained towards the stairs.

"Now, you don't know what came up. He may have found something and had to move on it and didn't have time to call."

"After six hours?"

Dulcy shoved her hand over her mouth to hide her grin.

"You think it's funny. I'll let him know how funny it is when I find him, I'll tell you what."

"You sound more like a jealous girlfriend than a business associate."

Reggie stopped, slapping her hand on the banister. Her whole body was un-tensed, hand on hip, chewing her lower lip like a stick of gum. She cocked her head at Dulcy and chuckled.

"Geez, you're right. What am I doing? I'm sure he'll be in touch. 'Johnny Boy' probably knows where he is, so we'll ask him."

"Get up those stairs before I get my hands on you," Dulcy teased, rounding the banister.

When they reached the hidden room, both girls stared at the rickety door, laughing nervously. They pulled out the stashed flashlights and candles from earlier and began reviewing each picture against Nelson Platt's list.

"This is frustrating not knowing what the hell we're looking for. I wish

'Johnny Boy' were here. Maybe he could give us a clue. Who do you suppose he was talking to back there?" said Dulcy.

"You're going to end up calling that to his face if you don't watch it. And I haven't the faintest idea. It's probably something to do with that maid again. I feel restless like I don't want to do this, and I don't want to explore the fireplace, and I don't want to sit through another cat and mouse session with 'Johnny Boy'... okay, sorry, now I'm doing it..."

"You just want to know where Tucker is, and you're not going to be able to focus till you find out. Let's go hunt down 'Johnny Boy.'"

"No need to hunt him down. He's right here," said a disjointed voice from the dark doorway.

* * *

"Ooo, you scared me. How long have you been standing there?" asked Dulcy, wincing.

"Long enough. What seems to be the trouble, ladies?"

"Who says you can never find a cop when you need one," said Reggie.

Laird stared at her but said nothing, secretly enjoying himself.

"Miss Winter, I have a note for you from Mr. Elliott that might answer your questions as to his whereabouts."

Reggie took the envelope and stared at it. There was nothing written on the outside and she felt a knot in her stomach as she slid her finger under the flap. She read quickly and then reread, unable to process the message in the scribbled lines. She passed it to Dulcy who scanned it, then dropped it on the table behind them.

"What's this about, Detective?"

"Ah – we're back to Detective then, are we? What happened to 'Johnny Boy'? Talk about shooting the messenger. Listen, ladies, I agreed with his plans. When he went to track down Landry, he had left the country with no explanation other than a bunch of canceled appointments and a tight-lipped receptionist."

"Then how did he know where to go? Why would he go to England?"

"Other than his business interests there?"

"Yes, because I don't believe there are labor problems in Manchester if that's what you mean."

"He paid a visit to the travel agency Landry uses and tracked him straight to London. Seemed like a good time to pay a visit to the families while he was at it."

"Oh, the travel agency. The one with the very helpful, young travel agent. I get it," said Reggie.

"I'm not sure that you do, but now that that's cleared up, shall we take a look at these pictures?"

"You know, I don't think I really feel like doing this tonight. It's getting late, and I had this idea I wanted to check out before all this happened earlier."

"You're not just saying that because you're mad at Tucker for leaving you out of his plans?" said Dulcy.

"Of course, I'm mad at him for leaving me out of his plans. Wouldn't you be if you were his assistant? I mean, what if there were labor problems in Manchester after all? Isn't that something I should be helping with?"

"I don't know. Aren't you mostly marketing or whatever?"

"I'm whatever. Anyway, when we were down here earlier, there was something about the pictures that made me think of Salvador Dali. What if these are positioned in such a way as to give us clues or tell a story?"

All three slowly began to revolve around each other, moving from one picture to the next.

"Nah," said Laird finally. "I don't think so. I see where you're trying to go, but I'm not getting anything."

"Sorry, Reg, me neither. Maybe we're just tired. It's been a long day. Why don't we start fresh in the morning? What time is it anyway?"

"It's almost 8 o'clock. Anybody hungry?" asked Laird, raising his eyebrows.

"I'm starving. I didn't get much to eat at all today unless you count a bit of clam chowder. I could eat. How about you, Reg?"

Reggie was still staring at the pictures on one end. They matched the pictures in the Brown Bag event, but they had a dimensional quality the others did not.

"No, not really. I think I want to head back to my room, maybe order room service, and crawl into bed. I didn't get much sleep last night after everything that happened. I appreciate the offer, though. Why don't we have breakfast tomorrow and then find some info on Dali?"

"Well, you happen to be in luck on that one. The Dali Museum is on the other side of downtown. If you really want to learn something, you can go on a tour. I definitely have to help these girls tomorrow, but I bet 'Johnny Boy' here would be willing to escort you."

"Oh, that would be great. Would you, Detective? I promise I won't call you 'Johnny Boy.'"

"Why don't we discuss it at breakfast? C'mon, we'll walk you back to the Plaza, and we can get something in the bar, Dulcy."

Once they were headed back to the inn, Reggie realized just how tired she really was. She stopped at the front desk to check for messages while Dulcy and Laird peeled off to the bar.

"Sorry, Miss. Nothing here."

She thought about the previous night's excitement. She would be glad to get into a hot bath, her jammies, and have something sent in. She turned the corner and stalled in front of her door, key in hand.

"This is ridiculous," she thought. "Wouldn't happen twice," and she slid the key in the lock and pushed the door hard.

She surveyed the room in the darkness. Everything seemed as it should, except for a blinking beam from the nightstand.

"Oh – a message!" she said, flipping on the light.

She leaned against the table, heart pounding, waiting for the voice and hoping it was Tucker Elliott. But when the message played, it was only the woman from the catering company calling regarding Dahlia's service. She scribbled down the number and plopped on the bed, staring around the room. She was appalled at the disappointment she felt. She was losing focus and needed to reboot. She could only assume she was overtired. She squeezed her eyes shut and wiped away a tear. She plucked at a tissue and wiped her nose, taking a deep, shuddering breath.

"Well, why don't I just sit here and feel sorry for myself? How pathetic. It's his company, and he can do with it however he pleases. He doesn't have to include me on a family visit even if he is tracking Landry," she muttered.

She flounced back on the pillows, grabbed one, and hugged it to her chest.

"Oh, no. I can't be falling for this man. I have a job to do. I thought I was flirting. Well, I won't do it. When I see him next, it'll be business as usual and no funny stuff. I won't let it happen. There, that's better," she said, yawning.

She settled back into the feathery pillows and shut her aching eyes.

"Just need to rest my eyes," she said and dropped off into a deep and dreamless sleep.

* * *

Chapter 31

Jack Butler: Wanna beer?
Ron Richardson: It's 7 o'clock in the morning.
Jack Butler: Scotch?
-Mr. Mom, 1983

Tucker had watched Laird drive away as he pulled out his itinerary and headed for check-in. Ironically, just days before, Dahlia had taken the same flight. He settled in his seat, pulling out a notebook. He viewed the few points he would open with and, satisfied with his battle plan, placed on his blinders and fell into oblivion. The plane landed in gray skies and rain, an appropriate welcome for the British citizen. He gathered his bag and headed for the terminal, checking the time change and sensing his stomach for the first time.

He always had a warm feeling heading home, but this time was different because of the loss of Dahlia. He concentrated on picking up his rental and headed out of the car park for the long country drive. He rolled down the windows as he hit the stretch of narrow road. When he felt the pelting rain had punished him enough, he pushed the button, rolling the window to a crack. The road was clear enough for a rainy morning, and he breezed through the roundabouts and narrow stretches until the Elliott homestead came into view.

He enjoyed the pleasure of coming home and looked forward to seeing his mother and father, even in the sad circumstances. He parked the car and circled to the kitchen door, preferring to pop into the back entrance. This would avoid the unrest that occurred when he visited. He also enjoyed teasing the kitchen staff, and at this time of day, something warm and tasty would come from the oven.

He slid through the back gate and the herb garden, which Myra carefully tended. He chewed on a sprig of mint as he popped the kitchen door latch. He was surprised to see so little activity as he searched the pantry and the mud room. The absence of the usual breakfast smells piqued his curiosity, and he grabbed an apple from the island bowl. He entered the dining area as Myra headed toward him, flowers and a vase in hand. On sighting Tucker, she screamed, dropped the flowers, and clutched the vase, ready to defend her turf.

"' Lor' Mr. Elliott, you did give me a turn. Whatever are ya doin' here? The missus didn't say anythin' as to your comin' home now. What's up with ya?"

"Sorry, Myra. I guess I should have phoned ahead. I was hoping to make it a surprise. Where is everyone?"

"They've gone to see the Porter's this weekend. So sorry, lad, as to Miss Dahlia. It was horrible news. We all were just that shocked to hear. Your Mum and Dad have been just strong as rocks, ya know. How are ya holdin' up, sir?"

"I'm fine, Myra. Did you say they went to the Porter's?"

"Oh, yes, sir. They just felt they had to go. They wanted to be with them and do what they could now. Not that I know what that could be, but sometimes ya just have to do somethin'."

328

"At the Porter's, eh? Well, Myra, I would like to clean up a bit before making that visit. Do you think you could whip up some of your famous egg casserole before I have to face them?"

"Of course, dear. Better on a full stomach, as I always say. Be right up for ya. You enjoy your bat,h and I'll tell Henry to get your car for ya."

"No, no. S'alright, love. I got one in town. Not to worry."

It wasn't long before Tucker was fed and watered, and Myra and Henry were waving him out the front door. He felt a pang of loneliness, leaving them to their warm, happy confines while he went to face the two grieving families.

The lanes were beautiful in their late summer splendor, lifting his spirits as he drove the few kilometers to the Porter residence. He swung the rental up to the front door and parked. He was looking forward to seeing his parents even though the meeting would be difficult. He had only spoken by phone to each couple. It was probably better to see them both at the same time.

He dismissed the lack of activity, steeling himself for the greetings as he approached the ivied entrance way and pushed the bell. He went over what he would say to them and was about to push the bell again when the door swung wide, revealing the reliable Jennings.

"Hello, Jennings. Happy surprise, I hope?"

"Oh, well, yes, Mr. Elliott. It's always a pleasure to see you. Won't you please come in?"

Tucker went to enter, but Jennings stood firmly in his path, and he stopped, confused.

"Jennings, I would love to come in, but you seem to be blocking the door, mate. Are you alright?"

Jennings did not look at the picture of health, and he coughed, staring rather wildly at Tucker.

"Sorry, sir. I seem to be in the way. Just tidying things up, you know, and if you follow me, I will seat you in the study while I inform the, er, family, that you have arrived. Would you care for a scotch, sir?"

"Jennings. It's 9:30 in the morning."

"Oh, quite, sir. You won't mind if I have one then. Just a small joke, sir. I would be happy to bring you some tea, maybe?"

"I really don't want anything, Jennings, except to see my parents and the Porters. Are they here?"

"Quite, sir. If you will excuse me, I will have them with you momentarily. Pardon me, sir."

Jennings backed out the foyer door, which is something Tucker had never seen him do. Something strange was going on, and he felt a wave of alarm begin. He yanked himself from the chair and paced around the room. He was staring absently at the leather-bound volumes and family pictures when he heard a loud noise come from the interior of the house. He stared at the door as if expecting it to burst open.

When all was still again, he wandered to the bookcase and pulled a volume of nursery rhymes from the shelf. He recognized quite a few of them and sat down in absorption, waiting for Jennings to return from his mission.

* * *

Jennings, who had quietly closed the study door and, covering the length of the hall at a very uncharacteristic speed, skidded to a stop outside the conservatory. He tapped lightly on the door, entered, and made his way through the foliage. He reached the far end, where George Landry and Dahlia Porter were seated among papers and dishes. Both were engrossed in their papers and barely noticed when he cleared his throat, addressing Dahlia in a faraway voice.

"What is it, Jennings? You look absolutely ghastly for so early in the day. Not nipping in the pantry, are you, love?"

"No, Miss Dahlia, but may I suggest something for yourself and the doctor?"

"Jennings, it's 9:30 in the morning."

"That has been brought to my attention, Miss."

Dahlia eyed Landry and then Jennings, pointing at each of them, then at herself.

"By whom, Jennings? There's only three of us here, yes?"

"Technically, it would be whom, Miss, and since we last chatted, we have been joined by a visitor. I took the liberty of placing him in the study. If you would please follow me."

"Jennings? Who did you let in here?"

But Jennings had turned on his heel and was heading for the door. Dahlia and Landry speechlessly followed as if in a gravitational pull. They followed the man's path, catching him up outside the study door.

"Jennings…"

Whatever fresh hell awaited, Jennings was at least enjoying himself. He swept open the door to an empty room and stood gazing in circles. Dahlia and Landry squeezed past either side of him, staring as well.

"Let me smell your breath. What have you been up to, drinking the silver polish?"

"He must be wandering out in the house, Miss. I left him here standing in the middle of the room," he said, pointing.

All three spread out into the foyer, heading in different directions, with only Jennings knowing for whom or what they were searching. Tucker popped his head out of the loo, listening closely. He thought he heard voices. He crossed the room in two steps, looking through the entrance. He was ready to give someone a piece of his mind once he found them.

He stepped into the foyer and listened. He thought he heard someone coming but couldn't determine from which direction. As he stood waiting for someone to show, three people popped into view; two of them wide-eyed and speechless, and one of them grinning from sheer delight.

Of all the people to wander into the hall, the least expected was the one who stood before him - Miss Dahlia Porter, recently deceased, hands on hips, and very much alive.

* * *

Tucker, Dahlia, and Landry stood staring in disbelief until Jennings gave a low cough and cleared his throat.

"Is there anything you require, Miss?"

"Scotch!" yelled all three from their respective corners.

Jennings bowed slightly, disappearing into the recesses of the house, leaving the three staring in awe. Once the truth had sunk in, Tucker ran for Dahlia, gathered her in his arms, and hugged her so tight she thought she would break.

"Never in my life has anyone looked so good. What have you done? Landry, how are you involved in all this? Someone needs to start explaining now," he said, regaining control.

"I'm sorry, love. I didn't mean to do it, it's just that the opportunity presented itself and I couldn't say no. As it turns out, I'm not the only one who has an interest in that house. It's been an open case for a long time. We'll get to the bottom of it, but we had to break a few eggs along the way, as they say."

"And a few hearts, I might add."

Dahlia looked like a child being scolded by her parents. Tucker pulled out the rumpled telegram, holding it up to her.

"Yes, love, that would be my work. I'm so glad you got it. Did you figure it out? Let's go sit. We can go over everything in the conservatory. Come on, George. Stop looking like the front of Mt. Rushmore."

"After you, Elliott."

"Oh, no, Landry. After you this time."

The three marched to the conservatory, Jennings in tow, with a large platter of refreshments. Once they were comfortable and Jennings had bestowed his last grin, they sat staring in embarrassed silence.

"Well, how are you, Tucker?"

"How am I? Well, Dahlia, I am a bit at full stretch at the moment. How do you think I am? Why don't you and the good doctor fill me in on your unusual partnership? I seem to be missing the more interesting details. Start any time."

Dahlia and Landry looked at each other, one waiting for the other when Tucker shook his head and began to chuckle.

"Sorry, but you have to understand my disappointment in you not trusting me enough to let me in on all this."

"It's so tough to explain, Tucker, but shortly after you arrived, things began to happen. I had had the police round at one point after I made the first complaint, and then when nothing came of it, I figured they were doing their bit to keep everyone happy. Right before the opening, I was feeling rather jumpy, so I rang them again, saying that even though things had been quiet, I was dead worried that something would happen. They asked me to come round downtown and speak to them there."

"You see, I had been in contact with a few people after the police visit, hoping someone might have information that wasn't in any record somewhere. One person would have an insight for me, which would lead me to someone else who would also have information, and before I knew it, I was beginning to see why someone might want to see the back of me."

"After the police listened to what I had been finding out, they told me about a little problem they have. It appears there is a rather old, unsolved case in their books that has to do with my tea room. It's a missing person's case involving a foreign businessman who disappeared back when the Hatfields owned the house. The tea room was the last place anyone had seen him alive while in the States. They weren't clear if he had business dealings there or if he was a family friend."

"It wasn't that he'd gone missing; that was the problem. Apparently, before he left his home country, he had stolen a rather large sum of money. The authorities were trying to find him and the missing property. They got nothing out of the Hatfields except that the man had been there but had since gone, and they didn't know where he was headed. The trail went cold, and it's still unsolved on their books," finished Dahlia.

"So, what had you been finding out that made them tell you about this case?"

"It seems I filled in a few gaps for them, enough to make them reopen the case because obviously, someone has just enough information to be dangerous."

"That I think we've seen. You've actually no idea just how dangerous," said Tucker.

"What do you mean?" asked Landry and Dahlia together.

"No, go ahead and finish telling me what you found out, and then we'll get to what's been going on at home, sweet home."

"Well, through a little snooping, I found that everything seemed to point back to the family. And at this point, the family is now only Mavis and Cord, which brings us to our main reason for being here. George is a bit of an amateur genealogist and knows a bit about how to research someone's family history. That's why it's so ironic that he fell into the part he played in all this."

"Back up and start from the beginning, please," said Tucker.

He was comfortable in his puffy chair, and the effects of a long plane ride, stressful morning, and the peatiness of his scotch were mellowing him beyond the annoyance he felt for Dahlia.

"Wait. Is that why you've been coming here, Landry? Researching Dahlia's family tree?"

"No, not hers, the Hatfield's, among others. As you'll see, it's with them that all this begins and will more than likely end."

"I'm sorry for interrupting, love. Please go on."

"Okay, I think in order to understand the story, you've got to go back to the beginning, which takes us to the early years of the city when Hatfield was becoming the philanthropist, entrepreneur, and business leader he's known for today."

"Alright, here's to Hatfield," said Tucker, enjoying the effects of his cocktail.

"Remember when you and Reggie were at the records hall, and you said there seemed to be some inconsistencies in the chronology, for lack of a better word, yes?"

"Oh, right, you would be reading along, getting the picture, and then there would be a hole in it. You could see that something was missing because the dates would jump forward, and the text wouldn't make sense like something had been lifted from the pile, you know."

"Well, there probably were things lifted, but as I started asking questions, I found a few things about the Hatfields that I'm sure he would rather have kept quiet."

"Such as?"

"I spoke to a few of the older population recently including a little old antique dealer shortly before my, uh, exit. I learned quite a few interesting tidbits, but our antique dealer enlightened me on a couple of details of which I was unaware. Mr. Hatfield has enjoyed the reputation of good Samaritan and town leader all these years, but he also delved into areas that aren't listed in the books, especially the good books."

"It appears our dear Mavis's father was a bit of a womanizer, a bootlegger, and a gambler, to name a few vices. He was certainly the top greengrocer in town, operating an above-board business, but he also had some side interests that were definitely less than legitimate. He had his fingers in building projects since he had money, but he also had an amazing stronghold on things that came into the ports, like liquor, weapons, and money. He apparently controlled and guarded these interests closely and roughly if need be."

"We think this could be the reason for some of the gaps. There are bound to be certain transactions our Mr. Hatfield wouldn't want immortalized. But as powerful as he was in these areas, he was extremely weak in one – women. We're still working on that angle, which is where our English genealogy comes into play."

"What are you talking about?" said Tucker.

"As I said, when we started, we figured this trip would fill in the gaps, or at least figure out a way to lay a trap and catch whoever is doing these things. We put the first part of the plan into action on my grand opening day. It was like a carefully controlled experiment with me as bait. George here didn't know what he was in for when he wandered into that ER room, I can tell you."

"So, you put it all on like a school play?"

"The police weren't thrilled with the idea, but I was going to do it whether they worked with me or not. I just wasn't sure how, so they had their chemist chap work up digitalin for my drink. It was in the ice, love. Once the ice melted, the digitalin was released, but only enough to mimic signs of cardiac arrest and shut my system down. How do you think the ambulance got there so fast? They were waiting around the corner with the antidote ready once I was wheeled in."

"A few special unit police chaps were floating through the crowd, but not enough to be suspicious. In case something happened, they would be on site. That's why Reggie was barred from entering the ambulance. I know she was wild with worry, and I felt just awful, but she had to be left out, literally. We ended up in the ER having a pow wow, getting me checked out and who should pop in, but George was going all militant on everyone, so we had to tell him. You can't be dead one minute then debriefing the next without an explanation."

"You have the picture of the scene, Elliott. I burst into the room expecting to see her flat-lining, and she's practically dancing on the gurney. Of course, I demanded to know what was happening, and since I had seen her alive and well, I had to become part of the plan. Keeping you out of the picture was the most difficult part. You don't go away very easily."

"You're quite the entertainer, Doctor. You must have really been enjoying the scene in the travel agency. Maria, by the way, is most accommodating.

She was very forthcoming on your entire routing."

"You were being very bothersome. I wasn't really acting. I was trying to get Dahlia out of the country where she would be safe and you wouldn't leave it alone. You really should think about a career in police work. You nearly found us out before she was even out of the city."

"Which brings me back to my original complaint. Why wouldn't you trust me enough to let me in on this?"

"Because the less people who knew, the better. I know you would want to help, and you would have to explain yourself to Reggie, and then there's Dulcy..."

"Alright, okay, I get it. What I don't get is what you were hoping to find."

Dahlia and Landry looked at each other and shrugged their shoulders.

"Give it to him," said Landry.

Dahlia pulled out an official-looking, rectangular paper. She passed it to Tucker, who scanned it, shrugged it, and threw it on the pile.

"This is a birth record, and I don't recognize any of the names. Who are these people, and what do they mean to all of this?"

"Well, we are now back to our little old antique dealer. It appears that old Hatfield was quite the womanizer. He loved his wife, but her health had declined even before the accident due to losing a baby, and she had sunk into a depression. Ironically, the outing which killed her was supposed to have lifted her spirits."

"But while she was dealing with her demons, Hatfield was dealing with the area ladies whenever he got the chance. There were numerous liaisons and one or two more serious relationships that did not end well for the poor women, notably one Sara Jane Brooks," she said, tapping the birth record with her finger.

"She was hushed up and sent away and landed here where she could cause no further trouble, or so Hatfield thought. What you see on this record are the names of two people you don't know. The third is another story."

Dahlia handed the birth certificate back to Tucker, who reread the entries and noted the dates, times, and locations.

"And the person whom I know?"

"The child," said Dahlia. "Look at the age of the child."

Tucker reread it and calculated the child to be somewhere around seventy years old.

"Who is this?"

"The main character in all this drama," said Dahlia as Landry looked on, slowly nodding his head.

"Are you sure? How did you come up with this?"

"It was something that was said, but I didn't really think anything of it till later when I found this."

Dahlia shot Landry a conspiratorial look, and he unclasped his hands, waving them in a yielding gesture.

"Don't quit now," said Landry.

Dahlia handed Tucker a yellowed, fragile piece of stationery. They watched as he made his way down the page, eyebrows raising from time to time, saying nothing.

My Dearest Alex,

It is with a very heavy heart but a vestige of hope that I write to you now. I have honored our agreement and stayed away since that awful day that I left for England, leaving you and our love behind.

You were more than generous to me, and I should have left it at that. I am very ill now and want to repair some of the sins I have done in my life. When I arrived here, I was beyond despair as to how I could have let things go so very wrong. I felt that you might never leave your wife but held out hope that you would ache as I did and send for me, but you didn't.

That ache turned to resentment and bitterness, and I found it hard to go on with my life without even the smallest joys to comfort me. I soon met a man who was kind and understanding, and he began to awaken the life within me that was so damaged. We became close, and I finally decided it was time to pour my heart out to him about our affair. I trusted that he cared enough for me to understand and stand by me after my most heartfelt confession.

Unfortunately, I had been mistaken and should never have discussed even the smallest details with him. He felt betrayed and sullied by my very presence. He left me and begged that I not try to contact him again. I tried to explain, but he felt dishonored and dirty, and I was again abandoned. This time, however, I was not alone. He left me, but not before I was indeed with child, the child I wrote to you about, claiming to be yours and taking money from you for him all these years.

My dear Alex, the child is not yours, and I must try to go to my grave with a clear conscience. I know that I can never make it right, but I can at least confess the horrible sin to you and make the truth known.

There is something else you must know. You may now know my son. He has always been a brilliant young man, and I could not keep the truth from him either. I confessed to him as well, and he has left me now too to find you as he saw his real father some time ago.

I never wanted him to know his real father since he abandoned him before birth. I never wanted this man to know anything about the child as I was horrified over his embarrassment of me. Clinton Peters has only known you as his father until most recently. I cannot stop him from seeking you out, and for that, I am also sorry.

Please do not be hard on the boy. He has had a very difficult life except for the money we received from you. I know he will try to contact you. By that time, I will be gone.

Be kind, and remember that I have always loved you.

Sincerely,

Sara Jane Brooks

He finished reading and turned the page over and back again.

"That's quite a story. Right out of a serial. Do you believe it?"

"We do. I know it seems far-fetched, but there is something else you need to see," said Landry.

Landry handed Tucker an old but legal-looking document. Tucker read the paper and turned it over, narrowly eyeing Dahlia and Landry.

"Is this real, legal? This is an annulment showing Clinton Peters having married Mazie Hatfield. What some people won't do. I'm afraid I'm a bit confused. So, she was married to Clinton Peters. Then it was annulled. She must have met Cord Cavanaugh fairly shortly after Clinton Peters. So, when does he come in?"

"Cord Cavanaugh was always there," said Dahlia. "Cord Cavanaugh is Clinton Peters. Or should we say Clinton Peters is Cord Cavanaugh?"

* * *

Chapter 32

Xenia Onatopp: The trick is to quit while you're still ahead.
James Bond: Now, that's one trick I never learned.
−Goldeneye, 1995

There were thick beams of light sprawling through the bay windows of Reggie's room. She lifted her head, then plopped it hard on the pillow. She did not feel rested. It was time to call Laird and head to the Dali Museum. She stared at the phone, but before she could pick it up, it rang, and on the other end was the man himself.

"Are you ready for an art outing?"

"What time is it?"

"It's 9 o'clock. I thought you might need some sleep, so I waited to call. I take it I woke you."

"Yes, well, no. I didn't sleep that well, but I'll be ready to go when you say. When do you want to meet?"

"How about a little breakfast, then off to the Dali?"

"I'll meet you downstairs in half an hour."

"So, what do you expect to learn here?" asked Laird.

"I don't know. There was something in those pictures that made me think of this place. It's probably a wild goose chase, but I feel like I need to do it."

"Well, let's go!"

They joined the tourists who were buying tickets and separated into a group led by a perky girl named Christine. As they entered the exhibit, Christine began her dissertation on the life and times of Salvador Dali. Reggie listened half-heartedly as she viewed the art, hoping to glean something from them. She had seen many Dali pieces and knew a cursory history of the man and his work. She had heard about the picture within the picture concept for which Dali is famous, but she had never seen it in such an alarming reality. This was what had drawn her here, and she recognized the carefully composed patterns as potential clues to the pictures in the hidden room.

"You haven't said a word. See anything interesting, I mean, other than some amazing work?"

Christine had stopped in front of a wall-size painting and was reviewing the unique design technique. Reggie and Laird were looking at a picture of a woman gazing out to sea in a highly visual and busy landscape.

"Now, if you read the name of the painting, it's Gala Overlooking the Mediterranean but back up twenty meters, and it's a portrait of Abraham Lincoln. So, what I'm going to ask all of you to do is just that. Back up twenty meters or sixty-five feet and see what you find."

Christine began shooing them backward en masse. When they came to rest, the sight before them was a larger-than-life portrait of Abraham

Lincoln, not viewable from a closer stance.

"That's incredible," said Laird, "and I'm embarrassed that I have never seen this before. I would never have imagined coming to an art museum for a murder investigation."

The sight mesmerized Reggie, and she was unable to answer him. She stared openly, but when the rest of the tour moved on, she did not follow. Laird was strolling along with the crowd but turned back to join her.

"What is it about this?"

"I don't know. It's so... compelling and captivating. I can't take my eyes off it. To think that someone can think this up. It's beautiful and frightening," she said.

"Frightening. That's a word that didn't come to mind, but everyone's different. Are we going to continue the tour or camp here?"

"Uh, we'll go on. Sorry. This is truly amazing. Alright, let's catch up, or they'll think we're planning a heist."

"Not to worry. I'll just flash my badge, and that'll be our get-out-of-jail-free card."

* * *

It was quite a bit later when Reggie and Laird emerged into the bright sunshine, mentally exhausted but better educated.

"I was very impressed, I must say," quipped Laird. "I didn't expect to enjoy it so much. But it is noon, and I need to get back to the office. Can you take it from here?"

"Oh sure, no problem."

"Okay, where can I drop you?"

"Oh, don't bother. I can walk; I feel like getting a little exercise."

"Mental or physical?" joked Laird.

"Both," she said decisively.

Reggie thanked him and promised to be in touch regarding arrangements for Dahlia's service. It was not the sort of thing Laird typically spent time on, but after the last tea room gathering, care had to be taken, and plans had to be exact. He would be on it, as would his men, with or without the knowledge of the others.

He trudged up the stairs, feeling bothered and restless. He had the familiar tingling of expectancy, the one he had when he was getting close. He threw his jacket on the chair, his wallet on the desk, and hit the intercom to Diane.

"No, sir, no messages. Expecting something important?"

"Maybe. I'll be in here, but when I go out, I'll give you a heads up."

Laird assumed the position for heavy mental activity, feet stretched across the desk and crossed uncomfortably, butt in the center of the cushion, body angle set for the perfect amount of oxygen to the brain. He let himself relax and saw a movie of events playing in his head. This was when the pieces floated into place, and the answers were presented orderly and meaningfully. He was straining over one particular thought when the intercom buzzed, and Diane's disjointed voice came through.

"Detective Laird? It's Mr. Elliott on the phone. Should I send it, or do you want to call him back?"

Laird toppled out of position and jumped on the intercom.

"No, no, I'll take it. Pass him through, please."

"Elliott! How's jolly old England?" he said, sounding anything but himself.

"It's merry old England to you, and it's full of surprises."

"What surprises?" asked Laird, hitching his chair and straightening to attention.

"Let's just say some pleasant surprises, but overall, an exciting, informative, emotional trip."

"Well, we knew it would be. Anything timely I need to know about."

"Our friend Mr. Cavanaugh has made a visit home."

The reference was not lost on Laird.

"A visit home? Sounds like I'm missing a piece of the puzzle."

"You're missing a few pieces, but what's more immediate is some information we need to track down. You need to bundle off to the hall of records and weed through the marriages, divorces, births, etc. You may also want to have another conversation with Mavis Hatfield. Seems she hasn't been totally forthcoming about the family. Also, check if there's any information on Sara Jane Brooks. She left for England in the 1940s. Dig around with some of the older characters there who might remember some of the local gossip. And round up Forrest Perkins. He's a squirrelly little toad who probably has the pulse of the entire city. I think all you need to do is give him the proper motivation."

"You mean like a warrant?"

"Whatever moves the man, Inspector."

"Alright, I'll get on all that. I was surfacing a few things myself. I'll be seeing Reggie later regarding Dahlia's service. You will be back for it. Sounds like a nice tribute. So, how are the folks? I know it's been a rough trip; I'm not trying to minimize it, Elliott."

Tucker was quiet before he resumed his end of the line.

"It's been unbelievable. I can't say more than that; I will later, but not just yet. Uh, how is Reggie?"

"You haven't been in touch with her?"

"No. There really hasn't been time. It's been very busy so far getting caught up on details and, uh, organizing. She alright?"

"That's some assistant you've got there. She's a real trooper, taking this whole thing and running with it. She's got an angle that may just break everything but she just doesn't have her arms around it yet. You should be proud of her, Elliott. She's got guts. No wonder she's your right-hand man."

"Sorry to have missed you. Things here are progressing. Will call again later. Cheers."

Her elation died away, and she crumpled the note and stuffed it in her pocket. She smiled at Traci, not feeling as chipper as she showed, and headed for the stairs.

"Miss Winter! Telephone! I can switch it to the house phone there if you'd like?"

"Yes, please, thanks, Traci."

Her heart pounded a few hard beats as she picked up the receiver.

"You didn't take your cell phone with you."

Reggie's heart slowed and sank.

"Are you my mother? You're not my mother, are you? You do seem to be acting a bit like her, but I don't think you're her."

"You're "she" is the correct usage, and I would have thought you would be in a better mood than when I last saw you. Doesn't look like you've made much progress," said Dulcy.

"Oh, sorry. It's just that I didn't sleep well, and you really need to stop correcting my grammar. Honestly, I do know how to use the English language, even though it may not seem like it.

"Start using it right, and I will. Hey, how was the museum?"

"You haven't talked to Laird?"

"No."

"It was amazing. I really enjoyed it, and I think he did as well. In fact, he mentioned something about being embarrassed at not having gone before."

"That at least establishes there are some human emotions under that overcoat."

"You know what? We need to start getting somewhere with all this. I don't know about you, but I feel like I'm so close to something, but all this other stuff is distracting us from accomplishing anything useful."

"Tucker didn't call, eh?"

"For your information, missy, he did."

"Well then, now we're getting somewhere. What did he say?"

"I missed the call. I was at the museum."

"Well, never mind. You need to come over here and get busy. I'm calling Laird and giving him that piece of foreign paper, and you need to look over these pictures again to see if you really learned something or if it was just a pleasant art outing."

"Fine. I don't have time for a bath, anyway."

"What?"

"Nothing," said Reggie, dropping the receiver and heading for the stairs.

* * *

Mavis was furious. She was actually pacing the floor – something a refined southern woman didn't do. What really was bothering her was Forrest Perkins. She would get him at some point for putting his nose into this. He went right off with that snooping girl whom she thought would help her while she had to put up with that vapid kitchen worker. Who knows what he told her! She thought for a minute. Maybe she had gone about this all wrong. No matter what happened, she needed him to continue as he had all these years, embarrassed and quiet. Now was not the time to tell the world their sordid history.

She was panicking, which wasn't like her, but only because that idiot had to call her and tell her that his documents, his documents, were missing from the English records hall. What a fool. She should never have sent him to do such an important job. If these people started piecing this together, they'd be on her doorstep before she could come up with a story. And he would be nowhere to be found. How did Mazie put up with him all those years? She really was a blind little sycophant. All those "business" trips. She congratulated herself again on what she had escaped.

She began to calm down, but only to give way to murderous thoughts. What if Cord conveniently didn't return from England? She wasn't sure how she'd pull that off, but if you had the means, you could fix anything.

She had to think rationally. Could she still salvage this? She needed to pull herself together and make a plan where she relied only on herself. Whatever happened to the others, she would come out okay.

She took a deep breath, closed her eyes, and turned to the fireplace. She picked up the poker and examined its end. That should do it. She grasped it firmly, heading towards the bedroom. As she reached the entrance, a slight sound from behind caught her attention. Did she hear something on the stairs? No, just the mice, probably.

She continued, poker still in hand, when again she heard a slight noise from behind, then nothing more.

* * *

"Miss Hatfield! Miss Hatfield! Can you hear me? Rivers, call a bus. Now!"

"No, no. I'm alright. Just a little dizzy."

She was trying to sit as the room swayed before her.

"You've got a nasty bump on the back of your head. Just lie back and try not to move. Did you see who did this to you?"

"I... I don't know. I'm not sure why I was here..."

She suddenly remembered and swooned, falling back against Detective Laird.

"Rivers! Did you make that call?"

"They're on their way, sir."

"Just relax, Miss Hatfield. Don't move. We're not sure of your injuries."

Mavis gave in, feeling the pain pulsate in her head. With that pain came another sensation: fear. Who really did this? She hadn't seen anyone. Through her haze, she tried to remember what she had been doing before she passed out. It was fuzzy, but she was headed somewhere. She peered through her lashes at her surroundings. Things were blurry and furry, and while she was scoping the area, her eyes fell on the bedroom floor, bringing back why she had been going that way.

"Get on the radio and find out where they are, Rivers."

"No need, sir. They're here."

To Mavis, it was like watching a play. It was almost amusing; the same nice young men who had been on the dais the day Dahlia died. She couldn't help herself, but she was smiling and even chuckling at the absurdness of her thoughts. The conflict of pain and dizziness caused her to hiccup, which startled Laird and sent him barking orders again.

"What's the holdup? Get her moving, now!"

As they hitched up the gurney, she reached out and squeezed his hand. She left him with a faint, sweet smile as they rolled her away. He nodded, maintaining an unreadable expression until she was out of sight. He stood motionless, then heaved a heavy sigh. He was tired, disheartened, and angry. And now he was again in a room that must be cordoned off and examined. He could only hope that this time, there would be something, even a minimal mistake. They had so little to go on everywhere else. He needed a break, even a small one.

He was frustrated that just as he had the opportunity to grill her, she managed almost to get herself killed right under his nose. He couldn't decide if he was angry over the lost opportunity or disgusted at being so callous over the attempted murder of the old lady. He pulled out his handkerchief and picked up the poker.

"Rivers!"

"Yes, sir."

"Get this to the lab," he said, pulling out his phone.

"Get me forensics. I need them at 112 S 3rd St. I'll be here till they arrive."

"Then I have something I have to do," he thought.

* * *

Chapter 33

Oswald Cobblepot/Penguin: I believe the word you're looking for is: Ahhhhhhhh!
-Batman Returns, 1992

Reggie trotted towards the door with instructions to Traci that if Tucker called again, she was to tell him she had gone to the tea room. She turned the corner of Third St. sighting Sea Gables about the same time her stomach growled. She had not eaten since breakfast.

She could smell the day's special as she slipped through the kitchen door. The girls were winding down from lunch, and she grabbed a roll from a basket on the island as she went to find Dulcy. She spied her in Dahlia's office, leafing through something.

"What's up?"

"Oh, hey. I was just looking through Dahlia's datebook. I found it while I was looking for something else. I'm surprised our Detective Laird didn't make off with this. It's interesting reading, really. I never bothered much with what she did on her own time, but now I'm wondering what some of these appointments were and if they could tell us something."

"Have you talked to Laird?"

"No, I have not."

"I'm sure he's on his way here. Well, after he went to his office, but I'm betting he's coming here next."

Dulcy had not looked up from the datebook but was engrossed in an entry that Reggie could only partially see.

"Find something good?"

"I don't know. It's dated the day before she died. It's with Hammond. Interesting."

"Why? Who is that?"

"Police commissioner. Wonder what that was about?"

"Maybe for her party. Maybe she went to him to monitor things during the opening."

"I think she had been to see him before when all this stuff started happening. They came over here once, but it didn't amount to much. They just sort of looked around the place and told her to keep in touch."

"Maybe she did."

Dulcy shut the book and gave Reggie a squinty stare.

"Do you recall any police here that day? I mean, other than the crew who came after... well... later in the day?"

"No, but I wasn't looking for any. I'm not sure I'm the person to ask, anyway. I barely know people here, and I was at the hospital for most of the time. Dahlia said nothing about the police, but I think we can safely say that she said little about a lot of things that day."

"Something about this bothers me," said Dulcy. "You know, I think I'm just looking too hard for something that isn't there. Here," she said, handing the book to Reggie and heading for the door, "maybe you can make something of this."

Reggie took the book and started scanning the pages. She noted several dates, times, and scribblings, but they held no meaning, and she laid the book back on the desk. As she did so, she saw a paper peeking out from under the phone. It was a list of ingredients, and she eyed it more closely to see if she recognized the recipe. On closer scrutiny, they appeared to be medical terms, and she wondered if Dahlia had been hiding some medical condition. Reggie pulled it from under the phone when the thing rang, startling her to the point of lightheadedness.

She waited to see if someone would pick it up from the front when it stopped abruptly, then patted her fluttering heart and went in search of Dulcy. She found her in the foyer on the phone, open-mouthed, eyes wide and staring, listening intently. Reggie finally sat down in the hall seat, waiting for the end of the conversation.

Dulcy hung up, staring at Reggie and shaking her head. Reggie's heart was sinking, wondering what else could be happening.

"I heard from John."

Reggie noted the softening in Dulcy's voice and wondered what was going on between the two.

"He said that, uh, he was just checking out a hunch he had. He went to see Mavis, and when he got there, he found her on the floor, out cold, not sure if she was alive or dead. She came around, and they took her to the hospital. He now has another crime scene and no leads. He's not a happy man."

"Whoa. Wasn't expecting that one."

"Nope. Me neither. That's not all, Reggie, there's more. They have an APB out on Cord Cavanaugh. I had forgotten about him, but they didn't. He didn't check in, and nothing turned up where they'd looked. He is officially a person of interest in pretty much everything."

"Okay. Well, now what?"

"John said to keep working on the pictures, and he'll be here when he can."

"Okay. At least it's something to do."

Dulcy caught her eye, and, taking her cue, Reggie marched up the stairs to the tunnel entrance. Trying the door, she found it locked. She was aggravated, feeling unproductive, disconnected, and ineffective. Her high from the art museum was wearing off; the effect had been transitory, and she could see it for what it had been. Like Dulcy, she was searching for something that wasn't there, and she was deflated and cranky.

She leaned up against the wall, waiting for the bathroom to clear. As if on cue, the door popped open, and a large woman wearing unflattering shorts, a sun-scorched hairdo, and frighteningly pink lipstick bumped her way out of the opening.

"Oh, sorry, I didn't know anyone was waiting. Reminds me of my grandmother's bathroom," she said, pointing over her shoulder. "Isn't it funny how a certain look and smell can take you right back to another place and time?"

Reggie stared at her speechlessly. She was right. What she was missing had everything to do with the senses. She was missing something, and it all started with the voice in the tea room just inches from where she was standing now. She was on the wrong path. She smiled at the woman and bolted through the bathroom door to the closet. The woman on the landing never realized her impact, only figuring that the poor girl in the powder room desperately needed a visit to her local urologist.

* * *

Tucker stared at Dahlia and Landry.

"Did I tell you how good it is to see you?"

"No, well, yes, actually you did."

Tucker sighed, rising to his feet.

"What is it?"

"We need to finish our arrangements and get out," said Dahlia.

"What's happened?"

"I knew we needed to settle our plans and get out of here, but now we really have to scoot," she finished, raising her eyebrows.

Tucker gazed steadily at Dahlia, waiting for the punch line.

"Mum and Dad, and your parents, love, are at the moment, cutting their lodge stay short because of a pipe bursting event. They'll be leaving first thing in the morning. Luckily, it was in the other part of the lodge, and they have enough water to make do till morning, but they don't want to be sitting amongst the workers for the duration."

"That speeds things up a bit. I suggest we get busy," he said, clapping Landry on the back.

Jennings brought them their meal in the conservatory. They had been working on their version of Dahlia's service most of the day and discussing the Peters/Cavanaugh connection.

"This is quite a setup. Funny how different our memorial service plans are from what I'm sure Reggie is doing. This is going to cause quite a commotion. Hammond will have to have his men positioned everywhere to make sure he doesn't get away," said Tucker.

"Or kill anyone," said Landry.

They had been so busy that none of them realized how hungry they were until Jennings appeared with a cart loaded with Shepherd's pie, whitefish, and a variety of veggie dishes and desserts. They were finishing the last bits when Tucker's phone rang, showing John Laird's number.

"Aw, you miss me, mate. That's sweet," quipped Tucker.

A scowl and a grimace replaced the smile on Tucker's face. He was saying very little, letting Laird control the conversation. He agreed to forward his travel arrangements and rang off. Dahlia and Landry waited for Tucker's response.

"Well, we may now know where Peters is. That was Laird. Apparently, he was following up on something I asked about and went round to Mavis Hatfield's home. He found her lying on the floor, out cold, thinking at first

361

she was dead. She had a fire poker next to her and a nasty knock on the back of her skull. Lucky to be alive from the sound of things. Over more, and we wouldn't learn anything from her, including what she's been up to recently and over the past four years."

"Shouldn't you be able to answer that, Landry? After all, you've been coming here looking into the family history. Surely there's something you can tell us about how we got to this point?"

"Ladies! I hate to break this up, but we need to move on," said Dahlia. "We need to make flight arrangements and put this plan before Commissioner Hammond. He has to approve it, or I'm going to stay deceased till further notice. Tucker, I think it might be time for you to bring Laird in now. He'll need to have an extra eye on things. I still don't want the others brought in on it, especially if Mavis Hatfield's been targeted. I was thinking she had something to do with this. Now, I'm not so sure. If we do anything about her at all, I think Tucker should call Reggie and get her to make a hospital visit. I think they've taken a shine to each other, and you said she had asked you for help when you first got to the tea room. Send Reggie in to do a little nonchalant nosing about. She can pull that off. Make her leave Dulcy behind. She's not got the patience for the indirect approach."

"I also think we need to enlist Perkins," she continued. "They've painted a rather dim picture of our historian, but from what I've seen from his brown bag lunches, he's managed to overcome his less-than-stellar past. I would say he has quite a following, almost like a septuagenarian rock star."

"I wouldn't go that far, Dahlia," said Landry. "He's made a respectable showing for himself, but I don't see any ladies falling over themselves to capture his attention. Or anything else he might have at this point."

"That may be true, but how do we know he hasn't masterminded the whole thing?"

"Perkins?!" said Landry and Dahlia together.

"No, not a chance. He hasn't got a clue on a good day, much less be bright enough to solve something no one else has," remarked Landry.

"Never say never," answered Tucker.

"Right. Is everyone clear on what they're to be doing at this thing?" asked Dahlia.

Landry had the start of a sketch going when Tucker's phone rang again. He raised his brow but hit the send button, a slight smile smearing his features.

"Hello, Mum. How are you?" he winked at Dahlia, listening intently.

"Yes, love. I am here. I wanted to surprise you. How did you find out? Ah, yes, Myra would definitely let you know, wouldn't she? Uh, what exactly did she say?"

Tucker grabbed a pen and paper and scribbled signals to Dahlia and Landry as the pips from the earpiece continued.

Can't wait to see me. *Driving in the morning. Meet at Porter's for breakfast.*

Porters send love.

Dahlia blew a kiss toward the phone, waving to her invisible parents. Tucker laid the phone down, rubbing his forehead lazily.

"I was hoping to be out of here in the morning. Now I'll have to make a show and then hopefully leave as soon as possible. My Mum, she loves a good surprise, that one. I reckon we'll have to delay the flight for a few hours."

"She's not going to let you run off the second they get home. You're going to have to do better than that, darling."

"Well, I'll reroute the flight in a second, but I really need to reach Reg. She's probably furious with me. I need to smooth this over and get her to Mavis. What time is it there, Dahl?"

"Let's see, 2 p.m. Probably at lunch. And yes, I think an apology..."

"What was that?" asked Tucker, stiffening and listening intently to something in the bowels of the house."

It seemed to gain in volume and was getting closer as they strained to identify it.

"For a quiet country house, this place is anything but," said Landry.

"It's Jennings," said Dahlia. "What's he on about now?"

Loudly and more plainly, they could indeed hear Jennings yelling through the house, making noises like a truck moving through a small space.

"Yes, ma'am. Drinks in the conservatory right away then!" he screamed, throwing open the doors and banging them against the walls.

The four of them stared in horror until Jennings yelled into the empty hallway.

"It's warm in the conservatory, ma'am. Wouldn't you rather take your drinks in the study? Much more comfortable, if I might suggest?"

Dahlia did not wait. She dove from her chair, curling around a pot of hydrangeas and coming to rest with her back to the window and her feet tangled in ivy. Landry stared, turning in time to see Mrs. Elliott marching into the conservatory, heading straight for the table. Inches away lay a prone Dahlia, exposed to all if they looked in the right direction.

Tucker hitched his chair around to hide her, waving at his mother and smiling as though not a care in the world. Landry said a prayer and closed his eyes as Alene Elliott swooped down on Tucker, arms wide and kisses flowing.

"Surprise! We're back!" she cried as she hugged him through a flood of tears, then reeled around back the way she had come, yelling for Mr. Elliott and the Porters.

Dahlia tugged at Tucker's pant leg from around the hydrangea bush.

"Is this published somewhere? So much for a solitary retreat. I may as well have booked in at the tube station. I'll get our flights and see you at Heathrow or at home."

She scrambled out the French doors, tugging the ivy from her feet. She slithered through the patio until she reached the gate unseen.

"Psst! Psst! Miss Dahlia!"

She wheeled around to see Jennings hanging out the kitchen door. He threw her a ring of keys, which she nabbed easily.

"The Elliott's car is parked near the east entrance for you. Leave the rest to me, Miss," said Jennings, vanishing from the door.

Dahlia felt like a felon. What could she put on her resume so far? Faked death, fleeing the country, breaking, auto theft, assumed identity, false passport. The list made her head hurt as she backtracked through the garden to the car. She had to crawl back under the conservatory windows where she could hear the Elliott's and the Porter's reunion with Tucker and the introduction of Dr. Landry, the esteemed doctor from the States. Feeling like an escaped convict, she took one last look, bolted across the lawn, and jumped in the car. She eased it through the gate, keeping one eye on the rear-view mirror, but all seemed calm. She hit the gas toward town, planning her strategy with each kilometer.

"Darling, it's so nice to see you. I hope we didn't frighten you by showing up like this. We thought it would be a fun surprise. Oh, dear, you look so tired. How are you bearing up, love?"

"Well, Mum, amazingly enough, I'm alright for now. Trying to keep busy. There were some work issues needing my attention, which gave me a good diversion and a nice visit with you. It's tough, but also very surprising," he said, choking up a bit.

"Surprising? I'm not sure I follow."

"Oh, well, there is a tremendous outpouring for Dahlia, and it's comforting to see how many are going to such great lengths to give her the best sendoff you could imagine. Gives one hope for humanity and all, you know," he said reverently.

Landry bowed his head and shut his eyes, afraid to look at Tucker through such a touching performance. Mrs. Elliott took it as a sign of grief and patted him gently on the shoulder.

"We all share your pain, Doctor," she said, sniffing quietly. "And that is why we plan to accompany you back stateside for the ceremony. We wouldn't miss it, would we, Delia?"

Delia Porter was speechless, as was Mr. Porter.

"I know it's short notice, and we said we'd wait till she was home, but you've convinced me, Tucker, that we must be present to honor her in the place she grew to love. I see how important it is," she said, beaming at the open mouths surrounding her.

"Yes, there's no one to make you feel the emotion of a moment like Tucker," said Landry sourly.

"Oh, that reminds me," said Mrs. Elliott. "I have something special to show you at the ceremony. Oh, Jennings, there you are. I need your help. Can you spare me a moment?"

"Yes, Ma'am, my pleasure."

"Would you please run to the car and bring me my case? The small valise with my initials. I think it's in the boot."

Jennings' pleasant countenance froze for a split second before he nodded and gracefully exited. He closed the wide doors with a devout smile. Laughter and tears continued from within, fading as he rounded the corner and leaned against the nearest wall. He reviewed his speech and marched out the front doors. He was going to put on a show just in case anyone was watching.

He strode to the drive, walked haltingly in one direction, then in the other. He walked further down the drive to the road, where he gazed in one direction and then in the other. He scratched his head lightly, placed hands on hips, and reviewed the expanse of house and grounds. He dropped his head, staring at the asphalt, then marched back into the house.

He chuckled as he adjusted his tie and headed to the conservatory for his next performance. He knocked politely and stood at attention before the families.

"Oh, Jennings, did you find my case?"

"I am sorry to inform you, Madam, that I did not find the case."

"Well, I know I put it in the car when we left, and I didn't take it out at the lodge, so..."

"I am also sorry to inform you, Madam, that besides not finding the valise, I also did not find any other property with which you came, including the car. It appears to have been stolen, as witnessed by Jacobs, who was bicycling by the time the vehicle departed through the gates toward East Sussex. I am sorry, Madam," emphasized Jennings with a slight bow of his head while inwardly accepting his award for best-supporting actor in a comedy.

* * *

Chapter 34

Clouseau: I believe everything, and I believe nothing. I suspect everyone, and I suspect no one.
-A Shot in the Dark, 1964

Reggie flew down to the hidden room as fast as she dared. It was a clammy, dark, and narrow strip, and the thought of what might be just out of her torch scope made her skin crawl. She stopped short of the fireplace, shining her light on the dusty bricks once more, hoping to spy something for a minute.

She ran her fingers over the rough surface, looking for signs of a recent intrusion, then turned to go when a sharp glint caught her eye. She was reminded of the metal fragment on the foyer floor the night of the cocktail party. She wondered if this had been there all along or if it was new since their previous visit.

She examined it closely in the torch glare. It was very similar to the piece she already had or the piece she had given to Tucker, she thought with disappointment. She could not compare the two until he returned. She pocketed it and continued on with one swift glance back at the musty bricks.

The door popped open with ease and once more she was gazing at the circle of pictures. She wished they could talk and tell her what puzzle piece was missing. She marched up to the nearest one, staring hard into the canvas. Her eyes finally glazed over, and she backed off to a more intermediate distance. She moved back and forth, hoping to achieve a rhythm or a pattern, but only managed a lilting waltz that would have been enjoyable had she had a partner.

She revolved in a slow circle, letting her eyes pass from one to the next. She set the flashlight in the middle of the desk and let the beam spread like a coating over the crooked ceiling. The light spilled down over the walls, then faded into nothing around the pictures.

The concept intrigued her, and she pushed the opposite door open and headed to the B&B, where she grabbed a kerosene lantern and retraced her steps. She lit the wick, turning the key to increase the beam. The room was filled with soft firelight, and she could see why Mr. Hatfield would have enjoyed the peaceful surroundings. The light flickered and danced over the private exhibit. Reggie backed up a bit, then a bit more, until she was standing just outside the doorway.

She closed her eyes and let the images burn on her retinas, just as she had done at the Dali Museum. When she opened them, she imagined she had seen another photo in the center etching. She stepped forward, then back, and focused her eyes again, not on the image itself, but its periphery. She was amazed at what she saw. Not only was there a main image but there was also a second one. It was crude, not the craftsmanship of Dali, but there nonetheless in its rough elements.

As she was picking out the image, she heard footsteps behind her, and Dulcy appeared behind a torch glow.

"Hey."

"Hey."

"What are you doing? Did you find something?"

"Maybe. Let's see if you see what I see. Stand where I am, and I'll take your spot. I want to see if you can make out what I just did."

"What am I looking for?"

"I'm not going to say. I want to see if you pick it out for yourself."

"Okay, so you were right here?"

"A bit over this way," said Reggie, sliding Dulcy to the right and centering her just off the threshold.

Reggie backed up as well and was gratified to hear a sharp gasp.

"Oh, my gosh! Is that what I think it is?"

"I don't know. What do you see?"

"Well, I'm not sure, but I'd swear it's a picture of Hitler!"

* * *

They took turns standing at various spots, picking out elements that created secondary images. It wasn't until they wandered back through the tunnel that Dulcy remembered to tell Reggie to call Tucker.

"How long ago did he call?" moaned Reggie.

"Only about twenty minutes. You can probably still get him."

Reggie went into Dahlia's office and dialed Tucker's phone. It rang, then went to voicemail. Disappointed, she replaced the receiver, staring at the jumbles of paperwork scattered in organized piles. Dulcy wandered in and sat on the chaise.

"No luck?"

"No. Oh well, I'll get him tomorrow. And by the way, I found something on the floor."

She reached into her pocket, pulled out the new metal fragment, and handed it to Dulcy.

"This looks just like..."

"Yeah, the one I found before. I'm sure they go together, but Tucker has the other one, so we won't know till he gets back."

They sat in silence, each processing what they had seen.

"What do you make of all that?" asked Dulcy, pointing down at the floor.

"Well, they paint a pretty brutal scene of the world at that time. I think it was Mr. Hatfield's way of expressing how he felt about the wars. They're really quite good, actually. Crude, but good."

"Yes, but what does it have to do with anything?"

"Nothing, maybe everything. I don't have a clue," said Reggie tiredly.

"What's the detective up to?"

"No idea. I should probably call him and get an update. Then I've got to go. I'm exhausted."

"Well, let me know if you find out anything important. I'm going back to the Plaza."

"I was thinking of going out to the B&B and just crashing there."

"Laird will have your butt if he finds that out. You won't get in anyway, not with Sgt. What's-His-Face on duty."

"I will if I use the tunnel."

The girls parted ways, with Dulcy heading to the B&B and Reggie off to the Plaza. Dulcy moved briskly through the tunnel, emerging in the closet. The whole place gave her the creeps, even though it was just as dark in the daylight.

She picked her way through the buckets and mops, cracked the door to the kitchenette, and slipped out to the stairs. She could see the sergeant standing out front under the dim porch light. She tiptoed along the corridor to the back of the inn, choosing a small room on the first floor not far from the scene of Mazie Cavanaugh's abrupt exit. She slipped in and turned on the bedside lamp, throwing the room into a soft, orange glow.

She punched Laird's number and waited through the rings, expecting to hear the familiar voicemail message. She was pleasantly surprised when an actual voice answered.

"Well, hello there. Fancy meeting you here."

"Wow, that's really clear. You sound like you're..."

She had the strange sensation of being the fly caught in the spider's web. She turned slowly and standing in the doorway was the man himself, dropping his phone in his pocket.

"Oooh, hey, how are you? Yeah, it's funny meeting like this. Thought you were working on what happened to Mavis. What are you doing here? Any news? Have you talked to Tucker, by the way? You know, I think..."

"Doing a little late-night investigating or something else, maybe?"

Dulcy felt a cold shiver dive down her spine. She felt exposed and also a bit threatened. She didn't like his tone, as straightforward and soft as it seemed. She also didn't like the look on his face. She had the sudden impulse to run. What was he accusing her of?

"You don't think I..."

"No, I don't, but I had to know. I have to suspect everyone, no matter how I feel about them."

And suddenly, John Laird was back, but it had been an eerie departure. He had chilled her to her toes, making her very uncomfortable. The suggestion of mistrust was ebbing, but her uneasiness lingered, and she found it difficult to move. She finally backed up and sat on the edge of the bed. Realizing his words, she folded her hands in her lap and gazed up at the detective adoringly.

"Oh, you caught that, did you?"

"You threw it out. It was a bit hard to miss. Or am I jumping to conclusions?"

Laird stared at her with an appraising look. Dulcy felt like a perp in front of the local copper. He was just a man trying to do a job, and she had stepped out of bounds into his murder scene.

"I scared you, didn't I?"

"Yes. Very much. I didn't like it, you know."

"No, I would think not."

Before she could explain further, he had crossed the room, enveloping her in his arms, holding her close to him. He kissed her gently on the forehead and held her even closer.

"I can't let you stay here."

"I know."

Grasping her hand, he led her from the room, switching off the light as he went.

"Goodnight, Sergeant."

"Goodnight, sir," said Sgt. Rivers as he watched them walk down the sidewalk.

He smiled, then frowned and opened the door covering the hall in several steps. He checked the doors, the steps, and the kitchenette.

"Odd," he thought. "Where did she come from?"

* * *

Reggie checked the front desk for messages from Tucker.

"Nothing, Miss," said the night attendant.

Reggie gave the boy a slight nod and hit the elevator button. As she waited, she thought about Mavis. Poor thing, alone in a hospital, her only family apparently on the run and no longer concerned with her. She felt guilty waiting for the lift to her comfy bed. She checked her watch. Eight o'clock. They wouldn't let her in at this hour anyway. Still, she felt unsettled and could tell she would not end up doing what she wanted, which was to go to her room, settle in for the evening, and rest and relax. She would go to the hospital and get to see Mavis, visiting hours or not. Damn, how she hated her second self. It would probably be what Tucker would tell her to do. She watched the numbers above the doors. They weren't moving. The longer she stood there, the more she resolved not to take the elevator. She looked away, knowing that the next time she saw the numbers if the floors still hadn't moved, she would walk away and head for the hospital.

She sneaked a peek up, cursing as the numbers remained stationary. She hitched her purse over her shoulder and turned to go. People were watching her. How long had she been there, and how much had she said out loud?

"Damn, I hate it when I talk to myself and others can hear."

She crossed the lobby, stopping short before bolting through the entrance.

"I suppose it's the same hospital where Dahlia went," she thought with a sharp, sad feeling.

She charged through the doors, bumping shoulders with a tall man who grabbed her elbow to keep her from reeling.

"Very sorry," he said, righting her.

Reggie looked up and laughed. Still holding her arm was John Laird, with Dulcy firmly attached to his other.

"What are you two up to?" she said, smirking, knowing Dulcy had been nabbed at the B&B.

"Uh, having a nightcap after all, and you?"

"Oh, just running out for a few essentials. Nothing to be concerned about."

"Well, you're welcome to join us if you'd like," said Dulcy, winking.

"I will definitely think about that, thank you," she said, exiting with increasing speed. "By-ee!"

"That was close," she thought.

* * *

Chapter 35

Highway Patrol Officer: Is anything wrong?
Marion Crane: Of course not. Am I acting as if there's something wrong?
Highway Patrol Officer: Frankly, yes.
-Psycho, 1960

Tucker knew what was coming but still wasn't prepared for what came out of his mother's mouth. Fortunately, at that moment, Jennings bumped through the door with the special-order scotch.

"Oh, thank you, Jennings; just what I needed," said Tucker, taking a long drought, at which point he noticed the rest of the room doing the same.

Mrs. Porter finished her drink in one gulp while Mr. Porter slung his back and reached for the bottle. His mother was gulping hers in a random, desultory fashion while his father finished his and was chewing away at the ice like a beaver on a log. Constable Downs reached for a glass, poured a healthy measure of bourbon, and threw it back. Landry was rubbing his forehead as if warding off a headache.

"Odd," thought Tucker, "sort of like Pavlov's dogs."

"Don't you have anything to say, Tucker?" wheezed his mother.

"Mrs. Benson drinks," spat Tucker, whereupon all occupants stared into their glasses and then thumped them on the table.

"Tucker!" squealed his mother.

"Lord, mother, everyone knows it, has for years. What the devil do you think she was doing at Waterson's? Probably picking up the week's supply. I think you've all let this get completely out of hand. You should be ashamed of yourselves for running amok on the word of a well-meaning but misguided individual. She is a busybody of the first order, shamelessly grasping for attention. I can see my visit here was premature and unwise. I have obviously upset you all, which was never my intention. Well, I think the only solution is to head back to the colonies. My business is finished, and I'm needed for the service. I'll be leaving first thing in the morning. No, don't try to stop me. I think this is best. Jennings!"

"Yes, sir!"

"Please help me with the packing in my room. Some of my things will need attention. Good night, all. Please think hard about what just happened here," he said as he turned on his heel and marched out of the study with Jennings in tow.

"What did happen here?" bleated the confused and slightly tipsy Constable Downs.

"That was brilliant, sir!" said Jennings with admiration. "Well done. How did you ever think of it?"

"Jennings, she drinks."

"Oh, I thought just her staff drank, sir."

"No, no, it's the lot of them. It's one big, soused household. Even Mr. Benson drinks, which is probably because of Mrs. Benson, but who knows? At the moment, I'm not terribly concerned. At some point, Mrs. Porter will have to fix it, but I'm sure you'll be able to help in your indelible way. I know one thing: I didn't have to explain where I was, figure out a lie to cover the car, and now I can leave and get back to help Reggie. I must say, it worked out beautifully, even if I do feel like a heel of the lowest class."

"There is one thing, sir," reminded Jennings. "The car. What shall we do about the car?"

"Why nothing. That's the beauty of it. I'll call a hired car for the airport, and you can go with me and bring back the Mercedes. Just say you went into town for something. Since the first missing car is already back in the garage, we should be all caught up on vehicles. Poor Mrs. Benson turns out to be the unfortunate boozing misfit we've painted her. It's not pretty, but it's functional. I shall most certainly be considered at the gates of hell for this one."

"Have you your tickets, sir?"

"Lord, no. I haven't called the airline, and I have to call Laird yet. And Reggie is expecting me to phone again. I'm afraid I have backed myself into a corner."

"Not to worry, sir. Allow me. I'll make all the necessary arrangements, and you will handle your phone calls."

"Oh, damn."

"What is it, sir?"

"Landry, poor sot. I have hung him out to dry. Jennings, do me the favor of booking him as well. Let him enjoy the Porter hospitality for a bit longer, then put him on the next flight out. Give me long enough to get back there and get things settled.

"Right, sir, consider it done," said Jennings as he saluted Tucker and backed out of the doorway.

Tucker was pondering his decisions when there was a slight rap at the door.

"Tucker? May I come in? It's mother."

"Yes, Mum."

"Tucker, darling, I'm sorry. It's all been just too much, you know. But when he called and said Dahlia had been seen, well, I think maybe we all just really wanted it to be so. Please don't leave on our account."

"No, love," said Tucker gently. "I'm not leaving on your account. I really do need to go back to the tea room. I have left Reggie in a rather precarious position. I feel guilty about leaving her to manage on her own."

"You know, Tucker, maybe you should take a good look at your lovely assistant. I mean, really take a look at her. I think you'll find something exciting there, but that's just me. I'll leave you to manage that on your own."

She left Tucker standing in the middle of his room, staring after her. She arranged for this woman to be his assistant. Now, he was beginning to wonder what she thought he needed assistance with. He took stock of what he had to pack. He pulled up Laird's number, but before the call could connect, there was another knock at the door.

"Come," he said impatiently, hitting the end button.

The door opened a crack, and Delia Porter poked her head through.

"Busy?"

"No, never too busy for you. Come in."

She pushed the door wide and glided gracefully through. She scanned the room and folded her arms across her chest as if suddenly chilled.

"Well, I must say, that was inspiring. Brave and impertinent, but inspiring. I guess we'll see you at the tea room?"

"Yes, absolutely. I'll call and fill you all in on the details. By then, you should have your flights fixed, and we'll get you rooms near us since there still isn't anyone booking into the B&B that I'm aware of."

"I appreciate it, Tucker. We'll talk later, love," she said, edging back out the door. "By the way, darling, where did the car end up?"

"In the garage," grinned Tucker.

"Oh, for the love of God," she said and was gone.

Tucker was waiting for Laird's impatient baritone but had to settle for voicemail. He needed this handled. He dialed Commissioner Hammond's number and had a quick but efficient conversation.

As he searched for Reggie's number, there was a loud banging at the door, followed by Landry's plaintive snarl on the other side.

"This place is busier than a tube station," he muttered.

Tucker flung open the door, preparing to take charge of Landry before the tirade could start. He shoved him across the threshold and threw the door shut.

"Listen, Landry, I know this is a bit much, but you'll just have to work with me. I've got Jennings booking flights, and I'm calling Laird to handle Dahlia once she lands. I'm getting out early, and you'll be following. You need to get back there and get ready."

Landry stared at Tucker, who was waiting for an explosion, but none came. The two men stared at each other, each daring the other to speak first. Landry gave a curt nod and soundlessly swept out of the room.

"This place is positively stark. I've got to get the hell out of here."

***

"Can you tell me what room Miss Mavis Hatfield is in?"

"Hmmm. She's in 301, but she's not allowed visitors. I'm sorry, but she's under guard till further notice."

"Um, yes, and I'm actually working this case with Detective Laird. I'm here to question her about the incident. I'm Regina Winter."

"You are not on the list, Miss Winter," said the nurse, staring through Reggie.

"No, I wouldn't be. I'm new."

"Well, I can't let you in without approval from the detective. Sorry, Miss."

"Thank you, I'll take care of it," and Reggie nodded and headed for the door.

A blast of hot night air slapped her face as she stepped to the curb, the same curb Tucker held her back from when a speeding car nearly clipped her. She gazed at the stars faded by the glaring hospital lights and wondered what Dahlia would have thought of all this. Reggie faced the building and stopped, looking for a lesser-profile entrance. Her gaze landed on a man in a cook's uniform opening a door, lighting a cigarette, and propping the door open with his foot. He let it go and wandered down the drive. Reggie reached for the handle and pulled and was amazed when it opened. She smiled brightly at the staff as she marched through the kitchen and into the main hospital. She hit the number three button, watching the floors light up and feeling the elevator jolt as it came to rest. She followed the arrows to 301, stopping at the nurse's station and eyeing the guard at Mavis's door. She recognized him as one of Laird's men and approached him with her best smile.

"Hello! How are you? Awful about all this, isn't it? First Dahlia, then poor Mavis's sister, and now Mavis. Detective Laird asked me to come down and check on her to see if she needed anything. Poor old thing, all alone in this place. Do you want to come in with me or are you okay here?"

The young man eyed her sharply, hit a button on his cell phone, and listened. He hit end and stuffed it back in his pocket.

"Go ahead, I'll be here."

"Thank you, Ronald," she said, glimpsing his name badge.

She poked her head around the door to see Mavis sleeping soundly, looking small and fragile in the large, white bed. She stepped closer and peered at the old lady's face. She was scanning the surrounding equipment when a slight sound made her turn back.

"What are you doing here at such an hour, dear?"

"I was worried about you. I heard what happened, Miss Hatfield. Who did this to you?"

Mavis flattened back into the pillows and sighed.

"I have no idea. I was... thinking about something. I went to my bedroom... I was almost there... I heard a sound. It was behind me... and then... nothing. I can't remember anything."

"What were you thinking about?"

She wasn't completely sure, but there was something on Mavis's face. It was a split second of panic, then a wall. She decided to take a shot in the dark.

"It's alright, Miss Hatfield. You just need to rest. I know the police are taking good care of things. They're going through your house as we speak with a fine-tooth comb."

"Oh, my dear, I hate for them to go to all that trouble. I probably just fell and hit my head. I haven't been feeling all that well lately. They really don't have to make a fuss."

"Well, Miss Hatfield, you do want them to make sure it's safe, don't you? What if you didn't just fall? They really have to get to the bottom of it. Plus, they found that poker beside you. Why else would it be next to you if someone hadn't been there?"

Mavis Hatfield was visibly agitated. She shakily tried to prop herself up as Reggie watched quietly.

"I do not think it is necessary for you all to waste precious time with my misfortunes. There can't be anything there that can help you with these murders."

Reggie was surprised. Who said anything about murders?

"Well, Miss Hatfield, we think you may be in danger because of something you know. Someone came here tonight to stop you from talking. What is it they think you can tell?"

"I wouldn't know, dear. I have no idea what someone would want with me. I have nothing and no one now and am of no use to anyone," she said, dabbing her eyes with a dainty handkerchief.

Reggie noticed there didn't seem to be any tears behind the hanky, and she gazed steadily into Mavis's eyes.

"Miss Hatfield, where did Cord go? No one can find him, and he's not supposed to leave the area."

She seemed guilty, or Reggie was imagining things. What else could she ask her?

"I have no idea where he is, nor do I wish to know. He is a horrible man and I never want to lay eyes on him again. I know he killed my Mazie!" she cried, bursting into heart-wrenching sobs.

Reggie watched carefully and saw that, this time, there were tears but also an insincerity that made Reggie feel as though she was watching a carefully constructed play. She felt like she was in the presence of an actress who was calculating every piece of dialogue and every gesture.

"I'm so sorry, Miss Hatfield. I did not mean to upset you. Would you rather

I left you alone?"

"Yes, maybe that's best. I'm sorry, dear. Maybe we can talk tomorrow if you wouldn't mind coming back? I just need to rest."

"Of course. I think Tucker might be back tomorrow, anyway. He was so worried when he heard about your accident. Detective Laird has been keeping him up to date while he's been in England."

Reggie had not been purposefully deceitful but was rewarded with a most interesting reaction. Mavis had been leaning back in her pillows, closing her eyes and almost purring. She now turned cold, hateful eyes on Reggie, her lips set in a hard, cruel line, teeth grinding. What had been a serene and peaceful closing to their interview turned wary and accusatory. To Reggie, the air seemed palpable with distrust and malice.

"What's wrong?" asked Reggie innocently.

"Nothing, dear. I was not aware that Mr. Elliott had gone to England. Is everything alright?"

"Oh, yes. Just a small plant issue he needed to handle. It also gave him an opportunity to see the Porters. They're very close, you know."

"Oh, yes, of course," she said absently.

"Well, I'll leave you to get some rest. I know when Tucker arrives tomorrow, there will be much to do before Dahlia's service. He's very specific on arrangements, so we'll be at his mercy till it's perfect. I understand he can be very determined."

Reggie found a swift turnabout in Mavis unexpectedly.

"Oh, my dear, I've been so selfish. I've forgotten that you have lost someone as well. I guess sometimes we get caught up in our affairs and don't see what's happening with others."

She should probably know better, but she decided to go out on a limb.

"Miss Hatfield, forgive me for asking, but I know that you were once engaged to Forrest Perkins. Now, please, don't be upset, but I just wanted to hear what happened from you."

"That was a long time ago and not worth discussing, dear. I thought there was more to him, but I was wrong. It was a mistake. I paid for it, and now it's forgotten."

"Oh, Miss Hatfield, I don't think it's forgotten at all. He has the utmost respect for you, and I think he still carries a torch."

"And how would you ever know anything about that?" she said heavily.

Reggie felt embarrassed because she would have to reveal her conversation with Mr. Perkins over lunch.

"Well, I just have a feeling that maybe it was all a mistake," she lied.

Mavis cocked her head and regarded Reggie quietly.

"You're lying, my dear. I don't know why, but I do know that you are, and for now, I am drained, and I shall have to ask you to show yourself out. This interview is finished," she said as she lowered her lids and lay still against the pillows.

Embarrassed and deflated, Reggie cast one last glimpse at Mavis and quietly let herself out of the sterile room.

* * *

"Oh, God, I'm such an ass," she said, slapping herself on the forehead. "I can't believe what a mess I made of that. I didn't learn anything, and I'm going to get in trouble with Laird when Ronald tells him how I lied my way in there. God, Tucker, why aren't you here to help me? I was going out for a few things. What if they're still there when I get back? He'll be lying in wait to see what I really did do. Where can I shop?"

Reggie strolled up to the Plaza swinging her drug store bag and humming a tuneless song, thinking about what she would say to Tucker tomorrow. She was marching towards the desk with hopes of a call from him when a voice behind her stopped her in her tracks.

"Find everything you needed?"

Reggie froze, thinking she would rather be in front of the desk personnel hearing nothing from Tucker than in front of John Laird explaining her recent quest at "questioning".

"Hey, hello, how are you? How was your drink?"

"Why does everyone I see tonight hit me with that same 'Hey, hello' guilty greeting? It makes me think you all have something to hide. Course, I know you have something to hide," he said, smirking at her.

"What would that be?"

"Oh, hey, awful about Mavis and her sister and every creature on God's green earth. You didn't really think he would keep that from me, did you?"

Reggie was so embarrassed she could barely look him in the eye.

"Did you learn anything useful?"

Reggie felt completely stupid. Who did she think she was? Indeed, she did not have more prowess than a policeman at conducting interviews. For some odd reason, she felt like she needed to do this on her own.

"Look, I know it's been a long day, and we've done a lot of work, but there's not a lot to show for it. Let's start over tomorrow," said Laird.

"I'm sorry I didn't tell you upfront. Truth be told, I wasn't sure I would even go through with it," she said, realizing that might actually be true.

"Not a problem. Just keep me in the loop. We'll find out what you learned tomorrow."

"Of course. Goodnight."

Laird watched her enter the elevator and push the button, satisfied that she was going to her suite. He looked to the ladies' room, pondering what it was that women did in there that took so long. He reflected on the other call he received this evening from Tucker via the commissioner. It was the shock of his life, and he was already planning on how he was to retrieve Dahlia. It would be a task keeping her in check until her service.

He began to wonder if he had been ditched. After all, he had scared her earlier, and he wouldn't be surprised if she were a bit upset with him. He was at the point of leaving when she slid up next to him, a mischievous look on her face.

"Where have you been, and what have you been doing? You look guilty and pleased all at the same time."

"I have been in the ladies' room with cleaning women who don't care who's there when they gossip."

"Am I to take it that you learned something of interest?"

"My Spanish isn't the greatest, but..."

"Do you have something for me or not?" said Laird, assuming police mode, "because if I need to detain those women, I need to know sooner than later."

"They're both a bit spooked and think maybe it isn't safe to work here when anyone can walk in and out with no questions asked."

"Doesn't sound like they have much to add. They're right, though; the security is lax, and that's how our murderer accomplished his goal without any trouble. Well, nice try," he said absently. "By the way, you just missed Reggie."

"Has she gone to her room?"

"Yes," growled Laird. "I watched the elevator. I don't think she'll be doing any more detective work tonight."

Dulcy was dying to run upstairs and see what she learned from Mavis but knew it was out of the question. She smiled politely, stifling a yawn, realizing how exhausted she was.

"Come on, I'll walk you to your car."

"Oh, right. Geez, I forgot. I was settling into my bedroom when you caught me. I'm going to need to move closer to the inn."

"I have a suggestion. I can supply you with closer quarters if you like. They come complete with armed guards. That way, I know you'll be safe and on the right side of the law.

"Hmmm. The right side of the law, huh? Should I come quietly, Detective?"

"Come any way you'd like, Miss Dandeneau."

* * *

Reggie tossed her purse on the bed and shuffled to the bathroom. She gazed at her face in the mirror, noticing the circles under her eyes. She hadn't been taking very good care of herself lately. She hadn't learned enough tonight to justify her reckless tactics, and she felt like a complete fool.

She reran the events in Mavis's room. At the time, it seemed so mysterious, but back in the dimness of her room. She felt she imagined all the questionable body signs and inflections from Mavis. All she really did was to harass a frightened old lady who had been knocked on the head and didn't have a clue as to why.

She washed her face, then plunged into the towel, brusquely rubbing her skin. She was more tired than she realized, and she loped back to the bedroom, shedding clothes as she walked. She didn't even bother putting on her nightie but fell into bed and pulled the covers over her head.

"I should have done that this morning when I woke up," she thought.

She tried to recount the day's positive points but felt herself drifting aimlessly. She was dozing and found herself far away, yelling for Tucker, but each time she called, a harsh ringing drowned out her voice. She yanked herself awake and realized that the harsh ringing was not a dream but the phone.

"Oh, God, what now?"

"I promise. I went straight to my room and went to bed. I am not questioning anyone else, I swear," she exclaimed.

"Well, nice to know you've been keeping busy while I've been away," said a warm, kind voice.

"Oh, Tucker. Where have you been? I'm so glad it's you. You never called me back!"

"Well, I am now. Let's say it's been harrowing."

Even in Reggie's sleep-drunk state, she couldn't make "harrowing" jive with a condolence visit.

"Again, with the 'harrowing' versus 'somber' thing. You people really have some strange death customs. Most people I know have a sedate, sad, contemplative exchange when they visit people experiencing a loss. You make yours sound like a cross-country bike trip on the A259."

Tucker decided to tell Reggie about the only part of the evening that would explain that remark and be true at the same time.

"Reg, you wouldn't believe it. It's been a strange and, yes, a harrowing evening. I tried to run into town for something, which is when I spoke to you. When I got back, the family was closeted in the study, cocktails in clenched fists, with the local constable making some wild claim that the neighbor had seen Dahlia drive from the estate into town. Of course, it's

Mrs. Benson, the one who drinks."

Reggie, who was now shaken from her sleep state and fully awake, had no idea who Mrs. Benson was or that she had a drinking problem.

"I had to calm them all down and insist that it was time I made for America, as it's obvious that I've upset everyone with my interfering presence, which is why I'm phoning you. I'll be home tomorrow; well, it's tomorrow now, but Jennings is dropping me, well, rather soon, and I'll be back before you've had a chance to miss me."

"Too late," said Reggie flatly as she realized how that sounded.

"Hey, Reg, that's lovely to hear, you know. I mean it," he said, deciding to keep this tack going. "It's been awful doing all this by myself. I enjoy having an assistant. And I'm sorry I left you there alone to handle all that. What have you been up to this evening? Sounds like you're in trouble, and my guess is Laird."

"You're forgiven."

"Thank you," said Tucker.

"I was thinking I was on to something earlier, but all I managed to do was upset Mavis and cause "Ronald" the cop, to tip off Laird that I was doing off-hours investigating."

"Brilliant. I was hoping you'd get on to her. Did you find out anything useful, then?"

There were no words to express what she thought she saw. She was imagining things.

"No, not really. I think... well... I thought I saw something in the way she was acting, but really, it was nothing."

"Tell me; I'm a good listener."

"I thought she seemed upset when I mentioned the police were searching her house and why the poker was there, and especially when I told her you were in England and concerned, she turned positively satanic. I'm telling you... hello?"

The silence on the other end was deafening. Reggie sighed and sank back into the pillows. She had done it again.

"No, just thinking, Reg. That's actually great. Can't wait to see you. We definitely have some things to discuss. There's something I really need to tell you as well," he decided.

"Okay," said Reggie quietly. "I guess I'll see you sometime tomorrow, then. Take care."

"You too, Reg. Cheers."

Reggie held the receiver in her hand for a minute, then dropped it on the hook. She nestled in the covers and imagined what it could be that he needed so badly to tell her. She drifted blissfully off to sleep with warm and cozy thoughts. Tucker looked at the clock. After a couple of hours of sleep he would be ready to finish this thing. He pondered the decision, then smiled. It was time to fill in Reggie on his most closely guarded secret.

* * *

Chapter 36

Topper Harley: So... I guess you've been with a man before... Ramada
Thompson: I'm a virgin. I'm just not very good at it.
-Hot Shots, 1991

The walk to Laird's apartment was quiet. Whether that was out of anticipation or caution, Dulcy wasn't sure, but she could see he was deep in thought. She loosely held onto his arm until he turned up a brick path leading to a well-appointed building. She wondered how she could have missed such elegant architecture as they walked up to the oversized double doors.

"After you," he said, holding the door for her.

Dulcy's insides flipped, and she patted her stomach to stop the butterflies. She smiled nervously, walking across the threshold into a beautiful foyer complete with Musak and paintings. Laird crossed the lobby to an oversized elevator with doors so spotless Dulcy could see the reddening of her cheeks in them. He pressed the button as the old-fashioned dial began moving downward.

The heavy doors opened noiselessly, and they slid in together without speaking. After an initial thrust, the elevator gained speed, landing them on the top floor. Dulcy's stomach lurched, signaling the deposit of the elevator and the return of the butterflies.

Breathing deeply, she walked out into a tastefully decorated hallway, Muzak again echoing through the space. She hung back as Laird unlocked the door, then followed slowly as he turned on a bank of overhead lights. In true cop fashion, he surveyed the perimeter, then shut the door behind her, locking it. All her bravado dissipated, and she was just a frightened little girl in a big, hunky cop's apartment.

Her earlier feeling of discomfort returned as she watched him scout the premises. She hummed an aimless tune to drown out the persistent voice in her head, urging her to run as she meandered through the tidy apartment.

"Would you like a little music?" he said, misinterpreting her mindless humming.

"No, not unless you do."

He handed her a drink that came out of nowhere, and she took it, grateful for something that had to do with her twitching hands.

"You have a beautiful place," she said with a voice that sounded nothing like her own.

He noticed it, too, and slid his arm around her back, gently guiding her to the couch.

"Relax. I invited you here; I haven't caught you squatting in a cordoned-off crime scene."

Dulcy burst out laughing, relieving hours of built-up tension.

"I'm sorry, it's just that I never do this," she said, thinking, 'said every female on the planet when they went home with a strange man.'

"You know I believe that? I think you spend all your time at that restaurant heating other people's cold tea. Maybe it's time you let someone tend to you," he said, taking her hand in his.

She smiled at him, twisting his fingers and noticing how large they were.

"You have huge hands," she observed, then reddened at the careless remark.

She just wasn't as comfortable as she thought she would be now that the opportunity presented itself. She winced and took a generous sip of her drink.

"You need to relax," he said softly. "Come with me, and I'll show you what my large hands can do."

He rose and held them out to her. She let him lift her from the sofa. He transferred them to one of his and led the way to the bedroom. Dulcy grinned in spite of herself and followed him.

It also was tastefully decorated, with an oversized king bed as the centerpiece. There were bay windows that showcased the glazed city lights in the distance. Dulcy was sure the blackness that lay beyond was the open space of the bay. She dropped his hand and moved to the window, gazing out into the twinkling of boat lights, streetlamps, and stars. He had left the lights off and stood behind her, taking in the view.

"Your dates must love this," she sighed.

"I don't know. No one's ever been up here."

She felt his hands on her bare shoulders, caressing her in long, slow sweeps. Her skin prickled, and goose bumps popped through her soft flesh. He also felt them and wrapped his arms around her, lightly rubbing her shoulders. He leaned into her, making her feel safe and comfortable. She finally allowed herself to give in. He nestled his face in her hair and gently kissed her on the top of her head. She stirred in his arms, and he pulled her toward him, kissing her gently.

"Come with me," he said, smiling.

"Whatever you say, Detective."

He led her to the massive bed, sitting her on the edge. He stepped to a masculine-looking writing table, where he emptied his pockets and dropped his phone. He reached down to an unseen spo,t and Dulcy saw a small cubby pop open. He dropped his gun in, and it snapped, hiding all traces of an opening.

Dulcy was mesmerized and not a little turned on. It was like giving yourself to James Bond. He crossed to the bathroom, emerging with a large bottle of something which he set on the nightstand. Dulcy was feeling more at home by the moment. He gave her a handsome smile and unbuttoned his shirt, revealing well-developed biceps and a shoulder line that made her feel weak. His chest was sparsely covered with hair, which made his chest muscles stand out even more.

He strolled into the walk-in closet ,where she could see his finely shaped backside as he stripped off the rest of his clothes and stepped into a pair of sleep pants. She always knew there must be something worth getting arrested for under that suit and overcoat. He returned and drew her shirt over her head, rubbing his hands with oil.

"Roll over," he ordered.

399

She rolled onto her stomach and felt his strong hands glide over her skin. He rubbed her shoulders and neck, releasing the tension before working his hands down her back and around her sides. He continued down her body along her legs, reaching for her feet. He carefully massaged each toe, then the soles of her feet, before making the return trip up her legs.

She felt her heartbeat quicken as he reached her thighs. He slowly rolled her onto her back, kissing her as he drew her arms over her head and clasped her hands in his. He moved again to her and kissed her tenderly. She was exhilarated by the rhythmic motion of him on her, and she pressed harder into him as they climaxed together. He kissed her again and rolled from the bed.

"I'll be back," he said.

She watched him move across the window light. She waited for him to return but could not stay focused. Her eyes closed gently, and sleep overtook her.

* * *

The day dawned brilliantly and sunny. Reggie had enjoyed blissful, dreamless sleep, Tucker Elliott's flight was flawless and uneventful, Dulcy Dandeneau awoke cheerful and rested in unfamiliar but cozy surroundings, and Detective John Laird whistled all the way to work, which, for him, was most out of character.

Reggie rolled over and squinted against the streaming sun from the open window shutters. She must have been truly tired of not closing and locking them, especially considering recent events. She yawned and sat upright, trying to decide what to do first. She lay back on the pillows and shut her eyes, rerunning last night's conversation with Tucker. What had they even discussed?

She decided to leave it alone in favor of caffeine. Having made this peace with herself, she relaxed in the solitude before beginning what she knew would be a nonstop day. With a loud, haranguing trill, the phone broke her reverie, catapulting her off the pillows.

"Well, ten seconds. Guess that's enough peace and quiet for today," and she reached for the phone, trying to decide whether to answer it or throw it.

"This better be good."

"Oooh, it is," cooed Dulcy. "Guess where I am?"

"Monte Carlo."

"Now you're just being shitty. I'm at Laird's apartment. We had a pajama party."

"Were there any pajamas involved?"

"Of course not."

"Oh, you slut, tell me everything. He caught you in the B&B, didn't he? That man is a pedigreed bloodhound where you're concerned. Are you sure he didn't have you micro-chipped when you weren't looking? So, what happened?"

"Yes, he did catch me in the B&B, and I'm not even sure how. I had slinked past Sgt. What's-His-Face and thought I was home free. I thought, 'Well, I'll just give Laird a call and see what he's up to.' I dialed his number, figuring I'd get his voicemail, right, when he actually answered from the doorway of the room I was squatting in."

"Ugh. That would have scared the crap out of me. What did you do?"

"I said, 'Oh hey, how are you? Fancy meeting you here,' you know that type of thing."

Reggie rolled her eyes and now understood why Laird had said, "Why does everyone I see greet me with that same guilty phrase?"

"But then he, well, asked me what I was doing, but not like out of curiosity. It was more accusatory if you know what I mean."

Reggie sat up in bed, cradling the phone closer to her ear.

"Accusatory?"

"Yeah, I think the actual phrase was 'Doing a little late-night investigating or something else, maybe?'"

Both girls in their separate beds pulled up the linens a little closer.

"What did he mean by that? What do you think he was accusing you of?"

"I don't know. It made me feel exposed and threatened. It was like he was someone else for a minute. Then he whisked it all away by telling me that he had to do that just to know, right and that he suspects everyone, no matter how he feels about them."

"Oh, the plot thickens. And so how does he feel about you, hmmm? Wait, he's not still there, is he?"

"Of course not. I wouldn't be talking like this if he were. He went to work. He left me a bagel and coffee on the nightstand."

"What, no rose?"

"Does he look like the rose type, Reggie?"

"No, not really, but you know, a rose, like in the movies."

"No rose. And he's not a very verbal individual, you see, so, never you mind. And what were you up to last night, you bad girl?"

"Why? What did he say about it?"

"Not much. We were having a drink, and his phone rang a couple of times, but on this one, he answered it, grunted a couple of times, and hung up. Then he said something like you were doing a questioning routine on Mavis Hatfield and that you'd maybe find out something, and he'd get with you when you came in. He also thought it might be funny to try and guess what you'd bring home from the drugstore. Because he knew you weren't going out for shampoo. So, what did you find out?"

"Nothing much. Now that I look back on it, I'm an idiot. All I managed to do was upset an old lady who'd been knocked on the head. I thought she was acting suspicious is the only thing I can say."

"How so? Did she say or do something? What do you mean?"

Now, Reggie was beginning to feel silly. Telling it would sound even worse.

"She became really agitated at one point when I said Laird's men were searching her house. She said there wasn't anything anyone could want there and that she didn't know anything about these murders. No one mentioned murders at all. Oh, I almost forgot. She accused Cord of murdering Mazie, and of course, she has no idea where he is. And then she started crying, but there weren't any tears. It was like this whole big act for my benefit. And the topper was when I was leaving. I told her Tucker was concerned about her and had been checking on her while he was away. If looks could kill! She didn't know he was over there. She backpedaled pretty fast when I mentioned him visiting the families. It was just the way she acted. It was all so... fake and rather poorly done."

"This is one big mess, isn't it?"

"Yes, ma'am. So, what's up today?"

"By the way, Tucker comes home shortly. He called last night before I went to bed. I thought it might be Laird making sure I stayed put."

"Don't think he didn't think about it. What did he say?"

"He extricated himself from the family, saying his presence had upset them and something about a loony neighbor calling the police saying she saw Dahlia drive into town from Porter's house. When he got home, they were all clutching cocktails with death grips in the study with the constable. He'll call when he gets here. It was a very long night for him. And listen to this - He says he has something he has to tell me."

"Do you think it has to do with the case or something personal?"

"I don't know, but we'll find out later today. By the way, we need to get up and move. Why don't we meet at the tea room before lunch starts and get another look at those pictures? We also need to check on the preparations for her service. I can't believe it's in a couple of days. I hope we'll be ready."

"I hope no one dies!" exclaimed Dulcy.

* * *

Laird sifted through his papers once more to see if he could glean anything from its hieroglyphics. Perhaps his brain was clogged with too many thoughts of Dulcy. He wanted to watch his step; he needed to keep his perspective. He still had three murders, a missing suspect, and a little old lady lying in a hospital bed. He reached for the phone and punched the Beach Drive Plaza's number.

"Winter Investigations, we snoop spring, summer, and fall," chirped Reggie.

"Very funny. Do you know I could have you brought in formally for questioning? I could even have you arrested for obstruction of justice. And my favorite, tampering with a witness."

"Well, arrest away," said Reggie. "The exculpatory evidence will show that I had no criminal intent in my actions. Therefore, I am not culpable."

"Reading law books in your free time, Miss Winter?"

"No, just a couple of old Perry Mason episodes."

"Get dressed. We need to get to work, and you have some explaining to do."

"Why do I feel like Lucy Ricardo caught without Ethel Mertz?"

"See you at the tea room."

The line was dead before she could get another word in, and she smacked the receiver back on the hook.

"Bet I don't even get breakfast."

***

Tucker gathered his things as they pulled up to the terminal. It was early, and he was beginning to feel the effects of no sleep and too much stress. He had left without goodbyes, knowing that he would be seeing them before they would even miss him. He set his watch back for a few hours to get himself on track.

"Well, Jennings, it's been quite a visit, mate. Don't know when I've had so much fun."

"Yes, sir. It's been a most interesting visit for us all. I should think home has never seemed so... felonious. I believe the only thing missing was the Keystone cops, sir."

"No, no, we had Constable Downs. Thank you, Jennings, for taking care of him and steering him out the door. He would still be drinking in the study if you hadn't convinced him that it was all just the ramblings of a mistaken woman."

"Poor Mr. Benson, sir. He will indeed be taken to the liquor cabinet after this incident. The man will need to settle in for the duration, as I fear Mrs. Benson will not give up on this episode for quite some time."

"Alright, Jennings. Thanks ever so much, and I'll see you in the States. You will be accompanying the family, I'm sure?"

"With all due respect, sir, I wouldn't miss it for all the 'tea' in England."

"Good man. Thanks again, Jennings."

Settled in first class, Tucker reviewed his flight times and sank back into the plush seat for a nap. He should have dropped directly to sleep, but he couldn't keep his mind off Reggie. How should he go about telling her? This is the type of thing on which he consulted with Dahlia. He smiled, remembering that just a couple of days ago, thinking of her made his heart sink. It also reminded him he needed to find her. By now, the commissioner would have contacted Laird and set things in motion.

He crossed his fingers and said a prayer to the gods that all would turn out well.

"Because here we go, ready or not!"

* * *

Chapter 37

Tiana: The dog just spoke to me.
Prince: If you are going to let every little thing bother you, it's going to be a
very long night.
-The Prince and the Frog, 2010

Reggie lounged a bit longer, knowing she had to get moving. Her obstinacy was partly due to being tired and partly due to being told what to do. She usually rebelled when that came up. She climbed into the shower, deciding to be a grownup. She'd call Dulcy when she got out and see what she wanted to do for breakfast.

Not far away, Dulcy was lounging lazily in Laird's bed, reliving the evening's highlights. She was basking in the glow when it occurred to her that she would have to go home for a new work outfit. She was not one of those women who showed up for work wearing clothes from the night before.

She reflected on how she really needed to move closer to the tea room. She would not be late to start the girls on lunch and was angry with herself for being so indulgent. She rolled over to the nightstand and dialed the tea room. This was not the start of the day she had envisioned.

After a brief conversation, she jumped out of bed and grabbed her things.

As she jogged out of the bedroom, she realized this was an opportunity to do a little private investigating herself. She slowed up, enjoying a long look around the apartment. After all, most people's homes spoke something about them.

She roamed from room to room, surveying each piece of furniture and each knickknack with an appraiser's eye. Something was bothering her about the place. She shrugged and threw on the rest of her clothes and raced out the door. She could run home, change ,and be back before anyone had a chance to think about her. She just hoped Reggie didn't get there first...

* * *

Detective Laird was regarding the back kitchen door like an old friend at this point. It was still early; lunch hadn't been started. In fact, most of the staff hadn't yet arrived. He smiled and pictured Dulcy waking up to a cream cheese bagel and coffee. Not bad, he thought, for a bachelor who rarely entertained.

He was glad the place was so lonely. He wanted to let himself downstairs and not answer any questions from staff or otherwise. He would be happy if they could conduct all this in the open. It was becoming tedious to squeeze down the rabbit hole to Wonderland. He felt his way along the well-trod path until he found the base of the fireplace. He stared for an eternity, waiting for something to jump out at him. When nothing did, he shuffled to the room and grasped the knob firmly, yanking it open with a groan of old wood and rusted metal. He shone his torch upwards, staring yet again at the carefully positioned art. The man definitely had talent.

He stepped further in, bouncing the light off the walls. Something made him stop at once. It seemed as though his eyes were playing tricks on him. He pointed the torch to the ceiling and stepped back to examine the dome-shaped pattern. The dimness of the cascade created shadows that fell in grotesquely misshapen forms across the walls and floor.

These misshapen forms seemed to be mimicking the art. He stepped forward, then back, just as the girls had done. What he saw was astounding yet repellent. He waltzed back and forth, adjusting his sight so his mind could interpret the outer picture as well as the inner. He readjusted the light and began at the left edge of the room.

Slowly and fluidly, he repeated the movements with each piece. As he let go of his conscious mind, the patterns began to tell a story. He felt inside his breast pocket for pen and paper and began scribbling cryptic notes. Having exhausted his ideas on the meaning of the pieces, he took a break to poke around the other entrance. They had been so preoccupied with the one side that they never thought to look on the other. He opened the door and shone the light, up, down, sideways, an in-between any crack larger than a hairline.

He stepped out into the tiny tunnel, sweeping the torch back and forth from wall to wall, searching for the strange or the obviously fresh. He let himself back into the room and gazed again at the covered walls.

He was thinking about wrapping it up when a slight sound on the other side of the room stopped him. As he watched, the door handle turned slowly. The wood creaked and groaned, and the door swung open to reveal Reggie and Dulcy. Laird flipped up the flashlight, catching them full in the face. Instantly, both women screamed to rival any star of classic horror pictures.

"It's only me. Stop carrying on, or you'll bring the whole place down here."

"You could give a girl some notice, you know," spat Dulcy.

"My heart is beating out of my chest," wheezed Reggie. "And I may have actually wet myself."

"Very nice. Listen, what did you find down here yesterday?"

"What do you mean?"

"These pictures. I know Dulcy said she thought she saw a pattern, but what about you, Reggie? What did you see?"

"I saw what Dulcy saw. I mean, we saw it together. It was a picture of Hitler if I'm not mistaken. Sort of a weird thing to be painting."

"Not for the time. Remember, there was a war going on when they lived here. But I now understand the Dali Museum's interest."

"Yeah, me too. But now that we see it, what's the significance? It was a great find, but it doesn't really get us anywhere except that he was a better artist than he was given credit for."

    "We're trying to find out why anyone would kill for what's in the house. Logically, this should be the key to that question."

"Who said anything about logic?" said Dulcy.

"I'm with you, but it's a good place to anchor," smiled Laird.

Reggie felt as though she was intruding. She watched the electricity between the two and was torn. She was happy for Dulcy but hoped the detective could keep his mind on the prize, the one other than Dulcy.

"I'm heading upstairs. I want to check on the rest of the stuff for Tucker. I'm still not sure when he's going to be here, but I better have things seen to," said Reggie.

"And I need to tend to the girls. We're closing in on lunch, and I need to be more helpful than I have been lately."

"You coming?" Dulcy asked Laird.

"No, not just yet. I think I'll stay here and... ruminate for a while."

"Too bad I know what that means, 'cause it sounds kind of dirty," quipped Dulcy.

Laird smiled and said nothing. The two remained still, grinning at each other in the low light.

"I'm going," said Dulcy.

"Wait, dinner later?"

"I'd love to. Bye," she said as she lingered a glance at him and disappeared out the creaky door.

Laird peeked at his watch and realized he had an errand to run or, better yet, a retrieval to make. He wondered if his apartment was the best place to hide a person who was supposed to be dead. He would have to find an excuse if Dulcy wanted to return to it after dinner.

With one last glance, he felt the beginnings of a theory that he couldn't get out of his mind. What if...? He gazed thoughtfully at the pieces, then opened the door. He stopped and whirled from left to right around the entire room. The pictures outside the pictures spoke volumes.

Were these telling a story, and about whom? Was this fiction or fact? He had no idea who the cast of characters were, but he had to find out. First stop—Nelson Platt at the historical society, and if he couldn't help,

412

he'd go to that twitchy historian, Perkins. One of them would know the answer to his question, but then would that tell him what was worth risking everything?

In his experience, what made people step outside the boundaries was - exposure or money... big money.

* * *

In a tiny, cramped room above a local feed store, a distinguished-looking gentleman sat pondering his future. Cord Cavanaugh saw his options to be limited. With Mavis in the hospital, he knew he was the key suspect in her attack. His inability to get back home quickly exposed the fact that he had skipped, and she had done nothing to disabuse them of this idea. She had saved her own skin and hung him out to dry. She was a bitter, unforgiving woman, and he couldn't reason why he had trusted her in the first place.

His sketchy, deteriorated mind skipped the fact that she hadn't given him any choice. She had dangled the proof of his complicity in his face, blackmailed him for it, and then ordered him to do the dirty work so she could walk off with the greater portion of the proceeds. If only he had been able to find the paper, but she was too bright for him. She had moved it, and not even the key to the box was helpful with an unknown hiding place.

His damaged thinking also did not take into account that none of what they were trying to claim belonged to either of them. It was something that had been stolen in the first place. He didn't know whether old man Hatfield had hidden it, but he knew it was there somewhere.

Once again, he would have to think up a way to access the tea room unnoticed, as he did on the night of the cocktail party. He had one last possible hiding place in mind, and all he needed was access. He had caught wind of the memorial service for Dahlia. That would be the perfect opportunity. If it wasn't hidden there, it wasn't in the house.

He needed to find out the times for everything. He put on his wig, hat, and sunglasses and marched down the stairs to the newsstand, hoping that somewhere in the paper, there might be a blurb about the service.

He at least had a tiny bit of luck left as he thumbed through the town events section and saw a piece on the woman, the service, and the tea room. Now that he had the timing in line, he could come up with a foolproof way to get in, get out, and get away for good. Mavis might know that he'd come back, but she would never know he was gone again. But this time, he would be comfortable for the rest of his life.

* * *

Dulcy was running around following trays of uncooked food, baskets of scone dough, and teapots waiting to go in warmers. The girls were like worker bees in a robotic fashion, setting a place here and wiping a table there.

She twirled around the kitchen, looking for something constructive to do. When she was satisfied, she went back to the office and read the few lines she had jotted down about Dahlia. They were better than she thought, making her a bit weepy.

She considered where Dahlia's body was at the moment. Was it still here? Or had it been taken to London? With the investigative tasks unfinished, she surmised that it was still downtown, awaiting release. She opened the drawer and picked up the other key that had turned up the day before and wondered what it fit. It had to be for something small, like an old-fashioned diary or lockbox. She decided it was part of the hidden treasures of the house that so far had escaped unearthing.

She held the key in her hand and felt the rough ridges. She could feel that it was more than a key; it was the key. She would find the lock that went with this, and she would do it before the service. It was the least she could do for Dahlia.

* * *

Reggie was moving so quickly that she hardly had time to think. She knew she would be seeing Tucker soon, but she was curious about a couple of things. Who were the people handling the refreshments? It seemed that the tea room staff were removed from the proceedings.

The police must be involved on some level, but she wasn't privy to that, which made her nervous. She decided that no matter what was planned, she would not be comfortable. She desperately wished Tucker would show up. She would do the best she could, but she still had unanswered questions: what would happen to this place once the service was over, and who were the people supposedly interested in buying it?

* * *

Dahlia had been cooling her heels in a back booth of a nasty, greasy spoon waiting on Laird. She supposed that the last place anyone would recognize her would be a seedy restaurant where she was sure that, at that very moment, there must have been drugs, murder, or both being done in the back alley.

She reexamined the bench to make sure she wasn't sticking to anything. She had refused the gracious offer of the waitress, or was it a waiter, to sample the steaming hot special of the day. Dahlia watched it go to a table across from her and felt relatively certain that the chef was an ex-prison cook.

She gazed at her watch again, hoping Laird would show soon. He could arrest her for all she cared, just as long as he sped her far from this place. She forced herself to settle down and concentrate on her paperback. At least it would take her mind off of her surroundings until he arrived.

* * *

Tucker cleared customs and headed to his gate. By now, Dahlia was safely secreted away by Laird, awaiting the final act. He pulled out his phone and hit redial on Laird's number. Hoping it wouldn't go to voicemail, he was thrilled when the man himself answered with his trademark curt acknowledgment.

"How are we doing?"

"I'm on my way right now. I had a bit of a hang-up in the tea room."

"Everything alright?"

"Yeah, everything's great."

"I reckon she'll be right mean by the time you get to her," chuckled Tucker. "She's not one to wait patiently, mate."

"You should see where I put her. She won't be mean. She'll be murderous."

Tucker winced.

"Bad choice of adjectives. Let's not bring the universe down around our ears right now, eh?"

"A bit touchy, aren't we?" said Laird.

"Let's just say the last few days have left me a bit on the edgy side."

"Not to worry, it'll all be over soon," offered Laird.

Tucker could not fathom why that statement made him feel so very uncomfortable.

* * *

"Reggie! I'm in the colonies again."

"Hey," she said breathlessly. "I've been waiting for you to call. I'm working on the details for the service. I have some questions, Tucker. I seem a bit out of the loop."

The ridge of hair on the back of his neck stood up as she softly spoke his name. Now, he felt even worse for having kept her in the dark since he found out the truth. He convinced himself it wouldn't have made any difference had she known; there was nothing on his end with which she could have helped.

"Well, I'm in New York, on my way, and will be there in, let's see, two hours and forty-one minutes, give or take."

"Do you need me to come get you?"

"No, no, I'll get a car. I want you to keep plugging away. Now, tell me, what can I help you with?"

They chatted for several minutes on the minutia of the event, speakers, catering issues, and music, and Reggie hung up feeling more in control than she had been. She turned back to the girl holding out napkins, picked a sample, and sent her on her way.

She glanced at her watch. He would be with her again in two hours plus. That gave her time to finish the preparations, run to the Plaza, and tidy up. She felt a small thrill of excitement and she thought about what it might be he wanted to tell her.

She flicked her hand as if swatting a fly and decided to put it out of her mind until later. She rounded sharply on a girl carrying vases, apologized for the near miss, and went off in search of Dulcy.

* * *

The door popped open before Laird could grab the handle and was held for him by a long-haired young man in filthy jeans and a t-shirt with a cigarette dangling from his lips. He thanked the man, who grinned back with the glassy, beer-eyed squint of the mid-day drinker and teeth that hadn't seen a dentist since he was a toddler.

418

Just as well, he thought. He didn't really want to touch anything he didn't have to. He surveyed the bar area more out of professional curiosity than anything else, then weaved his way to the dining room. He scoped out the tables, figuring she would have picked a booth to be inconspicuous.

Finally, his gaze landed on what he supposed could only be Dahlia. He grinned and shook his head, stifling a laugh as he made his way to the back. She was in a booth but sitting not quite next to the wall.

"Excuse me, Miss. Police," he said in his most resounding voice.

She lowered the book, peering over the top, and he saw the frightened gaze soften, then leer at him as recognition set in. She was dressed like an alien who had been given the wrong information before visiting planet Earth.

Her skirt was a loud plaid with a blouse whose herringbone lines resembled the test pattern on an old television set. She wore socks pulled up over her knees with platform shoes, worn jewelry, and a scarf on her head that looked like she had stolen it from a Russian field worker. Her sunglasses were more oversized than Jackie O's, and her lipstick was the shade of cotton candy.

"You look like a blind hooker. You're supposed to be drawing attention away from yourself, not trying to get arrested for vagrancy."

"I won't even dignify that with a response. It was bad enough I had to run out like a common thief from my own home but then not even having a decent choice of clothes... Well..."

Laird chuckled again and signaled the waitress for the tab.

"What are you doing?"

"Paying your tab."

"Oh, no, dear, there's no tab. I'm just hoping I'm not stuck to anything. You don't really think I'd eat here, do you?"

"Now, it's not that bad. There are lots of people enjoying their meals. Look around you," he said with a wave of his hand.

As he did so, he noticed only a few brave souls were managing the lunch menu. The rest were huddled over beer glasses in the bar.

"Let's get out of here."

He led her through the table maze and out into the bright sun, holding the door with his handkerchief.

"Now, if you allow me, I will take you directly to the apartment where you shall stay quietly put until show time."

"We're going now?"

"What else did you have in mind? What to knock over a liquor store before we go?"

"No! I'm starving," she hissed.

* * *

Chapter 38

Laird had finally retrieved Tucker and headed to his apartment, where a feisty Dahlia was anxious to fill Tucker in on the details of her exploits after their hand off at the train platform. At one point, Laird asked her to revive her rock star costume, of which she flatly refused to have any part. She promised Tucker that once alive again, she would take him to the diner for pie. Every diner has good pie, Laird had said.

"I'm sure their pie is brilliant," said Dahlia. "I would lay odds that the shoo-fly pie is made with real flies," which made them laugh in disgust.

They reviewed the details of the service with Dahlia and then left her to enjoy her first evening home with pizza, wine, and television. They left her ornery and cross, swallowed whole by the couch, arms folded across her chest like an Indian Chief on the receiving end of a bad trade. Tucker blew her a kiss and shut the door behind him.

"Oh, I feel awful running out like this. I must say it makes me a bit nervous to leave her alone here. You know, by herself and all."

"That's generally what being alone is, Elliott," said Laird, but he could tell there was something else on Tucker's mind other than leaving Dahlia.

"Okay, what's the deal?"

"Sorry?"

"There's something on your mind. Out with it."

"You're right, as usual. I've made up my mind to tell Reggie what's really going on. No, no, before you start in, hear me out. I think she has a right to know; it's the right thing to do."

"That's a good rationalization, Elliott. It wouldn't have anything to do with the fact that you have feelings for her, would it? Because lesser schemes have been blown to bits over this very thing."

Tucker stopped dead, scowling at Laird. He started to walk away, then turned on him with uncharacteristic aggressiveness.

"Look you, I won't have you or anyone else tell me how to read my gut instincts," stated Tucker. "They've served me well to this point, and I'm not about to ignore them now. So, let's just get in the car, meet them for dinner, and make sure everyone's on their mark. And by the way, where the hell is Landry?"

"Oh, Christ, you mean you don't know where he is? You two had this all worked out before you left."

"Yeah, well, I haven't heard a thing from him. I thought maybe he might have tried to reach you."

"No joy. Get in the car; I've got a call to make."

***

422

It was a happy reunion at the Beach Drive Plaza that evening. Dulcy, Laird, Reggie, and Tucker were closeted at a cozy table far from the noise and clatter of dinner plates and bar chat. Laird had reviewed the details of his people's placement for the service and then reviewed their parts down to the exact second of execution. They brainstormed possible complications, then satisfied they had covered their bases, changed subjects.

"I know I could have gotten the truth if I had just had more time," said Reggie, trying to convince Laird of her good intentions at the hospital.

"From which point, Reg, the point where you scared her or the point where she knew you were full of shit and kicked you out of her room?" asked Dulcy.

"Okay, fine. But you mark my words, there's something fishy with her, and at some point, it'll come out, you watch."

Laird's phone rang, and the three of them swiveled expectantly to watch him answer. He rose wordlessly, tossing his napkin, and without a glance, strode to the foyer, turning his back to them. All they could see was his head bobbing every so often, a shuffling of his feet, and a gaze to the ceiling before he slammed it shut and returned.

"Everything okay?" ventured Dulcy.

"Fine. Nothing to be concerned with. Just the creaking of law enforcement as it crawls along."

"No sarcasm there, mate," said Tucker. "Anything we can do?"

"No," stated Laird, leveling a look at Tucker, then signaling the waiter.

"Well, if you don't mind, it's still an early evening, and I would like to take

Miss Dandeneau here for an after-supper cocktail and let you two finish catching up on things," he said.

Dulcy rose, catching on and not altogether sorry. She knew Tucker and Reggie would like to talk alone, and she wasn't averse to spending more time with tall, dark, and handsome, especially if it led to more bagels and cream cheese.

"Well, nice to have you home, Tucker, and Reggie, I guess I'll see you in the morning. Last day before zero hour. You and I have some pictures to discuss," she said, winking.

Laird spoke to the waiter, nodded curtly to Tucker, and escorted Dulcy to the entrance.

"Hmmm," said Reggie.

"Have I missed something?"

"Oh, yeah."

Reggie gave Tucker a quick rundown on recent events between Laird and Dulcy, then waited for the appropriate reaction, but Tucker remained silent, tapping his water glass with his fork. Reggie was disappointed until she realized that maybe this was his way of working into whatever he wanted to tell her. "Tucker?" she said, peering into his face.

"What is it? Oh, is this what you wanted to talk to me about last night?" she asked innocently.

"Yes. There's something very serious I need to speak to you about."

Reggie felt the pit of her stomach bounce and her skin turn moist in the breeze of the ceiling fan. Up until now, she had felt a bit chilled sitting underneath it.

"I'm listening."

"Not here," he said, rising quickly and reaching for her hand.

She scooted her chair back in one swift movement as he was steering her away from the table. He led her out of the restaurant toward the elevator. He pressed the button, absorbed in thought.

When he seemed to wake up and notice Reggie standing close, waiting patiently, he grinned and laughed, gazing at her appreciatively. Reggie hadn't a clue as to what was on his mind.

But the reason for Tucker's perplexity was Reggie herself. He had tried to ignore what Laird had said, but it was insidious and crept into his consciousness, taking the space reserved for his discussion on Dahlia. The elevator opened, and he ushered her across the threshold.

"Where are we going?" she asked.

"To your room, of course."

Reggie dropped her purse, and Tucker instantly retrieved it.

"Sorry, Reg. I am so preoccupied I'm not being fair to you. I haven't checked back in yet, so rather than make you slog through all that, we'll hop up to your room. That works, yes?"

"Oh, of course. I'm sorry you just surprised me for a second. It's fine, really."

"Now, you're not very convincing. What's up?"

Again, for the eightieth time that week, she found herself feeling the complete fool, reading way more into this than was there.

"Well, you do know that I'm not on the third floor anymore, for one thing," she said.

"Oh, such an ass. Sorry; I completely forgot about moving day."

The elevator opened on the third floor, and a nice-looking older couple climbed aboard and stared at the arrows.

"Were you getting off here?" asked the woman.

"Thank you, but no," said Tucker. "My friend here is new to elevators, so we're having a demonstration."

Reggie could only politely nod and pretend she didn't speak English. The nice couple smiled and shook their heads indulgently while Tucker pressed the first-floor button. The man shot Tucker a look and quickly opted for the lobby. The doors opened, and they nodded politely to the pair as they exited. As the doors shut, Reggie reached around and smacked Tucker on the arm.

"Very funny," she said, then released into giggles.

"Wasn't that funny, eh?"

Reggie began to feel her normal, at ease self, happy to have the strained, serious air cleared. She decided that whatever he had to tell her, she would receive it in the calm, decisive business manner that he expected from her.

"I don't know. I think you made me nervous. It's been such a strange few days. I can't wait to tell you everything we've found. You won't believe it."

"Brilliant. I was thinking the same thing about what I'm going to tell you," he said, laughing.

"Really?" asked Reggie.

She smiled big though the bouncing in her stomach had returned. Tucker took her room key and unlocked her door. He halted her forward movement while he switched on the light and surveyed the room.

"All clear, Reg."

Reggie glided into the room, shed her wrap, and threw her purse on the desk. She turned to find Tucker eyeing her appraisingly. She felt overexposed.

"Please," she said, feeling awkwardly formal as she motioned to the couch.

He regarded her quietly, then reached for the phone.

"You know what we need? We need a nightcap. I think Laird had the right idea. What we need is a nice brandy, something old and aged and soothing."

While Tucker dialed the bar, Reggie wondered why they needed something soothing. What was he going to tell her? Oh, God, who died now? She was about to protest but instead smiled and sat silently, waiting for him to start.

"So, Reg, tell me about the pictures. It sounds as if you've each found something you and I couldn't."

"Well, yes. Remember the day I was going to go to the Dali Museum? Well, I did go. With Laird," she said, not waiting for a response. "It's an amazing place. It was just an idea, just a thought, but when we got back to the room, it made me look at those pictures in a totally different light. In fact, that was the key - the light. If you just played with the light a bit, you could see the picture within the picture. All of them are double-painted, like in Dali. And in one, we could actually see a crude likeness to Hitler. I don't understand that, but we all saw it. That's what Dulcy meant when she said we had paintings to review again tomorrow. I think if we look at them long enough, we'll eventually see it."

"See what?" asked Tucker.

"That I don't know, but it can't all just be coincidence. Why would you hide all that? It has to tie in; it has to mean something."

Tucker was ready to play devil's advocate.

"Well, Reg, I don't know. Maybe he was just an artist, with an artist's temperament and an unwillingness to share his work for fear of criticism."

Reggie couldn't decide if he had a point or if he was just stalling until the brandy came. She considered this idea. Just because it's there doesn't mean it explains all this.

"You could have a point. You know..."

But a sharp rap on the door cut the rest of her thought short, signaling the arrival of the brandy. A crisp, young man bearing a tray smiled graciously and crossed to the credenza.

"Is this good, sir?" he said, hovering above the table.

"Oh, fine, thank you very much," said Tucker, reaching for the bill.

"Compliments of the house, sir, welcome back."

"Give Maurice my thanks, please," said Tucker and watched as the efficient young man swiftly and soundlessly closed the door.

"Very nice," said Reggie.

He handed her one of the snifters and then stood swirling the amber liquid in his own. She followed suit, waiting patiently. Silence rewarded her, and after a few seconds, Tucker shifted his gaze, leveling it on her with a most serious expression.

"Oh, dear; here it comes," she thought.

Maybe it was worse than she thought. What could it possibly be that required expensive brandy, silence, and a series of somber glances? She wished he would say it.

"I wish you would just say it," she blurted.

"I know, Reg," he said softly.

He was staring past his brandy at the tips of his shoes.

"It's just that it's so complex. I really am not sure how to tell you this."

"Why don't you just say it," said Reggie, exasperated. "Oh, Tucker. Has someone else died? Who is it now?" she choked.

"Actually, quite the opposite," he said bluntly.

The trilling of the phone pierced the fabric of his suit coat, and he grimaced and checked the screen.

"Laird."

"Don't answer it," pleaded Reggie.

"You don't understand. I have to take this."

"I thought you were enjoying a nice after-dinner drink. Why are you calling me?"

Reggie watched Tucker's face blanch, and he drained his brandy in one swallow.

"I'll meet you downstairs, and you can fill me in. Right."

Tucker pocketed his phone and placed his glass on the table.

"Landry's gone missing," he said. "I know this is all very confusing, but I promise I will explain, and it will all make sense."

He closed her in his arms and hugged her tightly. He kissed her gently on the forehead and was gone.

Laird was waiting in the lobby, phone stuck to his ear as usual.

"Any news?"

Laird held up his finger, finished a call, and tucked the phone away.

"There was a man of ours on duty at the airport. We had him keep an eye out for Landry since he was right behind you. He had a description and a picture, and when he finally spotted him, he headed toward the taxi area. He ran after him but lost him. He called ahead to one of our cars, which then followed him to his office. Landry got out of the cab and went into the building. Our man waited, but he never came out. He questioned the attendant, who said he was out of the country, and it was the same story you got. When he said he saw him walk into the building, she became agitated, told him he wasn't there, and that she didn't know what he was talking about. He didn't believe her, so he searched the place but didn't find any sign of him. And that is where we are."

"Damn. Have you spoken to his wife?"

"Mrs. Landry insists that he called her from New York and let her know he was on his way. She was going out of town, which she delayed until he turned up."

"I think we can trust that she really doesn't know where he is. I know you haven't forgotten about Cord Cavanaugh. Where is he?"

"I don't know," said Laird, hanging his head. "I know he's somewhere close. I don't know where. You know he must be responsible for the attack on Mavis. Who else would it be? I don't want you doing anything stupid, Elliott, do you hear me? Let my men handle it."

"But I thought you weren't on this case, Inspector."

Laird froze, staring down Tucker. It was a split second before he regained his composure.

"I'm not on the Porter case," he stated, as though speaking to a child.

"Oh, right, right. Sorry. But how do you know where one ends and the other begins, mate?"

* * *

Reggie was exasperated. She sat on the edge of the bed, staring around her.

"Dammit! Now what?" she said, feeling helpless.

"I can't believe it! Just when he was about to say something finally. Dulcy. I have to find Dulcy."

Reggie dialed the number to the tea room. Even though dinner was over, someone had to clean up at least. It rang several times, and just as she was ready to slam down the receiver, there was a voice on the line.

"Sea Gables."

"Lisa?"

"No, it's Dulcy, Reg. Abandoned, as I'm sure you are as well."

"Yep. Just as it was getting good."

"Amen. Before I knew it, I was being dumped in my car, and all I could see were taillights. You know, I'm thinking this cop thing is sexy, but it's kind of like a roller coaster. Either way, at some point, you probably feel like throwing up."

"Ugh. That's a visual I didn't need. I don't know about you, but I'm a bit frustrated right now, and I need to do something. What do you say?"

"What do you have in mind?"

Reggie had no idea where Tucker was or if and when he'd be back. She grabbed her purse and headed for the door. She opened it a crack and peered out, anxious to spot any onlookers heading off to bed. She felt melodramatic; anyone seeing her wouldn't know what she was doing or why. Secrecy would only make her look guilty.

She straightened up, threw her shoulders back, and stalked off to the elevator. She remembered Tucker downstairs and about-faced to the stairs, where the only thing to see her might be a passing guest. She landed on the bottom floor in front of the exit door. She wasn't sure whether this led to the lobby or outside to the alley. She pushed the bar and felt the muggy night air slap her face and flap her dress around her.

It felt satisfying to be doing something, anything, but then she remembered that this was how she felt when running off to see Mavis. She winced as she remembered how that turned out. She surveyed the alleyway and bolted towards the tea room. What she would do when she got there was anybody's guess.

* * *

"What happens next, then?" asked Tucker.

"Nothing for you. I just wanted you to be up to date. You've had a long day, and you may as well get some sleep."

"Well, are you heading home?"

"Yeah, but I have a stop to make first."

"I want to check on Dahlia, so if you don't mind, I'll tag along."

"Suit yourself."

Reggie felt like an escaped convict. She pelted for the tea room, hoping she wouldn't run into anyone who would tell Laird she was out again. She slid up the exit and found Dulcy grabbing brandy glasses in the kitchen.

"What are you up to?"

"I thought we could use a little refreshment, something to help us figure out what we want to do. This is really silly, you know. I've got you down here, and it's all talk. What are we going to do, really?"

"It depends. How much trouble do you want to get into?"

"I can stand up to whatever you dish out. You stay in trouble anyway, so lead on."

"I have a feeling that we should double-check what we're being told. We need to use your police connection and find out what's really going on."

"You don't think he's telling us the truth?"

"I think he's working the room."

"Okay. Does that include me?" she said, glaring at Reggie.

"No, I don't think so."

"Good answer, but now I feel compelled to find out. He's not answering

434

his phone. You never know if you'll get him or his voicemail. Frustrating."

"What do you want to do?"

Dulcy smiled and handed Reggie a key.

"This is to his apartment. I swear there's something there that escaped me the other day. We need to check it out."

"Oh, no, we don't. That's not a good way to start a relationship, Dulcy. It's spying, right? Don't you think? Sort of? I mean, what if he comes back?"

"He won't. He kissed me goodnight and told me he would see me in the morning. This was going to take some time."

"And it's not spying. It's a fact-finding mission to help find out what happened to Dahlia."

"Well, when you put it that way. And you know he took Tucker with him so that I won't be seeing him again, either. If he stops by, he'll think I'm sleeping. Hey, I'm getting pretty good at this undercover stuff."

"Oh, right. Mavis thinks so, too. So does Laird and Ronald and..."

"Knock it off," she said, grinning. "I'm honing my private dick skills."

"Yeah, me too," she quipped and clinked her glass with Reggie's.

* * *

They were warm all over from the brandy break, equipped with bottled courage. They giggled as they checked up and down the street, then stepped across.

"Should we take my car?" asked Dulcy.

"No, how would you like Laird busting you for drinking and driving and breaking all in one night?"

"Oh, right. I think we'll stick with breaking and entering for now."

"Good call," smirked Reggie.

They slinked down the street toward the apartment, watching out for stray police. If they had rounded the corner just minutes earlier, they would have seen Tucker and Laird headed in the opposite direction. It was a lovely evening for a walk, and they found themselves on the stoop before they realized it.

"Nice place," said Reggie. "I've seen these before. Wonder what he pays for rent?"

"Well, I'm sure I don't know, but maybe you can go through his checkbook while we're here."

"Uh huh, and add invasion of privacy and trespassing to our list of sins. I like it."

They sighed and marched up the stone entrance. Their enthusiasm plummeted when they found the doors locked tight, governed by a buzzer system.

"Oooo. Didn't notice that when I left. Now what?"

"We wait a minute. Let's try... oh, duh..."

Dulcy pulled out the key, and the door silently released. With a grin, she pulled Reggie in after her. The entranceway was a brightly lit Spanish-style décor with local artwork around the perimeter and a faint hum of Italian Muzak. Dulcy crossed the foyer to the elevators and pushed the button.

Reggie was admiring the soft pastels of the Key West–style homes in the pictures and humming along to the Muzak.

"Reg, come on."

The doors slid open, and Dulcy pushed the last button.

"Nice. Top floor, top drawer. He lives well."

"Yes, he does. I'm sure he had a decorator do his apartment. It has that sterile, professional look but is nicely done. That's it. That's what was bothering me. There are no personal items. No family pictures, no magazine subscriptions, you know? It could be anybody living here. Whew! Glad I figured that out."

"Gee, Dulcy, lots of people don't put out pictures and things. He's probably never here. He works so much. Honestly, how much do you really know about him when it comes right down to it?"

"You know, you're right. I'm just jumping to conclusions. Once again, I'm making more out of this than there really is."

The doors slid open and deposited them in yet another Spanish-style hallway, brightly lit, Muzak in the background. Dulcy grinned at Reggie and inserted the key in the lock. The door opened noiselessly. Dulcy let out a deep exhale and swung it wide. She had figured that she could explain herself if she found Laird waiting on the other side.

What she hadn't figured on was the crossed-legged female relaxing on the couch. The recently deceased Dahlia Porter panicked, mouth hanging wide, wine glass dropping to the floor, chardonnay seeping over Detective Laird's beige carpet.

* * *

III

Part Three

Chapter 39

"Oh Gawd! What are you two doing here?!"

Dahlia flew off the couch, jerked them across the threshold, and slammed the door. The three gaped at each other until Dahlia grabbed them in a tight hug.

"I can't believe he told you. Wait till I get my paws on him. Bloody copper, I knew he'd cock it up. The time I've sunk into this charade."

She stopped, studying the two women. Something was amiss. These were no co-conspirators before her. They were chalk white and swaying where they stood.

"Ohhh, no. He never told you anything. You don't know, do you? You came here... What the hell are you doing here? What are you doing with a key to his flat, Dulcy?"

Dahlia's eyes popped wide, and she slapped her hand over her mouth.

"Oh my God. You're sleeping with him? You dirty girl, you. Tucker never said a word."

Reggie and Dulcy remained motionless except for a slight listing through this exchange. Dahlia turned them to the couch and sat them down. The pair made her a little nervous. They did not look well, and who knew when Laird would return. He would be furious with them. Dahlia didn't miss much; she saw all, and it wasn't a pretty picture.

"I'm sorry. I know you have a lot of questions. I'm not sure I should answer any of them now. It's a very long story, ladies. And it's a bit of a problem you finding out. It changes everything, doesn't it?"

Reggie opened her mouth and then shut it. Dulcy took Dahlia's hand in hers.

"I can't tell you how good it is to see you," she said, her eyes brimming with tears.

"It's just so..." she sniffed and shook her head. "I can't believe it. What we've been through. And all this time you were..."

"In England. At my parent's house, in hiding, and putting together plans with Tucker, Laird and Commissioner Hammond. He's a friend and there's an old case still on the books they'd love to resolve, and this gives them the opportunity to do so. Like I said, it's a long story and there's no time to explain. You should be getting along now. I don't know what to do with this, but I'll figure out something. Just get a good night's sleep and we'll sort it out in the morning. By the way, when did he give you that key? Come on, start spilling, darling, but make it short," she said, glancing at her watch.

"It isn't hard to figure out, is it? He came to investigate your 'death'," she said mocking quotation marks, "and one thing led to another, and I ended up with a key to lock up when I left the other morning."

"Hmmm," purred Dahlia. "Brilliant. Reggie, love, are you alright?"

"Uh, yes. I just had a vision of running after the ambulance when they took you away. I felt so helpless. I was thinking if I could rewind the clock, I would do things differently and... hey, wait a minute. You said you had a secret when you were heading to the podium. Was it the hidden room or was there something else?"

"That was basically it, but there is a bit more according to Tucker. Oh Tucker! You should have seen his face. It was classic, like something out of a BBC episode. Well, if you're okay, I really think you need to get moving. You lot can't be here when he gets back."

Reggie and Dulcy eyed each other guiltily. Should they mention Tucker? They were probably in for it anyway, might as well 'fess up'.

"What? There's something else, then?"

"You're right. We need to go because when Laird comes back, he might not be alone."

"You mean he may have Tucker in tow? That's possible since they left together. He may want to check on me again before he turns in. Time to be going, girls," she said, rising.

"We'll fix it tomorrow, I promise."

She reached for the door, but before she could open it, it swung in revealing Tucker Elliott and John Laird, looking very surprised indeed.

* * *

They looked like the three wise monkeys; see no evil, hear no evil, speak no evil. Each was stunned waiting for the large shoe to fall.

"Back it up, ladies," said Laird. "And what in the hell do we have here?"

"Hey, hi..."

"Oh, no, no, no. No more 'hey, hi, how ya doin', guilty, cover up the big boner error-in-judgment call. This changes everything. Sit down, ladies. As if I didn't have enough crap going wrong with this case."

"Which case, Detective, the Porter case or the Hatfield case, or the chambermaid case..."

"Miss Dulcy. Double checking the key to make sure it works?"

The man didn't miss much. Dulcy smiled and resumed her seat on the couch. She patted the spot next to her and glared meaningfully at Reggie. Reggie reclaimed her seat, followed by Dahlia who plopped down next to her.

"Well, the three amigos," said Tucker. "I left you safely tucked in your suite, Miss Winter. What have you to say for yourself, please?"

"Well, I... don't know," she finished. "I guess I was a little frustrated with how things went. I knew you had something to tell me and when you bolted out of the hotel... Oh! This is what you had to tell me, wasn't it? You were going to tell me about..." she said, eyes widening as her face flushed red.

She gave Dahlia a big smile and dropped her head on her shoulder.

"You were going to tell me, weren't you? Despite how the detective felt about it."

"Yes, I was. I just couldn't keep it from you any longer. It didn't seem right somehow because you're a smart lass, why wouldn't you have something to contribute? At least that's what I thought before your Mavis Hatfield exploits," he snickered.

"Will no one let me forget that?" she sighed.

"Well, now," said Dulcy. "That's interesting. Tucker was going to tell Reggie. Were you going to tell me, Detective?"

"No, I knew he wouldn't listen to me, so I thought I'd wait till he told Miss Winter here, then she'd run straight to you. Seemed like less work for me."

"So, here we all are. What shall we do with them, Inspector."

Laird looked like he had a good suggestion but kept his mouth shut. Reggie readjusted and Dahlia wriggled to a more comfortable spot. Dulcy looked at the floor, avoiding Laird's eyes, awaiting her dismissal. She was greatly surprised when he threw his keys on a side table and asked if anyone could use a drink.

"Not me, thank you," said Reggie. "Not for me," said Dahlia. "I've had a wonderful time with the Columbia winery this evening. I was hoping for more sleep. Must make it a point to visit Washington state soon, though."

"I'll have what you're having," said Dulcy, winking at Laird and hoping he would be amused and not angry.

Laird poured a scotch for Dulcy, himself, and Tucker. Dahlia changed her mind and fixed one of her own.

"I don't see the point of this at this hour," said Tucker. "What can we hope to accomplish?"

"This won't take long. Ladies and our gentleman," gestured Laird, "here's to a successful outcome and touching memorial service."

"Here, here," said Tucker raising his glass.

"Thank you, sir. So nice to be present for my send-off. One doesn't get this opportunity too often."

"Thank you for having me," said Dulcy. "One rarely gets to spend time with their employer once they're dead."

Reggie glared at Dulcy and stood to give her toast.

"To Dahlia. May you use your other seven or eight lives wisely."

"We'll meet over breakfast, except for you, Dahlia, sorry, and we'll rethink our strategy. You'll all have to be satisfied that there is no Porter case now. We have a lot of work to do. Now, Elliott, please take Miss Winter back to the Plaza and put a guard at her door if you must, and Miss Dulcy, I will take you to your car so you can be fresh and rested in the morning.

Dulcy looked disappointed but stood to go quietly.

"Miss Porter, go to bed."

"You *are* poopy," she said, giving Reggie a hug, followed by Tucker then Dulcy.

Reggie gathered her things realizing how tired she was. It had been a bit much. She had barely gotten used to Dahlia being dead, much less alive now. The group dispersed like a concert crowd when the lights went up. No matter how curious Reggie and Dulcy could be it was nothing to the exhaustion they felt after the last hour of drama. They knew it would be better in the morning. At least they hoped so.

* * *

It was a silent walk back to the hotel. Reggie felt so guilty she couldn't think what to say. Tucker was silent and she was sure it was due to his disappointment in her. She hung her head and marched through the lobby. Tucker acknowledged the manager, thanking him for his help while he was away. Reggie wondered what that meant but stayed quiet.

Tucker pushed the button and the elevator groaned and slid slowly downward. He leaned against the wall, tired but attentive. Reggie felt even worse than when she had been sitting before Laird.

"So, are you going to speak to me, Miss Winter?" he asked. "Or are we going to stand here and stare at the lift numbers?"

"You must be so disgusted with us. I wouldn't blame you if you just hated me," she said miserably.

Tucker regarded her for a minute then chuckled.

"Hate you? Don't you know, Love, this is what I live for? Why, if you didn't manage to create these most interesting situations, I should be eternally bored by each mundane day. You are the spice of life."

Reggie was sure he was trying to be complimentary but somehow it didn't feel that way. Even though she probably deserved it, she was offended at being made the joke of the day. She could feel the flush fill her skin and she turned from Tucker to face the elevator doors, wishing they would open quickly.

Tucker seemed not to notice, still amused at the situation. Reggie felt the opposite and her anger stung her and burned her face. Even though she was wrong, his condescending attitude was more than she could bear.

The doors opened and Tucker pressed first her button then his. Reggie angrily jabbed her floor again. A realization was dawning for Tucker, and he knew he was in trouble.

"Once again, Regina, are you going to speak to me or just march to your corner and I to mine?"

"I think the gloves are off. What do you think?"

"I think we need rest and a new perspective that comes with a good night's sleep. I suggest you take the sensible route."

"I guess since you have all the answers I should just do as you say."

"Pardon my directive, but please go to bed and rethink all this in the morning. I'm not trying to be difficult or rude. You have had a long day with a huge shock and have just as big of one coming up. I'll ignore the attitude for now and we'll get back on track tomorrow."

"You do what you wish," spat Reggie and stalked out the doors as they opened.

Without looking back, Reggie stalked down the corridor like a steam locomotive speeding out of the station. Tucker watched the doors slide shut and wished he could restart the conversation. She had had a traumatic shock and he glossed over it callously. He was trying to take control, but he did anything but. He pressed his button wondering how everything spun out of control so quickly.

* * *

Chapter 40

Breakfast at the Beach Drive Plaza was becoming a regular occurrence. Reggie was beginning to like it here despite the troubles of the trip. Now that she knew what had happened to Dahlia, the morning seemed brighter, food tasted better, and the company was more engaging, except for Tucker with whom she was still dismayed.

She was relaxed, refreshed, and ready to go as she had slept the motionless, dreamless sleep of the exhausted. She glanced at Tucker who seemed to be evaluating her as one would artwork or a business decision. Then she realized she was a business decision and decided to let it sit. He was just trying to work through it as well. They ate in silence until Dulcy could no longer contain herself.

"It's not that simple now, especially with Landry missing," said Laird.

"With you two knowing about the dearly departed, it changes the details of the service and the execution of the plan. We may just have to get along without him."

"Seems a bit cold-hearted. Is there not a concern for his safety?" said Tucker.

"Of course we're concerned for his safety, but we've got men working on it. He'll be found."

"Hopefully alive," stated Tucker. "And we need a medical doctor for this to work. Again."

"What do you mean again?" asked Reggie. "And what if something else horrible happens? We have a backup doctor, right?"

"The only happening I'm expecting is from the person who caused all this trouble. That's my main interest," Laird said.

"Are we sure about who that individual may be? What if we're wrong about Cord Cavanaugh? What if for some reason, it really isn't him?" said Dulcy.

"I haven't said it was Cord Cavanaugh," Laird said to Dulcy.

Tucker and Reggie turned in his direction. The three of them pondered this for a minute. Who else would it be?

"I need to keep my options open. I can't just pin the whole thing on him without proof. He is missing as well so for all we know, I could be targeting a person who has done a bunk, may be hiding, or for all we know, dead."

His blunt delivery made them uncomfortable.

"Knowing how much we'd like a quick end to all of this makes him a convenient candidate, but if you don't think he did it then we could be on the wrong tack with the whole thing."

"I didn't say he wasn't a prime suspect. He is, but we have to make sure we don't make any mistakes and that means an open mind and open eyes. My men are... hang on. Detective Laird."

Laird listened for what seemed an amazingly long time.

"Just keep me informed. Thanks."

"There. We're still missing a doctor. Anybody have any ideas on that? Elliott, all you had to do was make sure he made it home. What happened over there?"

Tucker eyed Laird with a quiet, yet disturbing glare.

"I trust Jennings with most anything. If he put him on the plane, which he assures me he did, then he got on the plane. What he did when he landed was in your hands, Inspector. Your men were on the detail on this side of the pond. What do they have to say about it?"

"We do not have him as you can clearly see. Now my concern is the whereabouts of Cord Cavanaugh. He's still out there and Landry's one more person we don't want to end up seeing in the coroner's office."

"So, do you think he did it?" said Reggie.

"I think he bears watching more than anyone else at the moment."

"Ok, what's the big plan," asked Dulcy. "I think I need to know since I'm the one with the responsibilities for the tearoom. Or am I? Things have changed on that, haven't they?"

"No. As far as everyone is concerned, you are the acting owner, manager, what-have-you for this event. The plan is relatively simple. This 'life celebration' is where the setup comes in."

"I'm going to ask my question once more," said Reggie. "Where the doctor is concerned – what do you mean 'again'?"

"What? Oh, well that takes a bit of explaining," said Tucker. "We need to start at the beginning with what happened the day of the opening. Landry had run off down the hall to find where they had taken her. Then he came out and said she hadn't made it. With me so far?"

Reggie was reliving the day seeing Landry walking down the hall, hands out, pitiful expression, the unbelievable announcement that she was gone.

"Yes, of course. It was surreal. I mean it looked bad, but you just refuse to believe it when someone says it's true. But it wasn't, obviously."

"No, Reg. He had walked in on a situation he was never meant to see. Being a staff doctor, no nurse or technician would think to stop him. There was supposed to have been someone to take him from Sea Gables to the hospital and handle it, but they missed him, and he came along with us. It was a comedy of errors and then, well, he had to be made a part of it all. Not willingly, mind you."

"Not very funny for a comedy," said Dulcy. "Sorry. But how had they done it? I mean she even fooled Landry. He really thought she was dead."

Tucker looked at the girls and deferred to Laird.

"So, they deserve to know?" he asked.

Laird shrugged.

"Let's just say it's a form of digitalis called digitoxin, which slows down the heart enough to fool even the best of physicians. In this situation, why would he suspect anything else, and they hurried her off before he really got a good look. It was a plan, ladies. She was in on it and so were the commissioner and his men."

"Were you?" asked Dulcy.

Laird gazed at her as if trying to make a decision.

"No, I was not. Not at first, I was sent, dispatched, like any other case. Then I started asking questions and the more I asked the less I got until I was told to back off completely. They put their own men on it and there was no way I was getting anything out of them. I would have been long gone had Mazie Hatfield not taken a very lethal nap."

"And I fully expected them to take me off her case, but they seemed satisfied to leave me alone and let me handle it. I have to say I was suspicious, and I knew something was up but what good does it do to question? I'd end up on a beat somewhere on the other side of the city, moving drunks home after hours. Since then, I'm a bit more enlightened as to why the big mystery and why all the secrecy."

"All you need to know is that it's a very old case involving a German war criminal," he continued. "He disappeared along with a lot of German money, and no one knows what happened to him. Some of the documents of the case went missing from the pile you two went through," he said nodding at Tucker and Reggie, "which filled in the gaps and wasn't exactly the legacy old man Hatfield would hope to have. There was a depot of weapons, money, and trade and somehow, he was at the heart of it."

"Those pictures tell a story, and we just have to decipher them to find out what happened. There's something else you should know. Cord Cavanaugh, or Clinton Peters, knows most of the story if I'm not mistaken, and thinks he has a lot to lose if we get there first. I just can't figure out why he hasn't moved sooner."

"I'm so lost," said Reggie. "What does he know?"

"There's a lot of paperwork connected with this case. It's here, it's in England."

"Sort of explains the article we found on the floor. Didn't I give that to you, Tucker?"

"Yes. I've got it. Something to do with Cord and Perkins and a very bad deal at the university that ended up chucking Perkins from his post of dean because of a plagiarism accusation. He claims to this day it wasn't and that he was set up by Cord Cavanaugh."

"Well, we can believe that a bit more easily now than I bet they could then," said Reggie. "He really has turned out to be quite the opposite of that retired, endearing southern gentleman."

"Well, he's nothing of the sort," said Laird. "He had his poor wife snowed completely. She had no idea who this man really was. Kind of sad to think you could go so long and not at least guess at it. I suppose you only see what you want to sometimes."

Tucker decided they needed motivation.

"Right then. What first?"

"I have to be downtown for a meeting in about twenty minutes," said Laird. "You'll have to start without me."

"Start what?" said Dulcy. "I haven't heard the whole story yet. What is it we're supposed to be doing and why all the secrecy?"

"You need to just relax. I want you and Reggie to go to the tearoom and make sure the decorations are in place for tomorrow. My men will be there helping hang them," he said meaningfully. "There will be tiny cameras in various places throughout the property. Make sure they're accomplishing that and then head down to the room so we can see if we can figure this thing out before it blows up in our faces tomorrow."

"But I thought you had a big plan?" cried Dulcy.

"We have a plan. It'll be just fine and will work no matter what, but we really need to know what those pictures mean. We'll catch the guy, but I just know that artwork will hang him, so to speak. Whatever they say, they say in detail. And when we have that, we'll have everything."

* * *

Laird took off toward his office leaving Tucker, Reggie, and Dulcy to head to the tearoom. The short walk to Sea Gables gave them a few minutes to get comfortable with each other again. Reggie was still angry with him but after all, he was going to tell her the whole story before she and Dulcy tripped up the works.

As they approached the door, they heard protests coming from the kitchen, growing louder with each step.

"What the devil is going on here?" asked Tucker marching into the kitchen.

"These 'gentlemen' are tearing up the kitchen putting cameras every-where," said Lisa angrily. "I get it, but do they have to rip up the walls?"

"No worries, I'll work with these men; you help Dulcy and Reggie somewhere other than the kitchen. Now, how can I help you gents?" asked Tucker.

The three headed to the foyer. Dulcy sent Lisa to deal with table arrangements then pulled Reggie into the office and shut the door. Dulcy dropped into the big chair and Reggie sat on the chaise, staring at Dulcy. Reggie had a familiar feeling that did not bode well.

"Oh, no, now what? You've got that look."

"I'm not sure but I think you just insulted me," said Dulcy. "I have to show you something."

Reggie hitched the chaise closer as Dulcy pulled out the small ornate key and handed it to her.

"Another one? Where do you suppose this goes?"

"I don't know but I had forgotten about it. I found it again the other day and should have asked Dahlia about it but, well, you know..."

"Let's go round to Laird's and see what she says."

"And how do you explain where we're going? We're supposed to be in that silly room doing I don't know what. I'm beginning to think it's just a room where a guy liked to hide from everyone."

"I know, me too. You know, maybe this key is what this is really about."

"Let's go," said Dulcy rising. "We'll find Lisa, tell her we have to run out for something and do this quick. We'll be back before Tucker even misses us."

Dulcy cracked the door, looked up and down, then motioned for Reggie to follow. They found Lisa, told her not to bother Tucker with their errand, then headed for the exit. Reggie quietly shut the door and they ran from the porch in the direction of Detective Laird's stylish apartment. One last glance showed a quaint tearoom, no Tucker Elliott in sight.

* * *

Laird was reading reports. Staff had been in and out all morning, updating him on events, giving him autopsy specifics, and general info. He still wondered about Cord Cavanaugh. There was still no news.

He reread Mazie Cavanaugh's autopsy findings. How a woman could be so blind was beyond him. But then again, maybe she just closed her eyes like so many women do. The more he thought about it, the more he knew she wasn't stupid. She had to have known something. He grabbed his things and was headed for the door when his ringing phone turned him back around. He gave it an undecided look, then marched back to answer it.

"Laird."

It was a short conversation; Laird listened intently, interrupting only to ask a question or two.

"Next time, call my cell. This isn't the best way to communicate but thanks for the info."

He stared at the phone then retraced his steps to the door.

* * *

Mavis Hatfield was being helped into her house by a woman police counselor. She had declined Tucker's offer to see her safely home. Mavis looked around making sure there was nothing out of sync. A detective, not Laird, had already examined the premises before allowing her to enter. From what she knew, there would be a guard posted until they found the "perp" and gave him new lodgings.

Mavis slyly glanced around for the poker. It was nowhere in sight, and she figured it had been taken as evidence. She was convinced it had been Cord who hit her but knew he would not return any time soon. He had not found what he was looking for and would revisit once he thought it safe. He would not know there would be a guard. This to her was an imposition, but then again, so was someone trying to kill her.

She only hoped she could keep the noise down when she pried up the floor to get the papers. She needed those to prove his guilt. She figured they were not focusing entirely on Cord leaving her to clean up her deeds and escape unscathed.

She thanked the policewoman who had tended to her so kindly, tucked her in bed, and advised her to stop worrying and rest. She would be back later to check on her and to let her know that even though the service was meant for Dahlia, they would not forget about Mazie.

The thought of Mazie gave Mavis a fleeting sadness. She found that she could only muster a minute's worth of regret seeing how Mazie had robbed her of her happiness so long ago. Mavis could not find it in her heart to forgive her, or Cord. She hated that he had never really loved her leaving her feeling naïve and betrayed. He had taken her virginity and left her with only deceit. She also thought of Forrest Perkins, the poor clueless bastard who lost his happiness right along with her. She had been so hard on him all these years. Not because he was guilty but because he had no backbone. He wouldn't stand up to save himself or her. She was forgetting the fact that the overwhelming evidence would destroy any man.

In these times, with newer investigative methods, his life would have been spared. He would most likely have been cleared and the right person punished. She pulled the covers back and crawled from bed. She went to the door and listened but heard nothing from the stoop. She returned to her room and quietly closed the door. She stared at the floorboard. How would she pry it up without her poker?

She looked around but saw nothing of use. She felt tired and nauseated. She went back to bed and closed her eyes. As she lay there, she remembered the will. She would be the one to deal with that now that Cord was in hiding. He would probably not be eligible to benefit, so she would be the sole heir. This thought cheered her immensely. She knew there had to be something of interest in it and the more she thought about it, the better she felt. She grabbed her purse from the nightstand and found the lawyer's card. Mavis's face spread into a nasty grin as she dialed the number.

"Yes, Attorney Becker's office? Yes, this is Mavis Hatfield. Attorney Becker asked me to call him regarding my sister's will? Yes," she said smiling. "I'll hold."

* * *

Reggie and Dulcy tapped lightly on Laird's door. After no answer, Dulcy turned her key in the lock. She gently pushed open the door surveying an empty room.

"She has to be here somewhere. She can't have left," said Reggie.

"Come on, let's check the kitchen," said Dulcy, shutting the door.

The kitchen was still except for a tea maker issuing hissing noises from a corner. Dulcy nosed around while Reggie went to look through the rest of the apartment. She was sure Dahlia was in the bedroom but didn't want to scare her. She went back to the kitchen to find Dulcy rummaging through the pantry.

"What the hell are you doing now?"

"Geez! Don't creep up on me like that. I'm just seeing what he's got in here. You know, I think he's probably a pretty good cook. Look at this stuff: capers, like six different kinds of gourmet mustards, a spice rack I would kill for, and just look at the tools. I don't even have stuff like this in the tearoom. I'm jealous."

"Will you get out of there and help me find her? Maybe we should just make a lot of noise, so she'll come check it out."

"Yeah, with one of Laird's guns or something. Let's just go out to the living room and call her name. We're making this more difficult than it has to be."

"Come on," said Reggie as she grabbed Dulcy's arm.

She threw open the swinging door and heard a sickening thump on the other side.

"Oh, no," moaned Reggie clutching Dulcy's arm. "God, I hope we didn't kill her."

"Yes, that would be embarrassing," spat Dulcy. "Well, open the door already."

Reggie eased the door open, but it struck something and stopped. They looked down to see a prostrate and unconscious Dahlia.

"Oh, for God's sake, get her up," said Dulcy.

"No, no, what if she's hurt and shouldn't be moved? We need to check her out first."

"Good idea. Make sure you didn't kill her."

"Me? I just opened the door. I'm sure she's fine, just a bit knocked out. She'll just have a headache, or neck pain."

"I'll tell you what the pain in my neck is, it's you two flattening me with a door then bickering over me. What are you doing here anyway?" she said, trying to sit.

"Ow! Shooting pain, shooting pain," she said lying back down.

"Oooo, you've got a lump on your forehead the size of a baseball. We need to get you some ice. Just lie still for a minute," said Reggie.

She ran into the kitchen and the two could hear her routing about for ice and a cloth.

"Guess he didn't take his key back after the other night," grinned Dahlia.

"Nope, still have it, obviously. Didn't say a word about it after we were here. So, I figured..."

"You figured you'd do some more snooping. What are you trying to find out about him anyway?"

"Nothing in particular. It just keeps nagging me that he doesn't have anything personal around. You know, pictures, trinkets, the type of things that tell you about someone."

"I get it. Now that you mention it, I don't see any of that either. I think there was maybe one picture on the shelf of his nightstand. Probably his mother but nothing more than that."

"Getting bored, are we? Looking at someone's nightstand things?"

"A little. Not much to do till tomorrow. Speaking of that, how's everything going?"

"That's just what we wanted to talk to you about. You know we wouldn't come over here and scare the shit out of you without good reason. There's something I found..."

Reggie bumped her way out of the kitchen and kneeled with a towel full of ice for Dahlia's head. She winced and grabbed the towel relieving Reggie of it with a scowl.

"Ow, that smarts, you know. What are you looking at?" she asked Dulcy.

"Nothing, just the towel. It's a Leron hand-embroidered toile napkin. Very expensive. Interesting for a bachelor on a cop's salary."

"I told you he probably had everything done by a decorator. It doesn't mean anything, and I think it's nice that he has..." added Reggie.

"Do you mind?" snapped Dahlia. "You two could make a criminal run back to jail. What were you going to tell me?"

"Oh, sorry. I found, wait..." she said, patting her pockets. "Did I give you the key?" she asked Reggie.

"No, I don't think so," she said, patting her pockets.

Dahlia waited patiently, Leron napkin growing wet from the ice and head starting to throb. She hazily put the napkin down and felt the bump.

"I hope you don't have a concussion," said Reggie.

"Yes, especially with Landry missing," said Dulcy, pulling out the small key.

"Yes! I found this the day I died," she said sitting bolt upright. "Well, you know what I mean. I didn't have time to figure out what it went to. I had to go out and do my death scene and I couldn't stall events trying to figure out what it was. I meant to get it to you but couldn't find it when it came time to go to the dais."

"So, you don't know what it means either," said Reggie disappointed.

"Sorry, love, wish I could say I did. But if anyone can figure it out, I know you can. Thing is, you better get cracking on it as we only have about... uh less than twenty-four hours," she said trying to focus on her watch.

"Are you sure you're alright? I mean you seem a bit fuzzy. I'm worried about you. How many fingers am I holding up?" asked Dulcy.

"I dunno," said Dahlia. "How many am I holding up?" she said, making a very rude gesture indeed.

"You're fine," said Dulcy. "Let's go."

* * *

Chapter 41

Events at the tearoom were carrying on in their absence. Reggie and Dulcy managed to slip back in with no one the wiser. The only problem was they knew nothing more than when they left. All they managed to do was nearly make Dahlia's death a reality and find some lovely kitchen implements in Laird's pantry. With no other plan, they headed down the rabbit hole where they were supposed to have gone in the first place.

They stood in the room, glaring at the pictures and changing focus to view the secondary portraits. Frustrated at seeing nothing more than the same puzzle pieces, they edged back down the path to try the fireplace again.

"There has to be something here," said Reggie. "I just know there must be an opening," she said, randomly prying bits of brick.

"Maybe not. Maybe we're going about this all wrong. We think it has to be here, but does it? I mean we couldn't seem to find anything even before we had the key. Finding that doesn't prove there's a latch or anything."

"I know but I feel it. I think I need to stare at it for a while."

"We've tried that already."

"I don't know; I can't remember that far back. We've wracked our brains so…"

"Wait. I think I hear Tucker and John."

The two stood by quietly. It seemed like forever before they came into view, and it gave Reggie a strange, queasy feeling in her stomach. Both men stared curiously at the women.

"What have you been up to?" said Tucker. "You have a very odd look about you, Reg, you alright?"

"Sorry, fine. Just thinking about something. How's the redecorating going?"

"This is a top-notch setup," said Laird. "There won't be a move made that isn't caught by one of these cameras. Better get ready for your close-ups."

Reggie and Dulcy stared at Tucker. They had been so caught up with where the key might fit, they had forgotten how behind the times he was.

"Reggie, why don't you take Elliott here into the room and review the items there? I'll brief Dulcy on her duties," he said, not taking his eyes off Dulcy.

Reggie rolled her eyes and pushed Tucker toward the room.

"Let's go, boss, I'll show you the strange things we've got going on there."

"I wasn't finished watching the strange things going on here," he said but she continued to shove him away from the fireplace.

"I really have missed a lot. They're thicker than thieves. Somehow, I didn't catch that before."

"Yes, well. It's been one crazy thing after another," she said coolly.

"Alright, may we call a truce?"

"Truce? I'm not doing anything," she said guiltily.

"No, stop moving, stop walking, hold still, will you?"

Reggie swung around and flared the light in Tucker's face.

"Put that down."

"Sorry", she offered, not feeling sorry at all.

"You're not sorry, I can tell. Look, I feel awful I laughed at you. I meant nothing by it. You know better than that. But you have to admit that sometimes you're just funny. It's one of those things I look forward to in a day. So please can we get back to business and stop this sniping?"

"Well, you were going to tell me about everything. I guess I can forgive you for thinking I'm funny. I am funny, you know."

"Yes, Reg, I know.

* * *

Tucker was swaying as he previewed the artwork, seeing the pictures and their counterparts in a new light. He scratched his forehead and stuffed his hands in his pockets. Reggie waited silently giving Tucker the chance to organize his thoughts. He moved between pictures leaning outward just far enough to catch the secondary images.

"Have you made a list?"

"A list of what? Oh, you mean like an inventory."

"Yes, like what Platt has at the museum. These must have names like the others. I wonder if the secondary images have names as well. Come over here, Reg, and help me pull this one down."

They gently lifted the painting placing it face down on the desk. On the back lower corner, there were numbers and initials.

"Refresh my fading memory, Reg. What was on the back of the ones at the museum?"

"The brochure had the painting numbers and beside those were names. They weren't hanging in any order, so there's the difference. A brochure of names instead of initials."

"Maybe there's a catalog he has with the names on it."

"Where would that be? We've poked about everywhere I can think of. Let's look at the other pictures here."

"What other pictures?"

"The ones all through the tearoom. You know I forgot all about the paper we found that fell out of the sun room picture."

"What paper?"

"I didn't show you the paper?"

Tucker registered the disgruntled boss' look and leaned back against the desk.

"I think I'd remember something like that, Reg. What paper and where is it now?"

"Laird has it. It dropped out while I was straightening the picture. I don't know if it can tell us anything, I think it's in German."

"Well, lucky for you I speak German. We need to get that paper and see what it says. Meanwhile, there must be a catalog here somewhere. He doesn't seem the type to hang them so particularly and not keep even a journal. Let's go look upstairs. Hopefully we'll find something interesting and then we'll go check out of the hotel."

"Really? We're checking out of the Plaza? I was just beginning to like it there. Are we coming back here?"

"Yes, we're coming back, and we'll put you in a beautiful room that doesn't include chamber maids, live or otherwise. The Porter and Elliott clans, complete with Jennings, will be arriving later and they'll be around to keep you company. You've not met Jennings yet, I believe."

"No, but I'm looking forward to it. By the way, which ones know and which ones don't?"

"Only the Porters and Jennings. She hid herself there from the beginning, only it wasn't easy, especially with my parents bargin' in trying to be helpful. It was really quite humorous.

Tucker relayed the whole story from seeing Dahlia alive to the stolen car and the sot of a neighbor swearing to Constable Downs that she'd seen Dahlia at the train station. We have smeared her reputation beyond repair, but it seems it was already frayed at the edges.

"So, now I know why it was such a crazy trip for you. I wish I had been there to see it. I would have loved every minute."

"I wish you'd been there too, Reg. Truth be told it wasn't the same without you, but then you probably know that."

Reggie was speechless. This was a place she was hoping to get to, and so was Alene Elliott. Now that he seemed to be responding to her, she was beginning to regret her subversive mission of getting him to grow up. She rather liked him "as is". Like a slightly irregular piece of fabric or a dented appliance. In addition to regretting her mission, she was beginning to grow fond of this man-child in dress clothes. This could be a problem.

"I know, so next time we'll stick together. I know how much you need me."

"That I do, Reg, that I do," and he smiled and reached for her hand to lead her out of the dark tunnel.

Reggie took it and wondered if those last words were spoken by the business Tucker or Tucker the man.

* * *

Dulcy and Laird were upstairs reviewing the proceedings. The staff had gone out of their way to produce an idyllic setting in the courtyard. Dulcy

470

was pleased with the transformation but also leery. It was beautiful last time as well, but the end result had thrown them into an emotional landslide. She followed Laird out to the B&B.

"Where are you going? Isn't this still off limits?"

"No. We're done now. We've opened it up and Reggie and Elliott will be moving back in later."

"And how long have you known about this, Detective?"

"Ah, Detective. We are in trouble now, aren't we? We sped things up to get it cleared before tomorrow. You can't have an event with a crime scene attached to it. We got what we needed. Even when I found you there, we were almost finished. Come on, let's take a walk," said Laird.

They stepped onto the back porch surveying the tiny white lights and the flowered railings. It seemed weddingish to Dulcy but glimpsing the pots of lilies on the steps and rails erased that thought.

Laird opened the door for her, and she entered feeling odd. She backed up and waited for him to take the lead. He understood and moved ahead of her past the kitchen cupboards and supply closet entrance to the tunnel. He grinned in spite of himself thinking of Sgt. Rivers' reaction on finding him and Elliott trampling over buckets and mops trying to enter the B&B.

It was refreshing not to have to duck yellow tape or worry with Rivers watching their every move. He started up the steps and turned to see her staring at him from the bottom stair.

"What's the matter?"

"What are you up to?"

"Come along," he said, taunting her.

She grinned and followed him rounding the banister head at a trot.

"So, what police matter lurks up here, Detective?"

"Oh, just a little matter of uh, oh just come see," he said.

She entered a beautiful suite with a sleigh king bed on a platform situated above the rest of the room. The claw foot tub was also on a platform in an alcove with ivy blossoming around it and leaded glass surrounding the recess. The décor was romantically unique with French doors opening onto a screened porch with an adjoining door to the next room. Best of all, it overlooked the garden and courtyard where all the events could be seen without entering the yard. Laird pulled her close and kissed her forehead.

"I booked this room for the weekend," he said. "Of course, it's business, you know."

"Oh, yes of course. Official police business, not monkey business," she said, kissing him gently. "You do know this is the bridal suite, Detective."

"It's a strategic location," he said, kissing her back. "We'll be watching every move out there."

"What about the moves in here?"

He grinned and slid his arm around her back and pulled her closer. He kissed her and moved his hands around her body, massaging her and coming to rest on her shoulders. She kissed him once more and pulled away from the embrace with one breathless motion.

"We can't do this now," she said. "Tucker and Reggie will be looking for us."

"I had no intention of anything else. I just thought you should see how we made use of your lovely suite. But I will be staying here. I'll be keeping an eye on the event and the guests. Last I heard, the Elliott and Porter clans would be occupying a good portion of the inn. They should be coming in soon; they're getting cars, so Tucker doesn't have to worry with their transportation. He let them know they could stay here rather than at the Plaza. I'd prefer everyone to be close anyway. Gives me that warm, fuzzy family feeling."

"Gives you the edge in watching them."

"The better to study them, my dear," said Laird.

Dulcy felt like she was in Granny's room alone with the big bad wolf. And she liked it.

* * *

Chapter 42

Courtleigh Bishop: My involvement was strictly limited to the extent of my participation.
-Mastergate, TV, 1992

Tucker and Reggie went room by room upstairs examining anything that could be another Hatfield. After scanning the area, he pushed her toward the bathroom.

"There are three pictures I want to come back for after the guests have gone," he whispered.

He was so close Reggie could smell his cologne and feel his breath on her neck. It made her lightheaded and she leaned on the banister to steady herself.

"Um, I think I know which ones you mean. Why don't we ask Dulcy where she keeps replacement pictures?"

They met Laird with Dulcy at the courtyard midpoint.

"Dulcy, do you have extra pictures somewhere? Stuff you stash away in case something breaks or needs replacing?"

"In the storage closet beneath the stairs. Why?"

"We've been doing inventory," said Tucker. "Not the ones in the room, the ones upstairs. We have a new theory now. We just need to find something that may not exist."

"Okay, if that's all then, what time are the families coming in?" asked Laird.

Tucker glanced at his watch twice before answering.

"Lord, how time does fly. If I remember rightly, they've already landed so we should be seeing them soon. Have you checked on the package in your apartment lately?"

Dulcy and Reggie turned attractive shades of red, eyed each other, and stayed quiet. Tucker registered the looks, folded his arms, and silently stared. They squirmed and looked everywhere but at him.

"Alright, Lucy, Ethel, what have you done now?"

"You take that back," said Dulcy. "I'm Lucy, she's Ethel."

"Something you need to tell us?" asked Laird, joining in Tucker's stare.

"Nope," chimed the two.

"We've some time before arrivals. Why don't we grab a seat in the B&B, wait for them, and you can tell us your story," he said, turning the girls to the back door and following closely on their heels.

"There's really nothing to tell," said Dulcy, once seated.

"We just needed to ask her a question, so we went over to your place," she said smiling.

"Just get to the part where the trouble comes in," he said flatly.

"We knocked her out with a door and were afraid we'd killed her for real, but we didn't," smiled Dulcy.

"Oh, I'm so glad," said Tucker. "I thought we left you to go downstairs?"

"You did, but then we started thinking and one thing led to another, and we had this question and the only way to get the answer was to, well, see her," said Reggie watching the door.

"What could possibly be so important that you would put..."

"Darling!"

Tucker looked up to see his mother in all her glory holding out her arms while the rest of the entourage piled up behind her.

"I'm not done with you," he said leaning in, smiling, but leaving her with a warning stare.

Reggie and Dulcy heaved a sigh of relief then remembered Laird. He was not watching the incoming crowd; he was eyeing them with a look that spelled trouble. Dulcy gave him her best smile while Reggie felt like a third grader waiting in the principal's office. She was not going to be a sitting duck. She caught Alene Elliott's eye and made a beeline for a hug and a kiss.

"I'm so glad to see you. It's awful being here like this, but I know you've been such a help to Tucker. It's been a terrible shock."

"I know. And it's wonderful to see you," she said in her ear. "Tell me about your trip," she said loudly, leading Alene away from Tucker and the group.

Dulcy took her cue and rose to greet the first guests to the B&B since the ill-fated grand opening.

"This isn't over Dulcy," grinned Laird as he rose with her.

"It is for now," sang Dulcy.

* * *

Once the families were settling in, Tucker took Reggie's hand and led her away from the herd. Laird and Dulcy were engaging in a heart to heart for which neither wanted to be present.

"Come along, Miss Winter. We'll settle our bill, and, on the way, you can tell me the whole sordid story."

"There's nothing sordid about it," she snapped, feeling miffed as she was being led away like a three-year-old.

"You don't mind if I keep a grip on you, do you, Love?" he said, holding her hand and keeping her close. "Just making sure you don't wander off anywhere. In fact," he said, "why don't we just stop into the Laird residence and have a chat."

"We don't have a key."

"I'm sure we don't need one."

They marched straight in as a fellow lodger headed out with barely a glance. He let go of the door into Tucker's waiting grasp.

"You do live a charmed life," said Reggie.

"No, love. I live a life of expectation. I expect to be able to get into the building therefore I do."

"Good attitude."

Tucker knocked sharply on the door several times which was opened at once by Dahlia, looking wary but glad to see them.

"Oh, yea! I was getting so bored. I've read his magazines and piddled about but it's really getting rather old. And I thought I wouldn't see you till later," she said, looking askance at him.

"Yes, well," he said, nodding at Reggie.

"Oh, I see. Yeah, well, nabbed you, did he?"

Reggie shook her head miserably and gazed at Tucker.

"It wasn't their fault, really," said Dahlia. "I would have done the same in their shoes, honestly."

"The beginning, please," said Tucker.

Reggie looked pleadingly at Dahlia, but she happily deferred to Reggie.

"Well, Dulcy and I were supposed to be in the room. We went into your office," she said motioning to Dahlia, "and Dulcy, again, had something she had to show me. She took out this small key and we were trying to

478

figure out what it fit when we decided to come and ask you since you're alive now and it was in your office. We figured if anyone knew what it went to, you would. So, that's how we got here," she said leaning into Tucker.

"We let ourselves in with Laird's key and went to the kitchen. We were trying to think of a way to let her know we were here without scaring her. But Dulcy was going through his pantry and his kitchenware and by the time she finished that, I'm sure you'd figured out you weren't alone and that's when we opened the door and..."

"Brained me. Yes. Well done, actually."

"It was sort of funny because it was exactly the kind of thing we were trying not to do."

"Yes, it was a real laugh," said Dahlia, rubbing her head.

"I'm so sorry. Does it hurt still? It was such a big knock."

Tucker leaned in and stared at the bruise on Dahlia's forehead.

"That's a bugger of a mark. You've got a whole other head there. Are you sure you're alright?"

"I'm fine; stop fussing. I think the worst part was Dulcy pressing that napkin thing to my head. That's what really hurt."

"And all for nothing," said Reggie. "You weren't even able to tell us anything. We really thought you knew," she said, trying to hide her disappointment.

"So, you were trying to find the..."

"The female end to this," Reggie said, holding the key up to Tucker.

He took the key and examined it. He stared absently into space then sat bolt upright beaming at the two.

"This key," he said. "I know who she is! Or what she is; I know what this fits."

* * *

The two could only stare as Tucker continued examining the key, picking the edges with his fingernail. Dahlia plucked it from him and passed it to Reggie.

"How could you know what this goes to? Not to be rude but you haven't even been here," said Reggie.

"Reg, remember that day I went down there to start going through the room with Laird? We were looking for a hidden compartment in the desk. That damn desk that has sat quietly this whole time hiding something important," he said, thumping his head. "It didn't even register when I saw it. Right side if I remember correctly," said Tucker closing his eyes.

"I can see it now; I didn't think much about it because we only had the one key, and it was too big to fit that. I figured there was another, but that's about all the thought I gave it."

"We need to go!" said Reggie. "We need to get in there and fit that key. C'mon, Tucker," she said, jumping up.

"I agree we need to try but we have a few things to do first. Dahlia, Love?

Great seeing you alive, as always. Keep ice on that and take something to keep the bruising down. Look in Laird's bathroom chest. We'll see you tomorrow," he said, giving her a big hug.

"Alright, Reg, off to the Plaza. We'll get that over with then we have to check in with the family. Duty calls."

"But when will we get into the room?"

"We'll see what we can do later. The Brits will be tired so maybe we can find time then."

Tucker took Reggie's hand and she waved and blew Dahlia a kiss as Tucker sped her to the door. The last sight Reggie had of Dahlia was a big smile, hands clasped in glee, and a twinkle in her eye.

* * *

The Beach Drive Plaza was a quick trip. The staff was gracious considering wherever these two went, trouble followed. It was a heartfelt farewell, but Reggie was sure they were glad to see the back of them.

"I'm sure they're glad to see the back of us," said Tucker as he paid the bellman and opened the cab door for her.

"How did you know I was thinking the same thing?" she said as she settled uncomfortably in the back seat.

"How is it that no matter what cab you get, it's always so awkward?"

Tucker adjusted sideways to face Reggie. He swung his long arm around her back and peered into her eyes. Reggie felt her heart skip a few beats and was sure he could see it pounding in her chest. She felt weak and exhausted and had a strong urge to lean over and kiss him. She had to get a hold of herself. She looked down at her lap and picked a thread from her clothes.

"Reggie," Tucker said quietly. "You're not going to fight me on this, are you?"

"On what?" she said, dazed.

"On going down to the room now. You know it might not be till tomorrow. I don't want you to do anything rash."

"Oh," she breathed. "You lost me for a minute. No, Tucker, I won't. I should expect it'll be late after dinner and goodnights," she added.

She didn't know what was wrong with her. She was finding it hard to keep control. She reached up and slapped her face brusquely.

"Okay, you've hit the edge," said Tucker. "I think you need rest."

"Maybe, but I'm not *over* the edge. Yet," she sighed.

* * *

The families were having a grand old time in the B&B salon. Rather than throw the lot of them on the tearoom, Jennings had ordered an Indian feast fit for a king. They were all jammed together passing food, laughing, and telling Dahlia stories, the perfect private evening before a public tribute. There were few others in the inn, so they made themselves at home.

"Oh! You two. Where have you been? Come and join us. We're having a wonderful time," said Alene. "The food is fabulous, and Jennings has taken us over as usual. I don't know what we'd do without him."

"Thank you, ma'am. Sir, Miss Reggie, please sit and allow me to get you plates."

He disappeared to the side kitchen. The thought of the tunnel entrance so close to him gave them an uneasy turn. He didn't miss much, and they craned their necks to observe him until Mrs. Porter reined them in.

"I think he's got it in hand you two," she said, eyeing them suspiciously.

Both sat silently back in the cushions. Delia Porter was not to be put off.

"So, what have you been up to? You've been gone for some time," she purred.

"Well, you know what it is to discharge a hotel," Tucker croaked. "Lots of goodbyes, hugs, stories, you know."

"Not anywhere I stay."

Jennings returned with their plates and cocktails allowing them to disengage from Delia and engross themselves in their food. Tucker peeked a few times to find the hoard taking little notice of them. Jennings presided quietly, smiling with satisfaction.

"Now Reggie," said Mrs. Elliott. "How have you been getting along, dear? I know this has been a trying time for you with all this going on," she said gently.

"Yes, it was an awful shock. You've really no idea," she said meaningfully.

"I knew you two would get on. I thought you would have a lot in common. Tucker is lucky to have you to help him through this. It's a very difficult time," she said, dabbing her eyes.

"That's a nice compliment, Mrs. Elliott, thank you. We've been managing as best we can."

Tucker felt awful for his mother. She was visibly upset but also an unrepentant busy body. He knew just where she was heading with this train, and he was getting off at the next stop.

"Has anyone seen Dulcy or Detective Laird?"

"Excuse me, sir," said Jennings. "The Inspector requested you meet him upstairs in the briefing room. You will find him and Miss Dulcy there. That includes you as well, Miss," smiled Jennings.

Tucker stood and lightly raised Reggie to her feet. This was noted by other occupants who sat by smiling silently.

"C'mon, Reg, duty calls."

"Yes, lots to do, lots of business things," she added.

Goodnights were thrown out quickly as they climbed the stairs. Tucker leaned over the banister precariously.

"Jennings! A little late 'tea' for the 'briefing room', yes?"

"Right away, sir, four scotches neat, arriving shortly."

Laird's suite is over here," he said, reaching for her hand.

She followed briskly along as his long fingers held hers lightly. He wrapped several times on Laird's door; the same wrap used at the apartment to signal Dahlia. They found Dulcy and Laird enjoying a moonlit gaze through the telescope. Tucker wondered what kind of reconnaissance had been going on before their arrival.

"Jennings is bringing scotch," he announced.

"Ooo, lovely," said Dulcy. "A perfect cap to a perfect evening."

Tucker and Reggie avoided each other's gaze, each knowing what the other was thinking about their perfect evening.

"Okay, these are monitors for the inside cameras which will also capture the ones outside. My men will be watching every inch of this place so when you flush out our suspect, we'll be there to get him. Our Miss Porter's entrance should seal it."

"Any word on Landry?"

"No, my men are still pursuing that. At this point I'm not sure what to think. It bothers me what happened from the time he got off that plane until now. With Cord Cavanaugh still out there, it gets trickier the longer he stays missing."

There was a polite tap on the door and Jennings entered carrying four deep amber colored glasses and a decanter.

"I take it you've had a chance to meet Jennings?"

"Yes, sir. The Inspector and I have come to an understanding on several tasks," he said smiling. "Will there be anything else, sir?"

"No, Jennings, on target as always. Good to meet you."

"Thank you, sir. If you will excuse me?"

"How are we getting Dahlia tomorrow?" asked Dulcy.

"I have several of my men retrieving her. She'll be dressed as a street person. She'll be equipped with a cart full of collected items along with a wire. She'll be observing everything from outside the fence so when her cue comes, she'll be on the spot. You three will pretty much be doing what you did last time. Just keep an eye out and make sure all the arrangements are being followed," he said to Dulcy. "You just be yourselves."

"To the Dahlia Porter Memorial Service," toasted Tucker.

"May it be the event of the season," added Dulcy.

"That's an understatement," murmured Laird.

* * *

The two were on their way to drop Reggie at her room when Tucker remembered the key.

"We forgot to tell Laird about the key."

"Oh, I think he would have wormed that out of her by now," grinned Reggie. "We have time before the service. It'll wait till then."

Tucker agreed and turned back toward her suite. He stopped at an end room pulling a key from his pocket. Her bags were neatly stacked in the corner and her clothes had been unpacked and arranged. Her nightgown lay elaborately on the end of the bed. She stared at it flustered and glanced at Tucker.

"Don't you just love Jennings," he quipped glossing over Reggie's embarrassment, and her nightgown. "He's done a first-rate job, as ever."

"I appreciate him doing this for me; I just hate to unpack."

"Yes, it's a nice gesture. Leaves you free to do other things. Well, I think I'll push off and find my room. You'll be alright then?"

"Oh, I'll be fine."

"Well, I'll see you tomorrow, Miss Winter," and he gave her a light peck on her forehead.

"Do find it in you to get a good night's sleep. It's going to be a wicked long day," he said.

"I promise," she said, searching his eyes.

And then it happened. She meant to give him a peck on the check but found herself kissing him full on the lips. It was a short touch; nothing too daring, but a kiss on the mouth just the same. It felt natural to do; she would do it again in the same circumstances, but a feeling of overexposure set in, and she moved away from him. She backed up to the door, a sheepish grin gracing her features. She felt the apology rise but nothing came out and she covered her mouth to stifle a giggle. His eyes never left hers and he followed her to the door bracing himself as he leaned in and kissed her back. It was a gentle, affectionate kiss. He pulled back and looked her full in the face.

"I rather liked that."

Reggie shook her head in agreement, but there was a large sign in her brain, red, octagonal, with STOP written across it.

"Can we explore this again? Maybe tomorrow?" she said, confused between her thoughts and her feelings.

"Of course, love."

Now she wasn't sure what she was doing. She felt she should stop before she crossed a line, a line where just on the other side, stood her mother, politely asking her what the hell she thought she was doing. It was horrible to have a conscience that looked like your mother.

"May I?"

Reggie blankly shook her head and Tucker leaned in again. It was a gentle kiss; this time, however, she could feel the passion behind the press of his lips. She drew her arms around him and held him close. She brought her face up to his and kissed him again. She now felt sure of herself, and the image of her conscience was fading into the distance. She didn't want to be safe here, she wanted to be dangerous. She gazed into his eyes and held him there for what felt like ages.

"I'm going with this kiss, and I'll see you tomorrow very early. It'll give you the chance to make sure this is what you want."

She nodded and kissed him, disappointed he was going but grateful for his understanding and patience as she was about to change her mind again. She would make it up to him. After everything was over and they had time, she would make it up to him.

CHAPTER 42

* * *

Chapter 43

Reggie closed the door and leaned against it smiling. Now she'd done it. She had kissed her boss, and he had kissed her back. The thought of it gave her butterflies. She waltzed to the window overlooking the courtyard edge and neighboring car park. She grabbed the nightgown lying nakedly on the bed like a Hollywood prop. She wadded it up and stuffed it in the dresser, unreasonably angry at its presence.

She peered out into the night, leaning against the sill. She gazed at the old building across from her. It reminded her of Rear Window where Jimmy Stewart stared into the lives of others from his wheelchair. People were still out walking dogs, closing up houses and lingering on doorsteps hoping for more than a peck on the cheek. She smiled and started to rise when a sharp movement caught her eye from the opposite building. She crouched down folding her arms under her chin to lean on the sill. She stared into the blackness but there was no more movement. She sat a few minutes longer drinking in the night sky.

Stars swam in front of her eyes, and she shifted her thoughts back to Tucker. She should have gone the dangerous route. She fell onto her bed in a lump wondering about him. She rolled off her spot and went to the kitchenette to heat water for tea. Cupping the mug in her hands she peered back out into the night, but the neighborhood was now quiet. She switched on the light and climbed on the bed. She restlessly sipped her tea hoping the soothing properties would invite sleep.

She wondered what Tucker was doing. Was he sitting on his bed second guessing himself? Of course not. He was a decisive man if he was anything. Once made, a decision was set in stone. She, on the other hand, continued to obsess over hers. Maybe she should just go to his room. She could change her mind; women did it all the time.

She re-situated, fidgeted, then finally realized she was never going to sleep. She decided she would go back to his room and if he was awake, she would knock. She ran over to the dresser thinking about what to wear. Something sexy, alluring, but not too much. Something sexually dignified. What the hell was that? She was obsessing again.

She was sure this was not what Alene had in mind when she hired her to keep an eye on Tucker. Her eyes rested on the contents of her emptied purse strewn across the dresser making note of her room key. Lying next to it was the little ornate key to the desk. Her eyes lingered there, and a new thought emerged.

It was still early, and she was wide awake. She could convince Tucker to go with her to the room. Even if he refused, she then had a second chance just to be with him. It was a win-win. She pulled something comfortable out of her drawer; something not terribly sexy, but not drab, but appropriate if they ended up in the briefing room. She pulled out a t-shirt and yoga pants and grabbed both keys from the dresser. She changed and surveyed the results in the mirror. Perfect.

She cracked the door peering down each section of the landings. All quiet both ways. She ran to Tucker's room. She stood outside his door straining to hear sounds. She knocked lightly three times and waited glancing anxiously each way. With each passing second, her nerve ebbed, and the idea began to seem foolish.

Now she was panicking for fear that he really would open the door. She had the key and was ready to go. She would only be a few minutes through the mop closet tunnel to test the key. If it worked, she would take Tucker down in the morning. If it didn't, she would have saved everyone time by eliminating another dead end. She could hear stifled voices in the salon.

"Oh, no," she thought. "If they're still in the salon, I'll have to walk past them. That won't work."

She tiptoed down the stairs and peeked through the banister. The Elliott clan had been replaced by an unknown foursome. But then another thought struck her at the bottom stair.

"The cameras. What if Laird was monitoring the cameras?"

She investigated the corners but saw only the mounts awaiting the devices. She walked through the salon casually acknowledging the foursome who nodded politely in return. She climbed into the closet hunting for the flashlights. She searched for the tunnel's release latch. She finally found it and felt it give way. She squeezed through the opening and closed the door behind her.

Alone in the dark, her nerve ebbed again, and she took a deep breath as she inched her way through the narrow passage. No matter how many times she did this, she would never get used to the creepy crawly feeling. She was standing at the door when she realized she might not be able to get in. Wouldn't it be locked? It wasn't the day they found it, but she was on the other side now. She shone the light on the doorknob and yanked it hard. She was amazed when the door popped open.

"Wow! That's odd. I guess we forgot to lock it. Good thing!"

She pulled it wide, flashing her light into the room. She sat the torch on the desk to create the dome light that encircled the perimeter. She gazed around the pictures for the hundredth time; one never knew when inspiration would strike.

Something was bothering her as she moved from piece to piece. The picture they removed was still sitting on the desk, but it was something else. She went around the room trying to remember what might be missing. And if something was missing, how could that be? No one had removed anything else. She turned her attention to the desk. It was ordinary; nothing ornate, antique, ostentatious, or even attractive. Its presence contradicted the fascinating work surrounding it.

She dismissed her thoughts and concentrated on the keyhole. She froze, thinking she heard a sound. She dared not move, waiting to hear it again. Uneasiness was welling inside her, and she rose from her crouch and went to the tearoom side door. She jarred it open with its usual pop, shining her torch a short way into the tunnel. She could see very little of the narrow, uneven passage. What she didn't see was the figure hiding, flattened against the wall just out of the sphere of the light until he was there standing before her. She could not believe her eyes.

"Why good evening, Miss Winter. And what would you be doing out of bed at this hour?"

To her shock and relief, standing just inside the tunnel was the good doctor himself, none other than George Landry. But her relief on seeing him alive and unharmed quickly faded as he raised a gun and leveled it at her chest.

"Now, Miss Winter, if you'll kindly step this way?"

* * *

Tucker shut off the taps and listened intently. Did he hear something, or was it his imagination? He stood in the bathroom entrance straining to hear. He crossed to the door and put his hand on the knob. He flattened himself against the door struggling to hear. Was that breathing on the other side? Maybe he was hoping Reggie had changed her mind and was standing outside. He yanked the door open but there was nothing but a slight murmur of voices echoing hollowly through the inn.

* * *

Tucker lay in bed staring at the ceiling, darkness still enveloping him and his suite. He grabbed his watch from the nightstand.

"Good enough," he said. "Six o'clock isn't obscenely early."

He crawled out of bed and pulled on his pajama top. If he was going to go skulking around the inn, he had better be fully clothed. He cracked the door and peered toward Reggie's room. He was satisfied that no one else was wandering about at this hour and he tiptoed down to her room.

He realized he had no plan once he was standing outside her door. Should he march in, trumpets sounding, wind blowing, music playing? Or knock quietly and wait to see if she answered. He hesitated while weighing his options. Big mistake.

"Oh, bugger. Company."

The time it took for him to decide was the time it took his father to visit the communal toilet. He had slipped out of his suite to find Tucker standing in front of the girl's door looking tentative and guilty.

"Son, if you're going to invade the enemy, you can't just stand there. As terrifying as it may seem, you either have to take the port by storm or retreat until you have a battle plan."

"You're always right aren't you, Dad?"

"By the time I get back from the toilet, son, I hope to find that what I have seen was only an illusion created by an old man's wandering mind after too much Indian food."

He smiled and ambled his way to the bathroom. Tucker watched until he was out of sight then tapped lightly on Reggie's door. He felt that if she had thought at all about last night, she would be awake hoping he would come to her door. He received no response, and he wrapped several more times, loud enough for her to hear wherever she was inside. He knocked again and called her name. He was beginning to feel pathetic when his father returned, passing him sporting a bemused expression. He leaned against the door with a grin and waved as if just waiting for her to answer. His father nodded, shook his head, and disappeared into his suite. Tucker could hear the click of the lock on his door.

He bent down to peek through the keyhole. One last jiggle showed him the door was definitely locked. He straightened up and tidied the front of his pajamas. He figured he must have been wrong in his thinking. He called her name one last time, then took his self-respect and his pajamas back to his room.

He lay in bed staring at the ceiling trying to fall back to sleep. He replayed the scene at her door. He was feeling rebuffed and embarrassed. Maybe she needed space. He was not foreign to this concept; many women were flustered by him. It was probably his intensity and passion once he made up his mind about something. Why was he really pursuing her? Maybe he needed to think about that. For her sake.

"Well, back to business as usual," he decided. "No need to create an issue with an employee. She's a smart lass, I'm sure she realized it too and is regretting her kiss, I mean decision, at this very moment."

Tucker had no idea just how much Reggie was regretting her decision. He stripped down and headed to the shower. He let the hot steam envelope him while he shoved away thoughts of her gentle laugh, her penetrating eyes, and the lips he had kissed. The feel of her hair, the smell of her skin, the taste of her, her arms encircling and pulling him to her were all things he needed to forget. As if to solidify his decision, he flipped the shower handle to the coldest setting and turned full front into it.

* * *

Tucker could hear the sounds of breakfast from the salon as he trotted down the stairs. It was an all-out feast, and he took attendance as he greeted everyone. Reggie was conspicuous by her absence, and he was feeling abandoned.

"So, Tucker, where's Reg?" smiled Dulcy.

"Oh, sleeping, I expect. Making sure she's rested for the big day. It is getting on a bit though, would you mind, well, when you're done, knocking her up and rushing her up a bit?" he said tersely.

"Oh, sure, Tucker," she said. "I'm actually done. She's just probably picking out clothes for the day. You know how she loves her clothes. I'll just run on up," she said, pushing in her chair while eyeing Tucker.

"Be right back."

The rest turned back to their breakfast and Tucker sat glaring at a big plate of delicious food. He pushed it away after only a few bites. This was duly noted by the senior Elliott who shot Tucker a concerned look with arched eyebrows as an exclamation point. Tucker marveled at how his father managed to put an entire conversation into one look. He pushed his chair back and gnawed on a toothpick.

"Elliott, I need to see you out in the courtyard."

"Yes, sir, Inspector," said Tucker, happy to escape the rest of family breakfast.

Without a word, he shoved his chair in and followed Laird out the back door.

"Well," said Alene. "He seems a bit restless this morning. I hope all this isn't too much. You know, just when he's given some time to heal, it almost seems as if we're making the wound fresh again. And the same could be said for you, Delia. Maybe this wasn't such a good idea. I just know how hard it's been on you all."

The senior Elliott was thinking about the fact that the memorial service wasn't the only thing that had been hard on his son.

* * *

Dulcy rounded the banister and took the stairs two at a time. She knocked twice on Reggie's door and barked her name. She knocked more forcefully and tried the handle. She was disappointed that she would have to wait for details from the night before when she spotted Jennings near the linen closet.

"Jennings!"

Jennings' head popped out of the shelves like a hummingbird at a feeder.

"Yes ma'am," he said as he hurried to her.

Something in her voice gave him a sense of urgency. He had heard Tucker earlier knocking on the same door trying to raise Miss Reggie.

"Hello Jennings. Would you please do me a big favor? Would you find Linda and ask for her master key for me? She has one to all the rooms."

"Right away, Miss. Is everything alright?"

"Oh, yes, fine. I'm anxious to get going and she's taking too long. I'm just going to sit and hurry her along."

"Oh, yes ma'am," said Jennings, marveling at the customs of American women.

While Dulcy waited for Jennings, she paced the hall taking note of the rooms filled for the weekend. It was a sellout from what she saw of the book. She headed back to Reggie's door in time to meet Linda jangling a large set of keys. She picked an ordinary model out of the midst and inserted it. The door swung open noiselessly and she thanked and dismissed Linda.

Jennings had disappeared like a phantom in the mist. She entered and knocked repeatedly to warn Reggie of her presence but there was no need. Reggie's suite was as bright and clean as an unrented room. She randomly checked the bathroom towels, sink and tub for signs of use, a practice she used to grade the work of newly hired maids.

"How odd," she thought. "Bed is made, towels aren't used, sink is dry. If I didn't know better, I'd swear she never slept here."

Then it dawned on her.

"Oooo, she stayed in his room. He was trying not to draw attention. I'll just run over there and hurry her up."

She knocked on Tucker's door and yelled into the crack.

"Okay, Reg, finish up. Tucker's looking for you and we have things to do. Meet me in the tea room, okay?"

Her response was the flap of a sheet and humming. Dulcy smiled and knocked again.

"Get in that shower now, girl."

As she ran down the steps, the maid stepped into the hall from the room next door folding a large bed sheet. She glanced around once, then returned to her duties.

* * *

Chapter 44

Marcus Penn: Assumption is the mother of all fuckups.
-Under Siege 2: Dark Territory, 1995

Dulcy walked out of the B&B in search of Laird. The blue of the fall sky always made her think of a Crayola crayon. The intensity of the color against the radiance of the sun made everything pop with a sharpness that seemed surreal. She met him and Tucker on the tearoom path deep in conversation. Unsure if she should disturb them, she skirted around and ran up the tearoom stairs. Tucker just missed her as he tried to rein her in.

"Probably finding more trouble to get into," he remarked to Laird.

Things were progressing nicely in the kitchen. Men in server uniforms with earbuds were testing equipment. She tried to spot one of the tiny cameras but saw nothing out of the ordinary.

"Wow, nice work," she said aloud.

"Thank you," grinned Lisa, mistaking her compliment. "We have been working our tails off here. And I'll tell you one thing, you'd think these police servers would be a pain but some of them are pretty good with a tray."

"As long as they keep the guests happy, I'm happy. Have we got any regular servers working this and please say yes?"

"Oh, of course. Our regular girls, you know."

"No, uh, agency staff?"

"Lord, no," said Lisa.

That's all Dulcy needed was more agency staff that weren't really agency staff that she would have to explain to Laird. Then again, she was sure he had thought of that.

"Look, I'm going upstairs to check on things. If you see Reggie come through, send her up, please."

"Not a problem," said Lisa, smiling slyly, like she knew what they were up to.

"No," said Dulcy. "She doesn't know anything. I'm becoming completely paranoid."

* * *

She was again standing in the musty, dank, circular room, staring at pictures, and feeling frustrated. She remembered something Reggie had said about numbers, initials, and cataloging. She looked at the painting they had taken down and saw the number and the initials.

As she examined more closely, she found a small mark on the right-hand side. It was barely legible and looked like 22/R, but she couldn't be sure.

It might have been another set of initials or the artist's personal mark proving the picture as an original.

"Interesting. Wonder if the rest of the paintings have a mark like this. Maybe if we go at it from another direction."

She stepped to the other side of the door and carefully lifted a painting off the wall. She laid it on its face noting a number and initials but no other markings.

"Well, it was a thought," she sighed.

She wondered if she should take each one down and check them when a glint of something under the desk caught her eye. She crawled back into the awkward space and squinted at something sticking out of the desk's side reflected in the low light. She reached up to touch it hoping it didn't move.

Her fingers traced something small and cold in the cramped space. She shone her flashlight into the area. It was the key she had given to Reggie, the key causing all the trouble at Dahlia's. So that's what Tucker was talking about and what Reggie must have been doing down here. But it had to be very recent, like this morning. She wasn't here last night; she was busy, Dulcy thought smiling.

"I bet she went to get us. She's got to be using the B&B entrance. Less 'Laird people' rummaging around over there."

She was about to turn the key then thought better of it. What if something horrible happened and she had to explain that to Laird as well. She still wasn't out of trouble for the apartment incident.

She backed the rest of the way out from under the desk straightening with a crack and headed for the B&B entrance.

"Nope, they all saw me upstairs and, in the courtyard," and she turned back to the tea room door.

"Rats. This is going to take a lot longer."

When she reached the kitchen, she found Lisa still putting finishing touches on canapes, dessert trays, and flower vases.

"Did you see which way Reggie went?"

"No, Dulcy, I haven't seen her at all."

"Oh, she's slick. She's definitely using the B&B entrance," she thought.

She bounced out the kitchen door towards Laird and Tucker who were still at it in the courtyard. As she came closer, Tucker moved into her path but kept talking with Laird.

"Wait, please," he said, turning her around.

Dulcy had no intention of leaving his side until they knew Reggie's whereabouts and what that key opened. She listened patiently, waiting to get a word in. Finally, she just interrupted.

"Excuse me, sorry, do you have a minute? There's something downstairs you need to see. Very important," she added, detecting hesitation from both.

"And has Reggie come out of there yet?" she said pointing at the B&B.

"No," they both replied. "What was she doing when you went up there?"

asked Tucker.

"She was just getting in the shower," grinned Dulcy. "But she has to be out because I think she's been down in, uh, you know."

"She didn't come through here," said Laird, glancing at Tucker.

"Why do you think she's been in there?"

"That's what I need you to see. And she must have gone through the B&B entrance which is why you didn't see her. But I found something under the desk just now," she said, turning her hand like a key.

Tucker and Laird both glared silently at her.

"Yes, so we need to go downstairs," she said enunciating slowly.

"If she was there..." Tucker said, eyeing Laird.

So that was why she wasn't in her room earlier. She had gone ahead without him. He would like to think her curiosity got the better of her. He was disappointed in this development. Must pay better attention in the future.

"Tucker? You alright?" asked Dulcy.

"Fine. I'm sure she'll be down in a minute. Let's go see what we've got."

"I think she came up here to get us. Shouldn't we wait for her?"

"Hasn't she already looked into it?" he said peevishly.

"It's possible, I mean the key is still in the lock. I think maybe she thought about it then realized she better have someone with her, you know, just in case.”

“She’s probably already gone back down,” said Laird, turning to go.

Tucker dialed his cell but after a dozen rings, hit end, tossing it in his pocket. He sighted Delia Porter at the back door of the inn.

“Delia! Did you see Reggie roaming about in there?”

“No, dear, I thought she was with you lot. I haven’t seen her since breakfast,” she said, joining them.

“Was she at breakfast with you?”

“No, I thought she was at breakfast with you.”

“No,” said Tucker flatly.

“How did she see her at breakfast if she didn’t have breakfast with them?” he thought.

“What a beautiful day. You couldn’t ask for a more lovely setting for a service,” she said, ignoring him.

“Well, sorry to run, got to get back to it. Keep my mother occupied, will you? Don’t want her with too much time on her hands. You know how she can be.”

“Not to worry. I have Douglas keeping an eye on her.”

“Cheers. You are A-one in my book,” he said, kissing her on the cheek.

She waved them up the path into the tea room.

"Now where is that young man with my mimosa?" she said.

* * *

No joy here either. Where is that woman, dammit?"

"She must still be upstairs. Come over here."

Dulcy pinpointed the key location as they peered into the recess. It was a tight space so only one would be able to see the key turn. Tucker leaned against the desk as Laird squeezed his bulk into the opening and pulled out a handkerchief.

"Well, turn it already," said Tucker.

"Dulcy, move that light up a bit; it's too hard to see."

Dulcy crawled down to him and threaded the light through the open spaces.

"I've seen this before," said Tucker. "Oh, right, Twister. First one to fall loses."

Laird turned the key and a drawer the size of a desk's inbox popped open between Tucker's legs where he was leaning.

"Bollocks!"

"Oooo," winced Laird.

Dulcy looked away stifling a groan.

"If you don't mind, I think you should pull it out of the desk."

Tucker grabbed the handkerchief, straddled the drawer, and turned to survey the contents. It was long, but not deep and full of papers. Laird poked a pencil through it and grunted. As he held up a layer of dusty, brittle sheets, a small envelope caught his eye. He slid it out and grabbed the corner, dropping it on the desk.

"Aa, Aa, Aa, no you don't," said Laird as Dulcy reached for the envelope. "I'll open it in a minute."

"But there's something in there."

"Really? There's something else in here, too. Just hang on, please."

Tucker watched as Laird picked through to the bottom of the pile then set the drawer on the desk.

"We'll go through these later. I don't see anything urgent except this."

He opened the top of the envelope and tossed the contents on the desk. The three stared in dismay. In the dim light, silently mocking them, lay another, small, ornate key.

"This is like Alice in Wonderland. Now what?"

"We can't do anything right now with a yard full of people," said Laird, sliding the drawer back in place and pocketing the third key.

"What else did you say you saw here?"

"I didn't but as long as you asked…"

She showed them the other markings she had found on the picture.

"It's like a hieroglyphic. I don't know what this means. Elliott, any ideas?"

Tucker looked over the picture, but Dulcy detected a lack of attention, his interest obviously still on Reggie.

"I also found this bomb in the desk and thought you might want to see that, too," she added.

"Alright, well I guess we should… wait…what?"

"I knew you weren't listening. You're too distracted over Reggie. Where do you suppose we look next? She's got to be around here somewhere."

"Let's go back to earlier when you talked to her."

"No, I didn't talk to her. I heard her get up and told her to get in the shower. I figured she would have to go back to her room to finish up so then…"

"Wait, wait, stop. She would have to what?"

"She would have to go back to her room to finish dressing."

"What are you talking about?"

"What do you mean?"

Laird leaned against the desk, careful not to bump the drawer area. Maybe they were getting somewhere now. The two stared her down making her extremely uncomfortable.

"Start over. If you didn't talk to her, why did you think she was in...where?"

"Uh, your room. I went to her room, and she wasn't there so I figured she was with you. When I knocked and called to her, I could hear her flapping around in the sheets and singing. I told her to get out of bed and get in the shower, which I assumed she did, but then she'd have to go back to her room for clothes and things. Right, or no?"

Laird leaned in with Dulcy for Tucker's response.

"Start at the very beginning and tell us exactly what you did when you went up there."

Dulcy retold the story, adding that she sent Jennings to find Linda who had all the keys.

"I let myself into her room thinking she might be in the shower, and I'd sit with her while she got dressed. You know I think Jennings thought that was weird? You know how women talk while they're getting ready? Don't you all do that over in England? I've been doing that since I..."

"Focus," said Laird, clearing his throat.

"Okay, I went in, and she wasn't there. So, I thought she spent the night with you so that's when I went to your room."

Tucker was shaking his head vigorously, now seeing why everything had been so confused all morning.

"Sadly, no, she did not spend the night with me. You've been laboring under a misapprehension. "We need to go check her room," he said halfway out the door.

* * *

Dulcy found Linda on the first floor and got the key. The two men were standing in front of Reggie's door waiting impatiently. She let them in and found the room exactly as she had before.

"Looks like housekeeping has already been in to clean," said Tucker.

"I don't think so. This was how I found it this morning."

"Really? Bed already made? Looks like she had some tea."

"That was there, too. See, we have this list we follow, just to review how the maids are doing? We check the bed, and the bathroom, especially to see that towels are hung correctly, sink and tub aren't left wet, and new supplies are out."

"And?"

"Everything looked fine. Except for the teacup and bag."

"What do you think?" he said looking at Laird.

"I think she didn't sleep here last night."

"Bugger. That's my guess as well. Bless me. I was probably the last to see her. I left her here and went to my room about 10:45. I was trying to be honorable. I shouldn't have been. I think our Reggie has gone missing. Laird?"

Laird had the phone out on his way down the stairs.

"She must have found something and gone off after it," said Tucker as he and Dulcy followed.

"Yes, but she should have been back by now," said Dulcy.

They stood in the foyer while Laird barked orders into his phone. They stared silently at each other and the floor, thinking about where she could have gone and what she could be doing. Tucker again admonished himself for his high principles.

"Detective Laird?"

"Yes, Rivers? Find anything?"

"Just this, sir. It was on the front porch of the tea room."

Laird closed his handkerchief around a small, round object.

"What is it?"

"It's a lipstick," said Dulcy. "It's Reggie's lipstick. Revlon Red, her favorite color. She never goes anywhere without it."

* * *

Chapter 45

Laird and his men were putting the wheels in motion to find Reggie. Unfortunately, the cameras and monitors were not set to go just yet, leaving them no information from which to start. Laird had given the lipstick to his men who were checking for prints. They had no idea why she was missing, only that the key was in the desk, and she was gone. Dulcy and Tucker closeted themselves in Dahlia's office to put their facts in order away from the ears outside.

"It's not your fault, Tucker," Dulcy was saying. "Why would you think she would go down there alone? We don't even know if she opened the lock. And if she did, maybe she found something that couldn't wait."

"Enough to bugger off then and there and not tell anyone? I'm not buying it."

"Possibly, but you know she thought she'd be back by now."

Laird poked his head in the room surveying the two downtrodden individuals holed up in it.

"Just thought you'd want to know we went over her room. She had a cup of tea at some point last night. The bag was fairly dry and the tea stone cold. She also used the sinks; the towel was just a bit damp and so was her toothbrush. Do you remember what she had on last night?"

"It was a shift dress, black, plain, no jewelry and flat, black slippers," said Dulcy.

Both men were gawking at her in amazement.

"Well, women notice these things."

"Do you think you could spot it in her closet?"

"Sure."

"We don't have all day, folks, the service starts shortly."

Dulcy picked through Reggie's closet until she came to a short, black shift dress on the end. She pulled it out, hanging it up in front of herself.

"Look familiar?"

Tucker leaned in for a look, bathing in the lingering traces of Reggie's perfume. So, she had changed before running off to who knew where.

"That's definitely it."

The black flats had been tossed on top of other shoes.

"So many shoes," said Tucker observing the covered closet floor.

"Of course," said Dulcy. "You don't think we go anywhere with just one pair, do you? These are my favorites," she said pointing to a beautiful pair of Italian black stiletto pumps.

Tucker secretly agreed; the memory of her in them not too long ago with a pretty black cocktail dress was burned on his brain. He also recalled how tall she was in them.

"Excuse me," said Laird. "If you two are done shopping, we need to carry on. If you'll pardon me, I need to go back to my men. We'll keep you updated on what we find. Meanwhile, keep ringing her phone and try not to worry. I'm sure she's fine. You know how she can be. Hospital? Mavis? Speaking of Mavis, she insisted on delivering a few words today. My men will be bringing her over soon. I suggest you be available to see her and get an idea of what she's going to say."

"I need to get back to the staff and get dressed. This day is flying by. What do we do about the key and the drawer?" asked Dulcy.

"We leave it for now," decided Tucker. "I'll have to check on the families, Dahlia, and keep tabs on Laird and what he finds out about Reggie."

"Then the room sits till after the service."

"Yes, it does," said Tucker sternly. "Don't go getting any wild ideas. Seems like every time we go down there, something else goes dodgy, or missing."

Dulcy was disappointed but knew he was right. Things did seem to go wrong where that room was concerned. They parted ways but Dulcy took one last look in Reggie's closet. She was trying to remember if there was anything else missing that she could see. She noticed a blank spot where a pair of shoes should be, but she was unable to figure out which ones.

She wandered over and pulled out a dresser drawer. There was a wadded-up nightgown on top but who knew what that meant. She supposed she should tell Laird. She turned to the closet and eyed the blank spot again. She couldn't put her finger on it, so she let herself out and returned to the salon to make sure the staff had finished cleaning the breakfast mess.

All was ship shape, so she slipped over to the broom closet and stuck her head in. Nothing unusual; brooms, buckets, mops, dust pans. Was something missing here as well?

"Hmmm, not sure. Maybe, but I can't tell," she thought, shutting out the light and closing the door.

"That's what's missing," she said, yanking it open again. "One of the flashlights! She definitely went this way. One's gone and I don't think it's in the room. Well, there's something, anyway."

She shut the door and went through the kitchen to the front. Alene Elliott was stepping onto the porch after a walk through the neighborhood.

"Hullo, dear. Alright? Such a beautiful area. Couldn't resist a little walk in the comfy clothes before dressing."

Dulcy held the door for her and noted how fit she was for her age. She was the picture of stylish comfort from her hat to her tennis shoes. Just perfect for a walk in any country garden.

"See you in a bit," she said as Alene briskly headed for the stairs squinting to read her watch.

Something about the encounter struck her but she couldn't think what.

She walked down the sidewalk wondering if Dahlia would arrive early and pester the public or if they would keep her back until the service was underway.

She noted some nice finishing touches that were courtesy of the department. She walked through the front to inspect the foyer. Everything was perfect and if she didn't know Dahlia was alive, she would cry from the beauty of it. Laird was in the kitchen, a now pleasant place for him to be, in her mind. She smiled remembering backing out of the supply closet to find him watching her wriggling and talking to herself.

"What? What's the joke?"

"No joke," she laughed. "Just a recollection."

"The supply closet?"

"Yes, you cop you, how did you know?"

"I laugh every time I think about it, which is every time I come in here."

"Oh, before I forget, speaking of supply closets, Reggie definitely went through the B&B entrance," she said, leaning in close and lowering her voice. "I found a flashlight missing, and oh, I also found a wadded-up nightgown in her drawer, which may not mean anything but thought you ought to know."

She was leaning very close and staring straight up at Laird who was smirking as she spoke. She was tickling his leg through his trousers while giving him her report. She walked her fingers across to the middle of his thigh and he backed off smoothly and laughed.

"Oh, no you don't. You be a good girl and go get dressed. And find out if

Elliott's heard anything."

She flounced out of the kitchen and down the stairs. Mrs. Porter was sitting in the sun sipping a rather sparkly looking mimosa. She looked like a cat enjoying the warm autumn day.

"Hello, Mrs. Porter. How are you?"

"Oh, I'm fine, dear. Just having a little champers before all this gets going. I just can't believe it.

Dulcy peeked again at her mimosa. It was actually pale and profoundly bubbly. She doubted there was any orange juice in it at all. She also doubted that Mrs. Porter had been told that she and Reggie now knew of her daughter's existence.

"Yes, ma'am. Well, I'm off. You haven't by any chance seen Reggie?"

"No, still looking for her, eh? You two seem to be missing each other today."

"That we do."

She steered toward the B&B. It was an eerie feeling; the dais was in the same place as before. She spied the band, also in the same place, but the faces were different. It was like revisiting a dream that starts out pleasant but ends in a nightmare. She felt a hand on her shoulder and Laird was beside her again, a comfort she was growing to appreciate.

"So, when's Dah... the street person making her appearance?"

"She's finishing her couture at present, so in a bit. Any luck with Reggie's phone?"

"No, well, I don't know. I left that to Tucker, and I haven't seen him for a while."

"Okay, I'll get with him. Don't worry, I'm sure she's fine. She has her own way of doing things, you know."

"Yes, I know."

If she could only believe that, she would feel so much better.

* * *

Dulcy found herself in unfamiliar territory. She had a large event underway with nothing for her to do. Ironically, she had taken ownership of the room Laird had busted her in the other night. What was just days ago felt so much longer.

She turned on the shower to warm up and opened the closet to review her outfit for the service; a pretty, no frills, short, black, sexy number but with enough decorum to work, pearls, which she loved and almost never got to wear, and matching earrings. She reached down to extricate her shoes and straightened immediately.

"The shoes! Alene Elliott walking in tennis shoes! That's what's missing from her closet. Her sneakers!"

Tucker could see Mavis Hatfield entering the courtyard on the arm of a capable officer. She was moving with slow, halting movements. A fleeting thought of Forrest Perkins had him hoping that when all this was over, forgiveness might be granted, and their relationship repaired.

He checked his watch marking the time. He had to speak with her but also needed to freshen up properly. His heart hurt hoping Reggie would return soon. Doubt crept in and he tortured himself for not being less of a gentleman. He sighed and heaved himself off the back step heading for Mavis. He was feeling desolate but by the time he reached her he was gracious, charming, and solicitous.

"Mr. Elliott, nice to see you again. This is all so familiar yet so disturbing. I'm sorry if that sounds callous but the recreation of the scene is a bit painful for me."

"I understand, Miss Hatfield. That's why I'm so appreciative that you agreed to speak. When would you like to talk?"

"Oh, just not first. I think I'd be too nervous for that, but I would like to get it done so I could enjoy the others."

"Shouldn't be a problem. Why don't we find you a seat out of the sun. Would you like something to drink?"

"Oh, yes, well let's see. How about a Pink Lady, please?"

"A Pink Lady. I'll see what I can do," said Tucker with a polite smile.

He chuckled as he asked the server if he had the means to make a Pink Lady. The man smiled graciously, reviewed his ingredients then told Tucker it would be his pleasure. His heaving back betrayed his laughter as he reached for his tools.

Tucker surveyed the courtyard, pleased with the smart decorations. Leaning against the bar, his mind went back to Reggie. He knew there was a problem but didn't know what he could do that would be better than the police. It was intensely frustrating. He replayed the scene in his room before she left. She would be here now if he had taken control. He couldn't stop punishing himself for it. These rationalizations were interrupted by the bang of a door and out popped Dulcy, bright, clean, and shiny for the upcoming performance. She lazily marched down the steps, and on spotting him, redirected herself to the bar.

"Starting already? Maybe I should join you. I'm nervous and where the hell is Reggie?"

"Nice segue, Dulcy. You look exquisite and your language is lovely. May I get you something? Miss Hatfield is having a Pink Lady. I shall have to try one."

"A Pink Lady?"

As if on cue, an over sized, fluffy drink, complete with cherries, whipped cream, and a dainty straw appeared in front of Tucker, set down by the politely smirking bartender. He evaluated the drink, then coyly slid it towards Dulcy.

"I have a reputation to uphold. I cannot be seen with such a thing in my possession. What would you like?"

"I'll have a Pink Lady. No, kidding, actually I'll just have a glass of champagne and after you deliver that cocktail, you need to report back here because I have something to tell you."

"Of course," said Tucker, beginning to feel like a henpecked husband, except he was fairly certain he didn't have a wife.

Dulcy observed the last-minute preparations and decided she liked being supervisor. She would visit the kitchen next and hope there was nothing for her to do there either. Tucker was back in no time, running his hands through his hair and distractedly watching the crowd.

"I know what was missing out of her closet."

"What?" asked Tucker, straightening.

"Tennis shoes."

"Sorry?"

"Tennis shoes. You know, trainers, you English type. I don't know what she brought to exercise in, but I'm sure if I dig through her things, we won't find any workout clothes either."

"Yes, she does yoga stretches so she says, though I've never seen it."

"I really should go and see what's brewing up there besides tea," Dulcy said absently. "Makes me nervous to have so much help and so little to do."

"Enjoy your champagne, then. You look stunning. It's a glow actually," he said.

"Thank you, Tucker. That's very heartfelt and I appreciate it."

Tucker nodded and slid away thinking about the glow. Reggie would have that glow if only he had followed his heart. This conundrum was foreign to him. He was always so in control. He vowed that when this was over, he would make sure that she had that same glow.

* * *

The courtyard was buzzing with activity. Servers rushing through the tearoom, staff checking on food and drink, and police keeping track of everything and everybody. This was not an invitation event; it was open to anyone who wanted to pay respects which included gawkers, publicity seekers, and sociopaths who preyed on the innocent.

Unfortunately, the person they were looking for was not an outsider. Dulcy had reprimanded Laird saying that when you sent Dahlia to the next life, selecting who was allowed to participate in the event was neither neighborly nor civic minded. To him it was only asking for more trouble.

"We're not asking for more trouble," Dulcy had said as she was arranging a central floral piece. "We've got plenty of trouble: a missing person, no, wait, two missing persons, a murder, not real but, another murder, very much real, another murder, also very real, an old lady knocked on the head, and someone who wants something out of here very badly. But those aren't really big things, I guess."

"The less unnecessary people the better; less to get in the way, less to keep tabs on, less to interfere in getting this guy, and do you know you look stunning?" added Laird.

"Yes, I've been told and how do you know it's a man? Could be a woman."

"That's right. It could be a woman as we well know. And never take anything for granted, Miss Dulcy," he said pointing a finger at her.

"I'll keep that in mind, Detective."

* * *

"Ow, that hurts," cried Dahlia. "Stop fussing, you twit. I'll have a word with Laird on you. Oh, I'll do it, stop."

"Excuse me, ma'am, it's just that Detective Laird was very specific on what he wanted as to your, uh, landscape?"

"I'll give you landscape. Just go sit and I'll finish. And give me the bloody shoes."

The scene in Laird's apartment had been volatile for some time. The men had managed to keep Dahlia intact up to this point. She was edgy and needed to be handled with care and that was what Lizbeth was for. Lizbeth, unfortunately, had gone to the ladies' room, leaving the men to tend to the finishing touches to Dahlia's "landscape".

Dahlia, on the other hand, was not so accepting when it came to being dressed in the latest in street wear, educated in the ways of the street, and various other necessities of her role. She calmed herself by remembering it was for her benefit and to be ungracious would be rude. When they finished, she looked the part of a street person; mannerisms and behaviors to be added.

"Now when we leave, you'll be on your own. Just know that we'll be watching every step. There's no way anything can happen to you because we'll be on it the minute it does."

"You give me such confidence. Too bad I feel jinxed before I even step out the door," she said icily.

The young man laughed, missing the point entirely. He was concentrating on timing and the element of surprise. They had strapped her with a wire to follow everything going on at her service. She would be listening in to what was being said and done on her behalf and it made her feel odd.

She was an outsider attending her own funeral and her destiny was in way more than just her hands.

She stepped in front of a full-length mirror to admire herself. She was quite authentic. With a pat to her hair, she glanced around at her bum, nodded approval, and marched out to her new surroundings.

* * *

An elderly man ambled outside the entrance of a shoddy apartment complex. He shut the foyer door listening for the lock click before turning to navigate the stairs. The cane bore into this hand as he leaned heavily on it. The gait needed to be just right to be convincing. He grasped the railing guiding himself down each step with care. He was leaving nothing to chance, but the excitement in his eyes belied his body language.

He had been waiting for this day for years. It was a moment of retribution, revenge, and hopefully, reward. The memories caused a physical reaction and as he reached the sidewalk, he stood up too fast, too fluidly. The men descended out of nowhere. He was sure he saw no one as he left the building, but it had been over before he had awoken that morning.

"Cord Cavanaugh? Alias Clinton Michael Peters? We're going to need you for questioning in the murder of Mazie Hatfield Cavanaugh. If you'll come with us, I think we can get this done quickly."

"I don't know what you mean. Take your hands off me."

"Don't make this more difficult, Mr. Cavanaugh. I don't want to have to send for black and whites."

Cord dropped the act and stood erect and defiant.

"I want to call my lawyer," he said, realizing defeat.

"You will have an opportunity for that when we get to the station. It's only questioning."

The disappointment of the catch was overwhelming. How could this have happened? He had been so careful. He had trusted no one and imprisoned himself in the squalid room like an animal. And he was deluded enough to think that without him, the secrets of the Hatfield home would not be purged.

The man coming around the corner swerved from the scene and crossed the street. It had been problematic, but he was able to sidestep this development. He briskly walked the few blocks toward an indistinct two-story brick house set back from the street and shadowed by overgrown sabal palms. He was lucky he had kept this property; it had come in handy.

As he neared the entrance, a swift movement in the side yard caught his attention. He dismissed it as the twins next door and continued up the walkway.

* * *

Reggie threw her long legs over the side of a lumpy mattress on a rusty frame and stumbled to the bathroom. She scrutinized herself in the slip of a mirror then turned on the cold tap and immersed herself in the chilled water. She blindly reached for a towel behind her and slapped the door by mistake. It swung, then hitched with an odd sound, a sickening sound. She felt sweat break out on her face. She didn't like the click it made and

525

she grabbed for it feeling panic rise.

The handle stayed steadfast, and she realized she was locked in from the outside. Did she do that or did someone else? Could the door lock by itself? Groaning with self-reproach, she surveyed her newest prison along with the change of clothing she had been given. This was a perverted twist of events. She was in a camisole and tap pants. She cringed at the thought of him putting his hands on her to remove the yoga pants and t-shirt to replace them with this set.

She ran her hands down the fabric and was impressed with the quality. She shrugged, rubbed her eyes, and splashed her face with more water. The bedroom was bad enough, but this was even worse. Her mind was foggy from whatever he had given her. She was having trouble grappling with reality. She wasn't even sure how she had come to be awake. What now?

"What time is it?"

Her watch was gone; taken away so she wouldn't know. All was quiet outside her prison. Now she was scared and alone and she knew things were progressing without her. No one would know where she was or what had happened. Self-reproach gave way to self-pity, and she wished again she had waited longer outside Tucker's door.

"Why did I let him be a gentleman? He gave me time to think, and I took it. Geez, I could just smack myself upside the head. And I even had a second chance."

She revolved in her tiny prison inspecting the items. It was just a bathroom. But it was a bathroom with a window, not much of a window, but a window just the same. She pressed her ear against the door listening. It seemed quiet, but she couldn't tell; her ears were buzzing, and her teeth felt like there were fuzzy mittens on each one of them.

The water had helped, and she blinked her eyes and shook her head trying to increase her consciousness. Escape was her focus now. She assessed the window and even though it was small, and she was in a lingerie set, she would have to squeeze through it and find her way back to the B&B. She wished she had been born with petite genes as she was probably more than the limited space could handle.

"I'll just use this," she said, stepping on the toilet and grabbing the towel rack. "I should be able to pull myself up and through."

She shinnied up and pushed on the window. It was stuck tight. She pulled up to investigate and found the trouble; it was painted shut and her only hope was to find something in the bathroom to release it.

She climbed down and searched for something sharp and flat to break the paint seal. She flipped through drawers, shelves, and the medicine chest which held nothing but an old tube of toothpaste, a few hotel shampoos, and soaps. She was losing hope when she spotted a pen on the floor.

"Probably won't work, but it's worth a try."

She climbed back to her previous perch and chinned up high enough to stab at the elderly paint before letting herself down to the toilet seat. She was in good shape thanks to her yoga work, but this was a stretch for anyone.

She had no notion of how long she had jimmied the paint but with one last jab, she dropped down to the seat and threw the pen in the sink. She chinned up again and banged on the wooden cross bars with the heel of her hand. There was a slight groan but no real movement. She thought she heard a door slam, and she froze.

She listened intently as someone was mounting the stairs, coming from who knew where. When no other sound was heard, she rested on the strained toilet seat, then renewed her fight against the window.

"I... will... get... this," she wheezed. "I'm getting pissed now."

She pulled up with a burst of energy and jammed it as hard as she could. She heard a lurch from the frame and stared at the rubbery, peeling paint.

"If that's not broken, then it's not going to be."

She gathered her last bit of energy and pulled herself up again. She leaned into it hard with her hand and the window released and popped up as if on a spring. She didn't care how it went up, just that it did.

She eased down gathering her breath and contemplating how she would pull her weight through the small opening. It was like stuffing an over-sized package through a mail slot, but it was her only shot and she wouldn't let the difficulty, or the lack of clothing, stop her.

"Let's just do it," she said breathlessly as she hoisted up and wriggled, kicking her feet against the wall and stabbing herself in the stomach and ribs with the jagged wood.

"Oh, I think... just about... just a little more," she gasped as her head appeared with her shoulders following through like a birthing baby.

"Oh, no. Shit. This is not good."

She had birthed through the window only to reveal that she was on the second floor and the drop was too much to handle.

"I refuse to give up after all that," she said, the stubborn, typical Reggie emerging from the drug induced coma to take charge.

She bumped the window with her head enabling her to see her surroundings.

"Oh, my goodness. Thank you, God, thank you Mother Nature. If Tucker could only see me now."

In front of her, not perfectly situated but good enough, was a tree with branches and a lesser drop than the window she was becoming stuck in. She squirmed more and stretched to reach the nearest branch. It was not close enough.

Grunting and brushing the stinging scrapes down her stomach, she inched out further, reaching harder for the branch. She glanced down, closed her eyes, and grabbed again.

"Ooo, Ooo, leaves and wood," and she opened her eyes.

The branch was solid enough, but she was still a bit away and the only thing left was to just fall and grab. She was out as far as she dared, still clinging to the bit of branch.

"Oh, here I go!" and she squeezed her eyes shut and swung like a monkey, scraping her shins as she cleared the window frame.

She screamed as the branch bowed and she dipped toward the ground. Her forward progress was arrested by another branch which caught her in the midsection adding insult to injury from the rotted window frame.

She picked a piece of tree from her hair and felt for blood. Soreness in her limbs was emerging and she hung briefly before cradling herself in a crook of the tree. She checked her wounds, none of them life threatening, then rested for a few seconds. She screwed up her courage and went for the drop below.

Once she hit solid ground, new problems arose. Where was she? How far was she from the tearoom? Was she close to downtown, and if so, what side? What would she do about clothes? Even in Florida this was unacceptable dress in decent company.

She took a deep breath and picked her way toward the front through the overgrown brush.

"I'll just run as fast as I can. With any luck maybe I'll find a cop."

She straightened her top which had slid sideways in the jungle swinging scene and pulled at her twisted pants to center them. She had no shoes, but her feet were tough from yoga, and she would manage. All she wanted was to get back to the tea room.

She bent down and gathered her breath, then ran headlong around the building. In her haste to escape, she neglected to make sure the coast was clear. She sprinted from her hiding place only to run straight into the arms of George Landry.

* * *

Chapter 46

"Oh, no you don't. No, no, I thought taking your clothes would have stopped any thoughts of running away. I guess you have a little more spunk than I gave you credit for," he said, wrapping her up in his arms.

Reggie was wrestling against his hold like a tournament tarpon.

"You son-of-a..." she choked then slackened as she felt the gouging of a gun-butt in her sore ribs.

She was marched to the door of her jail, mind racing wildly to devise a way out of this fresh hell. If she could only find a house number or street sign.

"Just head quietly up the stairs, my dear," he whispered closely. "No need for bravado. There's no one to help you and I guarantee it will only make things worse."

Reggie froze, morbid recognition making her as disoriented and queasy as the night of the cocktail party. She faltered on the step, repulsed and repelled by the man grasping her arm. His smile widened sickeningly while comprehension spread across her features.

"It was you," she accused. "I recognize that voice. It was you upstairs in the tearoom the night of the cocktail party. You grabbed me from behind and said... those things," she said clutching her pounding head. "But you saved me when I fainted, you helped Dahlia. We trusted you."

"And now you can trust me again. If you don't come along like a good girl, I shall have to call the police. They just happen to be down the street detaining a murder suspect and I could easily have you arrested for soliciting. Selling yourself for drug money. How sad. And since I now know how to get to the hidden room, I don't really need you, do I?" he said, shoving her up the stairs and back into the nasty, cramped jail from which she had just freed herself.

"Shame on you. Shame on you and screw you for that matter."

"Now, now, language, Miss Winter. I don't think your boss would be too impressed with that," he said disdainfully.

"And I don't think he'll be too impressed with you. He didn't trust you from the beginning, especially when you ran off to London. He was right about you all along. Must've been an amazing performance in Sussex. So, when did you decide to go to the dark side, Darth, early on or is this a recent development?"

"It can hardly matter now, but I was doing some business in Sussex when she spotted me. I had to think quickly, and it seemed that with what I already knew and her thinking I was helping, all I had to do was play the twitchy medical man who lost his nerve and went running straight to her. It really was an award-winning performance, if I do say so myself."

"You can say it, but you'd be biased," she said, hoping to stall him while she gained her bearings.

"I did take advantage of listening to them plot and plan knowing I could sweep in ahead and walk off with everything. It will be disappointing to Miss Dahlia's stunning resurrection, but sacrifices must be made."

"But if it's you, then they're flushing out an innocent person!"

"Oh, now you're just becoming a nuisance. This has all been delightful, but I think I need to be going now."

Fluttering in the pit of her stomach began anew. The service would be starting soon, and Dahlia's plan would be all for nothing.

"Oh, surely they've missed me by now?"

She thought about the Revlon Red she dropped at the front door. It was the last move she made before Landry stuck the needle in her. It was pathetic, but the only one she had been able to make. All she could hope was that someone would find it and see it for what it was.

She bent down to inspect the bloody mess of sheared skin on her shins and casually glanced around the room. She tried to locate her clothes, but they were nowhere to be found. Landry had turned and was rummaging in one of the drawers when Reggie threw herself at him. She neatly wrestled the gun away and backed to the door. Landry smiled and appeared unconcerned.

"So, going to shoot me? Have you ever fired a gun?"

"Your psychobabble isn't going to rattle me. I'll shoot if I have to and explain later. By now I've been missed, and you can bet someone is out there trying to find me," she said as she reached behind her and opened the door. "You think you have all the answers, Doctor? Well, you may have found out about the room, but you don't know enough to finish the job. And now I have the gun and you're going to be locked in this room and I have the most important thing of all."

"And that is," he said, a flicker of uncertainty passing across his face.

"The key."

"The key?"

"The key that fits the lock on the underside of the desk. And that, Doctor, is what we call a reversal of fortune."

"No, my dear Miss Winter, this is what we call a reversal of fortune," and with a nod of his head Reggie felt a crushing pain at the base of her skull. She could feel her consciousness ebb as she crumpled and collapsed at the feet of the dutiful but deadly Mrs. Gloria Landry.

* * *

Dahlia had tramped her way to the tearoom, shoving the jam-packed cart with all her might. It didn't help that it had one wheel which would rather go back from where they had come than to where they were going. It was a slow trip, but she brightened at the fact that she had made ten dollars on her trek across town.

She shoved and rested and shoved and rested until a faint crackling alerted her that the wire was within range. She pulled the cart to a stop and leaned on the handle.

"Can you hear me?" said a voice in her ear.

"Yes, I can hear you. It's a bit faint but you're there alright."

"Adjust the earpiece, then the sound should come in clearer," said Sgt. Rivers.

"Oh, right. Much better. Can you hear me?"

"Yes, you're coming in loud and clear."

"Brilliant. How does everything look, then? Is it beautiful?"

"Miss Porter, may we keep our minds on the job at hand? We need to keep focused. And it's very lovely, ma'am. You'll be pleased."

"I should be able to spot the entrance soon. Can you see me?"

"No ma'am, you're not in view as yet."

"I have to stop. These shoes are killing me. Where did you get these clothes anyway? I'm not this small, you know," she said sprawled on the curb clutching at the offending footwear.

"These... are... awful!" she said freeing her feet and tossing the shoes in the cart of cans, clothes, and crackers.

"I've changed my mind. This isn't going to work; I'm coming in," and with that she shoved the cart against a storm drain, pinpointed Sgt. Rivers, and bore down on the unwitting crowd.

* * *

"Any news on Landry?" inquired Tucker as he skimmed the front tables, reconnoitering with Laird near the dais.

"Not from my men but we finally talked to his wife again. She says he's been at their house in North Carolina. There was a call from the property manager who said there was some kind of plumbing problem and he had to go check it out. There's a landline but it's sketchy reception and cell service is basically for shit, so we're having it checked out."

"You believed him?"

"I have no reason not to," said Laird, eyes smoldering. "Tread carefully, Elliott, we're on it. Leave it for now," he said tramping up to the kitchen with Tucker following mechanically in his wake.

He was thinking about Landry. The last time Tucker had seen him he had not been pleased. He had scolded him and basically ordered him onto a plane, then left him in the dark. Stopping off somewhere before zero hour seemed like retaliation. Something wasn't right.

"I thought you were worried about Landry's safety. Why so cavalier all of a sudden?"

"A word, please," said Laird as he led Tucker into Dahlia's office.

"Can we not get into this here? We've got servers working the floor who aren't part of my team. I told you already that we have men on it. We finally heard from Gloria about 11:30 this morning. She hadn't talked to him but said he'd tried to call her from his cell, so he's off the mountain."

"She knows what we've told her which is enough to get him here and that's all. Now go look sad and mournful like you're supposed to and leave Landry and his properties to us."

Tucker watched Laird stalk off towards the front.

"Landry and his properties," grunted Tucker. "I can find his property here and probably faster than you right now."

He turned swiftly to the computer behind Dahlia's desk. He raced through his memory of when they were at the records building. He typed a few things into the computer and waited. Thoughts of Reggie went streaking by as he commanded the information to the screen.

"Property tax estimator, homestead and other exemptions, property record search. Here we go, property record search. Let's see what turns up under Dr. George Landry."

He poked and punched at the keyboard until he was satisfied he had a handle on the good doctor as well as Landry and Associates. Next, he went to corporate filings and analyzed key information from that website. He grabbed paper out of a small holder that said "Love, Wisdom, Peace, and Harmony" and began scribbling, never taking his eyes from the screen.

"I'll give them peace and harmony," he murmured and scrawled the last of the specifics on the back, stuffing it into this pocket.

As he opened the door, he heard raised voices and what sounded like a scuffle. He reached the foyer in time to see Laird leading a filthy person of indistinguishable gender up the stairs under vehement protests. He followed quickly and caught the tail end of Dahlia Porter disappearing into the upper reaches of the tearoom. He was impressed with her turnout but confused and angry that she was jeopardizing everything by walking through the front door.

He dashed after her glad that no one else seemed to take notice. She was convincing; just a gate crasher being hauled away from the scene. He saw the bathroom door shutting swiftly and headed for it. He turned the handle and felt the weight of someone on the other side. Laird was locking the door.

"What the …!?"

"It's only me," said Tucker pushing through then shutting it.

"What are you doing here?" Laird and Dahlia said at once.

"Listen," Laird and Elliott said at once.

"Stop that," shrieked Dahlia.

Tucker put his hands in his pockets and waited for them to stop. "If you're both done for now, we need to talk. There are things you need to know, things that may change our plan today," he said waving the paper in front of them.

"What are you talking about?" asked Laird.

Dahlia leaned up against the closet rubbing her feet, which still ached from the tiny shoes.

"I give, Love. I can't think of any more indignities you could hand me. First, you put me in these smelly clothes, shovel me into shoes the size a six-year-old would wear and then shove a trolley into my hands with aged beer cans and enough foil to call in an alien attack. Now you're saying we're going to change the plan. Whatever are you talking about?"

"Well, love," smirked Tucker, "you're awfully indignant for a person who seems to have tossed the plan as well."

Laird had been watching the volley with guarded interest. It was close to funny, but his neck was still on the line.

"Stop. This is not the time or place," he said pointing at Tucker, "and you are in trouble for pulling the plug on an operation which took a lot of man hours to put together," he said pointing at Dahlia.

"Me? In trouble? You must be joking. Can't be in trouble if you're legally dead."

"You're not legally dead so we move to Plan B," interjected Laird.

He sighed hard and hung his head. When he faced them, it was a compassionate, yet focused, Laird.

"Look, don't let this thing with Reggie cloud your judgment, Tucker. We'll find her."

"What thing with Reggie?" asked Dahlia.

Tucker stopped; she knew nothing about Reggie's disappearance.

"Sorry, Love, Reggie went, uh, missing this morning, and we're not sure whether she went off on her own or if something's gone wrong."

"Then why are we standing here worrying about who came in where when she could be in trouble or hurt or..."

She didn't need to say the rest. As Tucker turned toward the door, Laird turned toward the bathroom cupboard.

"You need to go this way," he smiled, and ushered Dahlia toward the cracked door of the linen closet and the tunnel entrance.

"But I don't want to…"

"We have some things to fix, and I don't think finding you out in the open will be healthy until we get a couple of things taken care of. Capiche?"

"Tucker? Are you going to let him do this to me?"

"It will only be for a small bit, Love. I promise we'll be right back. It's just till we can let you come out without giving my parents a heart attack. You do remember there are people here who will faint dead away at the sight of you? This really is the only place to put you for now."

Dahlia glared at him with all the venom she could muster. In the end, she knew he was right and marched into the cupboard and disappeared like a good white rabbit.

* * *

Tucker and Laird heaved an enormous sigh of relief both reaching for the bathroom door handle. They both backed away, then Laird waved Tucker before him to open the door to the rather busy bathroom.

"Nice job," said Laird. "I was dreading explaining this one to Dulcy."

"I as well. This is one I just know she wouldn't take well. It's not like we…"

Tucker and Laird were emerging from the bathroom to meet, once again, a confused Sgt. Rivers who had something very important to communicate.

"Uh, Detective Laird, sir," he said, face reddening beyond recognition while hoping something would swallow him whole, "I've been looking for you, sir."

"Of course you have, Rivers. What is it?"

"I just thought you should know that Miss Porter has broken plan and is somewhere in the building."

"She's somewhere in the building alright, Sergeant, now get back to your post and wait for new instructions," ordered Laird as he followed Tucker out of the bathroom.

"Maybe we should tell him..." began Tucker as Laird propelled him toward the stairs.

They had missed the fact that Rivers had remained solidly at attention.

"But there's more, sir," said Sgt. Rivers hoping to catch Laird.

"Yes, Sergeant?" said Laird impatiently.

"Greer and Wallace called to say that everything went down smoothly on Second Street. Cord Cavanaugh was taken into custody just about half an hour ago in disguise, like you thought, while making his way here."

* * *

Chapter 47

Taggart: What in the wide, wide, world of sports is a-goin' on here?!
-Blazing Saddles, 1974

Laird nodded and continued down the stairs. Tucker eyed Sgt. Rivers who stood soldierly by watching their exit. Tucker trotted after Laird to see him intercepted at the bottom by several official-looking gentlemen. He hung back straining to hear the conversation. When the group disbanded, Laird motioned Tucker toward Dahlia's office as he gestured to a man in the kitchen.

"Get me Jennings, Ben."

"Yes, sir. You'll be in the office, Detective?"

"Yes. Knock just once."

This was an unexpected turn and Tucker silently followed him into the room. Laird settled in the chair while Tucker perched on the desk edge facing him, arms folded, mouth shut.

"Going to let me go first, are you?" grinned Laird.

"Seems you have a bit more to share than I. Let's start with Cord Cavanaugh."

"Ah, yes, our Mr. Cavanaugh, or Clinton Peters or Michael Peters depending on what day it is or what scam he's running. We've spent some time figuring out his schemes and I can only liken it to a map of the London Underground. That should help you appreciate the complexity of it," he said smiling.

"You seem amused by all this, Inspector. Do tell? Because it isn't just Cord whoever-he-is. You're enjoying a joke, so what am I missing?"

"There's no joke, Elliott, in fact it's far from it. You know Dahlia was working with Commissioner Hammond, correct?"

Laird took Tucker's silence as agreement and continued.

"We've been working with him as well."

"We?"

Laird silenced Tucker with only a forefinger.

"In a minute, Elliott. We have piles of information on Cavanaugh but no evidence and anytime we thought we had him, he slithered away like the snake he is. Ironically, his wife helped him many times and only ended up dying for it. It wasn't his hand that killed her, but it was his order being carried out. That smooth, southern style is a well-practiced act that has kept saving his ass over and over."

"Until today."

"Until today."

"Lucky for us he made a few tactical errors. We knew he had to be in town."

"Because of Mavis."

"Yes. He did skip; Dahlia confirmed that, so she's our eyewitness. If that's the least we get him on, it's enough for now. We like him for the attempted murder of Mavis. My guess is she won't throw him under the bus since she's afraid he'll turn on her. She may have had something to do with the maid but that could be hard to prove."

There was a knock on the door and Ben sent in Jennings.

"You called for me, Inspector? Hello, sir," he said, nodding to Tucker.

"Jennings."

Tucker slid off his perch allowing Jennings to pass. He preferred to stand but was directed to the visitor's chair. Laird passed several photos to Jennings then leaned back and waited.

"These are the individuals, sir?" he said after sifting through them.

"Yes. I just want you to keep an eye on them and mix in like one of the staff. Listen to their conversations. There may be nothing there, but I'd feel better knowing they were tended to. Keep an eye on Gloria Landry. She'll be mingling and waiting for her husband to show. Catch her conversation to see if her story changes. If it does, contact me immediately."

Tucker's curiosity was getting the better of him. This was a new tack putting Jennings to work as detective.

"Should we let him in on it, Jennings?" asked Laird, reading Tucker's mind.

"Oh, of course, sir. Would you like to provide the details, Inspector?"

"Let's just say that in his youth Jennings had duties other than the Porter family. They were successful enough to gain him a bit of royal recognition. Correct Jennings?"

"Yes, sir. And you flatter me greatly."

"Why, Jennings, you old dog. Royal recognition, eh?"

"It is not widely known but is one of the qualifications with which the Porters were pleased. We may say that they feel an additional sense of security for my presence, sir."

Tucker felt a flush of embarrassment as he thought back to the Porter house. Jennings had told him how brilliant he had been in his handling of the Porters and the cars. But Jennings was being Jennings, polite and deferential but discreet regarding his own surprising accomplishments.

"You look puzzled, Elliott," noted Laird. "Make it quick, though. We need to get moving," he said, glancing at his watch.

"We. You said 'we' a bit back. What have I missed?" he said, striking back to his original point.

"It wasn't necessary to give you certain details but now that things may be finally escalating, you deserve to know the truth. It's not Detective, actually. It's more like Agent. Agent Laird, FBI. Nice to meet you, Elliott."

＊ ＊ ＊

Dahlia grabbed the flashlight inside the tunnel door and tiptoed down the stairs. Ironically, she regretted having tossed her shoes in the shopping cart. She passed the fireplace staring at the patchy brick and mortar half expecting something to jump out at her.

When she realized it held no secrets, she groped down the hall and let herself in the room. She panned the torch across the drawings, the lone desk, the decrepit paints, and the easel. She had hastily passed through here the day of the grand opening, noticing only the oppressive stench of dust and decay before finding the door opposite and feeling her way to the B&B.

"Oooo, lookie here. How beautiful," she said, moving the light in a circle over the line of drawings at the perimeter.

"What's this?"

She set her flashlight facing upward creating the light dome as others before her. She settled herself cross-legged on the desk arranging the light to evenly display the room.

She scooted further over the desktop and bumped into the drawer Laird had left out in his rush to find Reggie. She pulled everything out into a neat pile. The selection was mostly papers; a few old letters, some documents, an official looking document, an empty manila envelope, and what appeared to be a guide to the drawings. She laid all the paperwork aside except for the guide. She blew into the manila envelope double checking that it was empty. She checked her watch synchronizing her entrance with events happening above.

"Now, let's see," she said, uncurling herself and hopping off the desk.

Guide in one hand and torch in the other, the pictures were appearing in numbered sequence according to the booklet. There were numbers and letters following the description as well.

"I don't follow. This is number one but has a 22 R on this side. What if I jump down to 22? What do I find?"

She counted her way around to number 22. The description on the guide showed a rural setting with trees, farm equipment, and a newly plowed field.

"This isn't the picture in the booklet," she said, holding the torch closer. "This is a village green during a Saturday market. This is what, a watercolor? *The Presence of the Plow* is a charcoal. Something's wrong here."

She lifted the picture off the wall and set it on the desk. There were no long-standing must marks, no dust or grime. The edges were smooth and the backing taut and clean and they bore no distinguishable markings of any kind. She shone the flashlight on the piece on the desk. It was stained and weakened from years of neglect. The writing on the back was dim and barely distinguishable. Someone had replaced 22, but who and why?

She inspected the rest of the remaining drawings for authenticity. There were two others which had been switched. Her mind was a mass of confusion. She leaned against the desk feeling nauseated. She trusted them all. Who could've devised such a betrayal? She stood, unheeding of the filth beneath her feet making the rounds again.

"Alright, then. Who had knowledge and who had access?"

She checked the other desk drawers and the area where the hidden one had been removed. She flashed the light into the hole. There was something lying at the back, a lone specimen gone unchecked. She reached in and drew out a dull, dirty coin. She turned it over in the light but could read no markings in the dimness.

She tossed it into the drawer contents, then on second thought, placed it in the empty manila envelope. She crossed her arms, knocking the wire in the process.

"Oooh, I wonder."

She turned on her set and heard the crackle of minutiae from above.

"Rivers! Can you hear me? Rivers!" she hissed.

"Miss Porter?"

"Rivers, I need you to do something for me."

"Miss Porter, Detective Laird is looking for you to take your place."

"On my way, love. Listen, I need you to write something down for me, will you?"

"Yes, ma'am."

"Alright. In this order, please write: Reggie, Tucker, Dulcy, um, let's see, and Laird. That's it, I think."

"And what would you like me to do with this, Miss Porter?"

"Just hang onto it for now, alright?"

"Yes, ma'am."

"Thank you, Rivers," she said, switching off the wire.

"Of course, not Tucker," said Dulcy pacing," and that goes without saying for Reggie. I can't believe I wouldn't be able to trust Dulcy after all this time. Laird. What about Laird?"

A sweeping chill overtook her as she tried to piece together events. Laird had access to all areas. He was on the scene the day of, and he spent a lot of time with Dulcy. He was intimate with Dulcy, for God's sake. What did she really know about the man? She had been rummaging around in his pantry trying to find things out about him. She had asked *her* about him. What did any of them really know about Detective Laird? She felt panic rise.

"But he's a copper! How can it be him? He was working with Hammond. Surely the commissioner would know his own men. Wait! Landry, Landry, who came running to England at the first sign of trouble. I don't remember; does he know about the room? No, can't be him, he's missing. Is he still missing?"

"Rivers!" she said, switching on her wire.

"Yes, ma'am."

"Do you know if Landry is still missing?"

"I've been told that he's been located and is on his way here. Is there something you need to tell him?"

"No, Rivers, thank you."

"You're welcome, ma'am."

"No longer missing, but not here yet. That doesn't give him much access then."

She was horrified and panicked at the thought of her conclusion.

"I have to go upstairs. I have to find Tucker. We can't trust this man. We don't know who he is or what he's done. I've got to warn him against Laird."

* * *

"I said I would meet you there. Don't you know we cannot walk in together if I'm supposed to be coming from out of town? Don't fall apart on me now. Get your things in my car and be ready to go on my signal. You know where to park; the car will be picked up and disposed of. I have a stop to make but I want you to go on ahead. Act normal, chat with those snippy women you call friends, and above all, stay away from that nosy Elliott. Do you understand?"

"Yes, of course, George. I'm not an idiot, so stop treating me like one."

"This is it," he said, eyeing her keenly. "After this, we're out, we're done with this place. Nothing can go wrong. And they'll take care of that one," he said, throwing his head in Reggie's direction.

"You're obsessing over nothing. Just go on and leave me to it," she said impatiently.

George gave his wife a curt smile, a peck on the cheek, and threw one last glance at the window where Reggie lay motionless. As he climbed into his car, he caught Gloria staring at the same blank window and hoped she would keep her nerve. If he wasn't careful, she could ruin the whole thing.

She loaded her bags into the car, then slapped the trunk. He drove off watching her in the rear view mirror. She stared again at the window before heading to her car. He wondered if he shouldn't dispose of her now; there wasn't much call for women her age, but then again, it didn't really matter.

Gloria Landry stood at the driver's door still staring at the window. She had never been part of dirty work like that girl up there. She couldn't bring herself to think about it. Her fear for herself was overtaking her but she was in too deep to back out. She would do as she was told then look for a way out.

She sat gripping the steering wheel gaining courage, while up in her prison, Reggie was coming to and trying to move her uncooperative limbs. She relaxed and blocked out the pain using her yoga techniques. She tensed her toes, then relaxed them, followed by her calves then all the way up until she reached her neck which she raised gingerly.

But something was stopping her from sitting up and she tried to roll off the bed without success. The tied sheets strained and tightened leaving her worse off than when she started.

She checked her restraints chastising herself for tightening the bonds. She was secured to the rusty frame by her hands and feet. If she could maneuver them correctly, she could get free. At least the soft sheets could do no more harm than she had already caused.

She rotated her wrist slowly, tucked in her thumb and drew her hand upward. She felt the fabric tighten and cursed the Landry's. She found that if she could only get her teeth on the knots, she could get free.

She stretched forward as far as the ties would allow, bending toward her hands. She pulled with her teeth until she felt the cotton give. After a few minutes she was able to free her hands and then her feet.

Down on the street, Gloria Landry was rifling through her papers and making one last call. Reggie was glaring down at her when she heard the car start. She grabbed the doorknob to yank it open and threw herself at the door.

"Damn! It won't give."

She searched for something to hit it with but found nothing. She ran to the window. Gloria's car was still there. She gazed wildly around the room searching for an escape. She heard voices in the hall and ran to the door.

"Hello? Can you hear me?"

"Hello?"

"Yes! I'm stuck in my apartment. I seem to be having trouble with my door. Can you help?"

"Well, I'm not sure. Is it jammed?"

"I'm not sure. What do you think?" asked Reggie.

"Yes, it's jammed. I'll try to pop it open."

There was a crack and a bump on the other side, but the door stayed fast. Reggie tried not to feel defeated, but...

"Don't you have a key?"

"No, I can't seem to find it. I need to get out without it. It's urgent."

"Wait. I'll see if I can find Lucy. She has a master set."

"Thank you! I really appreciate your help. It's very important."

Reggie waited for what seemed like forever before she heard voices and a slight knock at the door. She returned the knock and heard the rasp of a key in the lock. The door swung wide and she was facing a wisp of a girl and a long-haired young man who burst into a large grin.

"Glad I could be of help. Have we met?"

"I'm afraid not, I'm Reggie but I have to hurry. Maybe another time," she said as she burst past them down the stairs three at a time.

She cracked the door in time to see Gloria Landry's tail lights turning left at the corner. She ran after her as fast as she could, careful not to get in any mirror view. She tried to gain her bearings as she ran. She could smell sea air now and figured she was down near the water and the Dali Museum. How ironic.

She ran after the car, keeping to the grass and side yards. As hard as she ran, the car was gone before she could determine a direction. She bent over in exhaustion panting for air. She forced herself on, stitch in her side when she came up a hill to see Gloria Landry's car stopped at a light. She hitched up her underwear and ran for her life.

* * *

Tucker stared between Jennings and Laird. Jennings was his usual calm relaxed self, beaming at Tucker.

"I am truly sorry for the delivery of that bit of news, but the fact of the matter is that this is an old case that we mean to see the end of."

Tucker grinned, staring at the floor. He raised his head, chuckling. He held out his hand, first to Laird and then to Jennings. As they were heading outside, Tucker remembered the paper with the Landry property information.

"Laird, hang on, you really need to see this, mate."

Jennings excused himself politely to eavesdrop on the attendees. Laird silently perused the paper.

"It's good information, Elliott. My men have been working the same angle. I don't recognize this name, though," he said pointing to the middle of the paper.

"That was an interesting find. I reckoned I'd just check her for fun. Turned up a hot one, I think. I'm not sure of the location but I believe it's local. I can check it out if you'd like."

"Mr. Elliott? Do you have a minute, sir," asked Sgt. Rivers beckoning him to the front room.

"I'll be out back. Don't do anything without consulting me," Laird said, fixing Tucker with an official stare. "I'll put my men on this."

"Right, not a problem."

"What is it, Rivers? Please tell me Miss Winter has turned up and we can solve this whole mess right now."

"Uh, no, sir, it's Miss Porter. She's requesting you meet her immediately. She says it's extremely important."

"I'm sure it is. Probably wants a bath and a new set of clothes. Listen, let's try telling her I'll see her in a few minutes. I've something to do."

"Yes, sir," said Rivers, feeling uneasy about having to disappoint the already irritated Dahlia.

"Miss Porter? Mr. Elliott says he will see you in a few minutes. He has something he has to do first."

Tucker lingered long enough to hear the response. Rivers was surprised at the number of words he didn't recognize or couldn't repeat. His ears were stinging by the time she finished.

"Alright there, Rivers?"

"Oh, yes, sir. She'll just wait till you get there."

"Cheers, mate," and he patted him on the arm and was gone.

* * *

Tucker weaved between the staff listening to the symphonic tones throughout the courtyard as guests were filling the area. The discordant sound of tears mixed with laughter struck at his soul and he longed to know where Reggie was.

Why was there no news of her, even from Laird? He watched as the man himself called over a short, dark officer to whom he handed Tucker's information. He meshed into the crowd and Tucker relaxed, gratified that the lead was at least being investigated.

He gazed across the courtyard where his parents were standing respect-fully with the Porters. His mother's handkerchief was at hand, and he could see that she had been crying. He felt guilty for her pain and wished he could tell her the truth. Jennings was bobbing through the guests, the epitome of graciousness while mentally noting every word. Tucker was sure his report would not only be descriptive but entertaining.

He observed Gloria Landry being descended upon by several unknown women. He marked her moves and when he at last caught Jennings' eye, his return nod satisfied Tucker that she was under surveillance. She continued to meet and greet as she made her way to the bar.

He watched what appeared to be an answer to a question from a distinguished-looking man. She checked her watch, shrugged her shoulders, and pointed to the street, pleasantly smiling, and shaking her head as she spoke. Tucker guessed she was discussing Landry's imminent arrival.

He moved to the bar and ordered a scotch. Some guests were milling about while others had selected their seats from the rows neatly lining the courtyard. Tucker downed the drink in one gulp, ordered another, and was moving away when Dulcy tapped him from behind.

"There you are," he started. "I was just…"

"Are we ready to go?" she asked nervously.

Tucker could see she was on shaky ground and wished to avoid any unnecessary episodes.

"Calm, please love. Laird has handled everything. Just take a deep breath and relax. It'll be fine. You'll be brilliant, I promise."

Dulcy smiled gratefully at him and sighed.

"Give me that," she said, plucking the scotch from him and gulping it down.

"Feeling better?"

He stared at the glass and grinned. As though he only had to wish for another, Jennings floated by and dropped one in his empty hand.

"Well done. Thank you, Jennings."

Jennings waved at him as he pressed through the crowd tailing some unsuspecting attendee.

"So, what will you open with? Are you reading something, or just waxing philosophically?"

"I have a poem, or rather lyrics. She gave them to me. You know, it's hard to be heartfelt when the deceased is ordering you around."

"I know you'll be lovely. Fantastic. The dog's bollocks."

"Now you're just being an ass," she said.

"I know, sorry. Oh, here we go. Laird's cue. Give us a kiss, love. Do us proud."

The soothing background music subsided as the gatherers began claiming the rest of the seats. Tucker took a spot by the dais while Dulcy climbed to the podium. The crowd silenced as she tapped the microphone and cleared her throat.

She thanked them for coming and bid them to pray with her. Tucker was bowing his head when he caught movement by the B&B. Mrs. Landry was still near the bar and as the crowd bowed in prayer, Tucker saw George Landry join her. Finally. He tipped his head hoping he would see and acknowledge him. Landry nodded, giving Tucker a two-fingered salute.

Once more his eyes found his parents and the Porters on the B&B porch. They had refused Dulcy's front row placement asking only to be part of the well-wishing crowd.

"I really don't think we should take center stage, dear. This is Dahlia's day and wherever she is, she's the centerpiece," Mrs. Porter had said, dramatically dabbing her eyes and sniffing.

She had blinked soulfully at Tucker who was thinking what a loss the West End theater folks were enduring without Delia Porter among them. Tucker surveyed the crowd, alert for the person who would make the wrong move.

"Shall we now pray, please."

Heavenly Father,
  You have not made us for darkness and death,
  But for life with you forever.
  Without you we have nothing to hope for;
  With you we have nothing to fear.
  Speak to us now your words of eternal life.

"That man is not who he says he is," bellowed a voice behind Tucker.

The crowd hushed, staring open-mouthed at the dirty, disheveled woman on the porch pointing a finger at Detective John Laird. The crowd turned toward him and stared, riveted by the turn of events. The grungy woman on the porch pulled off her wire and threw it to the ground. Tucker gaped at Dahlia in surprise and dismay. Dulcy was at the podium, head in hand, peeking through her fingers for the fallout. Jennings, shaken by very few things, exclaimed to the fellow mourner beside him "Don't you love a good funeral service?"

As she stepped forward and raised her arm, a fleeting figure blew by her heading straight for Laird. Another disheveled but bloodied woman clad only in underclothes raced to Laird's side and clung to him for dear life.

"It's Landry! He's behind everything and she's helped him," she said pointing her finger at George and Gloria Landry.

Tucker recovered and scrambled through the crowd, heading for Reggie with Dulcy following close behind. As shock turned to mayhem, Landry grabbed hold of his wife and backed up against the B&B porch, pulling out a gun.

"Now this can be easy, or this can be hard. Laird, call off your men. We'll just say our well wishes and be on our way."

"Okay, Landry, we'll do it your way. Jennings, you've got this one," and with that, Jennings dropped a rather large silver tray from his position on the porch onto George Landry's head.

Landry dropped the gun and slumped to the ground. Gloria watched in horror as he crumpled and lay motionless. She sneered at Jennings and shot out a hand for the gun.

"Oh, no you don't," said Dulcy as she lurched forward and threw a punch in Gloria's face.

Gloria joined her husband on the ground as the crowd let out a communal gasp.

"I never did like you," announced Dulcy.

Tucker folded Reggie in his arms as she began to sob. He stared curiously down at her lack of clothing but said nothing. Dahlia, still barefoot and bewildered, joined the group staring at the Landry's as they were led away by Laird's men.

Dahlia glanced up at the B&B porch having forgotten about her parents and the Elliott's.

"Oh, oops. Hullo, Mother, Dad."

"Hello, dear," said Mrs. Porter.

Alene Farthing Elliot, white as a sheet, slunk gracefully to the ground.

* * *

Chapter 48

Colonel Mustard: There's still one thing I don't understand.
Mrs. White: One thing?
–Clue, 1985

The paperwork took well into the night and Laird returned to the B&B tired but satisfied. He found both clans spread over the salon enjoying brandies and tea with Jennings presiding.

"If I forgot to say it earlier, Jennings, thanks. It was nothing short of brilliant, as you would say."

"My pleasure, sir. It was one of the most exciting funerals I've ever attended."

The Landry's had been hauled off to jail to the astonishment of the mourners. Mavis Hatfield had been reading over her tribute, in preparation for taking the podium when the deceased had begun to shout from the tearoom porch. Even with her elderly eyes, she still managed to recognize the young woman who had recently been pronounced dead. She absently folded the paper, tucked it back in her purse, and waited patiently.

Alene Elliott had been picked up, dusted off, and dosed with a hefty measure of brandy which Jennings just happened to have. Dahlia had been scrubbed and polished and given new clothes that neither smelled nor cinched her in unsatisfactory places.

The Porters had been apologizing and explaining to the Elliott's how Dahlia came to be crashing her own memorial service dressed as a street person. Alene had been going between tea and brandy but abandoned the tea at the explanation of the return from their lodge visit and Constable Downs' visit.

"And how is everyone doing? Tucker, how is Reggie?"

Tucker had been deep in thought and the mention of his name snapped him to. It did not escape him that Laird called him by his first name. He felt a slight touch on his arm from Dulcy who sat next to him, keeping a motherly eye out since his return from the hospital.

"She'll be fine. She's quite a tough bird. They gave her a sedative, so she's knocked out. It was a rotten experience; Landry is quite the villain as it turns out."

"Oh, don't we know it. The good doctor is anything but. Between him and Cavanaugh throwing each other under the bus we'll have everything we need to put them away for a good long while."

"That's all well and good but we still don't understand what old man Hatfield was doing down in that room. And we don't have a solution to this case for Commissioner Hammond, which means we're no further than when we started," moaned Dahlia.

"The pictures that were switched by Landry were found at the apartment house where he held Reggie. They'll be returned and we can start over. I know that sounds daunting, but we'll get to the bottom of it. Landry has no more idea of what they mean than we do. He'd pulled them apart and half destroyed them to find nothing."

"I have a couple of ideas, but I need all the pictures to test them out. We can start again tomorrow after some rest," smiled Dahlia.

Tucker had been conspicuously silent during this exchange staring blankly at the floor, head resting in his hands.

"Tucker, dear, what is it? It's all worked out well enough. Why so glum?"

"I just can't help thinking. What if she hadn't gotten away? What if they had gone back there after the service and she was still locked in that room? I can't bear to think what they were planning to do to her."

"You can't speculate about that, Tucker. Sometimes it's better not to know," said Dulcy. "I think you two should take a vacation, go somewhere fun where they'll wait on you hand and foot, then dive back into business. It'll be the best cure. Anyway, it's all over and she's safe."

Laird was watching quietly, but intently during this exchange. Dulcy eyed him appraisingly. She was beginning to understand this complex man. She surmised that he knew Reggie's fate but would never divulge it here in this company. Only later, in the full account of the recent events, would the truth be told.

* * *

A front swept through during the night bringing more fall-like conditions. The weather matched the mood of the guests as they awoke to a sunless day, punctuated by patches of fog and cooler temperatures. Breakfast was a more businesslike affair. Dulcy needed to get back to daily tearoom life.

Tucker needed to retrieve Reggie, and the families were embarking on a sightseeing tour. Ironically, their first visit was to be the Salvador Dali Museum.

Dahlia was brooding over the schedule of the day before attacking the portraits. Laird had stopped by early to coordinate the return of the pictures which were now evidence. Their importance in furthering the ongoing investigation kept them out of the overflowing evidence room of weapons, drugs, and personal belongings.

Laird had spotted Dulcy entering the B&B through the back porch and hurried to the front to intercept her. He could hear her speaking to someone near the salon and lay in wait for her in the hallway. When she didn't appear, his impatience won, and he charged the corner. She had heard him and was also lying in wait around the bend.

"Boo!" she cried as he popped into view.

He enveloped her in his arms and kissed her tenderly.

"Okay, you got me."

"I hope so," she said coyly.

He squeezed her tighter and kissed her forehead before releasing her and taking her by the hand.

"What's up for today?" he asked.

"It's time for me to get back to work. Dahlia asked me to be available in case she needed any help down there. That's infinitely more interesting than cucumber sandwiches and sugar lumps."

"What are you doing for dinner tonight?"

"I don't know. What should I wear?"

"Something dark in case we have to stake out a target," he said intently.

"Really??"

"No, not really. I think you should retire from private investigations. Your lust for intrigue makes me nervous."

"What about just my lust?"

"As long as it only applies to lonely, neglected undercover agents, we're good."

"Well then, back to the original question, I guess; what are we doing for dinner?"

"Pick you up at 7 o'clock. It's you, me, Tucker, Reggie, and Dahlia. Sort of a celebration."

"What are we celebrating?"

"Hopefully, the end of a very long search."

* * *

Jennings had accompanied Tucker to the hospital and was packing Reggie's things while Tucker made sure she was ready for release. He was reviewing wound care instructions with the nurse and having a final word with the doctor.

"Miss Winter, if you've had enough drama for now, shall we go back to the tearoom and have some real food?"

"Ugh, you should have seen what they gave me this morning. Looked like something the cat yakked up."

"We'll take care of that and then if you're done with crawling out of second story windows, we'll move on to something a bit lighter."

"If you would please excuse me, I have something to tend to in the lobby, sir," said Jennings as he slid out the door with the suitcase.

"The man knows how to make an exit," said Reggie.

"And when," replied Tucker gently lifting her and enclosing her in his arms.

"I was afraid I would never get the chance to do this," he whispered.

"I know."

Reggie's face was buried in Tucker's shoulder, wanting only to linger there.

"Let's get out of here," she said, smiling at him.

He smoothed a stray lock of hair trapped in a bandage and led her out, taking it slowly. She had shorn away a great deal of skin jumping for the tree and her shin bones were throbbing beneath what she had left of the raw flesh.

When they reached the main floor, standing at the exit smiling broadly was Jennings, a bright, cheerful bouquet in his hands. He held them out to her, a gesture which so touched Reggie she began to cry.

"Right this way, sir," he said pointing to a waiting car in the entrance way.

* * *

"What a bloody long day," sighed Dahlia. "I haven't spent a day like that in... well, never."

The five of them were relaxing in luxury, tucked away in a secluded section of an exclusive downtown restaurant. Having been denied reservations, Laird pulled a "cop" card flashing his badge. But it was the recently deceased, recently revived Dahlia Porter whom they had to thank for the exceptional accommodations.

"It is not every day we are lucky enough to play host to a living legend," sang Jean Yves, who was not only showing professional courtesy but a bit of curiosity about the most talked about memorial service ever.

Dahlia promised to have lunch one day soon and grace him with every detail of the harrowing experience. The Brits had spent their own long day as tourists, shopping, and lunching at a lovely restaurant by the beach, and had not made it back.

Reggie was looking brighter, and Dulcy was sure it was due to medicine which did not come in a bottle. Her battle scars would fade but her broad smile would last for the foreseeable future. They were relaxing back with their cocktails when Tucker finally pressed Laird for details.

"So, what do we know of our 'bad guys'?" asked Tucker lightly.

"Well, details are still coming to light, but this is an intricate and tangled mess which'll take time to sort out. Our 'bad guys' were into a lot of 'bad things'."

"Such as?" asked Dulcy.

"Cavanaugh, or Peters, if you will, has been telling us some very interesting stories. Dahlia and I have had conversations about what she's found, and after putting things together, amazingly enough he seems to be corroborating... so far."

"The papers I found down in the room were a bit convoluted, but he's been dealing in drugs, weapons, and then women dating back to old man Hatfield," said Dahlia. "Seems he just took over Hatfield's projects and added a couple of his own. Then he found out something about a big deal that went sour for the old man. So, with only one person who knew about it..."

"Cord Peters whatever," ventured Reggie.

"Yes, so not only did his mother blackmail the old man into thinking Cord was his son but after she set the record straight, he found himself a new secret and carried on the blackmailing."

"Okay, let me make sure I understand," said Dulcy. "His mother had the old man thinking Cord was his son, but she corrected this before she died?"

"Right so far."

"So, then he came here, met the old man, and married his daughter? How does that work?"

"He was furious with his mother for telling the truth. Suddenly she dies, the money stops, and he only has one blood relative left in the world; his actual father, the man who was with his mother but abandoned her when he found out what she'd been up to."

"Ugh, this is pathetic. Keep going."

"He comes to America thinking he'll ingratiate himself with the family under a new name and maybe manage to marry one of the daughters, which he does, but not before breaking the heart of the other. Mavis, of course."

"Oh, now this is getting interesting," said Reggie. "Are we about to find out what happens with Perkins?"

"Yes! Mavis finds out who Cord is somehow. She gets her hands on a letter not meant for anyone's eyes. And according to Cord," said Laird, "she still has a copy hidden somewhere in the house. She took it out of hiding to tease him after they'd been to the funeral home, but when he went back for it, it was gone. She had changed the hiding place."

"So, it was he who knocked her on the head," said Tucker.

"Yes, he's admitted to it. He was trying to take her down with him. He was trying to throw her under the bus as well," laughed Laird.

"Anyway," continued Dahlia, "she wouldn't give the letter back, so he turned on the charm. At the time she and Perkins were an item, and he was none too pleased about being replaced by some smooth-talking pretty boy. Cord was working her hard to get that letter when she ended up pregnant!"

Silence turned to gasps and pronouncements of "I knew it!" and Dahlia had to bang on the table to get back their attention. Renard floated by thinking she was crassly asking for service but was mollified when she apologized and ordered another round of cocktails.

"So now she has to go away with her sullied self, but she takes the letter with her. Cavanaugh was so angry that he wrote a scathing piece to the dean of the university where Perkins had just earned a professorship and exposed him for having plagiarized his thesis. For added effect, he also told the dean that he had 'seduced a girl of good breeding and put her in the family way'."

"Oh, my gosh," cried Dulcy. "But they can prove those things false these days, can't' they?"

"Well, maybe now, but Perkins was so mortified, not only over the thesis, but over Mavis, that he just barricaded himself in his papers and refused to have anything to do with any of them. Cord had presented a pretty strong argument, with proof somehow, and Perkins was stripped of his post and 'found to be wanting of integrity' so he checked out of society and started doing research projects for private individuals. It wasn't until recently that Platt was able to talk him out of his cocoon to come do the brown bag lunches. He's honestly a very knowledgeable person."

"And Mavis never forgave him," added Reggie. "She felt he just gave up on her and himself and has been frosty ever since. I think he would marry her today, poor thing, if she would say yes."

"By the time Mavis came back to town, Cord had set his sights on Mazie. She was an easier mark, less complicated and maybe even less bright than Mavis. He married her and the rest is history."

"But not quite," said Laird. "She may have been less complicated, but she was not less bright. She knew a great deal about what her husband was doing. And she let him. She liked money and her father disowned her when they married. But he couldn't get rid of him. There's something he knows but won't tell. He blackmailed Hatfield over it till he died. He figures if he can't get the money now, nobody gets it. And what can we do to him, put him in jail? He's already there and is going to stay that way. And by the way, he didn't murder Mazie, but he knows who did. And she's gone."

"So, who did kill the maid in my room?" asked Reggie.

"It could have been a different person, could have been Landry. We're not sure just yet."

"So, what about Landry?" asked Tucker. "How does he fit into all this?"

"Well, after old man Hatfield died, Cavanaugh did quite well for a while working with the established contacts and using his people, but time goes on and things change, and you need new people and fresh ideas and money. So, one day he meets this upstanding doctor fellow and the whole game begins again. Once a blackmailer, always a blackmailer. He finds out through one of his contacts that there's a guy who can help them out. A lot. He's a disgruntled employee, if you will, of Landry's. He's willing to drop on him in exchange for money and work. Cavanaugh approaches Landry with some fascinating private information and Landry suddenly has a new partner."

"But what do they do?" asked Reggie. "How do they make their money, and without getting caught?"

"It's like I said, we've been watching Cavanaugh for a long time. And interestingly enough, the tip we got on him came from Landry. Cavanaugh isn't that stupid. It didn't take him long to figure out how it all went down, and they started giving it up like free candy."

"Huh," said Dulcy. "But back to her questions: what do they do?"

"A little bit of everything. Whatever there's money in at the moment. Of course, there's your old standards; drugs, weapons, chop shops, and then there's women."

"What do you mean 'women'?" asked Reggie.

Tucker believed he knew the answer to this one and reached for Reggie's hand and held it tightly.

"It's all too frequent these days. It's sex trafficking. It's when a person is coerced, forced, or deceived into prostitution, or maintained in prostitution through coercion. It can also occur alongside debt bondage, as women and girls are forced to continue in prostitution through the use of unlawful 'debt' purportedly incurred through their transportation or recruitment – or their crude 'sale' – which exploiters insist they have to pay off before the can be freed. Sorry for the official verbiage but it's what they like us to use."

Reggie had turned white as the tablecloth and Tucker edged closer to her. She was gripping his hand like a vice, and he could feel the pounding of her heart on his shoulder.

"That's what he was going to do with me, isn't it?"

"I won't say no, it could have been, especially seeing how you were dressed. Or worse."

The table was quiet, each thinking about the horror of what that meant.

"We just need to get those pictures, figure out what they're trying to tell us, and screw him for being such a fuckwit," said Dahlia.

The table burst into laughter. It was blunt, but true.

"Renard! Let's order!"

* * *

Chapter 49

Jane: Can you please find somebody else to be creepy with?
-27 Dresses, 2008

"Is it okay to walk?" someone said.

"I think so," said Reggie. "Don't worry about me. It's a beautiful evening with a nearly full moon and I don't want to miss it."

"I came so close to missing everything," she said softly.

Her hand was in his and he squeezed it briefly. He was careful not to cause her any more pain. Her skin was shaved from both shins like a peeled carrot; scraped from the bottom of her kneecaps to the tops of her ankles. She had a deep gash on her cheek from the twig which caught her when she swung into the tree, and several bruised ribs from dropping onto the branch she used to jump to the ground.

The skin on her palms was raw and red and her big left toe was sliced from being caught on the windowpane while blindly jumping. He couldn't even imagine the number of bruises yet to surface. All he knew was that he would make damn sure she was tucked in safely tonight.

The five of them were walking past Laird's apartment on the route they had taken back to the tearoom. Laird had Dulcy by the hand and as they passed, he slowed their pace and peeled off. They scooted in the entrance and slipped through the door. Before anyone had noticed, they were gone.

"You're a bad boy, you are," giggled Dulcy. "Wonder how long it'll take them to miss us?"

"Reggie is on drugs and Tucker is afraid to take his eyes off her. Dahlia is looking at the moon and thinking about what she has to do tomorrow. They might be at the inn before anyone notices we're gone."

"Keeping me under surveillance, Detective? Afraid I might make away with valuable evidence? So, how do you plan on keeping me from escaping your lair, Laird? I'm one tough customer, you know."

"You need to stop watching late night TV. I think I can find something else for you to do," he said, guiding her into the elevator. "Want to see my handcuff collection?"

* * *

"So, they peeled off at his apartment, yes?"

"Of course, wouldn't you?" replied Tucker.

"I could do with an after-dinner drink, then, how about you?" asked Dahlia.

Tucker eyed her then glanced at Reggie. She was being a trooper, but he could see she was failing fast. He ushered her through the door and motioned for Dahlia to wait for him in the salon. He navigated Reggie to her suite. She happily handed over the key and let him guide her into the room to her bed. She sat bleary-eyed on the edge and smiled.

"Thank you."

"If only I could take away the pain, I would. Can I get you anything?"

"No," she said dejectedly.

Her eyes were filled with tears, and she took off her shoes and jacket. Tucker wasn't sure if he should stay or go.

"Alright, tell me. Why the sadness?"

"I nearly ruined everything," she said, tears leaking down her shorn cheeks. "I could have been sold as a slave and no one would have ever known what had happened to me. And he would have gotten away with it," she sniffed.

Tucker grinned then remembered how that had gotten him in trouble before. He handed her a glass of water with her last pain pill of the day.

"Please take this and know that if it hadn't been for you, we'd never know what he was up to. He would have gone on with just the word of Cavanaugh against him. You were so brave I can't even find the words. We almost let a truly awful man walk away to continue his atrocities against women and children. But you stopped it all."

She had laid her head on his shoulder as he softly spoke to her and when he brushed the hair from her face, her eyes were fluttering. He gently lowered her onto her pillow. He pulled the throw over her and softly kissed her forehead, then her cheek, then her lips. Her even breathing comforted him.

She would be fine. He kissed her one last time, a little longer, and as he turned to leave, she squeezed his hand, and a faint smile graced her lips.

He took the stairs slipping off his shoes at the bottom by the door. He padded into the salon where Dahlia had already burrowed in on the couch, sipping a dark liquid, and watching her toes as she wriggled them freely on the coffee table.

"Nice manners, darling. Remind me not to eat anything off that table in the morning, will you?"

He grabbed himself a single malt from the private stash in the pantry and plopped down next to her. They sat side by side, silently sipping, each waiting for the other to explain why they were there. She had bidden, he had followed, and neither was really sure why.

"As we were children, so we are adults," said Tucker. "Curled up together, warding off some unseen evil."

"Yeah, s'pose so," retorted Dahlia.

He reached over and grabbed her hand and held onto it tightly. They sat in silence and continued to sip their drinks. He felt the weight of her head lower onto his shoulder. There were still no words, but there was a small sound of sniffing coming from his lapel. He leaned his head onto hers and gave in to the overwhelming emotions.

* * *

Light shone through the window waking Tucker with a start. There had been a dream. He was with Dahlia, and they were children again. They were running over the moors and laughing. They had stopped in the middle and hid in a patch of heather. Something was after them but still they laughed.

The sky had been dark, then it lightened, and the sun burned bright, hurting their eyes. Tucker squinted at the surroundings, eyes stinging. He had a taste in his mouth like a peat bog. His neck cracked and when he tried to move, he was pinned by a great weight. He looked down and remnants of the night before became a full memory. Dahlia was stretched out over him, fast asleep and making ragged breathing sounds, interwoven with sharp snorts.

"Oh, Gawd! We're still in the salon. Dahlia, wake up!" he whispered loudly.

He pushed her off enough to try to wriggle his legs free, but she only slid toward the floor hanging off his knees. He slumped down underneath to catch her, and she pitched off the couch on top of him.

"What are you doing to me?" she moaned.

"We fell asleep in the salon, and you've pinned me like a wrestler. Can you possibly get off?"

The sound of footfalls froze them in their place. Tucker cringed.

"Well, nabbed in the process," said the senior Elliott. "All I wanted was a damn-all biscuit and you two have to be here crawling all over each other like ants on sugar."

It was too much for Tucker to be caught twice in one visit.

"Honestly, Dad, can't you just have a lie in once in a while?"

"Can't you just pick one bird and be done with it?" and with that he sauntered off to the pantry leaving the two in a knot on the floor.

* * *

Tucker sprinted up the stairs but slowed as he came to Reggie's room. He tapped lightly and called her name, thinking he would just check on her before showering. As he waited for an answer, his father passed him, shaking his head and muttering.

"Damn," Tucker winced. "Just can't win with this, can I?"

When he received no answer, he felt in his pockets, located the key Dulcy had given him and quietly let himself in the room.

"How about that, Dad?" he said to himself.

He peered around the door, but Reggie was out cold, still lying under the throw. He was relieved to see her and went to her side to watch her beautiful, grazed face as she slept. He tucked the throw underneath her making a cocoon and bent down to kiss her. She stirred and smiled but slept on and he tiptoed to the door.

* * *

Reggie slept way past 9 o'clock but didn't feel like getting up. When she reached for her watch, it was 10:15.

"Oooo, I must have dozed off. I need to get up and get down there."

She unwrapped her mummified self and sat up. She was creaky but sound and felt that after a good stretch and some breakfast she would be ready to take the tunnel again. She had not been in the room since she had surprised Landry switching the pictures. It would be painful, but she needed to do it for Dahlia and for herself. What was so important it was worth killing for?

The thought angered her, and she gingerly shifted and headed to the bathroom. As she crossed the threshold, she checked the lock and pushed the door open as far as it would go. With an appraising survey of the room, she slid off her clothes and climbed in the shower.

* * *

Dahlia had raced past the banister and rounded the top of the stairs in time to see Dulcy fumbling with the key to her room.

"Ahem!"

"Oh, shit, can you not do that?"

"And what have you been doing all night, you bad lass, you?"

Dulcy straightened and stepped toward Dahlia.

"Whew! Back at ya. You're a mess."

Dulcy reached in her purse and pushed a mirror in front of Dahlia's face.

"Ugh! Frightening. Thank God it's only you seeing this."

"You never answered my question. Where were you last night?"

"Well, I slept with Tucker. I'm just popping round to tidy up before going down below."

"Dahlia how could you?" she said, mouth open and eyes popping out.

"What? Oh, for Chrissakes, you twit. We fell asleep talking on the sofa in the salon. We were actually sleeping. What were you doing if you please?"

Dulcy just smiled, slid her key in the lock and popped the door open.

"I'm not saying anything since it can be held against me."

"Listen, love, I know what you've been holding against you, and it's got nothing to do with a chat," and with that she left Dulcy in the empty hallway.

Dahlia was the first to get to the room. She was so intent on putting her idea to the test that she decided to forego breakfast. The pictures in custody had not arrived but that didn't stop her from pulling the rest down and lining them up according to the guide. Tucker joined her and helped her lift them from their mounts and place them around the perimeter.

They had not yet moved any of the paints or easel but decided it was time to respectfully relocate them. He carried everything through the tunnel, piling them up before stowing them carefully. At the end of his second haul, he heard a sound from the other side of the door. He punched the latch and standing before him like a vision was Reggie, haloed by the light behind her. She stepped forward and he could see her full face now, embattled but beautiful.

"Hello," she said. "I wasn't expecting a welcoming committee."

Tucker couldn't help but smile, and he grasped her hand and gave it a squeeze.

"Hang on, I have things blocking the way. Wouldn't want you to trip and add more injuries to what you already have."

He moved the easel as she watched. She reached in and grabbed the paints, palette, and lineaments and set them aside. She gazed sadly at them feeling a loss she couldn't understand.

"Sad isn't it?" he said echoing her thoughts.

"Yes, but I can't say why."

"I believe it's pity for something that used to be fresh and new and helped create images of substance. It's a tribute in a way as well. They're still here even though the artist is long gone."

He was behind her and he closed his hands around her thin shoulders, stroking her battered arms.

"That's a nice way of looking at it. Gives you a sense of continuity, however strange the idea behind it."

"Yes, well, there's a lot we have to learn about this, love. Such as why would a man lock himself up for hours at a time painting pictures that no one would ever see?"

"At least not in this lifetime, anyway. But" she said turning into him, "I think we're about to find out. Are you ready for this?"

Tucker gazed steadily at her trying to read the message in her eyes. Was it fear, excitement, trepidation?

"The question is, are you? Are you ready, Reg?"

* * *

Dahlia had been doing heavy work down under the earth. The three of them hadn't mentioned where they would be to the rest of the family; they had left that to Dulcy.

There were twenty-four pictures lined around the room awaiting their arrival.

"What do you think? I've only arranged them according to what the paper says. Now we just have to figure out what it is they're saying, if they're saying anything at all, I mean."

The three of them stared at the pictures from every vantage point they could think of. The only thing they learned was that by mid-day they were hungry.

Tucker had been resting against the wall when he announced that he needed a break. He stood and rubbed the cramps from his calves. Reggie, sitting cross-legged, moved to stand but missed and sat back down trying not to laugh.

"Lovely, dear, and you so young," said Dahlia. "Why don't you both go up and order something and give it a rest for a bit. Bring me something back, please. I never did eat breakfast."

"And what are you going to do down here by yourself?" Doesn't seem right leaving you while we go up and have... well... food," said Reggie.

"Lord, don't worry about me. I'm going to go through these papers again and sort everything out in case I missed something."

Tucker gave Reggie a meaningful look and ushered her forward. There would be no changing Miss Porter's mind and they needed to do as she said. Reggie left under duress and Dahlia rearranged herself and started over.

Tucker put Reggie in front of him and lit the way through the B&B side of the tunnel. Once inside, Reggie reached for the closet door knob but Tucker grabbed it before she could turn it.

"Sorry, I know it seems strange but, I seem to be having rotten luck lately with... uh... doors. It's just that I'm having trouble getting them open and getting to where I'm going," he said, cracking it to a slit and peering through the tiny opening.

"I think I should help then, Tucker," she said. "You really need to get something in your stomach. You've been down in that hole too long."

She punched the door wide, narrowly missing Alene Elliott taking a shortcut out to the courtyard. Reggie was mortified while Tucker knew what this would mean. There wasn't any way he was going to walk out of a broom closet with Reggie that wasn't going to be misconstrued.

"Your father seems to know what he's talking about, Tucker. I didn't believe him but now I see I shall have to apologize. So nice to see you feeling better, Reggie dear."

She left the two standing in the closet, Tucker holding the door all but closed. Reggie laid a sour look on Tucker and stepped over him to exit the cramped closet. She threw open the door and heard a loud bang on the other side.

"Ow! What the bloody hell is going on?"

Reggie stood frozen, her hand over her mouth, while Tucker took a deep breath, and brushed past her, poking his head around the door to address the injured.

"Hullo Dad, following Mum into lunch? Feel like some company?"

Tucker grabbed Reggie's hand and pulled her out of the closet. Joseph Elliott stared, sighed heavily, and offered her his arm.

"Say, Miss Winter, have I ever told you about all the closets and cupboards in the Sussex house? If you like exploring, it's a marvelous place. You really should take a look at them some time."

* * *

Chapter 50

Ford Fairlane: You're just in time to see what I refer to as: solving the case. It's cute. I think you'll like it.
-The Adventures of Ford Fairlane, 1990

"I do believe my father is totally enamored of you, you know."

"Maybe a little bit," said Reggie. "Okay, maybe a lot."

Lunch had been delicious, and Lisa was sorry to hear that Dahlia was in her room with a headache.

"Should I take her some soup or a piece of quiche? It's good for the soul."

Tucker pushed his empty quiche plate away and thanked Lisa for her concern.

"It's alright, really. We'll run it round to her."

"If you think so," she said unconvinced.

Tucker smiled and winked at Reggie. The Elliott's watched them walk leisurely across the courtyard to the inn.

"Probably going back to play in that broom closet, you mark my words, Alene."

* * *

"You carry the lunch box and I'll hold the torch," said Tucker as they entered the tunnel.

The sight that greeted them in the room was a wondrous thing. Dahlia had remounted part of the paintings then hung more under those in a second tier, then set the rest in a third tier, encircling a portion of the room in a dazzling exhibit. It gave a flow to the images as they meshed together to make a scene.

"This is fantastic," said Dahlia, eating her lunch.

"Brilliant," said Tucker. "This is truly amazing. Still not sure what it is though, eh?"

"I was talking about the quiche. This is fabulous. This isn't my recipe, is it? Is this my recipe? I need this recipe!"

"They're trying to tell us something, that's for sure, but what?" added Reggie.

Dahlia had finished her lunch and was munching on a muffin when she ordered Reggie and Tucker to the side of the pictures.

"I think that just maybe, if we get a photograph of it as a whole we may be able to see it a bit better, yes?"

Dahlia took half a dozen shots and stood back examining the new gallery through the camera's eye.

"It's too small; not enough detail. We need to print these out and enlarge them to see what we get. I need to go up to the office."

"At least you don't have to hide from anybody when you go up," laughed Tucker.

"We'll just keep working on it," said Reggie, staring at the wall.

Dahlia turned to the tearoom entrance, stopped, about-faced, and crossed over to the B&B side.

"A little less conspicuous, I think."

"I dunno, I think you best watch out for my father, Dahl. He's beginning to have strange ideas about that supply closet. If he sees you coming out of it, he's either going to have a stroke or lock himself in it."

"Sounds like your dad," she quipped and was gone.

"Alright, then, whaddya reckon, Reg?"

Reggie was deep in thought. She was pacing, eyes darting over the artwork, chewing on a pen.

"Oh, no, you've got that look, the one that always brings trouble."

"I was thinking..."

"There it is. Trouble. Please, go on."

"Right before I put the key to the lock on the desk, and before that bastard Landry took me out at gunpoint, I'd been looking at the backs of the picture. The numbering and lettering had me so confused. It still does, but I've got this idea brewing," she said grinning from ear to ear.

"Ah, here it is, we've skipped straight to trouble. Never mind all those pesky in between steps."

"Oh, stop. I'll need your help, though."

"Right, an accomplice. Cannot get into proper trouble without an accomplice. So, what do I do?"

"Well," she said, fingering Tucker's shirt collar, "I need a big strong man to help me take all these down and re-hang them backwards."

"Right. If you'll just wait right here, I'll go find you one."

"C'mon, boss, let's get going. I'd love to have them all done by the time Dahlia comes back."

"Yeah, just as afraid of her as I am, eh?"

"Oh, probably more, yes."

"Alright, let's get cracking."

By the time Dahlia returned with the prints, Tucker and Reggie had removed each piece, turned them over and rehung them to face the wall. It was a mass of musty, deteriorated brown paper glaring blankly at them, with the exception of the hieroglyphics on the lower right side.

"My lovely images!" wailed Dahlia. "What are you two playing at now?"

Reggie was silent, scribbling frantically with the pen she had been chewing. She held up a finger, then continued to examine each piece and scribble violently. When she was finished, she turned the pad to them and beamed.

ANACCIDENTIKILLEDGERMANFIREPLACECOINSINBANKVAULT

"Oh my gosh! Oh, dear God," said Dahlia.

She grabbed the pad and began stabbing at the page. With tears in her eyes, she handed it back. Tucker read the printing over her shoulder.

AN/ACCIDENT/I/KILLED/GERMAN/FIREPLACE/COINS/IN/BANK/VAUL T

* * *

A trio of men, loaded down with camera equipment, were given explicit instructions by Laird to use a specific entrance inside a broom closet, to enter a hidden circular room where they would find twenty-four pieces of art they were to photograph according to the specifications given.

It sounded like a wild goose chase. Word around the department was that this was the old Krebs case finally coming to a close. The men stood in front of the broom closet, shaking their heads, certain they were in the wrong place.

"Hey, Sarge, are you sure about this? It seems awfully small. How we gonna get all this stuff down this little hole?"

The sergeant had loudly reviewed the details of the assignment and the consequences if not completed properly. He then abruptly hung up after requesting their presence in his office when they returned. There was no way out.

The three hauled themselves and their equipment through the opening and disappeared down the tunnel. They were not prepared for what they saw or for what came through the incomparable eye of the camera.

This would be one for the books; one that would be talked about in the station hallways for years to come. Feeling a surprising sense of accomplishment, the three packed up their equipment and headed for the tunnel entrance.

It was with a new respect for the artist and the human condition that the trio bumped their way up the tunnel and out into the broom closet. They baby-stepped to the door and awkwardly tramped through it much to the surprise of the distinguished-looking gentleman who excitedly exclaimed: "Upon my word! Alene! Alene! You've simply got to see this!"

The three stared after him, wondering if he were human or ghost, and hurried their way out of the Sea Gables Bed and Breakfast and Tearoom as fast as their equipment would allow them.

* * *

Tucker, Reggie, and Dahlia sat in the office like grade schoolers waiting for punishment.

"I know we're not in trouble but why does it feel so much like it?"

"Hey, how're you all doing? I heard; he's on his way. He was stuffing a muffin in his face when I last saw him. Sounds like we might finally be seeing the end of this," said Dulcy, more of a question than a statement.

"That reminds me," said Dahlia. "Whose quiche recipe is that?"

"Why, did you like it or no?"

"It was brilliant. And I didn't think it was mine."

"It was mine," smiled Dulcy.

"Really?"

"Really."

"Well, in answer to your question, it looks like a yes," said Tucker.

"We were having a look-see at these and once we started digging into them, we decided they'd better be turned over to Laird. Seems Commissioner Hammond will be satisfied after all."

Dulcy shot them a questioning look as Laird breezed through the door and marched straight to Dahlia's chair.

"May I?" he asked.

"Oh, why yes, of course, please, have a seat."

"You're like three detention brats in front of the principal," said Laird. "Quit it. Now, as it looks, you've found a possible murder scene. We haven't sorted it out yet, but we'll need your permission to dismantle the fireplace down under, if necessary."

"Obviously, yeah," said Dahlia, turning sheet white.

Tucker picked up her hand and held it in his. Suddenly it all had a different feel.

"And I'll return your photos to you," he said, handing Dahlia's pictures over the desk. "We've sent some men down to take additional photos. I'd like you to look at them when they're ready. I think you deserve to see the whole picture. You'll be amazed but also a bit repelled if that makes any sense. He was an incredible artist. It astounds me what he was able to create, locked in an underground room."

"This may sound crazy, but I think it must have been therapy for him for the guilt he felt. He may have been a lot of things, but from what we've learned, a cold-blooded killer is out of character. Anyway, we've been through the rest of the paperwork from the drawer. There was a copy of the letter from Cord's mother confirming that Cavanaugh wasn't really Hatfield's son. Oh, by the way, we translated the letter in German you gave us. It was an inventory of sorts, a bill of sale if you like. It confirms what they've known for some time, which is that this man Krebs, the German, had been dealing in weapons and liquor and whatever else he could make money on. Seems they had their own art scam running on the side, too. If it was illegal and you could make fast, big money, seems it was part of the plan. Hatfield oversaw operations but kept his hands clean of the dirty work. Any questions so far?"

All three shook their heads and continued to stare expectantly.

"Now, we talked last night about how Cavanaugh picked up his mother's blackmailing habit. Tucked inside a folded envelope that was stuck in something else was a letter."

Laird reached inside his jacket pocket and pulled out a clean white envelope with a slight hump in it.

"It was a bit delicate and faded but forensics was able to pull it out. This is a copy, but the main intent is very clear."

Hatfield,

I want to thank you for the opportunity to work alongside you as your partner in your various business projects. Now, I know you're thinking that I don't know, or will I ever, work for you and am, of all things, lastly, your partner. I believe you'll be wanting to change your mind by the time you reach the end of this letter.

You see, Hatfield, I am a man of many talents, just as yourself. One of these talents is investing. Maybe not investing as you see it but investing in talent and information. I've been watching your operations, along with an associate of mine, for some time now. My investment in his talent has provided me with information which I believe you will find very interesting.

We'll need to meet to discuss our arrangement, and my compensation, of course. I'm sure you're asking yourself why you would step one foot in my direction. The answer to that is simple; just tell me what happened to the German after last night's disagreement. Produce a living, breathing man named Krebs and I'll find opportunity elsewhere. Somehow I don't think you'll be able to do that.

Shall we say 7 pm down at the Knightwatch?

Regards

Cord Clinton Peters Cavanaugh

The three were speechless. Laird respectfully folded the paper and tucked it back in his jacket without looking at his audience. He stopped, placing his hands on the desk as if trying to account for everything.

"Okay, there was something else", he announced, staring straight at each one in turn. "They were rather hard to decipher, but they had been somewhat preserved inside another envelope.

"What is it, John?" said Dulcy sensing a change in atmosphere.

"They appear to be canceled checks to a Miss Olivia Hatfield, Chicago, Illinois."

"Oh, my... Mavis's baby! And he took care of her. But where is she now?" asked Reggie.

"That will be for Miss Hatfield to find out if she is so inclined. She already has a couple of tasks ahead of her. She's at the reading of Mazie's will as we speak. Since we have no evidence against her in any of the incidents, and since Cavanaugh has been charged as an accessory to murder, he's ineligible to inherit, so it'll all go to her, whatever it may be."

"But you said a couple of tasks. What else is there?" asked Dahlia.

Laird stared at her for a minute, then pulled out a small manila envelope and scattered the contents on Dahlia's desk. Once bright and shiny, a tarnished small key and a dim, discolored coin lay nakedly in front of them.

"Coins in vault," said Tucker.

"Coins in vault. She'll be going to the bank with you Dahlia since it's your property it was found on. But it's her father's money, ill-gotten or otherwise. I don't judge that part; I only uncover it. Well, that's about it. They'll be done with the pictures shortly so if you're ready, we can go over to the station."

* * *

They were seated in an indoor amphitheater surrounded by the photographers, desk clerks, police, and detectives. Dahlia's original idea of photographing the pictures had taken on a whole new dimension.

The team which had gone in and captured the "wall of art" as it would come to be known, had documented a masterful representation of a truly disturbing scene. These three men would have the distinction of uncovering a piece of surreal art that was not only a confession to a crime, but a most significant piece of work from an era where few were left who might remember the characters.

Dahlia, Tucker, Reggie, and Dulcy were front and center glued to the screen as the projectionist put each puzzle piece in place. The resulting effect was Dali-like craftsmanship. Where there was one picture, there was a second abstract image portraying a different scene, person, and place.

The room was overflowing; people sat in the gallery, stood at the back, and hung off the stair railings watching in blaring silence as the events on a midsummer's night began to play out like a slow-motion movie, each frame added in to make the whole.

"What do you see?" whispered Reggie. "I'm not sure if I can tell what it is."

"I think we need to focus on the central image our eye first detects," Tucker said as Dulcy and Dahlia leaned in to listen.

As they absorbed the up-close scene, they could hear gasps from the back of the gallery.

"Let's go," motioned Tucker.

"Why? What are we doing?" asked Dahlia.

"What did you think you saw?" asked Tucker.

"Do I have to say it here? It's a bit upsetting; I mean I'm not sure I want to say."

They were standing now, and as they talked, they noticed people around them moving and circling, some whispering to others, some just staring, some confused to the point of indifference.

The static scene on the screen was quickly becoming an interactive art project. The four made their way to the back of the room, taking the place of others who were switching to go down in front and up close. They readjusted their eyes to the outer image and collectively issued a sharp intake as the truth of the matter set in like a slap in the face. They quietly left the room, Laird watching then following. They were congregated in the hall, an aimless flock waiting for direction.

"Hey, you four. You okay? Pretty rough in there, huh? Come on, we'll go to my office."

The four followed him in a perfunctory fashion, wanting to be anywhere than there. None of them had ever been in Laird's office, including Dulcy, and they politely took in the décor, the beautiful water view, and again, the lack of personal items.

"I guess I understand the lack of personal stuff now," said Dulcy.

"What do you understand about it?" he asked earnestly.

"Well, they put you on a case, you move to a place, and when the case is done, you go home."

"I am home."

"What?" said Dahlia.

"I said I am home," he said louder than before.

"I'm not deaf, you goof, I'm looking for an explanation."

"I've been assigned to this branch permanently. I have family not far from here and my transfer request was granted. I have no personal nick knacks, or whatever you want to call them because I used a decorator, and she picked out the stuff. I haven't had a chance to totally unpack or shop yet. I could use some help if anybody has some time."

Dulcy sat down in the front desk chair smiling at Laird. The previous subject seemed to have been dismissed and she was ready to move on to new business.

"Okay, well, here we are. I know this is touchy but now you know the whole story, and now you know what we have to do next."

"How simply awful," said Reggie. "Am I to understand that the German man, what's his name, Krebs?

"Yes."

"This man Krebs was like a supplier for the black-market things old man Hatfield and gang were selling?"

"Yes, and that's why the German authorities were after him. He had stolen some valuable artifacts and artwork and was selling them illegally here. The things he took were property of the government and therefore not salable, on the open market anyway. They were tracking him down and had gotten as far as tracing him to Hatfield. Hatfield claimed he was a friend and a guest, but their visit had ended, and he had moved on. He said he didn't know to where."

"So, something went wrong one night."

"Yep. What he portrayed in living color for us was the argument, the fight, the fall, and Krebs dying as Hatfield looked on helplessly, all with Cord Cavanaugh watching. He had been willing to end the relationship but having to get rid of a body was another thing.

"What was so eerie for me was not only his painting it in such detail but the intricacies of the faces. The emotion of it stings to your soul. You could feel the pain when he fell, the fear from Hatfield, the greed from Cavanaugh. He really was a huge talent."

"I guess what was even more palpable for me was what went through his mind as he carried a heavy body to his own home and got it through that tunnel and then... "

Tucker reached his arm around Dahlia and gave her a hug.

"I think it might be appropriate to take her back to her family, Tucker. Maybe they can go to the beach for a couple of days, maybe something touristy. Something different the Brits never get to do. Give us time to deal with the fireplace."

"I think that's brilliant. Let me get you home, love, and we'll come up with something fantastic. Jennings is fabulous; he'll probably have it all planned by the time we get there. You know he loves the beach."

"Anything but the Dali Museum."

* * *

Chapter 51

"The universe might not always play fair, but at least it's got a hell of a sense of humor."
-Sex in the City, 2000

When Tucker looked back over the days that followed, they seemed as surreal as the Hatfield work itself. Jennings planned a three-day getaway at an elegant and exclusive beach resort. Dahlia and the Brits had been whisked away to enjoy sun, relaxation, and continuous spa treatments, well away from the overwhelming media circus at Sea Gables.

Once the attention was dying down, Dulcy was able to return to her daily routine and begin training Lisa to become management. She had stepped up to the plate through everything, including the ensuing aftermath as well as scooting the young man who had the nerve to show again regarding the sale of the property.

"You're back here? I heard about you. There's nothing for you or your company here, so hit the road. And don't show yourself again," she had yelled at his back as he retreated through the courtyard gate.

Dulcy could not do enough to encourage her. This also gave her more time to help Agent Laird decorate the apartment with his personal flair. The dismantling of the fireplace had been a monumental and sad task.

With the space below so limited, they had to excavate the area to make room for manpower and equipment. In the end, it was spacious enough to comfortably accommodate the cluster of people and tools needed to complete the job. Due to the detail provided in Hatfield's mural, the team was able to go straight to a latch in the fireplace which released the stairway opening.

True to the images portrayed, the now decayed and decrepit remains of Dietmar Krebs, were discovered. A victim of foul play, the body was buried without ceremony in a brick tomb of no consequence in a house far from his native Germany. Placed beside him were his papers and a confession, faded and dirty but written in Hatfield's scrawling hand.

As he lies, one day so shall I
   By my hand he goes to find peace
   I live on awaiting whatever fate I'm due
   My very life mocks me and I run frantically to nowhere
   Guilt is my constant companion
   My only escape, a chamber of horrors
   That I have created
   My vision, my artistry, my compulsion
   My pride, my masterpiece, my confession
   It will lie in wait, long after my life recedes
   And one day, the images will reveal all
   And I will be released

The team had carefully bagged the missive and removed the remains. They followed the staircase and discovered a latch at the top which released the first-floor opening. The gap had been sealed to keep the burial secret, along with any other entrance to the lower level that had been there when built. Hatfield had taken to using the bathroom or the B&B entrance to complete his work and the fireplace tomb had been immortalized in charcoal and oils, then forgotten.

Once the discovery was confirmed, the tearoom had been descended upon by reporters, forensics teams, curiosity seekers, and the regular lunch crowd hoping for a meal at their favorite restaurant.

Dulcy had been happily overwhelmed by the increase in business and publicity for the tearoom. The circumstances were gruesome, but she had no control over that. Until recent events, Sea Gables had been a quiet lunch and tea spot with a few unexplained events which made patrons a bit nervous. She could see it becoming a main destination rather than just a place people stopped into by accident. It was an exciting prospect, and she was looking forward to the changes that would inevitably follow.

* * *

"I have a marvelous idea," said Reggie as she and Tucker were lunching at the tearoom.

He narrowed his eyes and lowered his fork.

"Oh, Lord. How much is this going to cost me?"

Reggie looked around at the full tables and the line at the door and smiled.

"I don't think it will cost you a thing, boss," she said, twinkling her bright, almond eyes at him.

"This is a historically preserved location. More than likely, there are grants and such that can be used to do a little work around the place."

"Ah, there it is, a little work around the place. Alright, love, what's brewing in that fascinating head of yours?"

"I've been thinking. With all the attention this is getting, I know this might sound a bit ghoulish, but in the scheme of things, that hidden room is a pretty nifty spot."

"Oh, no, you're not thinking..."

"I can see it now, white lights on the floor and ceiling of the tunnel, an elevator entrance in the B&B. Of course, we'd have to get rid of the broom closet."

"My father will be devastated."

The senior Elliott, upon having seen the team of photographers wandering out of the closet, had demanded an explanation and had been taken down and given a tour of the room by Laird himself. Satisfied with the arrangement, he had thanked him and puttered off to find something else to occupy his time.

"Well, I think he'll manage. It's cozy and despite the issue with the fireplace. I think it could be a beautiful and romantic private dining area. Very exclusive, you know?

"God help me, I actually think you might have something. We'll talk to Dahlia when she gets back. She'll be in later today; she has to go to the bank with Mavis. Anyway, it just might be a brilliant plan. Oh, can't believe I forgot this. I spoke with Nelson Platt and he's very anxious to have the pictures. He wants to do an opening and put them in a permanent display. We'll see what Dahlia has to say about that as well."

"Oh, Tucker, I don't think so. That whole scene is a bit much for public consumption. And they should be on the walls for the diners to see, with a disclaimer, of course."

"Some say neither were the holocaust images, but in the end, it's art."

"Oh my," said Reggie under her breath.

"Sorry?"

He followed her gaze to the hostess desk where standing arm in arm were Mavis Hatfield and Forrest Perkins.

"Shall we?"

"Oh, I think so," Reggie said, taking his hand as she scooted out of her seat.

"Hello Miss Hatfield, Mr. Perkins."

"Oh, hello dear, how are you?"

"The question," said Tucker, "is how are you? You've been through quite a bit here."

"I'm strong and able-bodied, so I'll manage," she said, showing the queenly bearing that had been dampened during the drama of recent events.

"I had no illusions about my father. I knew there were certain... activities that were going on. I chose to close my eyes to them. I was young but old at the same time if you can understand that. I have given all my documents to Agent Laird," she said abruptly. "That should be a final nail in Cord's coffin. It's not in my nature to be vindictive, but I feel a certain freedom in all this. I can now live in peace."

She paused and reflected for a moment, then eyed Tucker, then Reggie.

"Mazie left me his money. It was quite a lot, you know," she said, almost purring.

"Well, Forrest, are you hungry?"

"Ravenous, Mavis."

The two watched them walk away, arm in arm, ready to start over.

"You're awfully quiet, you know. Makes me think you've got crazy and dangerous thoughts brewing in that scratched up noggin of yours."

"I was just wondering what we do now. It's been so exhausting and constant since we got here, I'm not sure what to do with all this free time," Reggie said.

"I have an idea," he said, smiling wickedly.

"Hello! I'm back. Did you miss me? Give us a kiss," said Dahlia descending on Tucker and Reggie like a bird on a fish.

"You're looking well, love, all tan and rested and rubbed. Just saw Mavis inside. She's lunching with Perkins."

"Lord luv a duck! I can't believe it. All is forgiven?"

"It's a start."

"Listen, I've got to go to the bank with Mavis. They found the box. Did you know? There's a letter that's been waiting since Hatfield died that says only the person with the key can access it. Of course, with all the publicity they know who it belongs to now but you two have to come; I don't want to go alone. Please?"

Tucker and Reggie glanced at each other and chuckled.

"Wouldn't miss it, love, right Reg?"

"Absolutely," she said. "I am wild with expectation and giddy with anticipation."

"Yes, love, but what about the bank visit?" she said softly in her ear.

* * *

The bank executives had removed the box from the vault and presented it to both women who were apprehensive but curious. The key was handed to them by Laird and once the box was opened, a heaping amount of gold coins lay undisturbed by time.

"But how much is there?" asked Mavis.

"Well ma'am, these are minted with about .999 percent gold, so they are extremely valuable today. You probably have about $250,000 here. Excuse me but there is also this," he said, handing Mavis an old, yellowed envelope.

"I just don't think I can," she said, holding it out to Tucker. "Please read it to me."

If you are reading this, I am long gone and you have solved the puzzle of the pictures. I hope it's my dear baby girl Mavis reading this. You were always the responsible one, which is why I want you to know that I never wanted to hurt anyone, especially you. Below is the last known address for your child. I hope we can forgive each other for how we both

behaved. Please try to find her and let her get to know you. This money is yours, some ill-gotten, but not all. Use it for whatever will make your life happy.

I love you.

Papa

Tucker handed the letter back to Mavis as the tears streamed down her cheeks. She wiped them away with her handkerchief and straightened herself to her full height.

"Dahlia, this money is yours. I have no wish for it, and I would like to see you be able to make this tearoom everything you've ever dreamed of. Maybe you can find a way to display Papa's work somewhere. It was conceived in guilt and shame but is deserving of appreciation."

"No, I couldn't..."

"I will not discuss this further, Miss Porter," and she placed the key in Dahlia's palm and folded her fingers over it. With a faint smile, she walked out of the vault and the bank without even a turn of her head.

* * *

Dahlia was busy in a meeting with her newly formed team of Dulcy and Lisa secreted away in her office. Once again, Tucker and Reggie found themselves with time and no prospects. They started their way to the B&B.

"Tucker, dear, are you coming to dinner?" said a disjointed voice. "This is it, we're on our way home tomorrow. Come join us for dinner."

"Actually, we've just made other plans, Mum, but thanks."

She walked the length of the porch and wrapped her arms around Tucker giving him a tight squeeze.

"We will see you at Brooklands for the gala, I hope. It's a very big event, you really need to be present, dear. Reggie, make sure he gets to where he's supposed to be and dressed correctly, please," she said, enveloping him in a tight hug.

"Take good care of him for me please, love," she whispered in her ear. "You've done marvelously."

"You know I will."

* * *

"Jennings is an absolute treasure," said Reggie as she looked in wonder at the beautifully laid table complete with linen, candles, flowers, silver, china, and the most scrumptious dinner she had ever seen.

"Fancy eating in tonight?" asked Tucker as he held out a chair.

She had no idea how hungry she was, and she ate like it was her last meal. Jennings appeared out of nowhere when they were finished and removed any trace of an exquisite feast.

"Thanks, mate. You are amazing as always. See you at home next?"

"With great pleasure, sir. Miss Reggie, looking forward to seeing you as well. Goodnight," he said with a pleasant nod as he vanished.

The light was dimming earlier every day in the late fall sky. Reggie padded over to the window and blissfully watched the shadows fall over the courtyard. She saw Laird round the fence and trot up the back tearoom steps. Reggie smiled; she knew Dulcy would be out shortly and they would be having a late supper.

As they came out the back porch, they stopped and shared a tight embrace and long, sensuous kiss. Reggie knew she should have looked away but somehow couldn't seem to leave her spot.

"What are you up to?" asked Tucker as he came up behind her and encircled her body.

"Oh, nothing. Just watching people having sex on the back porch."

"Sorry?"

"Dulcy and Laird were kissing on the porch. They're gone now."

"Really? How were they kissing? And tell me slowly."

Reggie laughed and leaned back into him. He brushed her long hair aside and kissed her neck. He moved in a slow circle, from mid-neck around to her ear.

"Was it like this?"

Reggie's body was tingling from head to toe, and she shivered involuntarily.

"Alright?"

"Oh, yeah, it's just that you found my really, really sensitive spot."

"Well, now, where would that be? Would it be here?" he said, pecking her neck and grazing his lips across her shoulder as he slid her dress strap down.

"Uh huh."

"Or maybe here," he said as he kissed her shoulder wrapping his hands around her middle.

He kissed her neck back over to her ear and felt her lean more heavily into him.

"Oh, my goodness, you're making my knees weak."

He released her waist and slid his hands down her hips turning her to him. He grabbed her by the wrists and laid her arms over his shoulders. He pulled her to him and kissed her lightly as he swept his hands up her back. They stood, toe to toe, forehead to forehead taking each other in.

She looked beautiful. He raised his head and smoothed the hair from her face. He touched the stitches on her cheek and leaned in and kissed them. Then he kissed her lids, her forehead, the tip of her nose and then her lips. His hands roamed over the softness of her back, and he held her close again.

He kissed her and swept both legs up and carried her to the bed. He lay her down gently, being mindful of the tattered shins, still raw and painful. His body was silhouetted in the dim light as he lay down next to her. She laid her head on his shoulder and pressed her cheek against him.

"You alright?" he whispered, wrapping her in his arms as though she might disappear.

"I'm fabulous. I thought we'd never get to this."

"Ever, or just this afternoon?"

"Maybe a little bit of both."

"Fancy a hot bath? I'll wash your back and loofah your bruises."

"I don't think you have a big enough loofah."

"Let's just see what else we might have to work with, eh?"

"I'll run it," she said sitting on the edge of the bed observing her sheared shins.

She strolled to the bathroom where she turned on the taps and watched the flow of the water.

"Don't start without me," he said, lazily rolling off the bed.

"Back at ya, boss."

Dahlia had been in a daze since returning from the bank. She felt guilty and exhilarated at the same time. She knew she shouldn't accept the money, but what she could do for the tearoom was a long and growing list. Dulcy and Lisa had offered their congratulations and ideas which only served to add to her confusion.

She was alone in her office, something she hadn't been able to do in quite some time. She put her feet up, pulled out her idea pad, and organized her thoughts. She needed a pow-wow with Tucker and Reggie. She hadn't seen them but remembered Tucker had put Jennings to work setting up a room service dinner.

"Oooo, I need to go see how it went. Hope there's leftovers."

She crossed to the B&B entering through the back door. She greeted guests in the salon then trotted to Tucker's room.

"Tucker, it's Dahlia. Open up, love."

She waited a minute then leaned in and listened. She could hear the tinkling of Reggie's laughter and water running in the bathroom. She listened more closely and heard Tucker's voice over the beat of the water saying, "Which bruise now, Regina?"

Dahlia shook her head, grinned, and went back the way she came.

"Finally," she muttered as she hopped down the stairs.

* * *

Chapter 52

Alex Rogan: We did it.
Grig: Yes, we did, didn't we.
-The Last Starfighter, 1984

It was a busy night at the inn. Dahlia retreated to her office to consider her windfall and find something to eat in the kitchen. The Brits were packing and rushing between rooms making sure they had everything. Tucker and Reggie were still relaxing in the sitting room of the suite when she needed more to wear than a towel all night. She would need to go to her room for fresh clothes. Tucker was against this idea, but Reggie was adamant and headed for the door.

"Please check for passersby before roaming the halls," he said. "I've had damned unlucky experiences with that this trip."

Reggie regarded him questioningly as she opened the door. Heading for the stairs was the senior Elliott himself, carrying a gaggle of shopping bags and a bottle of port.

"Well, hello Miss Reggie. Just having a last glass downstairs if you care to join us. If not, have a lovely evening," he said observing her towel and winking.

As he descended the stairs, Reggie overheard "Finally" escape the old man's lips.

"Ugh. That was embarrassing," she thought, tiptoeing down the hall.

All spruced up and ready to go back to Tucker's room, she took one last look in the mirror. She thought she looked well this evening considering everything. She seemed to have a soft glow about her. She poked her head out the door checking for roaming Brits, then scurried back to Tucker's room. She knocked lightly then slipped through the door.

At the other end of the hall, Mrs. Porter was taking ice to her room for their nightcaps later. She watched as Reggie sped down the hall and flew into Tucker's room.

"Finally," she thought as she went in to deposit the ice.

* * *

The next morning was hurried and frenetic. Cars had been arranged, bags had been stowed, and schedules had been coordinated. Jennings had decided to stay back and make sure nothing was left behind. Little did they know he was going back to the beach to coordinate a schedule or two of his own. Tucker and Reggie stood by hugging and kissing and promising to be at Brooklands in due time for the gala. They had a different look about them this morning and Tucker's mother was trying to put her finger on it as they pulled away from the inn.

"Ah," she said with a dawning realization. "Finally."

* * *

Dahlia was left standing in the courtyard drinking in the sunshine and waiting for the last two to leave her to her busy new life.

"Well, love, it's time to say cheers and see you soon. I also have to say that your memorial service was one of the worst I've ever had the misfortune to attend, Tucker. Sorry."

"Well, then, we'll just have to do better next time."

She held her hands out to him, eyes moist and lips trembling. He held her tight until she dropped her arms and released him.

"Go on with you, then. I'll be alright now."

"I know."

"Reggie, put your thoughts on the romantic dinner idea and email them to me," she said, hugging her to the crushing point. "I love the idea. I think it will be brilliant."

They watched and waved as she disappeared into the tearoom. Laird had stopped for a quick good-bye, a scone, and a stolen kiss from Dulcy. He was still dealing with the fallout of all the drama and was expecting nothing less than a frantic day. Dulcy had cried and told them they must come back soon.

"I don't know who I'll get into trouble with now. I'm really going to miss you," she said, hugging and kissing Reggie. "And we've decided to rename your suite 'Tucker's Plot' since without you we honestly don't know what would have happened to this place. It's yours to call home anytime."

He was overwhelmed and, for once, speechless. They waved and blew Dulcy a kiss as they drove away. When they were out of sight, she shook her head, grinned, and said "Finally."

* * *

Chapter 53

About the Author

Jacqueline Farthing Galvin, also known by her pen names Jacquie Galvin and Mama Galvin, is a versatile author. She is the President and CEO of Live Life's Rich Moments. Jacqueline has been on a literary journey for over thirty years and has self-published over 100 works across various genres.

Her works include captivating short stories, heart-racing mystery thrillers, informative feature articles, and descriptive travel narratives.

Jacqueline's literary journey started at a unique intersection, where she skillfully balanced her passion for writing with running a freight business and excelling as a medical representative.

One of her most recent literary gems, the award-winning *Grace for Grant: A Journey with an Old Soul*, masterfully navigates the deeply moving odyssey of her family, marked by the loss of her 19-year-old son, Grant.

You can connect with me on:

🌐 https://www.jacquelinefarthinggalvin.com

⬛ https://www.facebook.com/farthinggalvin

🔗 https://www.instagram.com/jacquiegalvin

Subscribe to my newsletter:

✉ https://jacquelinefarthinggalvin.com/bookclub

Also by Jacqueline Farthing Galvin

Murder for Afternoon Tea - Episode II - Welcome to my Underground Lair

Detective John Laird's investigation into a fatal collapse uncovers missing staff, vanishing witnesses, and buried secrets. When he's pulled off the case, Tucker, Dulcy, and Reggie dig for the truth, only to uncover lies and betrayal. Who's missing, who's dying, and who's lying? Find out in Episode II - *Welcome to My Underground Lair.*

Murder for Afternoon Tea - Episode III - Finally

In Episode III of *Murder for Afternoon Tea*, the final showdown unfolds. Detective Laird reveals his true identity as his team scrambles to find Reggie, who escapes captivity just in time to expose the killer. Chaos erupts as a gun-wielding culprit takes a hostage, but Jennings saves the day, uncovering buried secrets and righting old wrongs. Relationships are mended, and mysteries solved, setting the stage for the next adventure: *Death in Paradise: Secrets of the Croquet Club.*

Death in Paradise: Secrets of the Croquet Club

In the third *Tucker and Reggie Mystery*, a restful getaway to Useppa Island turns deadly when croquet mallets become murder weapons. As the Mayhugh company head is found dead in a banyan tree, motives abound on the shrinking island. When more victims fall, Tucker and Reggie set a trap to catch the killer, but will they reel in the truth—or become the next targets? Find out who survives and who wins the deadliest match yet!

Grace for Grant: A Journey with an Old Soul

In this memoir, Jacquie recounts how her nineteen-year-old son, Grant Galvin, faced a life-altering series of events when a suspected stroke landed him in rehab, only to experience a heart attack shortly after. As baffling symptoms spiraled out of control, his family found themselves navigating a whirlwind of diagnoses. Mischievous and curious, Grant's antics left both trouble and laughter in his wake. But when an outburst led to his hospitalization on his birthday, chaos took over. Step into Grant's world of supernatural phenomena, spiritual connections, and medical madness. You'll laugh, cry, and be glad you joined the journey.